A WOMAN OF TRUE HONOR

TRUE GENTLEMEN BOOK EIGHT

GRACE BURROWES

Print ISBN: 9781941419946

Ebook ISBN: 9781941419939

To the many, many, many good guys.
You are the real heroes.

CHAPTER ONE

A man raised with six brothers should have been impossible to ambush. Valerian Dorning's excuse was that the typical fraternal skirmish involved a pair of fists, and those, he'd become adept at dodging.

Miss Emily Pepper's weapon of choice was a pair of lips—hers—and luscious, soft lips they were too. Valerian's body had no inclination whatsoever to escape her fire and, had surrender been honorable, he would have gone peaceably into captivity after at least fifteen minutes of heroic struggle.

His gentlemanly honor, alas for him, was yet in evidence. "Miss Pepper..." he murmured as she tucked in closer. "Emily..."

She was a well-formed young woman, which Valerian noted in less genteel terms every time he clapped eyes upon her. Now, purely in defense of his sanity, he laid his hands on her person. Her biceps seemed a safe enough place to grasp her, except that she twined her arms around Valerian's neck, and his hands landed on the sides of her ribs.

Her breasts—more luscious softness—were mere inches from his touch, while his self-restraint was threatening to gallop off into the next county.

"Miss Pepper, we must not."

Though *he did*. For one glorious, demented moment, Valerian kissed her back, reveling in her blatant desire and in the sheer perfection of her body pressed to his. He dreamed of Emily Pepper, he longed for her in the darkness, and he subjected himself to long, cold swims in the millpond trying to exorcise her from his imagination.

This utter folly masquerading as a kiss would make Valerian's nights only more tormented. Miss Pepper's hands roaming his back conveyed equal parts eagerness and determination, and when a fellow had never been particularly sought out by anybody, much less by a comely female with a lively mind, a wonderful sense of humor, and a fiercely kind heart, he was easily felled.

Her questing hands wandered south, giving Valerian's bum an exquisite squeeze.

"*Miss Pepper.*" *Do that again.* "We must not forget ourselves."

She did it again, and Valerian forgot whose royal arse sat upon the British throne. When she clutched at his backside, she brought her womanly abundance into greater proximity to Valerian's chest, and the battle to deny arousal became an utter rout.

He stepped back lest he have to depart the picnic with his hat held over his falls.

Miss Pepper kept her arms around his neck, her breath coming in soft pants that sent Valerian's wayward imagination in all the wrong directions. What she lacked in subtlety, she made up for in dearness.

"I have bungled even this," she said, gaze fixed on his cravat. "You are trying not to laugh, aren't you?"

If anything could drag Valerian's attention from the rise and fall of Miss Pepper's charms, it was the note of misery in her voice.

"I beg your pardon?" Why must her hair be such a soft, caressable brown? Why must her fingers stroking his nape bring poetry to mind?

"I cannot even manage a stolen kiss with a gentleman bachelor. My dancing is a horror, my laughter too boisterous. I will never be accepted even in *Dorsetshire*."

Valerian took her hands in his and managed another half step back. "You make Dorset sound like a province of Lower Canada. I assure you, your neighbors all hold you in very high regard." They held her father's money in high regard. From what Valerian could tell, the local gentry weren't quite sure *what* to make of Miss Pepper herself.

Fools.

"I will not attend the summer assembly." She dropped his hands and turned so she faced the woods that backed up to the garden of the Summerton estate. "I refuse to be made a laughingstock."

"Nobody will dare laugh at you." Unless, of course, she fell on her pretty fundament. Valerian had suffered the indignity of a public tumble himself, having been tripped by some brother or other, and he well knew the capacity for merriment that the publican's punch could inspire.

Also, the blinding headaches.

"They won't laugh at me to my face. Shall we take a stroll to the stream, Mr. Dorning?"

Wandering the woods together was not quite proper, except that other guests were also enjoying the shady paths winding beneath the trees. The occasion was meant to feature the out of doors, and the estate where Valerian's brother dwelled with his new wife was beautiful in any season.

Valerian offered his arm, Miss Pepper curled her hand into the crook of his elbow, and they set off at a sedate meander.

"I will miss you if you don't attend the assembly." A partial truth. Valerian would not miss watching every bachelor, widower, and squire stand up with her. He would, though, miss seeing her smile at all the babies and children. He might also miss hearing her laugh at some lout's attempt at humor, especially if he were the lout amusing her.

Miss Pepper had a genuine laugh, one that conveyed warm-heartedness and a convivial spirit. She also had a temper, and Valerian liked that almost as much as he liked her sense of humor. Too many women pretended they never had grounds for offense, and too many men were content to believe the ladies' fictions.

"You are being gallant," she said. "If I'm not at the assembly, the general opinion will be that I think I'm too good for my neighbors' company. I am getting off on the wrong foot with them, and I don't know what to do about it."

Earlier in the year, Emily's father, Osgood Pepper, had purchased a local estate sunk in debt. She was overseeing refurbishment of the manor house, one of many properties she would inherit upon her father's death.

"The local folk don't know what to do about you either." The uproar in Valerian's breeches was subsiding to a familiar ache, and turning his mind to Miss Pepper's social situation helped reduce the ache to a pointless yearning. "Country life comes at a slower pace than what you're used to in Town. Here your fortunes won't be decided in the space of a few Wednesday-night gatherings at Almack's. You have time to ease into the community."

"You're saying if I don't attend the summer assembly, I can simply show up at the autumn gathering?"

"Or winter, or next spring... Though the summer gathering is in some ways the best."

"Why?"

"Because the engagements are announced at the spring assembly, typically, and summer is when the courting couples preen and prance about. The weather is usually pleasant enough that most people walk both to and from the gathering, and the whole business has a more relaxed, congenial air. I do hope you'll come."

As one of the many Dorning offspring, Valerian had been raised with certain expectations. First his father and now his brother held the title Earl of Casriel, making the Dornings the ranking family in the neighborhood. Dorning Hall entertained its neighbors at a summer fête and a Yuletide open house each year, and the Dorning brothers were expected to stand up with the wallflowers at any event that featured dancing.

Hospitality was expected of a Dorning, even a penniless bachelor Dorning. *Especially* of such a fellow, in fact, for it was among few valuables he had to give.

They reached the stream, which today ran a placid course between grassy banks. "Why did you kiss me, Miss Pepper?"

She took the bench that some obliging soul had placed by the water a century or two ago. "Why did I *try* to kiss you?"

"I'd say the venture was a success. May I join you?" The bench sat in shade, and the view across the stream was a sunny pasture on Dorning land. Mares cropped grass, tails whisking at the occasional fly. Foals napped at their mamas' feet or frisked about with each other like enormous milk-drunk kittens.

"Please do have a seat," Miss Pepper said, arranging her skirts. "A kiss is not a success when the gentleman's primary reaction is dismay. I should apologize."

"Please don't. I'm simply out of practice in the kissing department. My dancing is much more reliable."

He'd made her smile, and that was... that was worth all the thwarted yearning in Dorset.

"I don't know how to kiss, and I don't know the country dances," she said. "Papa's finishing schools and governesses made sure I learned the ballroom dances, just as I have passable French and can mince about in a fancy riding habit without tripping over my hems. That education is inadequate for the challenges I face now."

Miss Pepper wasn't much of a horsewoman. Valerian had seen that for himself, and her ballroom dancing qualified as passable at best.

"Dances can be learned," he said, "as can the equestrian arts that figure so prominently in rural life. You picked up French, after all."

"I did not *pick up* French, Mr. Dorning. I gathered it, one word at a time, over years of hard labor at the hands of experts. Most of my governesses concluded that the daughter of a cit could not be very bright, and I came to agree with them, at least as regards languages."

Why did you kiss me? He could not ask her that again, though neither could he explain the sheer nonsense that came out of his mouth.

"I hold dance classes every Wednesday evening for the four weeks before any assembly. The young people like an excuse to stand up with one another, and few of us want to attempt our first waltz on a crowded dance floor." He did not dare inform her that he charged for those classes on a donation basis.

Nobody was obligated to pay anything, but those who could afford to did put a few coppers in the jar. He needed the money, though not desperately enough to insist on payment when many of his neighbors were one bad harvest away from needing it more.

"You suggest I make a limited spectacle of myself?"

"I suggest you have some fun with our younger neighbors, who tend to be less hidebound and serious. Come a bit early, and I'll get you started. One can practice the waltz with a single partner, and other dances require only four couples. The country dances, though, often form lines, and that means learning them in company."

"You won't let me fall on my backside?"

Her question was endearingly in earnest. "No guarantees, Miss Pepper. Anybody can take a tumble—I have myself—but I do promise to help you up."

"*You* have fallen on the dance floor?"

"Went sprawling before the entire company. My brother Hawthorne gave me a hand up"—Hawthorne's boot might have precipitated Valerian's fall, purely by accident, of course—"swatted at me a few times, and gave me a shove in the direction of my partner, who like the rest of the group, was laughing uproariously. I made it a point to conquer the dance floor thereafter." And the drawing room and any battlefield where a man could be felled by manners or deportment.

"Very well," she said, rising. "I will join you for these tutorials, and we shall see what progress can be made, if any."

They ambled back to the garden, where the buffet had been set out, and still Valerian had no answer to his question—why had she kissed him?

"Shall I come for you on Wednesday afternoon?" he asked.

"Please. My driving skills are as wanting as my dancing abilities. I will look forward to our next meeting, Mr. Dorning." She bobbed an abrupt curtsey and left him standing by the fountain.

"Margaret likes her." That comment came from Valerian's brother Hawthorne, who was the host for the day's gathering. "Margaret has a very discerning nature. Witness, she married my humble and handsome self."

"When will you stop sneaking up on an unsuspecting brother?"

"When my unsuspecting brother stops focusing so intently on a lady's departure that he becomes oblivious to all else, though I grant you, Miss Pepper has a comely form."

Hawthorne, the tallest and most muscular of the Dorning siblings, was a farmer at heart. He might have been admiring a yearling heifer's well-sprung barrel, so dispassionate was his assessment of Emily's attributes. When it came to his darling Margaret and the two little girls he was raising with her, though, he was anything but dispassionate.

"The lady needs a few pointers regarding country dances," Valerian said. "I am happy to provide them."

"You look happy." Hawthorne slung a muscular arm across Valerian's shoulders. "You look overjoyed, awash in ebullience, a testament to—*oof.*"

Valerian had elbowed him hard in the breadbasket, which had the desired effect of dislodging Hawthorne's arm and the agreeable result of improving Valerian's mood.

"Marriage has made you soft, Thorne."

"Softhearted," Hawthorne replied, gaze going to his smiling, strawberry-blonde wife.

Spare me from besotted siblings. "I will leave you to your wedded bliss and thank you for a pleasant gathering. Please make my farewells to Margaret, would you?"

"Make them yourself. What is so urgent that you must be among the first to leave?"

Valerian wanted to study up on his country dances, though he knew them all by heart, and he wanted time to think. Had Emily Pepper's kiss been simply another attempt to acquire a needed skill?

A plausible explanation and a very lowering thought.

"I do occasionally have matters to see to, Hawthorne. My manuscript wants polishing, for example. My thanks again for a lovely afternoon." Valerian made a perfectly correct bow and sauntered away, offering parting words to a few neighbors as he gained the path that led to Dorning Hall. When he was safely into the woods, and thus out of view of the gathering, he crossed the stream and turned his steps along the track that led to the millpond.

Even on this gorgeous summer afternoon, the water would be frigid, or at least it had been that morning.

"MR. DORNING SAID he'd teach me to dance." Emily offered this explanation to Briggs, who as usual sat embroidering by the parlor window.

"You know how to dance, miss." A neutral statement of fact that somehow conveyed a world of censure. Briggs had been with Emily for years, and they had been long years from Emily's perspective.

"I know some dances, true," Emily said, for it was always best to agree with Briggs where possible. "I know the ballroom dances one needs at Almack's." Not that Emily had been admitted to that great citadel of snobbery. "Other dances are popular in the countryside."

"A lot of hopping about, clapping, and twirling," Briggs said. "Not very dignified, if you ask me."

Which Emily had not. "I can attend without you." Emily pretended to rummage in her workbasket, though she was heartily sick of embroidery, lace, and knitting. A lady of the manor was expected to ply her needle for the beautification of said manor, apparently, until that lady was barmy with boredom. "I'm sure Tobias and Caleb will want to go."

"You think a pair of glorified London clerks will bother with a rural assembly?"

"They won't have a choice when I ask them to accompany me. They are gentlemen."

Briggs sniffed and snapped off a thread.

Tobias Granger and Caleb Booth were Papa's left and right hand, respectively. They had worked for him since their boyhoods and had stuck by him through every tribulation. Emily was certain they had generous bequests in Papa's will, and their loyalty to his various businesses—and to Papa himself—was beyond question.

To Briggs, however, Tobias and Caleb handled money, albeit indirectly, which put them in all but trade and made them only nominal gentlemen. She had been born into modest wealth, and clung to the standards of her upbringings long after that wealth had been squandered.

"Those two pester your father the livelong day with their silly business. It's as if nobody explained to them how the king's post works."

"They are still in the office with him?" The evening meal approached, though Papa would have taken a tray at his desk if Emily had permitted it.

"The three of them have been at it since you went larking off to yon picnic this morning."

Emily closed her workbasket gently. "I am at present the female head of this household, Briggs. I am expected to socialize with our neighbors. I'll see you at supper." Why Briggs had not chased Caleb and Tobias out of Papa's office, Emily did not know. Very likely, Briggs was protesting Emily's decision to attend the picnic, which was ridiculous. Briggs had declined to accompany her, pleading hay fever, when in fact the true ailment was likely disdain for rural pastimes.

Emily left Briggs to her sniffing and stitching and took the steps up to the next floor. Living in a stately home was an adjustment for a woman who'd grown up in very modest dwellings and then in a modestly appointed London town house.

Here, servants dashed up and down steps at meal times, desperate to get hot dishes to the table at least warm. That was a near impossibility when the kitchen was situated on the opposite side of the house from the dining room.

Whenever Papa worked in the estate office, a footman waited outside the door, ready to fetch a book or a file from the library if need be. The maids were so numerous Emily had yet to learn all of their names, and the housekeeper expected daily consultations on everything from the linen stores to how much more summer ale should be brewed.

"And I know nothing about any of it," Emily muttered, rounding the landing. The steps seemed to grow more numerous each week that Emily bided at Summerfield House—or Pepper Ridge as Papa had christened the estate—but on no account must she use the more convenient stairs designated for the footmen or the maids.

"And if a footman is found on the maids' stairs, I am to sack him." Briggs had offered that directive, though how was Emily to come upon such a bold fellow when she herself was relegated to only the public stairways?

She reached the top of the steps and had to pause to catch her breath. Fatigue dragged at her—studying plans for the renovation of the master suite had run late last night—and morning had begun early so that she could fit the Summerton picnic into her schedule.

"Where, in my usual fashion, I made a prime fool of myself—again." She moved off in the direction of Papa's office, dredging up a smile and a bouncy step.

She hadn't meant to kiss Valerian Dorning, but there he'd been, looking scrumptious in his riding attire, all alone on the path, the picture of affable gentlemanly composure caught in a moment of quiet contemplation. Emily had seen him dance in London, had seen the longing gazes the young ladies of Mayfair had aimed in his direction. He was manly grace personified, had exquisite manners, and his discretion was to be trusted utterly.

And for the space of three heartbeats, *he had kissed her back.* The pleasure of that moment had been sublime, the mortification that followed it hellish.

Why did you kiss me, Miss Pepper? Emily had been unable to admit the truth.

She tapped on the door to the estate office and pushed her way inside. Tobias and Caleb sat with Papa at the reading table, which boasted a plethora of ledger books, two abacuses, and a pen tray full of pencil shavings.

"Out," Emily said, "the pair of you. Papa, for shame. I set foot off the property, and you are back to the very ways that resulted in your falling ill. I won't have it."

Caleb assayed the affable smile that went so well with his medium height, auburn hair, and general good humor. Tall, blond Tobias kept flicking wooden beads from one side of the abacus to the other.

"In a moment," he muttered. In the opinion of most young women, Tobias would doubtless be accounted gorgeous. He had Nordic coloring, heroic features, and an English gentleman's exquisite sense of fashion. He was also, alas, about as warmhearted as an icehouse.

"Out. *Now,*" Emily said as sweetly as possible. "Papa, you are to rest before dinner."

Papa sat back. "But it's only..." He flipped open his pocket watch. "Oh dear. Tobias, Caleb, best do as Emily says. We've been very naughty boys."

That oh-look-at-the-time humbug was for show, an attempt to dodge Emily's wrath, but she was too tired to do more than hold the door for Papa's conspirators. Papa's health had improved significantly. His color was better, and he had more energy, but he was still of spare build and not a young man.

Caleb and Tobias went muttering on their way, Tobias scowling,

Caleb offering a sheepish bow, leaving Emily a clear field on which to upbraid the true culprit.

"I am glad you feel so much better, Papa—"

"But you worry for me anyway. I know, child. Sit down. You look to be in worse condition than I ever was."

Why, thank you, Papa. "I haven't time to sit. I must have a look at the master suite before the workmen leave for the day. Come, I'll walk you to your bedroom."

Papa bided in an apartment across the corridor from Emily's old rooms on the ground floor, which put him as close as possible to the servants belowstairs and spared him from much use of the staircases. The arrangement had seemed like a good idea, though in reality, if Papa needed anything—a cup of tea, his reading glasses—he had simply hailed Emily to send for "one of those strapping fellows in livery." She had moved to rooms on the next floor up, leaving Papa a hand bell with which to summon the servants.

The sound of that bell haunted her nightmares.

"You may be off about your business," Papa said, rising. "I could not keep up with you for all the wool in Wales. Must be the good country air putting such a spring in your step, eh?"

Never had the coal smoke of London called to Emily more sincerely. "I have much to do here, Papa, but not so much that I can't walk with you for a moment."

He sent the ledgers a longing glance and went gracefully to his fate, offering Emily his arm. "You should have been a man."

Papa meant that frequent comment as a compliment, but each time he said it, Emily suffered a little deeper cut. She would never be a man and had better sense than to wish to be one.

"What were you, Tobias, and Caleb working on?"

"Redesigning the hold of the merchantman I bought off that grouchy marquess in Sussex. If Caleb is right, we can substantially increase the cargo capacity without any loss of stability."

"What does Tobias say?"

"That Caleb's an idiot, though of course Tobias is ever polite about his insults."

And Tobias was occasionally right. "Might you seek the opinion of a master shipwright before you start buying materials, Papa?"

"Suppose I should, shouldn't I?"

"Neither Caleb nor Tobias has set foot on a merchantman under sail, to my knowledge. They mean well, but their expertise has limits."

"Huh." Papa stopped outside his apartment. "We'll let that be our little secret, shall we? Find me a shipwright, then, and he can take a look at the plans."

"Of course, Papa." Pepper Ridge was close enough to Weymouth and Bournemouth that finding a shipwright shouldn't take too much effort. "Have a nice rest, and I'll see you at supper."

Papa paused, hand on the door latch. "When you have a spare moment, I have a matter to discuss with you, but it will keep for now. Perhaps you ought to grab a nap yourself, Emily, when you've finished inspecting the master suite."

Emily patted his arm, which wasn't as bony as it had been even two months ago. "A fine idea, Papa, and whenever you can spare *me* a moment, I will be happy to discuss any topic you choose."

She dearly hoped Papa sought to discuss a business topic with her. Insurance contracts fascinated her, subrogation language was a pure delight, and terms relating to liquidated damages could entertain her for hours. Compared to those challenges, she was utterly bored with the herbal inventory, the ale calculations, the litany of difficulties put forth by the head carpenter working on the renovations, not to mention Briggs's sniffing and sniping.

Cook's endless explanations for what sauce went with what joint or why certain cheeses could not be served with certain fruits had also grown tedious, and Emily had lost all patience for the master gardener's dithering over roses.

She dredged up another smile and prepared to deal with the

master carpenter, but she also took a moment on the landing to recall those precious moments in Valerian Dorning's arms.

The truth was, she'd kissed him for the least defensible reason: *She had simply wanted to*, from the first moment she'd met him. In a sea of duties, tasks, and obligations, a stolen kiss shared with an attractive, charming gentleman had loomed before Emily like an indulgence sweeter than sunshine and birdsong.

And Valerian Dorning had kissed her back. Briefly and gently, but he had.

CHAPTER TWO

So thoroughly had Grey Dorning, Earl of Casriel, adjusted to married life that when his countess decamped for a visit with her former in-laws, Dorning Hall—Casriel's home since birth—felt unwelcoming. Beatitude had told him to enjoy having "the place to himself."

"As if I could," he said, rapping on the door of the cottage Valerian now occupied. "My whole life is spent in the company of my siblings, and now they desert me."

Valerian himself opened the door. "That is entirely unfair. You either urged us to get married or banished us. Nonetheless, I will welcome you to my home as if you are the prodigal himself. Have we heard anything from Oak?"

Oak, the family artist, had taken employment with a Hampshire widow who had a collection of paintings in need of restoration.

"From Oak? I've heard not a damned thing." Valerian had urged Grey to write to Oak, but pining for Beatitude took precedence over fretting about Oak in Grey's opinion. He passed over his shooting jacket, which he preferred for other activities because it was spectacularly comfortable.

"Does nobody dress you?" Valerian said, swatting at the sleeves and hanging the garment on a peg beside the door. "You are weeks ahead of the grouse season."

"I am comfortable. I can move my arms. What smells so good?"

"Beef roast. We have time for a drink before our meal. Do you truly feel abandoned up there at the Hall?"

Grey could never admit as much to a sibling. As Valerian had said, the younger Dorning brothers had been sent out into the world more or less on the end of Grey's very own boot, lovingly applied to their respective backsides.

In the fashion of elder brothers faced with inconvenient realities, Grey seized on the least embarrassing truth. "Her ladyship's absence is keenly felt."

Valerian led the way to a small parlor, one nonetheless graced by a bouquet of daylilies and faintly scented with verbena.

"Grey, repeat after me: *I miss my wife.*"

"You needn't gloat."

Valerian had only two decanters on his sideboard, both good crystal and nearly full. "A tonic to settle your lordship's nerves," he said, passing over a glass of claret. "I don't gloat to see you besotted, I rejoice. You went up to London with all the enthusiasm of an innocent man facing transportation. You came strutting back thoroughly in love with your wife. Gives one hope."

Casriel lifted his glass. "To your health and to your own hopes, whatever they may be."

Valerian sipped his wine. Like Grey, he hadn't changed for dinner. This was a bachelor household, and they would wear their damned boots to table if they pleased to, but somehow, a country gentleman's casual turnout looked so much more... *more* on Valerian. His cuffs and cravat bore a touch of lace, and the weave was beautiful. His sleeve buttons, cravat pin, and watch chain were the only gold on his person, and yet he conveyed elegance in his very lack of jewelry.

"I hope for a good meal in good company," Valerian said. "Catch me up on the family news."

In truth, Beatitude had become the epicenter of family correspondence, mostly because both Daisy and Jacaranda—the female Dorning siblings—were conscientious about their letters. Jacaranda bided in Town with her husband, Worth Kettering, and thus kept an eye on Sycamore and Ash and, to a lesser extent, Will. Daisy had married a local squire and poked her nose periodically into Grey's, Hawthorne's, Valerian's, and Oak's business.

"You catch me up first," Grey said, sinking into an exquisitely comfortable reading chair. "Has Daisy made any inspection tours of your home?"

"I pay my calls on Daisy on Thursday," Valerian said, taking the second wing chair. "That way, I can see the children on the nursery maid's half day. How long will your countess be gone?"

"Too bloody long. I should pay a call on Daisy. One of those brigands is my godson."

"And Daisy is our baby sister. Drink your wine, Grey."

Coming here had been a mistake. The Hall was lonely—might as well admit it, damn the very notion—but Valerian dwelled in near solitude in this cottage and yet managed to give the place an air of domestic comfort. He'd always had the ability to seem at ease, to take matters in hand, whether those matters were the appointments in a tenant cottage, fashionable repartee, haying teams, or a trio of feuding brothers.

Valerian owned his own estate, a tidy manor bequeathed to him by an aunt, but he let the land out rather than dwell even that short distance from the Hall.

Grey sipped a lovely glass of wine and resented its quality. "Where did you come by this vintage? It's quite good." Better than the everyday on hand at the Hall, possibly better than the company wine at the Hall too.

"I translated some recipes from the French for the publican's wife. She mentioned that she was bored serving only English fare, and I offered to find her a few dishes easily prepared and not too costly. The wine was a gesture of appreciation on her part. My next assignments are recipes for Italian crème cake and French chocolate drops."

"The coach passengers will appreciate your work. Beatitude enjoys chocolate drops."

Valerian's smile was damnably kind and knowing.

Grey downed his wine and rose. "I miss my wife."

"She doubtless misses you, too, and the reunion will occasion much joy. Tell me about tomorrow's cases."

The thought of welcoming Beatitude home was so very cheering —she'd promised an absence of no more than ten days—while the prospect of the Monday-morning parlor session was nearly grim. What fool had decided that the ranking family in the shire should also periodically supply the neighborhood's magistrate?

"One would think having eight younger siblings would result in a temperament suited to the magistrate's job," Grey said. "I find instead that my upbringing has exhausted my patience with petty squabbles. I fear I should not have had Thomas Springer bound over for the quarter sessions."

"Nonsense. He stole from a widow and did so on a lark when he has never known want in all his sixteen years. His family should let him stew for another week or so before they make reparation suffi- cient to get the case withdrawn. His youthful peccadillo will remain that—an embarrassment, rather than an outright scandal—and you will have spared him far more serious consequences a few years hence."

An accurate and sensible summation—also comforting. "His father over-imbibes. I suspect Thomas was trying to earn his father's notice."

"So have a serious talk with the senior Mr. Springer about how a boy's conduct reflects on his antecedents and a good paternal example being the best gift a lad can inherit. Then ask him if he'd like you to approach the widow to hint at the possibility of reparation."

"I'm the magistrate. I cannot approach anybody."

"You can approach her to ask after her well-being, Grey. You need not oversee the negotiations. I can do that."

This case had cost Grey sleep for the past week. Young Tom Springer had no real harm in him, but neither had he any sense. Valerian's suggestion, by contrast, was the embodiment of good sense.

The evening progressed with most of the conversation over dinner relating to the cases to be dealt with on the morrow. There were six, and by the time Valerian was serving the Italian crème cake, Grey knew exactly how he would dispose of five of them.

"And have you any suggestions regarding the allegations brought against Jenny Switzer?" Grey asked.

Valerian topped up Grey's wineglass and sat back. "She's charged with mayhem, if I recall, for taking a swipe at Squire Rutledge?"

"Served him a good slap across the face. The surrounding facts are in dispute."

"No, they are not," Valerian said, carving off a slice of cheddar and passing it to Grey. "Rutledge is a philandering old boor. He has to find maids through the London agencies because none of the local women will allow their daughters to work in his home. He made a grab at Daisy once when she was fourteen."

"If somebody had thought to tell me that, I might have cited conflict of interest and sent the case elsewhere." The wine went perfectly with the cheese, not too sweet, a hint of effervescence, a nice, light note on which to end a pleasant evening, though the Switzer case was anything but light.

Jenny was fifteen. She would not fare well at all if incarcerated or sent to the quarter sessions.

Valerian served himself some cheese. "The crime of mayhem requires not simply injury, but permanent disfigurement or disability to the victim, does it not?"

"How do you know that?"

"Because I helped Ash learn his law. Somebody had to quiz him. Sycamore was too busy annoying all and sundry, Oak was off painting, Hawthorne was pulling up tree stumps with his bare hands, and so forth. Will the blow Jenny dealt leave a scar?"

"She barely scratched him, more's the pity."

"Then dismiss the charge for lack of foundation. I will send word to Miss Pepper at Pepper Ridge that a young lady with a reputation for hard work and sound morals is available for employment. That will spare the combatants awkward moments on market day or in the churchyard."

Pepper Ridge—formerly Summerfield House—was more than ten miles distant from Dorning Hall by the lanes, and did indeed patronize a different church and market town.

"You're sure about the definition of mayhem?"

"Absolutely certain, and Rutledge won't argue with the king's man in any event. He's lucky you didn't charge him with attempted rape."

"Had I done that, Jenny would have suffered, and no jury would have convicted him."

"Perhaps, but there's merit in giving Jenny's account the credence it deserves, Grey, and to letting Rutledge know his misbehavior won't be tolerated. When you dismiss the charges against Jenny, put the fear of God into Rutledge for provoking a young maid into defending herself. Would you like to bide here tonight?"

Grey would like to bide at the cottage for the next week, where no empty corridors made the hours drag and no whining neighbors could bother him with their squabbles and disgraceful behavior.

"I will take myself home. This is exceptionally good cake."

"I wanted to try the recipe I translated to make sure I got it right. My cook/housekeeper has the Sabbath free in addition to her half day, so I had the run of the kitchen."

"*You* cooked this meal?"

"I like to cook, and I wasn't about to serve the Earl of Casriel cold sandwiches and ale for a Sunday meal." Valerian corked the wine, portioned a quarter of the remaining cake into a bowl, and rose.

"Some sustenance to see you through tomorrow's ordeal." He walked Grey to the front door, as a considerate host should.

"You mentioned Miss Pepper," Grey said. "How is she settling in?"

Valerian put aside the cake and wine to hold Grey's coat for him. "It's early days. Dorset is not Mayfair, and Pepper Ridge requires a lot of attention."

And that was a telling dodge. "You were seen walking with her at yesterday's picnic."

"Hawthorne cannot keep his mouth shut, while Oak sees much and says little. We are blessed in our brothers."

"Does one conclude that you and Miss Pepper are congenially disposed toward each other?"

Valerian passed him the cake and the wine. "I like her, I suppose she likes me. I also like a pleasant meal, a ramble across the fields, a lively fiddle tune. She is in want of allies, and I know how that feels. Try not to eat all the cake on the walk home."

He bowed Grey into the night air, and while Grey still missed Beatitude terribly, the ache had dulled to a patient misery. Half the remaining wine and a few nibbles of cake on the walk home helped soothe even that discomfort.

Not until Grey was preparing for bed an hour later did it occur to him to wonder how a man with *eight devoted, loving siblings* could know what a want of allies felt like.

THE SUNDAY CRÈME cake had been an extravagance, but Valerian had been in a self-indulgent mood since leaving Emily Pepper at the Summerton picnic on Saturday. He'd taken his plunge in the mill stream—a near-daily ritual of late—and then trudged home to resume kicking himself for offering to teach Miss Pepper the country dances.

"Because I am an idiot," he muttered, turning his gig down the lane that led to Pepper Ridge.

The London publisher who'd shown an interest in his manuscript had been merely polite. His note had been nearly perfunctory. No talk of subscriptions, serialization, or—damn it all to hell—*money*. Sycamore had either ignored or missed Valerian's hints that he was available to assist in the management of Sycamore's club, but then, Ash was fulfilling that role quite well.

Leaving Valerian to man the exalted post of dancing master without portfolio.

Pepper Ridge rose up at the end of the drive, an edifice that to outward appearances exemplified the stately country home at its finest. The interior told another tale, much like a well-dressed bachelor's empty pockets contradicted his fine attire.

Valerian brought his horse to a halt at the foot of the terrace steps and handed the reins off to a groom. "Clovis might appreciate a bucket of water. I should not be long."

"Very good, guv'nor. Come along, horse."

Valerian had arrived early. Having two sisters, he was well acquainted with a young lady's notion of time when an outing required dressing for the occasion. To his surprise, Miss Pepper received him almost immediately.

She bobbed a curtsey, frills and flounces flapping at her hems and bodice. "Will I do, Mr. Dorning?"

God save the poor woman. "You would do superbly for an evening at Almack's." Her dress bared most of her arms and a considerable expanse of her décolletage—not the done thing for an informal late afternoon gathering—and the heavily gathered and embroidered underdress was overlaid with a silk demiskirt that fell to about six inches above the underhem.

The dress was both too much and not *nearly* enough.

Miss Pepper smoothed a hand over her skirts. "We are not bound for Almack's."

"Shall I be honest?"

"Somebody had better be. Briggs claimed this was precisely the outfit to make a fine first impression."

"That shade of soft blue is lovely, the material is gorgeous, and the workmanship exquisite."

"Put me out of my misery, Mr. Dorning. I've chosen poorly, haven't I? Poorly for Dorset."

"You have chosen well for a London formal dinner." Though even for an occasion such as that, the ensemble was overdone and not particularly flattering. "Let's have a look at your dressing closet. I'm sure we can find something better suited to rural socializing. How do the renovations proceed?"

"I have no idea." Miss Pepper took off up the stairs at a good clip, lacy trim fluttering. "I look in on the job at the end of every day, and the head carpenter claims they are proceeding quite on schedule. If that's so, shouldn't I hear hammers banging and saws sawing?"

"Incessantly." Grey was preparing to demolish the family wing of Dorning Hall, and even that effort resulted in a ceaseless din.

"The master suite is three doors down on the left," she said when they'd reached the top of the stairs. "Note the silence. By this hour of the afternoon, the workmen usually bestir themselves to make some sort of racket, but much of the day I'm not sure what goes on in there. They have removed the old wallpaper, taken up the worn carpets, removed the fixtures and the wainscoting, and carted those away, too, but that has taken them nearly two weeks."

That list of preparatory tasks should have taken a competent crew a day, possibly two. "Let's drop in, shall we?" Valerian started for the master suite before his hostess could stop him. "Our dower house at Dorning Hall was struck by lightning last autumn. I oversaw the selling of the salvageable brick, stone, timber, glass, and fixtures. I can assure you, tearing down a single set of rooms for refurbishing should not take two weeks."

He opened the door without knocking and interrupted what appeared to be a game of dice.

"Taking a break, gentlemen?"

"So we were," a tall, spare man with thinning blond hair said, getting to his feet without any apparent haste. "The afternoon break, as it happens. Back to work, lads. And who might you be, sir?"

The *lads* glanced around, then produced awls, hammers, and nails.

"Let's have this discussion in the corridor," Miss Pepper said as one of the men began to pound a nail in what Valerian was certain was a random location. Miss Pepper marched out, her fancy dress earning stares all around.

"Mr. Dorning, may I make known to you Mr. Prentiss Ogilvy. Mr. Ogilvy, Mr. Valerian Dorning."

"From Dorning Hall?" Ogilvy asked.

"The very same. You've been at work for the past two weeks, as I understand it."

The Dorning name took some of the shine off Ogilvy's arrogance. "Give or take. These old houses can't be hurried, I always say. We're making fine progress, though, like I tell the miss here."

His speech wasn't that of the Dorset countryside, and Valerian hadn't recognized any of the men working for him.

"Where do you hail from, Mr. Ogilvy?"

Ogilvy winced as a crash sounded from the master parlor. "Over Portsmouth way. We go where the work is, and Mr. Pepper was powerful eager to get this job started."

"And when will that be?" Valerian inquired.

"Beg pardon, sir?"

"When will you start on the job? From what I can see, you've been sitting about for two weeks, doubtless swilling some fine Pepper Ridge ale, and pretending that a day's worth of demolition takes a week to complete. Perhaps between rounds of dice, it does."

Ogilvy grasped his dusty lapels. "Now see here, Mr. Dorning, the Ogilvys has been carpenters and masons since Good Queen Bess's day, and if the structure isn't to be damaged in the stripping down, then care must be taken."

The ale on Ogilvy's breath would have knocked Valerian's horse onto its muscular rump. "You disposed of rugs and fixtures for Miss Pepper. How carefully did you account for the proceeds?"

Ogilvy's gaze darted to Miss Pepper, who was remaining admirably silent. "Proceeds, sir?"

First the invocation of Good Queen Bess, now the echoing. The man was a crook and a stupid one.

"I'm sure the contract you signed obligated you to account for any salvage sold on behalf of the owner. You are entitled to a commission —fifteen percent is the highest I've seen—but not to loot the premises. Where is your accounting?"

"The, um,"—Ogilvy ran a finger around the inside of his wrinkled neckcloth—"the carpets and such haven't sold yet. I sent them to Portsmouth to get a better price."

"Did you send the books too?" Miss Pepper asked, all eager good cheer.

"Them books are in the stables in crates."

"Because," Valerian said, "storing old books in a horse barn is sure to safeguard their value, but for the attentions of the rats, mice, and other vermin, to say nothing of the damage stable cats can do. You may go back to work, Mr. Ogilvy."

As Mr. Ogilvy slipped through the door, the noise coming from the master suite spiked, then receded to a thumping din.

Miss Pepper paced off, skirts swishing. "I told Papa that a crew available on short notice was a crew with little to recommend it. I told him to read the blasted contract, because I haven't had the time. The salvage was to be sent to Dorset, not to a booming port town nearly seventy miles away. Portsmouth has access to every trade route frequented by British ships. Nobody there has need of my old carpets or door latches. I had *no idea* that I was due the proceeds of the salvage."

"Miss Pepper?"

"I knew better than to trust Ogilvy. I *knew better*, and I did not listen to my own instincts." She stalked up the corridor, coming to a halt outside a door with lambs and geese carved into the panel. "I sat in that stuffy parlor and let Briggs lecture me on the finer points of pall-mall, which I have no intention of ever playing, and which she has not played for at least fifteen years. I am good at reading contracts —very good—and I should have been..." She rested her forehead on the door, the wind abruptly dropping from her sails. "Forgive me, I am in a temper."

"I adore your temper."

Temper put a little color in her cheeks and fire in her eyes. Temper cut through her careful manners and the subtle watchfulness she carried beneath her polite behavior. Perhaps she had kissed Valerian in a temper of some sort, for kissing also animated her.

"You do not adore my temper."

"A gentleman never argues with a lady, but in this case, I must. What's to be done about Ogilvy?"

"Nothing will be done. Papa is too pleased to be once again embroiled in his mercantile adventures, and I am to entertain myself with putting the house to rights. If Ogilvy takes a year to do a job that should last only a month, Papa won't mind."

She pushed open the door and led Valerian into a sitting room done up with gold and azure fleur-de-lis wallpaper, dark blue velvet curtains, and the delicate, ornate furnishings popular in the previous century.

"My dressing closet is through the bedroom," she said. "Briggs will be horrified that you're in my private apartment, but she's very likely having her nap at this hour. She's perpetually horrified lately. Dorset doesn't seem to agree with her."

Miss Pepper's movements were brisk, her tone equally matter-of-fact, and yet Valerian was certain he was in the presence of an upset female.

"Do you *want* to spend your time refurbishing the house?"

"So the likes of Ogilvy can condescend to me and deceive me while wasting Papa's money? He has done little in the two weeks he's been here, as you noted, Mr. Dorning, and this house has more than two dozen bedrooms. The thought of spending years... No, I do not want to spend my days pretending I have authority to refurbish this dratted hulk of a dwelling."

Not merely an upset female, a furious female. "If you don't want to take the house in hand, what do you want to do?"

Valerian had followed her right into the confines of the dressing closet, a room about eight feet square. With rows of dresses lining two walls and trunks and wardrobes on the other two, the space was crowded indeed.

"I am a dab hand at business, if you must know, Mr. Dorning. Lately, Caleb and Tobias have taken over the jobs I used to see to in that regard. What I want..." Miss Pepper stood close enough that her light floral scent blended with the lavender sachets fragrancing her wardrobe.

"Yes?" Such soft brown eyes she had, and such storms brewed in her gaze.

"Is to kiss you again."

CHAPTER THREE

The Dorning family members were noted for their striking eyes. On some of the siblings—Emily had met a half dozen of them—the shade was nearer that of periwinkles or bluebells than a plain blue. On others, the hue was cerulean, more brilliant than northern summer skies.

Valerian's eyes were a regal blue, the hint of purple so subtle, it likely changed with his attire or his mood. More impressive than the color, though, was the force of his gaze. When he looked at Emily, he gave her his attention with a calm, complete focus that said she'd captured his interest utterly for as long as necessary to convey whatever sentiment she pleased.

Better still, his eyes gave away a hint of his own feelings. When Emily announced her desire for another kiss, he neither mocked her nor turned up chilly.

If anything, his expression became bashful. "While I am flattered beyond telling at your"—he gazed about at silks, muslin, velvets, and lace—"your declaration, a kiss shared with a man such as I can lead nowhere."

"Such as you? You are an earl's son, a gentleman, a neighbor of sorts…" A handsome devil who ignored his own good looks and dealt always in honesty and decency.

"Miss Pepper—Emily—I have *no prospects.* None."

He could have produced any other objection—*I care for you only as a friend, your antecedents and mine are from different strata, my affections are elsewhere engaged, a lady of such forward manners has no appeal to a man of my breeding*—and Emily would have been less surprised.

"What need has an earl's son for prospects?"

The peerage made a great show of titular succession, giving the heir a courtesy title and much deference, but from what Emily had seen, the entire lot of them got on quite nicely. Officer's commissions, government posts, mercantile apprenticeships with wealthy uncles, diplomatic engagements—if a job paid well and carried influence, an aristocrat's younger son generally held it.

The nobs looked after their own, and the rest of the country managed on the land, means, and business left over.

"In my position," Mr. Dorning said, "a man's prospects, or lack of them, define him. Shall we find you a comfortable afternoon dress that allows you freedom on the dance floor?"

"The afternoon dresses are in this section." Emily gestured to the rack behind him, where a dozen lovely long-sleeved, modest creations hung side by side. "I favor the blue."

"Then save the color blue for the assembly itself. How about this one?"

He'd chosen her favorite. "Briggs says that raspberry color is too worldly for me." The shade was a red-leaning purple, like ripe berries or the last streaks of a gorgeous sunset. Emily had fallen in love with the fabric, a light cotton with a graceful drape.

Mr. Dorning took the dress from the rack. "The color flatters nearly everybody. I have a riding jacket of this shade, and I cut quite a dash in it. In the country, we aren't as particular about who can wear what hues on which occasions. If a cloak grows worn and would make a lovely underskirt, then practicality wins out over Mayfair sensibilities. I'll wait for you downstairs."

He bowed and moved toward the door, as self-possessed as if he'd encountered Emily at some London musicale.

"What about my kiss?"

He stopped, turned, and approached her. "I must think on that notion—torment myself with it, if you want the truth—but until I can better reconcile the obligations of honor with the selfish clamorings of a mere mortal man..." He kissed her cheek, a soft, delicious, leisurely press of lips. "There's a kiss. Now you cannot accuse me of denying a lady her wishes."

His smile held a hint of impishness, and Emily realized she had just been flirted with. Gently, subtly, and ever so charmingly.

"Away with you," she said, flapping the dress at him. "Or you will make us late."

Prattle, her lady's maid, soon had her changed out of her fancy gown and reunited with Mr. Dorning in the guest parlor.

"We must make haste," Emily said. "If Briggs catches me in this outfit, she will order me to put the other on, and we will be late in truth."

Mr. Dorning offered his arm. "Then to horse, Miss Pepper, lest the domestic despot throw you into the fashion dungeon."

They had made it nearly to the front door when Briggs emerged from the family parlor and planted herself in the middle of the corridor.

"Miss Briggs." Mr. Dorning offered her a genteel bow. "Good day."

"Sir." She nodded at him and turned a puzzled regard on Emily's dress. "What prompted this... this departure from the agreed-upon plan?"

More than the question itself, the tone ripped at the pleasure Emily took to be on an outing with Mr. Dorning. That he would hear her addressed like a wayward schoolgirl brought a hot flush of mortification to her cheeks.

"The dress is quite pretty, isn't it?" Mr. Dorning said. "One of those ensembles that might not make much of an impression hanging in the wardrobe, but is marvelously attractive on the right woman. Never fear, Miss Briggs. Though the local lads will gawk, they will be on their best behavior, or I will deal with them severely."

He sketched a bow and opened the door for Emily.

"Good day, Briggs," Emily said. "I'll see you after supper." And just like that, she was out the door and sitting next to Mr. Dorning in his gig. "Why do I feel as if I've been liberated from the hulks?"

He clucked the horse into a trot and steered the vehicle down the drive. "Because that woman has more confidence in her own judgment than she ought. She had you decked out to impress the patronesses at Almack's, not to hop around the village assembly rooms."

"Briggs means well." *But listening to her would have made a fool of me.* "In London, she urged me to accept the suit of Mr. Anthony Beerbaum. I refused, and we've been at cross-purposes ever since."

He turned the horse smoothly onto the lane. "I am not acquainted with Mr. Beerbaum."

"He's a fortune-hunting nobody with, as you say, more confidence in his own opinions than he ought to have—and he has an endless store of opinions. Fortune hunters tend to be wealthy in their opinions. They have considered perspectives on everything from my eyebrows to the embroidery on my hems."

"Because," Mr. Dorning said, "gazing at your hems as they partner you allows their eyes to stray over your person without offering outright insult. I hope you left every one of them with broken toes. Would you like to take the reins?"

Broken toes? That was the proper response to a disrespectful gaze? *Broken toes?* "Do you teach your dancing students to break a man's toes for rudeness?"

"Absolutely." He said that in all seriousness. "If you don't want to ruin your gloves, you can drive bare-handed or wear mine. The horse's name is Clovis—king of the Franks, founder of the Merovin-gian Dynasty—and he's a perfect gentleman."

Emily was still marveling over the concept of breaking a man's toes. "I don't know how to drive, Mr. Dorning. Papa puts a coach and four at my disposal, and I've never had the need to drive myself."

"You are in Dorset now," he said, putting the reins in one hand. "Take my gloves."

They effected the exchange, with Emily drawing off her own gloves and putting on Mr. Dorning's. He then showed her how to hold the reins, how to communicate with the horse so the beast dropped from a trot to a walk, how to navigate a turn.

"With a sensible equine, the driver has little to do," Mr. Dorning said, "rather like a good dance partner. You look after your own feet, and your partner manages the rest. I think you have natural talent as a whip, Miss Pepper."

"I am terrified," Emily said, though she was exhilarated too. "At any moment, Clovis will shy at a rabbit and go careening off across the fields. We will be dashed to the ground, and I will break my head upon a rock."

She was only half jesting.

"If Clovis panics, you hop out of the coach at the first opportu-nity. You might turn an ankle, but you will not break your head. A bolting horse can sometimes be controlled by a rider, but when drag-ging a conveyance behind him, the same animal is harder to contain. Take the left turning into the village."

The gig went a little wide, but Emily managed the turn. "I like this. Ladies in the country drive themselves?"

"You should probably take your companion along for anything but a trip to the home farm to fetch honey for your cook, but yes. Ladies in the country drive themselves."

"Perhaps the country isn't all bad."

"You did not care for London, and you are skeptical of the coun-try. Where would you like to be?"

Like most of Mr. Dorning's sallies, that question was insightful.

"I am exactly where I want to be at the moment, sir." She signaled the horse to a walk and then brought him to a smooth halt outside the village livery stable.

Mr. Dorning handed Emily down and dealt with the hostler. A lone fiddle was tuning up somewhere nearby, and a dozen people strolled the green in pairs.

"I'm nervous," Emily said. "Not only because my dancing is less graceful than a bear's, but also because I'm neither fish, nor flesh, nor good red herring."

Emily braced herself for platitudes: *Nonsense, my dear. You'll be the toast of the evening. Your dancing is exquisite.* She'd heard them all and told herself those compliments were meant kindly.

"Then be yourself," Mr. Dorning said. "Simply be yourself, and that will be adequate to any challenge you face here today."

Novel advice, and she suspected Mr. Dorning followed it himself.

He knew everybody, of course, and handled the introductions faultlessly. Then Emily was walking through the steps of the dance pattern while Mr. Dorning used his cane to beat a steady rhythm on the plank flooring, and the fiddler offered a dirge-like version of the dance tune.

I am enjoying myself. The thought popped into her head as young Mr. Woodmore Troke collided with Miss May Cheaverton, amid warnings from the onlookers to "Watch out, Woodie!" and "Tack left, Maysie, or he'll sink you for sure!"

The couple remained upright, more at peril of capsizing from laughter than anything else. Through it all, Mr. Dorning called assurances, dance steps, the occasional sly jest, and advice, until the dancers were moving at a proper tempo. They learned three dances, though everybody but Emily appeared to know the first one fairly well.

When the time came to wander back to the livery, Emily was tired, but in a good way—for a change.

"They've seen those dances done many times," Mr. Dorning said, backing Clovis into the gig's traces and fastening the harness buckles. "Old Roger de Coverly is often the opening or closing dance. He gets the blood moving or, in the alternative, ends the evening on a jolly note."

The hostlers were busy with other customers, and Mr. Dorning dealt with the horse as if he was used to serving as his own groom.

"My blood is moving," Emily replied. "I cannot say when I've enjoyed an evening more." They'd finished up with punch and cake at the local inn, which Mr. Dorning had paid for from coins in a jar discreetly positioned near the fiddler's feet. "Was I to compensate you for this evening's instruction?"

He stood unmoving by the gig, while the horse flicked an ear back and forth. "The jar is for donations. I pass a bit to the fiddler, pay for the punch and cake, and there's seldom much left over. Let me hand you up. Would you like to drive?"

Emily climbed into the bench. "I would. No need to lend me your gloves. Was my question awkward?"

He took the place beside her, making the vehicle rock. "My answer was awkward."

Ah, so that's what he'd meant about having no prospects. He'd meant he had *no money*. Emily took up the reins and clucked to Clovis, who seemed to know the way back to Pepper Ridge. The summer sunset was lovely, the evening air a fine antidote to the exertions of dancing.

Emily remained close to Mr. Dorning when he handed her down in front of the manor house. "I meant what I said earlier."

"I beg your pardon?"

"I have never enjoyed myself on an outing more, Mr. Dorning. I will look forward to learning more dances next week."

He stepped back. "I will look forward to that as well. Your servant, Miss Pepper." He bowed very correctly over her hand and waited for her to open the front door before driving off.

She watched him go, her heart light. He had no money, but never had a problem been easier to solve, for she had pots and pots of money and nobody to share it with. She assayed a little pirouette before skipping up the steps, much too happy to deal with Briggs, Papa, or the housekeeper's latest recitation of domestic drama.

~

"OSGOOD IS ALMOST his old self again," Caleb Booth said, pouring two brandies and bringing one to Tobias. "Good to see him enjoying the work and giving orders once more."

"To Osgood Pepper's health." Tobias Granger lifted the glass, the toast sincere. Osgood had taken a pair of grubby boys from the mill floor and made successful merchants of them. Of course, they were in part to thank for Osgood's own success, but the initial generosity had been Pepper's, and he remained generous with them still.

"To his health and to his determination to bide in the country." Caleb took a sip of his drink. "I did not see this sudden penchant for ruralizing coming, Toby. This house could put up a regiment comfortably, and the distance from the bedroom to the dining room is a morning constitutional."

Caleb was doing what he always did. Playing the jovial confrere while tiptoeing up to a delicate topic. Tobias found that strategy tedious and preferred that Caleb either keep his schemes to himself or air them directly.

"Osgood knows what he's about, Caleb, and his present priorities work to our advantage, so adapt your opinions accordingly."

The library was splendid, if a bit shabby. Old books had one scent —vanilla and leather—a library full of neglected old books another. A hint of dust and mildew, a touch of bygone hound about the carpets. The ceiling boasted a fresco of cherubs, billowing clouds, golden trumpery, and a buxom, spear-bearing female in a white robe, while the globe in the bow window was seventy years out of date.

"How does rusticating in the back of God's own wilderness work to our advantage?" Caleb asked, giving the globe a spin.

Caleb's tone was mild, his features pleasant. He showed the

world a cheerful, tolerant mien, and for all Tobias knew, Caleb *was* cheerful and tolerant. He was also a shrewd, ambitious, hardworking businessman, though not nearly as astute about people as he was about buying and selling cloth.

"Osgood wants Emily to marry into the gentry," Tobias said, "or so he used to claim. No peer-for-sale will do for Emily, and in that regard, Osgood is wise."

"He is an indulgent papa," Caleb allowed. "We know that. We also know none of the fortune hunters stood a chance with dear Emily."

"And thank God for that, but the squires and baronets don't stand a chance with her either."

Caleb slouched against the casement of a tall window, the fading sun catching the fiery highlights in his auburn hair.

"We can pray that is so, but I lack your confidence, Tobias. Some of these country gents have Town bronze, plenty of means, and impressive physiques."

"But they are country gents. Emily has spent most of her life learning to move among the peerage without causing offense. She's out of her depth here, and she knows it. We will be her dear, familiar friends. Ready to escort her anywhere, deflect the presuming bumpkins, and remind her of the splendors of the capital should she tire of ruralizing."

"She does seem a bit out of sorts lately, but then, Osgood gave us all a scare." Caleb gazed out over the front drive, his expression distracted.

Had Caleb truly been unhappy to see Osgood fading, or had he been relieved? "I've done some reading on foxglove medications," Tobias said.

"Oh?"

"Sometimes, the cure is temporary. Sometimes, the patient gets a reprieve, and then the dropsical symptoms carry him off with little warning."

Caleb used the edge of the window casement to scratch between his shoulder blades, like a bullock against a sapling. "When I die, I hope it's with little warning. A decline like Osgood endured was hardly dignified." He tossed back the last of his drink. "You are still convinced Emily will settle on one of us?"

"We are all she has. The nobs consider her a mushroom, the squires consider her a nabob's princess, the nabobs threw their sons at her in hopes of getting their hands on her money. We care for her, we know her, we understand her."

"You don't mention that we like her."

Caleb apparently more than liked Emily. Tobias had no idea whether the affliction was romantic love, physical attraction, or an amalgam of the two with a soupçon of old-fashioned greed, but Caleb watched Emily with a covetousness he usually reserved for the inventories of failing competitors.

"More to the point," Tobias said, "Emily likes us. She will soon see the advantage of choosing one of us for a spouse." In which case, he and Caleb had long ago agreed that the loser should cede the field with good grace, and the winner would recall that good grace when it came time to administer Osgood's vast estate.

A pragmatic plan that saw to the security of all concerned, which was really what Osgood himself wished for.

"If we are such obvious superior choices," Caleb said, "who is driving Emily up the lane?"

She hadn't been at supper, which was served at an ungodly early hour in the country, but then, women could keep to their rooms for any number of reasons. Tobias went to the window and watched a one-horse gig come to a halt at the foot of the steps. The beast in the traces was glossy and well built, but a bit on the unprepossessing side. No matching white socks, no braids in his mane.

"That is one of the Earl of Casriel's host of brothers," Tobias said. "They clean up nicely but haven't a proverbial pot between them."

"The youngest owns The Coventry Club in Town. He has a pot or two, I'll wager."

"That's not the youngest. They are all named for plants.

Hawthorne Dorning married the woman who used to be lady of this manor, if my interrogation of the footmen is to be believed. The spare trains dogs, of all things, and there's a painter in the batch. The Dorning family suffers from the increasingly common ailment of having more pedigree than means. Come away from the window, Caleb."

The Dorning fellow bowed correctly over Emily's hand, and when the front door banged closed, he climbed into his humble conveyance and tooled away.

"But where did she *go* with him?" Caleb muttered, pouring himself another drink. "Why go anywhere with a fellow whose idea of a well-spent day is to fish, nap, swill ale, and converse with his hounds? These country types have no ambition."

"A pleasant drive at the end of a summer day strikes me as more appealing than another supper listening to you, me, and Osgood discuss engineering modifications to make steam looms more efficient. Emily is simply bored with rural life and trying to be gracious to the bumpkin-ry. One of us will eventually take her to wife, and all will be as it should."

Caleb appeared soothed by that recitation, though he tossed back the rest of his brandy before sauntering from the library, a man with no apparent destination. He would attempt to catch Emily on the stairs and fail—she moved at nothing less than a forced march these days—and he'd try to pry the details of her outing from her if he did catch her.

Tobias, by contrast, rose early enough that he and Emily were the first down to breakfast most mornings, and they had a good half hour to confer—as a cordial husband and wife often conferred—regarding the day's schedule.

Emily hadn't even mentioned an outing with the Dorning fellow —Elderberry? Setwall? What *was* his name?—which confirmed that she put no importance whatsoever on Dorning's company.

In an abundance of caution, Tobias would ensure that remained the case.

~

A PARADOX HAD VISITED itself upon Valerian the day he'd hugged his brother Oak farewell. Oak had taken a post in Hampshire restoring paintings for some parsimonious widow, a fine use of both his charm and his artistic ability.

The result was that, of the seven Dorning brothers, only Valerian and Casriel remained at the family seat. The irony of feeling thronged by louts and boors for most of his life and missing those same louts and boors terribly was cruel.

The spare, Willow, had married an earl's daughter, Lady Susannah Haddonfield. They were awash in marital bliss and puppies, for Willow loved dogs and dogs loved him. Fortunately, the favor of a few well-placed aristocrats meant polite society loved to pay extravagantly for Will's canines and for his services as a trainer of hounds.

Ash, who had read law, was in Town as the second-in-command at Sycamore's club. Sycamore, the youngest, had struck out into the world without much gentlemanly education and was apparently thriving all the better for it as the proprietor of a gaming establishment doing business as a supper club.

Hawthorne had taken on the challenge of converting Dorning Hall's vast botanical riches into a commercial venture, and in the process he'd married Mrs. Margaret Summerfield. They bided on a property of hers that shared a boundary with Dorning Hall, and Hawthorne had never looked happier.

Sitting in her lovely parlor, Margaret looked rather pleased with life too. "I will tell Hawthorne you stopped by, Valerian, and he will be sorry he missed you. More lemonade?"

"No, thank you. I must be going, but I did want to—"

"Uncle Valerian!" Before he could get to his feet, Valerian was stormed by a little girl in a wrinkled pinafore. Adriana climbed into his lap and squeezed him about the neck. "Were you coming up to the nursery to see us?"

Greta, smaller, quieter, and less robust in her mannerisms, hung back by the doorway at her governess's side.

"I was indeed," Valerian said, rising. "Greta, good day." He bowed with Adriana clinging to his neck, which occasioned giggling from Adriana, a smile from Greta, and a look of patient humor from Margaret. "I am burdened with a bag of lemon drops," he went on, "and they grow ever so heavy in my pocket. If only my hands were free to retrieve the bag."

Adriana scrambled down. "You're free now."

"Margaret?"

"They may each have *one*."

He withdrew the bag and held it out to Adriana, who snatched a sweet like a trout after a fly. Greta was more deliberate, and the young governess, who blushed becomingly, somewhere in between.

"And for you?" Valerian held out the bag to his hostess when the children had gone whooping down the corridor.

"You are so sweet," Margaret said, rising to select a treat for herself. "I do believe you are the girls' favorite uncle."

The compliment stung, though Valerian wasn't in truth any sort of uncle to the children at all. "I am the uncle they know the best, all the others having found gainful employment elsewhere."

"And yet," Margaret said, taking the bag and holding it out to him, "you somehow have the coin to buy the children a treat."

Valerian had exactly three shillings on his person and not much more than that to his name. He did own Abbotsford, but the property produced no income at present.

"With all the other uncles flown," he said, "somebody must drop by to spoil them. I did have a question for you, though."

"Have a lemon drop, Valerian."

He took one to humor her, but in truth he'd counted them out and figured he had about six visits' worth in the bag.

"My question regards Pepper Ridge, or Summerfield House, as it will likely be called for the next fifty years."

Margaret wrinkled her nose, which made her resemble Greta

facing a plate of mashed turnips. "I don't miss the place. I didn't spend much time there if I could help it. My former brother-in-law was no sort of house steward, and that became increasingly evident."

"If you were to make a list of matters to address in an effort to restore the house to its former glory, how would you go about it?"

Margaret rolled up the bag of lemon drops and passed it back to him. "This has to do with Miss Pepper, doesn't it?"

"With being neighborly. I gather her father's improved health means she's more or less on her own putting the house to rights, and she has no experience with a dwelling that size."

Margaret returned to her chair, so Valerian took a seat as well. This was the point of his call, for he'd no real need to observe the good cheer, laughter, and comfort in which Hawthorne and his family dwelled. Hawthorne's air of contentment was palpable from twenty paces upwind.

"The problem as I saw it," Margaret said slowly, "was a want of leadership in the senior staff. The cook and housekeeper get on well, which means they spend an inordinate amount of time in the housekeeper's sitting room, ostensibly discussing menus, but in truth gossiping. When the upper servants set that kind of example, and the butler and first footman are no better, the entire staff mills about, criticizing each other, nattering about nothing, and slacking. The hard workers are compelled to slack lest they be condemned for making others look bad, and the whole house suffers."

Valerian had written exactly this in the chapter of his book on managing domestics. "Are they capable, the senior staff?"

"Capable, but unmotivated. I should call on Miss Pepper, shouldn't I?"

"In a social capacity, I'm sure that would be appreciated, but you cannot be seen to undermine her authority or criticize her as lady of the manor. Perhaps if you took Lady Casriel with you, or Daisy, or both?"

"We should call on her," Margaret said. "I have been remiss, what with"—she smiled at her hands—"being a newlywed."

Valerian rose rather than allow her to extol the virtues of the married state. "I'm sure Miss Pepper would appreciate a call. Please give my regards to Hawthorne."

"I certainly will." Margaret escorted him to the door, and he was tapping his hat onto his head when the inevitable question came. "How is your manuscript coming along?"

He said the same thing he'd said the previous Saturday when Hawthorne had asked him. "Quite well, thank you. The revisions are complete, and the next step will be publication."

"I look forward to reading it someday. Thank you so much for calling."

Valerian bowed over her hand, made his escape, and paused only long enough to wave in the direction of the nursery windows before swinging into the saddle and cantering—not galloping—down the drive.

He hadn't been exactly honest with Margaret regarding his manuscript. Publication was one possible next step. The more likely eventuality was that nobody would want to print the damned thing, nobody would sign up to buy it, and months of hard work would never see the light of day.

That possibility constituted failure.

Complete, utter failure, and it was by far more likely than publication.

CHAPTER FOUR

In London, the great mass of unvouchered wretches who were denied access to Almack's regarded Wednesday evenings during the Season as drudgery. They hosted or attended consolation entertainments and by mutual agreement ignored the shame of exclusion from the sanctum sanctorum.

Emily gave her appearance one last appraisal in the cheval mirror. What woman in her right mind preferred tepid punch, dry cake, and gossip to the fresh air and friendly company to be had in Dorset?

She had done as Mr. Dorning had suggested and saved the blue dress for the upcoming assembly, which meant this week's choice was a pale green muslin with three-quarter sleeves that ended in small lace cuffs. The bodice and collar were also edged in cream lace, but only edged.

"I cannot believe Prattle laid out such an unimpressive ensemble for you," Briggs said, coming to a halt on the threshold of Emily's sitting room. "I will have a word with her. When you are new to the neighborhood, appearances matter. I thought I'd made that plain to her, but she is merely a lady's maid."

Briggs hadn't knocked before entering, though if Emily remarked that presumption, Briggs would sulk until Michaelmas.

"I chose this outfit," Emily said, turning from the mirror. "I tried to impress all and sundry with my sartorial splendor in London, and my plan failed. If last week's outing is any indication, I am well advised to reconnoiter the neighborhood before I trot out the French fashions and expensive evening gowns."

The plan to win the tolerance of London's hostesses through an abundance of lace, jewels, and embroidered flourishes hadn't been Emily's, but rather, the confident advice of *the best* modistes and milliners. Blaming them for bad guidance now served no purpose.

Briggs closed the door gently, and even in that simple task—by the posture of her shoulders, her downcast gaze, the soft sigh she permitted herself—she signaled resignation.

"Do you know how frustrated you become with your father?" Briggs asked. "You tell him to rest, to partake of good food, to moderate his consumption of spirits. He pretends to listen, then does as he pleases much of the time, and that course brought him perilously close to ruined health."

Papa had actually come perilously close to death. "Papa is an adult. He can be reasoned with, but his decisions are his own."

Briggs crossed to the dressing closet and opened a wardrobe. The dress hanging on the door was a cream dinner gown with puffed sleeves and intricate pearl embroidery all over the bodice. The ensemble was both exquisite and hideous. By candlelight, the pearls turned Emily's bust into a beacon worthy of a Channel lighthouse.

"Mr. Pepper is a man," Briggs said, taking down the dress. "He need never consider who will have him for a spouse or who is measuring him against some comely schoolgirl with a winsome smile. Beyond a certain point, wealth is a burden, miss. I have explained this to you. A fellow doesn't want to be seen as a bought-and-paid-for ornament. You lack the standing to attract the notice of a truly wealthy aristocrat. You lack the beauty to turn the heads of important young men. You must fish in a shallow river, among wealthy gentry and not-quite-venerable money."

Briggs carried the cream confection from the dressing closet, holding it as carefully as if it were a holy vestment.

"I am not an angler hoping to catch my supper, Briggs. I've mentioned that to you before." In the gentlest-possible terms, of course.

Briggs tilted her chin up and closed her eyes, a martyr beseeching the heavens for patience. She completed her *tableau vivant* with a grand sigh and a pitying gaze aimed at Emily.

"If you fail to marry before your father goes to his reward, your fortune could be held up for decades—decades, I tell you—in chancery. That fate is one your good father would spare you. I daresay either of his minions would willingly accept you as a spouse, though you know my opinions regarding that pair."

Emily took up the reticule and parasol made to complement the green dress. "Marry Caleb or Tobias?" Briggs had muttered something similar a few weeks ago, and Emily had ignored the comment as one borne of Briggs's penchant for dire imaginings.

"Why do you think they have remained single all these years? Your father trusts them, you know them, and they are familiar with your family's circumstances."

Briggs hung the pale dress on Emily's bedpost, where the pearls sewn across the bodice caught the late afternoon sunshine pouring through the window.

"My family's circumstances are hardly remarkable, Briggs."

"Don't lie to yourself, miss." Said ever so quietly. "You have wealth, your father is respected to the extent a merchant can be respected, but your brother's disgrace reflects poorly on all concerned. I know of what I speak, having been similarly shamed by my own brother's poor choices. Your brother's situation must be disclosed to any man who offers for your hand, though both Mr. Granger and Mr. Booth already know the particulars."

"Then they know Adam was innocent." And how had this

dreadful topic come up in the middle of an otherwise pleasant afternoon?

"Your own father testified against him and saw him transported."

"Old news," Emily said, snatching up the bonnet she'd chosen for this outing. "And Papa regrets his decision." She hoped he did, though he never mentioned Adam by name or otherwise. Adam was dead to him, and Adam was none too happy with Papa.

"You have time to change that dress," Briggs said. "You needn't go about in public looking like a dairy maid."

The green dress had been Emily's idea, a rebellion against all the modistes' suggestions and flattery.

"That is unworthy of you, Briggs. I am decently clad, comfortable enough for dancing, and certainly not in the mood to belabor odd notions such as marriage to Caleb or Tobias. I bid you good day."

Emily forced herself to leave the room at a decorous pace, but fleeing Briggs's fulminating glances and fraught silences was nearly as compelling a motive as spending another pleasant few hours in Mr. Dorning's company.

She took herself to the second guest parlor, which had a view of the drive, and tried to re-establish the sense of happy anticipation she'd enjoyed before the confrontation with Briggs. Like a pesky housefly, Briggs's reminders refused to depart Emily's awareness.

That Adam's situation could affect Emily's marital prospects was a disturbing notion she'd managed not to dwell on. If Papa learned that Emily corresponded with her brother, Papa would be furious, but Emily refused to believe her brother had been guilty as charged. An occasional letter seemed the least consideration she could spare her only sibling.

A clatter of wheels on the crushed-shell drive sent thoughts of Adam back into the mental cupboard where Emily usually locked them. Five minutes later, the butler announced Mr. Valerian Dorning, who looked positively resplendent in country riding attire. His boots were clean, but lacking the champagne shine the Town dandies affected. His cravat was a neat arrangement, no cascades of lace or starched grandiosities of height. His coat was a soft brown that made a nice contrast with his striking blue eyes.

"Miss Pepper, a pleasure."

The words were the most uninspired of civilities, but Emily believed he meant them. He bowed over her hand and offered her a smile that conveyed not mere approval, but genuine warmth.

Emily dipped a curtsey. "Mr. Dorning, the pleasure is mine."

She aimed a look at the butler, who was trying to hover by the doorway. He withdrew, and then Emily was alone with her escort.

"Have I chosen appropriate attire?" she asked, stepping back and twirling. "You must always be honest with me, Mr. Dorning."

"Your ensemble is quite fetching, and I am being not only honest, but restrained in my compliments. Clovis awaits us on the drive, and I suspect you are ready to try your hand at driving again."

Emily preceded him from the room and was soon seated next to him in the gig. He steered the horse around the circular driveway and turned him onto the lane, then passed Emily the reins.

"I have looked forward to this outing," Emily said, clucking the horse into a trot. She had worn riding gloves, but she needed a pair of driving gloves, for she intended to become a proficient whip.

"I have looked forward to another dancing practice as well. A little socializing in the middle of the week is good for us, I think."

Emily knew what to say in response. First, agree with the gentleman. Second, flatter his insight, his wit, or his knowledge. Third, ask him another question designed to allow him to show off his opinions and education. Flatter, smile, repeat.

Mr. Dorning would know that silly exercise for the insult it was.

"Do you know what I think is good for us?" Emily replied, guiding the horse around a curve in the lane, then drawing back gently on the reins.

"My heart beats with anticipation to know your thoughts, Miss Pepper."

She brought the horse to a standstill in the shade of a towering oak. "A kiss shared on a quiet country lane."

Mr. Dorning gazed out over the summer-ripening fields and pastures, his expression caught between humor and something uncomfortable to see.

"Miss Pepper, while I esteem you greatly, I must remark on the lack of variety in your topics of conversation."

He was teasing her again, flirting gently, and Emily did not want to be teased or flirted with. She did not want to be instructed regarding her marital prospects, or scolded regarding her choice of dress. She wanted to be noticed by a man whom she could esteem, one who took her situation to heart and dealt with her honestly.

Mr. Dorning apparently wanted to get on with his afternoon appointments.

"Then I will cease prosing on about a topic which is so clearly of no interest to you."

She gathered up the reins and would have given them a stout shake, but Mr. Dorning's gloved hands covered hers.

"You mistake the situation, Miss Pepper."

No, she did not. She was attracted to a fellow who was doubtless used to the daughters of cits tossing themselves at him, and today was just another day when Emily Pepper had made a cake of herself.

"I have overstepped, Mr. Dorning. It won't happen again. My upbringing is ever a disadvantage in polite company. You needn't make excuses for me."

He gazed down the deserted lane, giving Emily perhaps her last opportunity to admire his profile. He was handsome, but he was also self-possessed, kind, good-humored, and a true gentleman.

"I am attempting to make excuses for myself," he said, slanting her a look, "and largely failing."

"You have done nothing inexcusable."

"Not yet, perhaps." He wrapped the reins around the brake and took off his gloves. Next, he removed Emily's gloves, drawing them from her hands slowly, as she watched him in puzzlement.

He cradled her cheek against the warmth of his palm, then slid a hand around to her nape. "I am about to take unforgivable liberties, Miss Pepper."

"Good. I am about to do the same with you, Mr. Dorning."

And then, heavenly days, he took the most wonderful, glorious, breath-taking liberties Emily had ever enjoyed.

VALERIAN'S CHILDHOOD had ended shortly after his tenth birthday. On that occasion, he'd been reading away a summer morning in the crook of an enormous hemlock when his parents had chosen to quarrel on the bench beneath the tree.

The earl and countess were frequently at odds, and Valerian's first reaction had been resentment that they'd interrupted his peace with their bickering. Mama and Papa argued, they even shouted at each other on rare occasions, and when hostilities were at their worst, Papa would spend long days far afield on the estate collecting botanical specimens.

Because Papa also spent long days far afield in the same pursuit when Mama was in her less bellicose moods, Valerian concluded that parents vexed each other in the normal course—his parents, in any case.

Eavesdropping was rude, but so was interrupting, and once Mama began her cannonades, no sane boy revealed that he was within earshot of the battlefield. What's more, Papa was giving as good as he got.

"You have enough bonnets and furbelows to last into the next century," Papa declared. "I will not stint on the education due our children for the sake of your vanity."

Mama sat up very straight, though her expression was obscured by a straw hat sporting nesting sparrows and silk roses. "For shame, my lord, that you would begrudge your countess a few fripperies. Oak has no need of a drawing master. He draws well enough from sheer natural ability. You want to make the boy into your personal botanical illustrator. Admit it."

Oak could draw anything, from caricatures to portraits to land-scapes. He sketched in papers secreted in his hymnal during services. He drew patterns in the dirt with sticks. Despite that prodigious talent, he longed to make what he called *art*, about which Valerian knew exactly nothing. Painting fusty old gents in frock coats or beldames in enormous skirts wasn't a very exciting ambition.

"Oak could do worse with his talent than to illustrate learned treatises," Papa shot back. "People pay money for such a skill, and those herbals and plant guides serve a greater purpose than keeping your milliner in chocolates and lace."

Mama shifted a foot farther from Papa on the bench. "Talk of money is vulgar. Our sons are gentlemen, and you would have Oak in trade. I despair of you, my lord. You own thousands of acres, enjoy a fine income, and yet you expect me to economize like some shopkeep-er's wife. If you encourage the boy, he'll end up as an itinerant drawing master. Is that what you want for him?"

If Mama expected her goading to escalate the battle, she was bound to disappointment. Papa took off his hat, ran his hand through his hair—he was going thin at the top, much to Valerian's consterna-tion—and rested his arm along the back of the bench.

"The world is changing, my lady," Papa said. "Already, the cits and nabobs are buying up the old estates fallen on hard times. England has lost one set of colonies, and the wars on the Continent can't go on forever. The most ambitious of our yeomanry are off across the seas to someplace where they can purchase their own prop-erties. Idle gentlemen trading on blue blood and family connections are increasingly of no use to anybody."

An odd silence ensued, one indecipherable to a boy whose arbo-real perch was growing uncomfortable.

"You are not idle, my lord." Mama's tone was as conciliatory as Valerian had ever heard it. "You are one of the most respected amateur botanists in the world."

"I thank you for that observation, and I hope our children can make something of my legacy, but the younger boys must be prepared to make their way in that world. Hawthorne loves the land, Willow has a knack with the beasts, Ash has a head for figures, and Sycamore has an adventurous spirit. Oak, thanks be to the Deity, has talent, and I intend to see that talent developed."

What about me? Valerian caught himself before he shouted that question down to his papa.

"I suppose a year or two of instruction couldn't hurt," Mama said. "Drawing is a polite accomplishment, and Oak isn't very musical."

I love music. Valerian also loved dancing and singing, and it wasn't as if he was completely inept at sketching either. The stable master said he had a fine seat and good hands with his pony, and Vicar allowed that he was an apt pupil.

Whatever *apt* meant.

"I'm glad you see my point," Papa said, rising and extending a hand to Mama. "Our boys will be more than idle gentlemen, useful only for making up the numbers at literary salons. I want sons I can be proud of, men of purpose who pull their own weight and make a contribution." He drew Mama to her feet and peered at her bonnet brim. "That is an interesting rendition of the damask rose, your ladyship. I shudder to think how much silk went into its creation."

"It's a pretty decoration. Think instead of how pleased I am to wear it."

They kissed then, which was ridiculous considering that they were old and married. They strolled off, arm in arm, leaving Valerian with much to consider. He set aside his book and remained in his tree when what he wanted was to yell at his parents: *I'm here. I've been here all along, and I am going to be a man of purpose who makes a contribution too.*

Instead, he'd remained silent until his parents were out of sight, and only then did he climb down from the tree.

Many summers later, sitting next to Emily Pepper in the gig on a deserted lane, Valerian felt that small boy reproaching him. He was not a man of consequence, and he made no contribution. Such a fellow had no business kissing a lady as if she were the answer to his every prayer and fantasy.

And yet, Valerian kissed her anyway.

LONDON WAS APPARENTLY full of men who knew only how to fumble, flatter, and bumble in a lady's presence. Emily sat upon the bench of Valerian Dorning's lowly conveyance and learned more about her own body in three minutes than she'd gleaned in the previous three years of waving her fan and waltzing.

She liked the touch of Valerian's fingers on her cheek and chin. He stroked her face slowly, as if memorizing the texture of her flesh and contours of her bones. His caresses made her insides melt like beeswax beneath a candle flame, while her heart felt as light as the flame itself. His lips were soft when they brushed against hers, and his chest was all hard muscle.

Emily pressed against him, hungering for a closeness entirely inappropriate to a country lane. That was another revelation: His kisses could make her lose sight of common sense, of *everything*, save the rise of desire and the frustration of having too little privacy.

When he eased away, Emily rested her forehead against his shoulder. "I think you had best take the reins, Mr. Dorning."

"I think I had best apologize."

"If you apologize for kissing me, then I will apologize for taking similar liberties with your person."

He took up the reins and merely held them, while the horse stood in the middle of the lane, one hip cocked.

"You will not allow me to be the gentleman in this, will you?"

Emily had no idea what he meant. "If kissing disqualifies a fellow from the ranks of gentlemen, I can name you a dozen London swells who should be denied membership in the better clubs."

He slanted a glance at her, the most annoyance she'd seen in him. "A *dozen* men have kissed you?"

"To get their hands on my fortune, they'd kiss my cast-off boots."

Mr. Dorning shook the reins, and Clovis ambled forth. "I don't want your fortune. Your fortune is half the problem."

Then I'll give it away. Instinct kept Emily from saying that. Valerian Dorning was no callow swain to be impressed by grand gestures, and besides, that money had been hard-earned. Tossing it to the wind would alarm Papa and do little good.

"If my fortune is half the problem, what's the other half?"

"My lack of one. You cannot entertain the addresses of an idle ornament, Miss Pepper."

"You and I have kissed. You could at least call me Emily."

Clovis trotted on, and soon they'd be at the village.

"I will call you Emily when we are not in company if you will move a proper distance toward your side of the bench. I cannot think..." He nudged her with his shoulder. "I can think of nothing else but you when you sit so close to me."

"Good." For Emily could think of nothing but him. She shifted a few inches away, which did absolutely nothing to curb her unruly thoughts. "If I marry, my fortune becomes my husband's."

"No, it does not. Your fortune very likely remains tied up in trusts, available solely to you or to the beneficiaries you designate. Generally, your children benefit from such a trust, most especially your daughters, but you could also leave that money to charity."

He sounded very confident, but Emily wasn't so sure. "Then why were all those fellows slobbering over my hand in Town?"

"Because you are sensible, kind, intelligent, pretty, devoted to your papa, and in every regard a lovely woman."

Maybe Valerian Dorning always sounded confident of his conclusions. Maybe he didn't know the extent of the Pepper family fortune.

"Might we stop at the posting inn?" Emily asked as they drew into the village. "I forgot to mail a letter this morning." Not quite true, of course, but Emily distrusted the discretion of the staff at Pepper Ridge.

"I can take it in for you."

"That won't be necessary. I'll only need a moment." Though the letter would take months to reach its destination. She popped down from the gig before Mr. Dorning could assist her, darted into the posting inn, and slipped the letter into the hands of the innkeeper's wife. Emily passed along an extra coin to buy the lady's silence and was back outside in less than a minute.

She'd managed to mail two other letters like this one since arriving at Pepper Ridge, and each time, she expected some comment from the innkeeper's wife. Each time, that good woman merely smiled and slipped the letter into the coaching pouch without a word.

County life had its advantages.

When Emily emerged from the inn, her escort was lounging against the side of the gig, looking delectable and distant.

"Will you waltz with me this evening?" she asked. "Briggs would scold me into next week for such a question."

"Then Briggs deserves a scolding." Mr. Dorning handed her up onto the bench. "A companion is not a governess."

"I must practice saying that, so when I trot it out in a discussion with Briggs, I sound confidant. Will you waltz with me?"

"Of course." He swung up onto the bench and sat a proper distance away. "I will waltz with all the young ladies and maybe even with a few of the young men."

He did that, partnered the less graceful youths in the role of teacher. The result last week had been much hilarity and even some improvement in the lads' dancing skills.

"Pair me up with the worst cases," Emily said. "Lord knows, I've stepped on plenty of masculine toes from time to time. I deserve to have my toes trod upon once or twice for the sake of another's education."

Mr. Dorning guided Clovis to the livery and helped Emily down from the gig. By the time he'd put his gelding up in a roomy stall with a pile of hay, she heard the violinist tuning up in the assembly room.

When Emily would have taken Mr. Dorning's arm and joined the couples strolling on the green, he instead kept hold of her hand.

"Those men—the dozen who did more than slobber over your hand—did they... Were they...?" He looked around and bent two inches closer. "My means are limited, but my family has influence. I can see any Town swell ruined, if need be. My brother Sycamore is diabolically clever in that regard, and Casriel and his countess know everybody. My sister Jacaranda is on familiar terms with the Regent himself, and—"

Emily squeezed his hand to silence him. "You don't believe in dueling?" Tobias and Caleb had both fought duels, though Emily wasn't supposed to know that.

"If a lady's name is associated with a matter of honor, the lady's reputation suffers. In my opinion, a man's consequence makes a better target than his physical person. If, however, those advances were welcome, then I am entirely overstepping, and you must laugh at my presumption."

Emily was not at all inclined to laugh. "Mr. Dorning, a lady suffers untoward advances in the course of a London Season. Either her behavior has given rise to confusion in the minds of her admirers, or her admirers are a lot of bumptious dunderheads who will never pay any mind to her preferences. Those men tried to kiss me. I was not at all motivated to kiss them back."

Mr. Dorning straightened as the violinist went into a flourishy, trilling cadenza. "You kissed me. Several times."

Emily patted his cravat and linked her arm through his. "I did, didn't I? And if you are very lucky, I might step on your toes this evening as well."

He escorted Emily to the green and deftly handled renewed introductions. In the course of the evening, Emily did indeed step on his toes. More than once.

～

MARIE CUMMINGS WAS PRETTY, sensible, and the mother of three boys whom Valerian truly enjoyed. When she'd been widowed five years ago, she and her sons had continued to farm an excellent patch of ground, and she always greeted Valerian with a warm smile.

He liked her, he admired her, and because he owned the patch of ground she farmed, he avoided her assiduously at any but the most public venues.

"I do believe," she said, taking the seat beside Valerian and surveying the dancers, "that this is the happiest hour of their entire week. The young people enjoy these lessons even more than they do the assemblies."

Marie was hardly elderly. Valerian put her age at mid-thirties, and a very healthy mid-thirties at that.

"I enjoy these sessions," Valerian said, which was the truth. He also earned a bit of coin when they went well. "Do you know Miss Pepper? I would be happy to introduce you to her."

That was apparently not the direction Mrs. Cummings had intended the conversation to travel. Beneath the stomp of the dancers' feet and the music of the fiddle, a slight pause ensued.

"I have wondered if you prefer men," she said quietly. "You've never so much as flirted with me, never offered a naughty smile. Then I see you with Miss Pepper, and I know exactly whom you prefer. She and I met in the churchyard, and I quite like her. Take this."

Mrs. Cummings passed him a folded and sealed paper, and Valerian slipped it into his pocket.

"I am to convey that note to somebody on your behalf?" Better that than let her cherish odd notions where Valerian was concerned.

"Convey it to your banker, Mr. Dorning. That's the rent I haven't paid you for the past five years."

Five years ago, Mrs. Cummings had been sorely grieved to lose her husband of twelve years. Her sons had been in the unruly stage prior to adolescence, and farming without the aid of a spouse, even farming good land, had been a challenge few widows would have welcomed.

And yet, she'd taken on that task rather than uproot her family or rely on the charity of her relations.

Hounding a widow for rent had been beyond Valerian. She and her sons had needed a place to live, and he lacked the hard-heartedness to turn them out of the only home the children had known. Because he owned only the one property, he used no steward or land agent, but instead should have collected the rent himself.

He'd let the matter slide, asking Casriel to send the Cummings family some help at planting, shearing, haying, and harvest, and making sure they were included in the list of families receiving Boxing Day baskets.

"I can tear up the bank draft," Valerian said. "Young men eat like horses, and horses eat like horses, and no farm ever—"

She touched his sleeve. "I'm marrying Stephan Carter. When he learned that you were treating my tenancy like a life estate, he insisted that we settle up with you. He said he wants to be the only man taking care of me and mine."

Carter was an upright soul with a hearty laugh and a prosperous freehold not far from Marie's farm. He was not yet forty, and his sons seemed more interested in seeing the world than growing crops in Dorset.

"You, madam, have done a marvelous job of taking care of your-self and your offspring."

"Because you were generous, Valerian Dorning. The rest of the village took its cue from you. You went on as if widows embarked on farming in the ordinary course, when we're instead supposed to become poor relations or remarry posthaste. You made sure I had help from Dorning Hall, just as any other tenant or neighbor is aided at the busy times. The miller, the blacksmith, the shearing crews— they all treated me fairly because you set that example."

The set was ending, and across the room Emily Pepper was clapping heartily as her partner bowed his thanks for a dance more enthusiastic than graceful.

"You worked hard," Valerian said. "Your boys worked hard. I have been lucky to have such a conscientious tenant."

The applause died down, and the fiddler sent Valerian a questioning glance.

"You really are a kind man," Mrs. Cummings said, rising. "I will vacate your property once the harvest is in, and I hope you will attend my wedding. The boys are well behaved around you, and my oldest is ready for these dancing lessons you offer. I'm not sure how that happened, but Stephan says his children also grew up on him when he wasn't looking."

Valerian rose as well, the paper crackling in his pocket. "Phillip will be welcome if he cares to join us next week. He might want to dance at your wedding, mightn't he?"

"He'll want to drink as much punch as he's able, more's the pity." Mrs. Cummings pressed a kiss to Valerian's cheek and gathered up her shawl. "Thank you, Valerian, for your many kindnesses. Don't wait too long to pay your addresses to Miss Pepper. She really is a fine young lady."

Valerian bowed, and Mrs. Cummings headed for the steps, her business with her landlord concluded—her soon-to-be former landlord.

CHAPTER FIVE

"We must have Valerian up to Dorning Hall for a proper meal," Beatitude, Countess of Casriel, informed her husband. "I have missed him —I miss all of your siblings—and he should not be a stranger to his niece."

She held that niece, Lady Fredericka Gardenia Dorning, against her shoulder, the child having obligingly fallen asleep immediately after her supper. If she ran true to her breeding—she was a Dorning, after all—she'd awaken just as Grey was climbing into bed with his lady wife later that evening, and all thoughts of a pleasant marital interlude would be shoved aside—along with Grey himself—as her ladyship heeded the summons from the nursery.

"I had supper with Valerian last week," Grey said. "He is managing quite well, as he always does. Let me have that baby."

Beatitude passed the infant over, tucking up the blankets, then sinking into a rocking chair. "Your daughter grows heavier by the fortnight."

She did, bless her chubby little heart. "Is it time to ween?"

"Now that she and I are home, it's time to add some gruel to her

diet. Nurse says she'll sleep better, and that has become a consumma-
tion devoutly to be wished."

Indeed. Grey had given orders that the nursery was to notify him
if the baby grew fussy and the hour had passed midnight. He then
brought the child to her ladyship, burped the little stoat when her
appetite had been satisfied, and returned her to her crib. The nursery
maids had grumbled at first, while Beatitude had stopped looking so
exhausted.

She watched as Grey made a circuit of the playroom with the
child dozing in his arms.

"You are considering how to present something to me," Grey said,
"something I won't like. If you want to go to London to do some shopping, I will escort you up, but I cannot think the summer air in Town
is healthy for you or for the baby."

"I've had enough travel for the nonce," Beatitude replied. "But
you mention that Valerian is managing quite well. I wonder what he's
managing on."

As did Grey. Charm, most likely. Dorning men learned early how
to trade in that commodity.

"That is Valerian's business. My brothers are of age, and a very
wise countess encouraged me to set them loose upon the world." The
baby was fast asleep, but Grey kept up the slow, rocking walk. The
thought of turning his infant daughter loose upon the world someday
nearly unmanned him. Tabitha, Freddie's older sister born on the
wrong side of the blanket, had already gone off to finishing school,
and Grey had to limit himself to writing her only weekly.

"I said to set them loose," Beatitude replied around a yawn. "I did
not say to abandon them to the elements. That baby is always so good
for you. Did you know Valerian has received no rent from the
Cummings's farm for five years?"

The baby sighed, the sweetest, most contented sound a father
ever heard. "I beg your pardon?"

"Marie Cummings has not paid rent to Valerian once in
five years."

Grey took the second rocking chair, careful to maintain the rhythm he'd established in his perambulations. "How do you know that?"

"Marie's sister in Hampshire is a neighbor to one of my cousins' wife's cousins. That sister has noted that Marie was the object of considerable charity from her landlord here in Dorset. I gather the first year would have been the last for Marie as a farmer, but for Valerian's generosity."

"That farm is one of the best tenancies in the shire." The house was commodious, too, sturdy and handsome, fit for a large family. More of a modest manor than a mere farmhouse, and several parcels of the arable ground were sublet to other families. "Why the devil hasn't Valerian collected any rent?"

"Because Marie was left with three young boys? Because her husband died suddenly and with a crop in the field? Because you set an example of gentlemanly decency for your brothers, and Valerian, of all of them, heeds that example most assiduously?"

"It's *my* fault Valerian is pockets to let?"

Though to forgive five years' rent, and never mention a word about the debt, surpassed any example Grey could have set. He was both proud of Valerian for that gesture and peeved at himself for not learning of the situation earlier.

"It's partly your fault he's such a lovely man. We must find him a wife."

We must do no such thing. Valerian would be appalled at such meddling. "We must put this child to bed."

Beatitude rose, yawned again, and stretched. "I love the long evenings that summer brings. I do not love the short nights."

"I love you." Grey stood to steal a hug, both mother and child in his embrace, both sleepy, both inexpressibly dear. "Valerian cannot support a wife, and he'd never marry a woman he could not support."

Beatitude straightened and took the baby gently into her arms. "Have you read his book?"

"I started it once or twice when I chanced upon the manuscript in the library." Not that he'd been snooping, of course. "A lot of witticisms dressed up as fashion advice, from what I could gather." He accompanied Beatitude into the next room, where a nursery maid dozed in a chair beside the crib.

Beatitude laid the baby in the crib, touched the nursery maid's shoulder, and took Grey's hand. He stood marveling at his sleeping offspring, beset by the thought that Valerian would make an excellent father. Not something he could say with ease about all his brothers.

"Are we dressing for dinner?" he asked when he and Beatitude were in the corridor.

"I'd rather not. It's just us, and only Wednesday. You are already fretting about your parlor session on Monday and will doubtless get back to reading law as soon as we're done with supper."

"There's so much law to read." Though a magistrate was not a lawyer. He was, instead, a man of property and good judgment, bringing as much common sense to his adjudications as legal expertise.

"So have Valerian appointed magistrate. He has the time and the temperament, while you dread the whole business."

Grey considered that suggestion all the way to the bedroom he shared with his countess. "Valerian has common sense." And Grey did dread the whole business, more each week.

"Valerian is liked and respected. He's accustomed to sorting out noisy, feuding, obstreperous siblings, and he could use the income."

"The income is nominal." Expenses only, though some magistrates managed to turn expenses into a tidy sum. "Valerian would not cheat the ratepayers with fictitious sums." A point very much in his favor.

"Of course not, but he could defray some of the costs of maintaining his bachelor household, nonetheless. Paper and ink, for example, are not cheap, but a magistrate must have them. Coal for heating a parlor one day a week. A portion of the upkeep for a horse, because a magistrate must familiarize himself with crime scenes and go forth to make arrests. He must occasionally confer with other magistrates in the district and host them at his house as well."

Grey hadn't charged for most of that, because it hadn't occurred to him to do so. "You learned economies as a widow." He held the door to their sitting room. "I like this idea. I like it a lot." He loved this idea, in fact.

"I like you too," Beatitude said, hugging him after he'd closed the door. "I heartily dislike how you get quieter and quieter as Monday draws near. You avoid chatting up the neighbors at services on Sunday because you fear they will bring up a pending case. You are not the best resource for the job, Grey. You took it on out of duty because you, too, are every inch a gentleman."

He wrapped her in his arms and rested his chin on her crown, grateful beyond words for his marriage. Valerian deserved a chance to marry, to have children, to enjoy the comfort and pleasure of a wife's companionship.

"I'll ask him if he's interested. Even if he took on the job for six months, that would leave me free to focus on demolishing the old wing of the Hall. Tabitha will be home soon, and I want to spend as much time with her as possible. I haven't been socializing nearly enough for a man with a new baby to show off, and you are right: Valerian has the temperament for the post."

Beatitude kissed his cheek and slipped away. "When will you ask him?"

"Tomorrow. Tomorrow morning."

She turned her back and swept her hair off her nape. "If you'd undo my hooks, please?"

Grey loved this part of being married, the simple domesticity, the shared privacy. He tended to Beatitude's dress, and when he would have stepped back, she remained with her back to him.

"My stays too, Grey. I'm inclined to have a short nap before we go down to supper."

"A short nap is an excellent idea." He kissed her nape and thanked the Deity once again for the wonders of married life. As it happened, Casriel and his countess did not go down to supper for a good hour, and when they did, they descended to the dining room quite in charity with the world—and with each other.

THE REST of Valerian's evening was spent over ale and sandwiches at the posting inn, and though he was friendly to everybody, he shared smiles and glances with Emily more often than he should have. The gathering broke up, and then it was time to take the lady home.

The drive to the village had been one of contrasts: the tremendous pleasure of sitting beside Emily, the even greater wonder of kissing her and being kissed by her. But despair had come along for that journey, too, because an honorable man without means was a man doomed to bachelorhood. He would grow old making up the numbers at house parties, dancing with the wallflowers, and wishing some venerable auntie would leave him even a small competence.

With money in his pocket and the prospect of a property of his own where he could dwell, some of his despair ebbed.

"Who was she?" Emily asked as Valerian guided Clovis away from the livery. "Not that it's any of my business."

"Mrs. Marie Cummings, soon to be the second Mrs. Stephan Carter. She was widowed a few years ago, and she and her sons continued to work a Dorning tenancy." Valerian dodged the whole truth because he wanted time to consider the improvement in his fortunes. Marie and Stephan seemed well suited, but engaged couples quarreled, and bank drafts could be stolen.

Still, the rent on the Cummings farm had been fairly high, owing to the size and quality of the holding. Five times "fairly high" was a sum that could be invested, and Valerian's brother-in-law Worth Kettering was brilliant at managing investments.

"I ought never to admit this aloud," Emily said, "but sometimes I envy widows. They have the benefit of marriage settlements and the freedom society grants few other women of standing."

"Provided they are discreet."

Emily arranged her skirts, the movement conveying impatience. "Not *that* kind of freedom. I realize many married women are granted a certain latitude once they've filled their husband's nursery. I meant freedom to own a business, to manage their own finances, to *run* a business." She fell silent. "Perhaps I ought not to have partaken of the ale."

She'd had a mere lady's pint, and that after two hours of exertion.

"Perhaps you ought to speak your mind more often, Emily Pepper. Finish your thought."

"I know polite society would consider my view of marriage old-fashioned. Why marry a man and then cast him aside for another? Why marry a woman, for that matter, and treat her like a morning hunter? Sufficient for the start of the ride, but once she tires, toss her aside for any number of afternoon mounts. Now I'm using equestrian analogies to describe marriage. Shall we discuss the weather?"

"I like that you have the courage to discuss more substantial topics than the weather. Did you enjoy yourself this evening?"

Another twitch at her skirts. "More than I have at any London entertainment. Your neighbors aren't afraid to laugh. They *know* each other, they haven't simply been introduced at a boring old ball. Papa has this kind of camaraderie with his business cronies, while I..."

Kissing Emily Pepper was glorious, but conversing with her, with the true, honest Emily, was in some way equally precious.

"While you?"

"The last time I had true friends was at finishing school. Several of us were partners in adventure. We visited back and forth over school holidays and came to each other's aid when difficulties arose. What little French I have is thanks to my schoolmates, not to the tutors Briggs later inflicted on me."

This topic—how women developed friendships—had never

occurred to Valerian. He had been sent to public school and university, where the inevitable youthful associations had arisen, but he also had a platoon of brothers, a horde of neighbors, and the welcome any well-born bachelor enjoyed at Mayfair entertainments.

Emily Pepper had neither siblings, nor neighbors of longstanding, nor a titled family's connections.

"Are you still friends with the young ladies you knew at school?"

"Likely not. The last of our little group married two years ago in Edinburgh. Papa was too concerned with showing me off around Town for me to attend. Then he grew too ill for me to go visiting."

The bank draft in Valerian's pocket was no great fortune, but to a man who dealt in pence and shillings, rather than pounds and ponies, it was enough to shift his perspective, however slightly. Perhaps Emily needed a shift in perspective as well.

"What are *you* concerned with, Emily? What would you *like* to be concerned with?"

She was quiet for a while, as the village fell behind them and the western sky turned from orange to mauve. A nightingale caroled in a nearby hedgerow, and a half-moon crested the horizon. The moment was purely beautiful, romantic in a way that had little to do with kissing.

What would Emily Pepper think of a man who'd spent months working on a manuscript for an etiquette book? What would she think of Marie Cummings's decision to take up farming?

"I used to be much more in my father's confidence," Emily said. "I was his amanuensis—Briggs insisted my penmanship be faultless— and then I became his confidante about all matters mercantile. Things changed, and now Tobias and Caleb are his constant companions. They are hard workers, they know the mercer's craft, and they are devoted to Papa, but sometimes, I suspect their devotion is to Papa's coin, rather than his best interests."

"You would be good at running a business."

She glanced over at him, her brows knit. "Do you flatter me, Mr. Dorning?"

"You don't need to be flattered. You are sensible, honest, familiar with the cloth trade, and determined to honor your father's successful legacy. You are also in the habit of protecting him, particularly given his recent poor health. He should be grateful that you bother to question the motives of his business associates. When nobody else looks after us, family should be trusted to do so."

"Does your family look after you?"

"That's different."

She nudged him with her elbow. "Because you are *a man*?"

"You are teasing me."

"And you, sir, are changing the subject."

"Trying to." He turned Clovis up the lane that led to Pepper Ridge, though why must the manor house be such a short distance from the village? "I've sent my manuscript to my brothers Sycamore and Ash. They are developing a broad circle of London acquaintances, and I am hopeful they can find me a publisher to print the book."

Valerian didn't talk about his book with anybody unless he was directly asked.

"You've written *a book*?"

"You make it sound like some great accomplishment. Every schoolboy can put pen to paper."

"You make it sound like a trivial undertaking. Part of the reason I haven't kept up with my school friends is that writing a letter is such a laborious process. One must be tidy and witty and informative, but not dull or presuming. My handwriting must be that of a perfect lady. You have written *an entire book*."

"Which nobody is interested in publishing thus far. You should correspond with your friends, Emily. Even a note recounting your remove to Dorsetshire, your father's improved health, your renewed attempts on the dance floor. Tell them how you go on, and they will write back, if they're your friends."

Valerian drew Clovis to a halt at the bottom of the manor house steps and climbed from the gig. He assisted Emily to alight, and when he would have stepped back to bow his farewell to her, she kept hold of his hand.

"I will write to my friends, and I will keep an eye on Papa's business dealings, as best I can. I caught him redesigning the hold of a merchantman without consulting a shipwright, and Caleb and Tobias were abetting that folly."

Valerian was developing a dim view of Caleb and Tobias, but perhaps that was jealousy at work. They were guests at Pepper Ridge, sharing meals with Emily and sharing an interest with her in a trade about which Valerian knew next to nothing.

Emily drew him up the steps. "What is your book about?"

The fading light was a blessing, for Valerian was blushing. "Manners, etiquette, polite conventions. How to go on in a social sense." Perhaps he needed to add a chapter on when and how to go about kissing a young lady—or why to refrain from kissing her.

"Social conventions are a brilliant topic for a book. Not everybody can afford fancy finishing schools, and the people teaching at those schools aren't the people pouring tea in Mayfair. I've made many errors because my deportment instructor hadn't been to London since German George's day."

Nobody had ever, ever called Valerian's "little project" brilliant, but then, his family were the only people to learn of it, and they were all to the manor born.

"I hope some publisher regards my scribbling as similarly inspired. I also hope you will join me again for next Wednesday's dancing practice." The two hopes were equally compelling, though Valerian was still a younger son without prospects.

He did have a potential home of his own, though, and he did have a few pounds to his name.

"I would not miss next week's practice for all the silk in China, Mr. Dorning. If I am very diligent, and my partners patient, I might eventually master the quadrille."

The overhang of the entranceway cast Emily's smile in deep

shadow, and yet, in Valerian's heart, a light glowed. They leaned toward each other at the same time, lips brushing softly.

Foolishness, that. "Good night, Emily. I'll see you next Wednesday."

"Good night, Valerian. I want to read your book."

Valerian wanted to stand in the shadows and kiss Emily until dawn, but Clovis chose then to stomp a hoof and swish his tail.

"I'm flattered, though I have only the one spare copy of the manuscript. You must promise to take very good care of it if I lend it to you."

She squeezed his hand. "I would guard it with my last breath. Until next week."

Valerian waited until she'd ducked through the front door, and then he waited another few moments simply because the night had taken an unexpected and wonderful turn. Emily thought his book was brilliant, she'd called him *Valerian*, and he was to see her again next week.

His attraction to her was no longer cause for despair; indeed, it had become the spark lighting a small, cautious flame of hope.

EMILY REMOVED her bonnet and tarried before the mirror in the foyer, examining her reflection. She was delaying the ordeal of chasing Briggs from her private sitting room, for Briggs was doubtless perched like a cat at a mousehole, waiting with scolds couched as pointed questions and long-suffering sighs.

"A companion is not a governess," Emily muttered, slipping off her gloves. "And Valerian Dorning is not a fortune hunter." She took off her cloak and hung it on a peg, glad for once that the staff was less than punctilious about their duties.

"So you've endured another evening of the stomping, sweating Dorset locals?" Tobias asked. "While I admire your generosity of spirit, I hope your toes are none the worse for your outing."

He'd come down the stairs too quietly for Emily to have noticed his descent.

"My toes often came to grief in London, if you must know. The purpose of the dance lessons is to ensure everybody who wants to can acquit themselves well at the assemblies, myself included."

Tobias seemed amused, though he wasn't smiling. "And the friendly pint at the posting inn afterward? Does that also aid one's skills on the dance floor?"

Emily might have tried to end the conversation with some pleasant remark about being neighborly. She might have politely pleaded fatigue. She might have agreed with Tobias, because that would be the easier course.

And where had all that agreeable, sweet, biddable behavior landed her? She was consigned to Briggs's company, cut out of any business discussions, and assigned pointless renovation projects about which nobody cared.

Perhaps you ought to speak your mind more often, Emily Pepper. "Are you spying on me, Tobias?"

The humor in his eyes faded. "I do believe the country air is making you contrary, Miss Emily. Apologies if I have given offense. I occasionally deliver correspondence to the inn, and I happened to overhear a tavern maid gossiping with some plowboy. They look forward to both the dancing lessons and the flirtation to be had thereafter."

Happened to overhear, meaning he'd eavesdropped. "I've suggested Papa have a master shipwright review your plans for the merchantman," Emily said, starting for the staircase. "Neither you nor Caleb made that suggestion."

Tobias fell in step beside her as she mounted the steps. "A ship-wright to fuss over a few simple changes will take time, and time is money. Caleb will be difficult over the delay, as only he can be, but if it's important to you, I will second the motion."

Emily had already won Papa's consent. She did not need Tobias's gracious offer of support. "If those few simple changes unbalance the cargo hold, and our ship is damaged or lost as a result, then the time saved by cutting corners now is wasted, isn't it? If our haste causes preventable loss of life, then we are at fault, are we not?"

"Dancing puts you in a bad humor, miss."

"Depending on who partners me, you might be right, but that has nothing to do with irresponsible hurry where Pepper Shipping is concerned. Papa has agreed to send for a shipwright, and Caleb has nothing to say to it."

"Caleb probably doesn't see it that way."

To blazes with how he sees it. Emily could not bring herself to be quite that honest. She instead stopped at the top of the steps and rummaged around mentally for how Valerian would couch the point she needed to make.

"I appreciate how hard both you and Caleb work and how loyal you have been to Papa during his bout of ill health."

"I am happy to be of use to a man who has done so much for me," Tobias replied.

Emily suspected he meant that. Tobias was short on charm, but to Emily, that made him easier to deal with than Caleb. Caleb had a ready sense of humor, an ability to turn the conversation in a light direction, and a tendency to not take himself too seriously. Caleb was more of a friend than Tobias would ever be, though Emily trusted neither of them.

"You are well compensated for your loyalty too, Tobias. I am Osgood Pepper's daughter, and now that his health is improved, I intend to resume my duties as his amanuensis and assistant."

She made that decision as the words left her lips, and she would explain it to Papa at the first opportunity.

"But Osgood has a pair of secretaries now, miss. We brought the Walmer twins down from London, and between the two of them, they handle all the correspondence and reporting."

Emily knew the Walmer twins by sight, but she did not *know* them. They had been employed in the Manchester office and brought to London only as Papa's health had faded. Now the two young men bided in guest quarters, ate at the second table, and mostly kept away from the public rooms.

"Then I will read what they produce and ensure it meets with Papa's wishes." She'd done that before all the trouble had flared up with Adam, and caught many an error too.

"Might we discuss this someplace less public?"

Tobias was a creature of strategy and action, all logic and ledgers. That he'd ask for privacy was disquieting.

"In here," Emily said, leading him to the second informal parlor. "Whatever you have to say, Tobias, please just say it. You and Caleb cannot be trusted to honor my father's health limitations. You keep him at his labors when he has promised to rest. You leave him sitting at the desk when he should be enjoying fresh air and sunshine. You ply him with port far into the evening so that you can discuss business, business, and yet more business. I won't tolerate it any longer."

To say the words felt good. Shouting them would have felt better.

Tobias wandered across the room, coming to a halt before a woodcut of a hare in snow. Such art would not adorn the walls of a London town house, but Emily liked the exquisite detail of the print and the hare's sense of calm sagacity.

"You are right, of course," Tobias said. "We have been too pleased with Osgood's renewed vigor to insist that he heed your concerns regarding his health. I think you underestimate, though, the extent to which his newfound joy is precisely because you are more interested in matters social and domestic."

This was said gently, even carefully, as bad news should be delivered.

"You're saying Papa is *relieved* that I'm less involved in his mercantile enterprise?" A sense of betrayal accompanied that question, because Tobias's suggestion fit all too well with Emily's own sense of the changes the past few years—and the remove to Dorset—had brought.

Tobias glanced at her over his shoulder. "Osgood hasn't said anything directly, but he's implied that you feel responsible for your brother's wrongdoing. Osgood is worried that you've tried to take your brother's place in the business, when you should be finding a husband and setting up your nursery."

How could an evening go in such a short time from unalloyed joy to utter rage? "My brother has a name. Adam is alive, and in two years he will be free to return to England. The courts found him guilty, and you and Caleb aided them in doing so. I will never believe Adam stole from Papa's business, though I understand the evidence presented was damning. In no way do I feel the need to atone for a wrong Adam did not commit."

"You are so loyal," Tobias murmured. "I admire that about you tremendously."

"If you admire my loyalty, then try to show a little more of it yourself. Make Papa observe mealtimes, send him up to bed at a reasonable hour. Have at least some of your blasted discussions out in the garden or on the terrace. I will not sit idly by while you and Caleb make Papa ill again."

That wasn't exactly fair. Older men grew frail in the normal course. Papa had been lucky to come across medication that had abated his symptoms, lucky to have encountered Margaret Dorning, who knew how to prepare and administer that medication.

"I can do as you ask where Osgood is concerned," Tobias replied, "but you will still hover and fret, when what Osgood wants, what he wants more than all the fast ships and beautiful cloth in the world, is for you to take a husband and be happy. You refuse to even make the attempt, Emily. How loyal is that?"

Tobias again spoke softly, reasonably, and Emily wanted to slap him. "You may have a point, but taking a husband does not necessarily result in happiness. The wrong husband is worse than no husband at all."

"And instead of looking for the right husband, you insist on maintaining a correspondence with the son Osgood has disowned. Your father would be very hurt if he knew that."

The parlor, Emily's favorite, abruptly felt too small. "I don't need

you to tell me how my own father would feel. Papa made a grave
error where Adam is concerned, and in time, I hope he can
admit that."

"Does Adam reply to your letters?" Tobias's question was posed
casually—too casually.

"He has not for some time. Because of his skill with languages
and numbers, he's managed fairly well as convicts go, but his situation
is difficult. How exactly did you learn that I write to my brother?"

Tobias next became fascinated with the landscape over the
mantel, a bucolic study of a shepherd with his flocks. While the sky
was pale blue and replete with fluffy white clouds, the shepherd and
his charges dwelled in a dark forest below. To Emily, the painting
raised a question: What manner of sheep dwelled in forests? What
manner of shepherd kept his sheep beneath the shadowed trees when
sunny fields were nearby?

Tobias faced her, his expression conveying more patient humoring. "I spotted a letter to your brother on the first occasion when I
took my correspondence to the inn," he said. "The inn's mailbag
spilled. I was clumsy with it, trying to shove my letters in with all the
others, and the lot went cascading over the table. The innkeeper's
wife was wroth with me, and well she should have been."

Two hours of dancing hadn't tired Emily, but this discussion was
tiring her. "I trust you will keep quiet about my personal correspondence." She made that a statement, not a question.

"Your secrets are safe with me, Emily, but I don't think you'll find
Caleb quite so accommodating."

Emily had started for the door, though the significance of Tobias's
words stopped her. "I beg your pardon? Is Caleb also prone to spilling
mailbags that just happen to include my letters to Adam?"

"I trust not, but Caleb fancies himself in love with you. If you'd
give him a chance, he might well be that right man you alluded to
earlier. If you accept Caleb's suit, you can keep an eye on your father,
remain attached to the business, and start a family. Caleb is a decent
fellow and good company. Far more sociable than I am."

A more accomplished lady might have been able to hide her reaction, but Emily was only an heiress, not a lady by birth. She burst out laughing, even knowing that deriding any man's romantic aspirations was unkind.

"I'm sorry. You have taken me very much by surprise. I could no more marry Caleb than... The idea is absurd. He's a fine fellow, and he has many delightful qualities, but he's not... He hasn't..."

He doesn't listen to me. He doesn't ask me questions I ought to be asking myself. He doesn't warn me against my own impulsive nature, though warning me must cost him.

Caleb is not Valerian Dorning.

"Feelings can change," Tobias said mildly. "I will leave it to Caleb to make his sentiments known to you if and when he deems such a declaration appropriate."

Tobias was back to being amused—or pleased. Emily couldn't tell which. "If Caleb is shrewd," she said, "which I believe him to be, he will not burden me with unwelcome announcements. Please heed my demand regarding Papa's health, Tobias. That must take precedence over all other concerns."

She made it as far as the door before Tobias's voice again stopped her. "Your request, you mean? Your suggestion that Osgood pay more attention to naps and mealtimes?"

"My demand," Emily said firmly. "My utterly clear and sensible demand. Good evening." She drew the door closed quietly behind her, but all of her good cheer from the time spent with Valerian was gone.

Tobias had been smiling at her as she left the parlor, and though the result was to illuminate features more handsome than most, the effect on Emily was profound unease. She was climbing into bed when she was assailed with the awful notion that *Tobias* might be thinking of courting her.

She fell asleep and dreamed of waltzing with him, something she'd done on several occasions previously. In slumber, the prospect took on the quality of a nightmare for no reason Emily could discern.

CHAPTER SIX

—————————

Morning brought with it both an oppressive overcast, which was unusual for Dorset in summertime, and a corresponding dampening of Valerian's spirits.

The money Marie Cummings had conveyed was not that large a sum when invested in the cent-percents. The manuscript sent to London apparently hadn't impressed anybody. Translating recipes and giving dancing lessons was no way to make a fortune, and Clovis needed new shoes.

Valerian took his morning tea tray to the back porch of his little cottage. The view was lovely on sunny days, and even today the air was full of birdsong and a hint of a breeze. Birdsong and breezes made no sort of dower portion, though, not for a woman of Emily Pepper's means.

"Clovis needs new shoes, I need new boots." This grim reality had become apparent as Valerian had applied polish to his footwear before going to bed. He'd already had his boots resoled twice, and he might be able to make do with that economy again.

"Are you now given to talking to yourself?"

Grey stood on the garden path, looking every inch the country squire—almost.

"The sapphire in your cravat pin is a bit overdone for daytime in the country, Casriel. I like it on you. Join me for a cup of tea?"

The earl climbed the steps to the porch, his boots gleaming—less than a year old no doubt.

"How do you happen to have a fresh pot of tea at the ready when you didn't know I'd be calling on you? You even have a second cup on the tray."

Good God. Valerian had put together his own tray, lost in imagining a call from Emily Pepper, which was ridiculous. So far gone had Valerian been in his make-believe socializing that he'd put service for two on the tray.

"You were overdue for a visit," he said. "The next parlor session approaches, and Hortense Blevins is accused of stealing Milly Anders's best petticoat from the wash line. I have a suggestion about that."

Grey took a seat at the small table where Valerian had set the tray. "I was hoping you would."

"Offer to cut the petticoat in half." Valerian slid into the other chair. "Take a leaf from Solomon's book. The woman who did the fancy embroidery on the hems and seams will object to the destruction of her artwork, and you will know to whom the petticoat truly belongs. Or ask both ladies to bring you samples of their best stitchery, and their responses to your request will shed light on who has nothing to hide and who has turned to backyard larceny."

Grey helped himself to a slice of buttered toast, slathering it with jam. "What if they bring me chemises and stockings and whatnot? How will I examine such garments without dying of mortification? This is good jam. I thought we were out of pear preserves at the Hall."

"That's not from the Hall. Hannah Weller gave it to me. I translated a treatise for her from the Latin, all about gout and humors and black cherry tisanes."

"Sounds dreadful, but not as dreadful as taking ladies' undergarments into evidence. Do you enjoy translation work?"

"I enjoy being useful to my neighbors." *And having a steady supply of preserves, too, of course.*

Grey put down his toast and put aside all pretense of Elder Brother Out for a Ramble. He sat forward, forearms braced on his knees.

"I said that very thing to my countess the other night. Valerian is quite well liked, I said, in part because he's such a generous soul, and well blessed with tact and consideration."

"Thank you." Though this effusion of fraternal flattery was leading up to something. "Your tea." Valerian passed over the first cup after putting in a dash of sugar.

"You have the knack," Grey went on, "of seeing what's needed and being about it. You are also well read in the law, an accomplishment I cannot claim and do not aspire to. I suspect you could also examine delicate embroidery far more knowledgeably than I can."

"While you sit in the Lords, a purgatory I would not wish on a sworn foe."

"Just so." Grey dunked his toast in his tea. "It's about the magistrate's post, you see. You're perfect for it, and I am *not*. The whole business was inflicted on me because Papa took his turn at it, though I doubt he was any more suited to adjudicating squabbles than I am. You know the law. You hold property outright, unlike Hawthorne, who loves the land but has none of his own. Might you be interested in becoming the king's man? You're a decent fellow with some time on your hands."

A decent fellow with time on his hands, who stayed up late translating recipes, polishing his own boots, ironing his own cravats, and dreaming impossible dreams where Emily Pepper was concerned.

"I am not exactly at loose ends, Grey." Books didn't write themselves, and if a publisher came along willing to print the completed book, the author was still expected to find subscriptions for it and to make any needed revisions.

The earl slurped his tea. "I thought you'd finished up your little project."

Emily Pepper thinks my little project is brilliant. "I've finished with the first draft. What's involved in the magistrate's duties?"

"I hardly know, I'm so poorly suited to it. You listen to a lot of complaining neighbors. About every two months or so, you are called down to the posting inn where somebody has knocked somebody else about the head. Spats and tiffs, brawls and bad behavior."

"Sounds like having a lot of brothers."

Grey finished his tea. "You would see it like that, but then, you liked reading law. Ash said you had a better head for it than he did."

An observation Ash had never passed along to Valerian. "I like solving problems and being of use."

"There, you see?" Grey held out his empty cup. "You are perfect for the post, and being magistrate will help defray some of your household expenses."

Valerian poured his brother another cup. "I thought the magistrate worked for free, happy to contribute his efforts to the common weal."

"He does contribute his efforts without remuneration, but he's not expected to contribute his paper and ink, his horse, his coal, or his personal conveyance. Reasonable expenses are compensated."

Valerian sipped his tea and tried to ignore Clovis's need for new shoes. The farrier had already reset the front pair once...

"I will think on this, Grey. I'm flattered that you'd ask me, and I do like to be of use, but I also have some ideas in mind for another book, and writing a book takes time."

The earl downed his second cup at one go. "You are being coy. You can do your scribbling in the evening, when lesser mortals, such as my humble self, are condemned to perusing the law books hour after hour. If I threaten to thrash you, would you agree to take on the magistrate's job? You could arrest me for assaulting a judicial official."

"You're a peer. You are harder to arrest than most."

Grey rose. "I knew that—I think. Please do consider taking the job, Valerian. If you don't like it, we can pass it on to somebody else."

"Somebody such as?"

"I don't know. The time of year is wrong to impose on anybody working his acres, but only a landed man will do. That reminds me, Beatitude says your tenant is walking out with Mr. Carter. Will you move into Abbotsford should Mrs. Cummings vacate that property?"

"I don't know." Valerian got to his feet as well. "I might simply rent the place out again."

Grey peered at him. "Hawthorne wants your southern fields. Says Dorning Hall hasn't the drainage to grow some of the medicinals that will make us the most money. That reminds me..." Grey pulled a folded piece of paper from his pocket. "Your share of our first quarter's earnings. Margaret's recipe for baby soap is apparently quite popular."

Valerian slipped the bank draft into his pocket, the morning acquiring a sense of unreality. "Baby soap?"

"More tallow and scent, less lye, or something. Not as harsh on tender skin. Margaret said women will claim they are buying it for their infants and godchildren, while in fact using it themselves. All quite clever, and quite beyond the imaginings of a mere rural earl. Beatitude likes it, which decides the matter." Grey moved off toward the back door, apparently intent on walking home across the fields. "Worth Kettering says your accounting system is nothing short of brilliant, and that is high praise indeed."

"My accounting system?"

"It's certainly not mine. Don't you recall? You sat us all down as the first load of pretty sachets went off to Town and told us in no uncertain terms that successful businesses kept accurate, detailed books. Your sermonizing inspired me to review the estate ledgers, which were admittedly a bit out of date."

And that was likely a euphemism. Casriel was more conscientious than the previous earl, but he was also smitten with his countess and new daughter, and more drawn to Town and socializing than Papa had been.

"I consulted Kettering before I set up the ledgers," Valerian said as they reached the back porch. "We need to know precisely which items are selling well, at what time of year, and where." Any clerk could follow that logic, as could any bachelor with pockets to let.

"Whatever you did, it's working. Hawthorne is full of plans for more products and larger markets, but a word with him about Abbotsford would be appreciated. I haven't your knack for dealing with sibling quarrels." Grey paused on the porch steps. "Looks like rain. We could use a good soaking shower. Beatitude likes rainy days."

That nonsensical observation had his lordship smiling at his mahogany walking stick.

"Wait here," Valerian said, ducking back into the house. He retrieved a jar of pear preserves and passed them to his brother. "Hannah's pear jam is not to be missed. We might consider selling some along with our plum blossom soap and rose sachets. Make gift baskets for the Little Season."

Grey put the jar in his pocket. "My brothers are geniuses. Why Beatitude has thrown in her lot with a plodder like me I will never know. Think about the magistrate's post, talk to Hawthorne, I must be off."

He jaunted across the garden, a plodder who had nonetheless conducted a briefing on the family business, delegated a serious responsibility, and passed along some family gossip, all while pretending to simply enjoy a cup of tea.

"I haven't said I'll accept the magistrate's job, Casriel."

"You are taking the decision under advisement while you consider all the relevant evidence. You are perfect for the post, and you know it." Grey touched his hat brim, bowed slightly, and let himself out the garden gate.

Valerian resumed his seat at the table and took out the bank draft. He stared at the folded piece of paper for a moment before cursing softly and opening it.

He had to rub his eyes to make sure he was seeing clearly. "Ye prancing unicorns. Ye rose-scented cherubs." The sum would keep a small family of country dwellers for a year. Not lavishly, but... comfortably. And this payment was based on the *first quarter's* earnings.

Valerian's thoughts became a jumble of emotions, with *Clovis can have new shoes* flitting through his mind right next to *I can have new boots.*

Better than that, Hawthorne could continue to work the land, which rose to a vocation for him. Ash would have some income, so he needn't lark about town on Sycamore's coattails. Will, the family dog lover, could raise his offspring and his puppies secure in the knowledge that the Dorning fortunes were prospering. Will might not accept any of the proceeds himself—Valerian was having second thoughts—but he'd allow Grey as the patriarch to set up trusts for any progeny.

Rain began to patter softly against the porch roof, while Valerian stared at his garden and considered how an estate overgrown with botanical plantings had become, against all odds, the profitable venture Grey had claimed it could be.

Grey, the plodder, the mere rural earl.

Hawthorne let himself through the garden gate, apparently oblivious to the rain. "Has Grey stopped by this morning?"

"He has. How are Margaret and the children?"

Hawthorne sat in the chair Grey had vacated. "Well. Did Grey leave you a bank draft?"

Valerian nodded. "I am dumbstruck."

"I am relieved—and dumbstruck. Will you rent some of the Abbotsford acreage to me?"

Brothers. "Probably, but first I need to consider a few matters when my head has stopped spinning. Let's step into the parlor, shall we?"

Hawthorne rose. "Celebrating our good fortune?"

"Steadying my nerves."

For a big man, Hawthorne moved quietly as he followed Valerian into the parlor. "Margaret's expecting. My nerves could use steadying. Why are your nerves in a state?"

"Congratulations." Valerian passed him a half-full glass. "You might be looking at the next magistrate, though I haven't given Grey my answer yet."

"He hates that job, hates it with a dutiful, gentlemanly passion. I would hate it too. What's this?"

"Brandy. Good for warding off the chill when a day turns damp."

Hawthorne took a sniff then a sip. "When will you decide about Abbotsford?"

"Soon. Marie's leasehold won't run out until after harvest. To your health and to Margaret's well-being."

Hawthorne saluted and tossed back the rest of his drink. "You'll take the magistrate's job? The entire shire would thank you. They hate trooping up to Dorning Hall for the petite sessions, and Grey hates sitting in judgment of anybody."

"It's not sitting in judgment, it's solving problems, but I must consider the post before I accept it." Valerian wanted to accept it, wanted badly to accept it, but even more he wanted to discuss the whole situation with Emily Pepper, the sooner the better.

LAST NIGHT'S discussion with Tobias had apparently inspired him to avoid the breakfast table, which suited Emily quite well. The conversation had served another purpose. By the time Emily had gone upstairs the previous evening, Briggs had been snoring gently in a reading chair, a history of millinery fashion on the carpet at her feet.

Emily had tiptoed past, changed into her nightclothes, and sent a maid to wake Briggs only after Emily herself was abed.

When did I become such a sneak? Valerian Dorning encouraged her to speak her mind, and then—why should this be so remarkable? —he listened to what she had to say.

Briggs bustled into the breakfast parlor, already dressed for the day despite the early hour. "You should have wakened me last night. In future, I expect you will." She took the place at Emily's right hand, her customary choice.

Good morning to you too. "A history of hats would be enough to cause anybody to nod off. Did you sleep well?"

Briggs poured herself a cup of tea, set the pot down, and stared at the steam wafting up. "I did not, to be honest. When next you attend those dancing practices, or whatever they are, I will accompany you. My conscience has been troubling me for allowing you twice to flaunt convention by accepting the escort of a strange gentleman. It will not serve, miss, even here in Dorset."

Emily sprinkled cinnamon on her porridge, the scent soothing a flare of temper. "You make it sound as if a map of Dorset should include a warning about monsters. Mr. Dorning is hardly unknown to me. We have been introduced, we have stood up together, he has greeted you most cordially. Would you care for some toast?"

"No. Thank you."

Very well, battle over the breakfast table it would be. "Briggs, he is an earl's son. He is a gentleman. He is exactly the sort of fellow Papa expected me to encounter here in the country."

"Encounter, perhaps, but throw your cap at? I beg to disagree." She managed to make even taking a sip of tea an act of condemnation.

Emily slapped a double pat of butter into her bowl of porridge. "I understand now why a lady of means often chooses to break her fast in her own bedroom, enjoying a quiet hour to herself upon waking."

"Don't be impertinent. I have only your best interests at heart, and Mr. Dorning hasn't a feather to fly with. He's handsome and well mannered, I'll grant you that, and he has connections, but a woman cannot live on waltzes alone."

You may be excused. The words popped into Emily's head, a tantalizing and shocking show of temper.

No, not temper. *Authority.* Emily was the female head of the household, for now at least, and entitled to respect.

"Briggs, I appreciate your concern, but I must ask you to refrain from questioning my judgment where the company of neighbors and friends is concerned. Mr. Dorning knows the surrounds, I do not. Mr. Dorning is an accomplished dancer. I am not. Mr. Dorning was raised in this shire, I am the newcomer without any sense of local mores or history. You lack those assets as well, and I'd think you would be grateful that a man with better things to do has taken a kindly interest in my situation."

"Pass the toast, please."

That was petty of Briggs—also a little sad—issuing a command that flatly contradicted her earlier stated preferences.

Emily set the toast rack and the butter by Briggs's elbow. A change of topic was in order. "Do I mistake the matter, or does Caleb seek to engage my affections?"

"He'd be a fool not to. Caleb understands the value of coin, he's a hard worker, and he gets along well with your father, but he's not gentry. Your father hopes most fervently to see you married to a wealthy squire, which, it must be said, that Dorning fellow is not. Should you be using so much honey, miss?"

Emily had only begun to drizzle the honey onto her porridge. She let a goodly dollop drip from the wooden whisk while she sorted placatory replies, considered yet another change of topic, and wondered when a loyal ally had become something else entirely.

How would Valerian handle a companion grown into a martinet?

Firmly and kindly, that's how. "Briggs, I have the sense that Dorset does not agree with you, while I enjoy the countryside more and more the longer I'm here. You have only to ask, and I will write you the most impressive character ever penned by the hand of mortal woman. Your loyalty and common sense have seen me through many a tribulation, but please recall that a companion is not a governess."

Emily rose, retrieved a tray from the sideboard, and set her tea and porridge upon it. "I wish you good morning. I'm off to the study to review my father's correspondence."

A turgid silence greeted that announcement, which bothered Emily not at all. Briggs was shrewd. She'd sulk a bit, offer a grudging apology, and revert to her stolid, somewhat grumpy self.

Again. When had this pattern originated, and more to the point, why was it repeating with greater and greater frequency?

"And what's to be done about it?" Emily murmured, pushing open the door to the study. The room was blessedly empty, not even the Walmer twins yet in evidence, so she took a place at the reading table and started on the stack of outgoing correspondence, her porridge disappearing in bites between letters.

She was halfway through the stack when a footman brought in a tea service and a pot of coffee. "Shall I take your tray, miss?"

"Good morning, Richard. Please do."

"That builder fellow, he's asking to see you."

London servants would have endless reserves of dignity, but Emily preferred the slight judgment that colored Richard's tone. The honesty. He did not care for *that builder fellow* and neither did Emily.

"I'll see Mr. Ogilvy later today." The pattern in Papa's correspondence was disquieting, and Emily wanted to finish the stack before Caleb, Tobias, or Papa joined her. "When does my father typically come down?"

"Mr. Pepper likes a leisurely start to his day. We don't usually see him in the study until midmorning. With the rain, I suspect he'll tarry in his rooms a mite longer."

Emily got her own habit of rising early from Papa. That he'd taken to resting in the morning should have cheered her, except it didn't. Late nights and lazy mornings were the habits of a young man about Town.

"We need the rain, don't we?"

"That we do, miss. Doesn't do for the pastures to dry out, does it? We end up short of butter and cheese come winter." Richard bustled off with the tray, the exchange extraordinary in two regards.

First, weather was a casual topic in London. The streets might be muddy, the night foggy, but those factors were mere inconveniences. Here in the country, the weather was akin to divine judgment. Families thrived or failed on the frequency and quantity of the rains. A harsh winter could decimate flocks or carry off beloved elders.

The country version of weather was more compelling, more genuine. Talk of weather here was not meaningless as chatter about the weather in Town was.

The second characteristic making Emily's conversation with Richard remarkable was its friendliness. Her direct interactions with the Pepper Ridge staff were almost exclusively through the butler and housekeeper, and those two worthies were holdovers from the previous owner's household. Richard was new to his post, and his cheerful attitude and forthcoming nature were a pleasant change from the taciturn butler and fretful housekeeper.

Emily went back to reading Papa's mail, though the longer she read, the more questions she had. Not until well past ten of the clock did the Walmer twins creep into the study, and by that hour, she'd read every item of outgoing and incoming correspondence.

And she was unhappy with both.

WITHOUT AN ESCORT, a lady would not typically call on a bachelor, but a bachelor was under no such constraints where the lady was concerned. Valerian assured himself of this as he trotted Clovis up the Pepper Ridge drive.

The horse had been fidgety under saddle the whole way, shying at puddles and balking at hedges, suggesting even a dumb beast knew calling before noon wasn't the done thing. Still, the day was mild, the rain had tapered off, and Emily might enjoy a quiet hack across the fields before the sun climbed too high.

That reasoning even sounded somewhat credible.

Valerian passed his reins to a groom, who took a good five minutes to appear from the stables. The butler was waiting in the foyer, though his dark suit was wrinkled about the knees and sporting shiny elbows.

Did Emily see those small lapses? Did they bother her?

"Have you a card, sir?" the butler asked.

Valerian passed over the requisite item. "I am happy to wait in the green parlor. I know my call is somewhat early."

The old fellow shuffled off without seeing Valerian to the guest parlor, another lapse.

Valerian was heading for the stairs when the sound of raised voices stopped him. A man was in a right taking about something—the words *no longer your concern* came through clearly—and as Valerian listened, a woman replied in equally strident tones.

And that woman was Emily Pepper.

He reversed course and passed the library, opening the door to the study without knocking. "Excuse me, I was looking for the guest parlor and must have lost my way. Miss Pepper, good day."

Emily was toe-to-toe with a red-haired fellow in business attire. Another man stood near the window, his expression guarded. Two clerkish-looking youths—identical twins—looked as if a tiger had sprung in through the window and prowled between them and the door.

"Mr. Dorning." Emily curtseyed.

Valerian bowed. "Might you introduce me? I apologize for intruding, but wouldn't want to slight the civilities now that I find myself in company."

A flush rose over the red-haired fellow's collar. The taller man's resentment was more subtle, and perhaps tinged with amusement.

Emily trudged through the introductions. Mr. Caleb Booth of the red hair and Mr. Tobias Granger of the height and watchful gaze knew enough to bow and offer platitudes, but through the whole of the introductions, Caleb Booth kept hold of a sheaf of papers covered in handwriting.

Maybe a tactical retreat was in order. "Miss Pepper, if my timing isn't inconvenient, would you offer me a turn in the garden?"

She didn't want to leave. Valerian could see that. She wanted to not only continue the altercation, but to win it.

"Do see to your guest," Tobias Granger said. "We'll be about our business here. A pleasure to meet you, Mr. Dorning. Emily has spoken very highly of you in the capacity of—what was it?—dancing master?"

Valerian winged his arm at Emily. "Mr. Granger, I was raised with six brothers and, because the Almighty likes to give a man a challenge, two sisters as well. If that's your idea of a clever insult, you are much in need of practice. I enjoy dancing, I enjoy the company of my neighbors. I enjoy providing an opportunity for the young people especially to set aside their cares for an hour or two. Demean those undertakings, and you reveal yourself to be a stodgy, graceless boor. When next we meet, I trust your invective will be more inventive. Miss Pepper?"

Emily had taken his arm, Caleb Booth was smirking, and the twins were frankly goggling.

"I want those letters," Emily said. "They are my father's correspondence, and I have every right to read them."

Booth's smirk became a condescending smile. "Now, Em, you needn't bother—"

Valerian snatched the papers from him. "The more siblings a man has, the faster his reflexes. You must have been an only child, Mr. Booth, but that should be no impediment to good manners. *A gentleman never argues with a lady.*"

Valerian passed the papers to Emily, who swept from the room with him as if processing from her presentation at court. She maintained her composure until they reached a turn in the corridor and encountered Osgood Pepper.

"Daughter, what on earth has you in such a state? Mr. Dorning, if you are responsible for the fire in my Emily's eyes, I suggest you put your affairs in order."

"You had best put your affairs in order, Papa," Emily shot back, thumping his bony chest with the papers. "Those geniuses you employ to oversee your business affairs have let the insurance lapse on our two largest warehouses. Fortunately, our solicitors were sufficiently dismayed to write to you directly about it."

"The insurance?" Pepper's brows knit. "Are you certain?"

Warehouses without insurance were disasters waiting to happen, as Valerian well knew. Publishers frequently went out of business because a warehouse fire destroyed an entire inventory overnight.

"Perhaps," he said, "this topic is better suited to a more private location?"

Pepper scowled at him. "What *are* you doing here, Dorning?"

"Mr. Dorning saved Caleb's life," Emily retorted. "I was ready to do him a serious injury when Mr. Dorning intervened. Tobias is equally deserving of my wrath. I can understand that an occasional bank draft gets lost in the mail, or a notice is set aside through inadvertence, but two warehouses, Papa? The two that are most likely to be full of expensive inventory?"

A shadow of confusion passed through Pepper's eyes. "I am nearly certain I signed bank drafts made out to the insurance company. I will remedy the oversight immediately. Perhaps when I was so ill, I failed to see to the matter."

Emily stepped back, gaze troubled. "Then you failed to attend to two notices for each policy, failed to take action when cancellation warnings were sent out, and failed to heed the solicitor's letter as well. At death's door, Papa, you would not be so negligent."

"Then perhaps the Walmer boys were a bit lax," Pepper said. "In any case, I won't let it happen again. Is that my correspondence in your hand, child?"

"I am not a child, Papa, and yes, this is the correspondence that I found sitting on the reading table. Some of it is more than a week old, and I gather no replies have been drafted."

"More oversights to remedy, then," Pepper said, holding out his hand. "You can take your handsome caller into the garden, and I will be about my business, eh?"

Emily did not want to hand over the letters. Valerian could see that as clearly as he could see the paternal pride that drove Pepper to demand their surrender.

"If we're to enjoy the garden," Valerian said, "you'll want a bonnet and shawl, Miss Pepper."

She let her father have the correspondence and took the steps at a brisk pace. When she was out of sight, and her footsteps had faded, Pepper was back to scowling.

"If you think to marry her fortune, think again, Dorning. No impecunious younger son will get his hands on my Emily if I have anything to say to it. She's all I have, and though I may be old, I take her welfare quite seriously."

"As well you should," Valerian replied mildly, "but Caleb Booth was hollering at her—I heard him from the corridor—and Granger did nothing to intervene. This altercation took place before a pair of clerks, who also failed to come to the lady's aid. Even you must admit that two warehouses full of inventory at risk for loss are worth your daughter's concern. Miss Pepper is taking your welfare quite seriously, sir. Rather than thwart her, perhaps you might allow her to support you until such time as she is willing to cede the field."

Pepper rested his weight against the newel post, suggesting the man ought to be carrying a cane, despite his protestations of renewed health.

"You don't understand, Dorning. Emily means well, but ever since... she worries excessively. Warehousing any inventory is a calculated risk. There were years when I could not afford to insure anything, not even my silks, but luck was with us and we're doing better now. Emily needs to get married and have some babies, and I do not mean get married to the likes of you."

Plain speaking, indeed. "Emily needs to know that you and your business interests thrive. She is wholly devoted to you, and until she is assured that you have matters entirely in hand, I doubt she'll be marrying anybody."

Pepper's gaze drifted up the stairs. "Just like her mother. Stubborn as hell."

"Devoted," Valerian countered. "Bright, determined. We call it stubbornness only when the ladies try to talk sense to us."

Pepper rolled the letters into a cylinder and smacked Valerian in the chest. "Charm will get you a turn in the garden, Dorning, and not much more. Break Emily's heart, and I will make you sorry."

"And the same to you, sir."

Pepper grinned, revealing an attractiveness that must have been more evident before his health declined.

"I do like a man with backbone, and I do not like fellows who raise their voices to my Emily, though she'd provoke a saint to shouting. Her brother was the same way."

Pepper shuffled off just as Emily appeared at the top of the steps, a blue shawl over her arm and a wide-brimmed hat in her hand.

"You are worried," Valerian said as she descended. "Give your father time to ponder his options and then inform him of your chosen course."

Emily paused, two steps up from the bottom. "Simply tell him I'll resume reading his correspondence?"

"And then do it. No bargaining, no exceptions, no negotiating or backing away from your word. You do this out of concern for him, not because business letters hold some odd fascination for you. If he's made an error of this magnitude, and two clerks and two flunkies didn't catch it, then he needs your help now."

Emily came down the last two steps, slipped her arm through Valerian's, and then leaned in closer, giving him her weight for a sweet, unexpected moment.

"I hate to fight. I fought with Briggs at breakfast, I fought with Tobias last night, I fought with Caleb this morning. I expect I'll fight with Mr. Ogilvy this afternoon. I never aspired to be a lady pugilist."

"Sweet heaven forefend. Let's stop by the master suite before we visit the garden, and perhaps your encounter with Mr. Ogilvy won't be as contentious as you fear."

She straightened. "You are very dear, Valerian Dorning. I hope Papa wasn't too rude?"

"Your father was appropriately protective of you."

Emily took Valerian's arm and turned back up the steps. "He should be protective of his inventories. We had a warehouse fire ten years ago. I had just gone away to school, but I could tell from my mother's letters that the lost inventory wasn't the half of it. The shopkeepers and modistes, the theaters and court drapers all shared in the disruption, even if they didn't lose any goods. Their customers were inconvenienced, their businesses suffered. The other mercers charged them extra to fill our orders, knowing the matter was one of hardship. Papa vowed then never to take that risk again."

"Could he afford to lose a warehouse or two?"

"He could lose ten warehouses. That's not the point. I cannot lose him."

They reached the top of the steps, and now Emily, too, seemed tired.

"Do you miss your brother?" Valerian asked. "I certainly miss mine, and they are all extant and in great good health." Ash was prone to the mulligrubs, but he was physically hale.

"My brother is quite alive, thank—who told you about Adam?" Emily came to an abrupt halt outside the door of the master suite. The fire was back in her eyes, the steel once more in her spine.

"I hope you will."

CHAPTER SEVEN

"The earl's brother is going to cause trouble—more trouble." Caleb made that announcement while goggling out the window, doubtless hoping to spy on Emily and Mr. Dorning strolling in the garden.

The rain had obliged the doting couple by moving off, while Tobias's mood was anything but sunny. Work on *his invective*, indeed. That Dorning had offered the set-down with good humor made the insult even worse.

As Dorning had known it would.

"We've had this discussion," Tobias said. "Valerian Dorning is a Dorset bumpkin, a younger son without a groat to his name. Emily is bored, and Dorning is a novelty. Come away from the damned window. You're not her nanny." Caleb was becoming troublesome too, and Tobias had to do something about that.

Caleb remained by the window, though he let the curtain fall back into place. "She's not out there yet. Probably taking tea with Dorning behind a closed door. Emily grows restless, true enough. I thought women were supposed to delight in lavishing great sums on wallpaper, carpets, and door carvings."

Emily Pepper was not *women*, something Tobias was coming to increasingly appreciate. She was twice the businessman her brother had been, maybe twice the businessman Caleb was too.

"The insurance payments should have gone out on time, Caleb." Osgood had been in high dudgeon over that *error*, his temper reminiscent of his old self. His competitors considered the name Pepper appropriate, as did any suppliers who disappointed him.

"Bank drafts go astray in the king's mail all too often, or perhaps the clerks were less than conscientious. You and I have been preoccupied with refitting the new merchantman, running a London business from the cow pasture God forgot, and humoring Osgood. No wonder we haven't had time to curry Em's favor."

Tobias remained lounging on the desk rather than peek out of windows like a lovesick schoolboy. "She doesn't like to be called Em."

Caleb ambled across the library. "She told you that? Most women like pet names."

"I'm glad to hear you're an expert on *most women*, but trust me when I say Emily bristles each time you presume upon her Christian name, particularly when you do it in front of others and in a condescending tone. If you mean to court her, respect is imperative."

Caleb's brows rose. "My regard for Emily is entirely sincere. I esteem her above all other women."

"Excellent, but does she esteem *you* over all other men? Will shouting at her before me and a pair of clerks win you that objective?"

And what would Caleb have done had Dorning not intervened? Laid hands on Emily? In that event, Tobias would have laid hands on Caleb, and Osgood might well have sent both of his loyal minions packing.

"I blundered badly." Caleb's boyish chagrin would have done the late, great Mr. Garrick proud. "My apology to the lady will more than make up for my error, I assure you. I did remind Osgood about the damned insurance policies. He became testy, and I let the matter drop. I won't make that mistake again. Still, one oversight is no reason for Em—*for Emily*—to stick her pretty little nose where it doesn't belong." Caleb gave the globe a spin, then shoved his hands into his pockets. "We ought not to leave Osgood alone for much longer."

"Is that a suggestion for me to take myself back to the study so you can resume spying on Emily and her swain?" Though nobody appeared to be strolling in the garden as yet.

Caleb's ears gave him away. He could control his features, but a redhead's tendency to flush with temper or excitement was apparently involuntary, at least in his case.

"I do not spy, Tobias. I safeguard the lady's good name. Emily has a chaperone. Blasted Briggs seems to spend more time hiding behind books and embroidery hoops than doing her job."

And that was another problem. "Briggs bears watching. I've set the housekeeper to befriending her, but I know from experience that task is very uphill work."

Caleb consulted an ornate pocket watch. "Shouldn't you be competing with me for Emily's affection, old man? If you're attempting to charm her, your effort is too subtle by half."

"My strategy was honestly to let you fall on your sword—which you were well on your way to doing when Dorning intervened—and then I would step in, the reasonable, respectful alternative." The best strategies were always the least complicated.

"I will *wield* my sword rather than fall upon it," Caleb retorted, wiggling his eyebrows. "You stand around all puckered and proud, barking at the clerks and toadying to Osgood. That won't win the fair maid. I am far from perfect, but I will make Emily an excellent husband."

"You had better."

Caleb slid his watch back into its pocket. "You're ceding the field? Any tradesman knows that if you offer the customer a choice, or several choices, the result is more likely to be a purchase than if you show her only the one product or one product at a time. Even if you're to be the lesser choice, you have to make some sort of effort, Tobias. Most women like to be pursued, even if they aren't particularly enamored of the pursuer."

"Perhaps you ought to write a book about how *most women* prefer to be courted."

"Don't pout," Caleb said, striding for the door. "Emily likes me. She always has."

"She needs to more than like you. My esteem in the lady's eyes has suffered a bit of a setback. If you allow Dorning to steal a march now, we both lose, and Emily ends up married to a prancing whopstraw. Worse, Dorning might harbor ambitions toward Osgood's enterprises."

"Isn't that what fortune hunters generally do? Harbor ambitions? I don't hold that against a man, harboring more than a few ambitions of my own."

"This fortune hunter is brother to the fellow who owns The Coventry Club in Town. He's brother-in-law to Worth Kettering, whom some refer to as the king's man of business. He's an earl's son and the current earl's brother. Osgood has all but lost his firstborn son, and if Dorning has a head for numbers, he could step into Adam's shoes."

"No, he could not. You and I have already stepped into them, and there's an end to it. Tell me about your setback."

"Emily and I had an uncomfortable conversation when she returned from dancing yesterday evening."

Caleb waved his hand. "And?"

"She is corresponding with Adam."

"We knew that. Loyal sister, dutiful sibling, doubtless combined with a soupçon of guilt. She wanted Adam to be found innocent of wrongdoing, but the jury disagreed. All very sad, especially for Adam, but fortunately, very five years ago too."

"That we know of her letters became apparent in my discussion with her, and she was most displeased. She has taken great pains to keep that correspondence private."

"And we have taken great pains to see that it is not. Adam hardly ever writes back, but then, mail between here and the penal colonies is not reliable. Apologize to her for overstepping and climb back on the horse."

This air of brisk dispatch was something Tobias frankly admired about Caleb. Caleb never bothered denying a fault, but instead, admitted his mistakes, apologized, and got on with the business at hand.

Perhaps courting a woman shouldn't be *business*, though. A troubling thought.

"I will mend fences as best I can," Tobias said, "but you have some fence-mending to do as well. We haven't spent years toiling in Osgood's warehouses so Valerian Dorning can waltz off with Emily's fortune."

"I don't think he's that sort," Caleb said, pausing before a pier glass to examine his teeth. "I think Dorning is more the kind to waltz off with a lady's heart, and I wish him the joy of that thankless enterprise. Do we blame the Walmers for the unpaid insurance premiums?"

"We let the matter drop. Osgood apparently forgot to send the bank drafts up to Town, and Emily has brought that to his attention. You should know I've suggested we have a shipwright look over our plans for the merchantman. Osgood seems amenable to that notion."

Caleb brushed a hand over his hair, straightened, and scowled at Tobias's reflection in the mirror. "Was that necessary?"

"No, but recall your lessons on how to handle ladies shopping for fabric. You initially ask the customer for things she can easily agree to: 'Mrs. Smith, won't you please step this way, hold that fabric up to the light, consider this combination?' Mrs. Smith obliges out basic good manners. Then, when you ask her to make the actual purchase, the habit of acceding to your requests benefits you and your bank balance."

Tobias was first out the door, knowing Caleb would follow rather than lurk at the windows.

"So you've asked Osgood to summon a shipwright, and he said

yes." Caleb pulled the library door closed and set off down the corridor. "What's the next request?"

"To allow me to take a hand in the renovations." Emily would be grateful to be free of that burden.

"And the next?"

To send you back to London. "Perhaps to hold a ball so Emily has something besides wallpaper and men's business dealings to interest her. I know not what my specific request might be, but an inventory of goodwill with one's employer is always a valuable asset."

"Maybe you should write a book, Tobias. *Aesop's Fables for the Aspiring Merchant.*"

"And maybe you should keep your mouth shut and pay closer attention to Osgood's unpaid bills."

Caleb shoved him, but the gesture lacked any sense of bonhomie. Yelling at Emily had been foolish, and Caleb knew it. Briggs was no sort of ally, and Osgood was in a justified temper.

While Valerian Dorning escorted Emily among the roses. About *that* situation, Tobias could think of all manner of clever invective.

HOW ON EARTH had Valerian Dorning learned of a brother whom Emily had been forbidden to mention to her own father? She wasn't to speak of Adam under Osgood Pepper's roof, wasn't to mention him in company. Adam had been not only transported for supposedly stealing from the business, but also banished from the Pepper family for dishonorable conduct.

And the banishment was far more painful for Adam than being sent halfway around the world to endure seven years of penal servitude.

Valerian Dorning's eyes held a question, and he expected answers Emily wasn't ready to give. Not yet, maybe not ever.

She pushed open the door to the master suite instead and marched into... what looked like a den of thieves. One knot of men was gathered around a set of dice, another held hands of playing cards. A dented silver flask was quickly slipped into the pocket of a fellow lounging against the stack of lumber.

The lot of them regarded her with the sort of arrogant glee naughty schoolboys turned on the first former who'd never dare report organized cheating.

"Mr. Ogilvy," Emily said in her haughtiest tones. "Explain this idleness."

Ogilvy set aside his cards and bestirred himself to rise from an overturned half barrel. "Good morning, Miss Pepper. We wasn't expecting you."

"That is not an explanation."

Valerian Dorning sauntered up on Emily's right, and, bless the man, said nothing. He merely gazed about, looking like a headmaster condemned to the company of dull-witted scholars.

"We was taking a break," Ogilvy said. "A respite from our labors, like it says in the Bible."

Perhaps confrontation became a bad habit, or perhaps Emily refused to be disrespected when Valerian Dorning was on hand to witness the insults.

"Are you the Almighty, Mr. Ogilvy, creating an entire universe such that you've earned the right to decree your own Sabbath here in my father's house? The hour is not yet noon, and every man and boy in this room sits idle when there's work to be done."

The cards disappeared, as did the dice, while Emily's temper only grew.

"A short break, miss," Ogilvy said. "One in the morning and one after our nooning, just like it says in the contract."

His smile reminded Emily of Caleb's, and that comparison did nothing for her composure.

"Mistake," Valerian said quietly, shaking his head. "Dissembling before the lady is a serious mistake, Ogilvy."

Was that amusement in Valerian's voice? He certainly didn't sound upset.

"I can read," Emily snapped, "in several languages, as it happens. The contract you signed was based on one my father has been using for several years. The terms contemplate no morning break. They contemplate no sitting about dicing and gambling while pretending to take pride in a job well done. They contemplate no quarter for thieves and charlatans."

Half a world away, Adam faced all manner of privation and shame, and as far as Emily was concerned, he'd done no wrong, while these thieves diced and drank for pay.

"Now see here, miss," Ogilvy said, stepping closer. "There's no call for hysterics. I brung the bank draft for the books and whatnot. Thought you'd be pleased to have the coin, and now all I get is a cross female thinking she knows how a job is to be managed. You'd best run along and let my men get back to work."

Valerian snorted. *Snorted.*

"The bank draft," Valerian said. "You ought to surrender it before you're ejected from the premises, Ogilvy." He wiggled his fingers peremptorily, as if anything that had been in Ogilvy's grasp was not to sully Emily's hand.

She liked that bit of playacting, liked it very much. She liked even better the suggestion that she sack the lot of these fools.

Ogilvy fumbled in his pockets, first found his flask, and eventually located a piece of paper and passed it over.

"You," Emily said, walking past Ogilvy, "are a smirking, shirking reptile parading about as a tradesman. I have had enough of your sly tricks and disrespect. Pack up your tools and leave. Send a final invoice to my attention, and I will consider it for the sake of those unfortunate enough to be in your employ. You have fifteen minutes to vacate this house."

Silence greeted that announcement. Silence and, for Emily, a sense of immense satisfaction.

"You heard her," Valerian said pleasantly. "Stow the tools and away with you. The rain has let up, so you can all troop off to the inn where I'm sure Mr. Ogilvy will buy you a round in consolation for your self-inflicted misfortune."

The oldest of the workmen rose and collected a hammer from atop the stack of lumber.

"You can't do this, miss," Ogilvy sneered. "You aren't a party to that contract, and my agreement is with Mr. Pepper."

Valerian considered the bank draft. "Ogilvy, you are either very brave—which I doubt—or very stupid. Do you honestly believe that Osgood Pepper will take your dishonest word over that of the woman he has raised to have the finest instinct for business? The daughter who will inherit the lot of his properties and enterprises?"

Valerian held the bank draft up to the light, as if he suspected a forgery. "You were lucky to get this job," he went on, "and through your own graft and slacking, you have lost it. Find some dignity and leave, or I will be very certain to tell Mr. Pepper exactly what I've witnessed on every occasion when I've seen your work site—if one can call it that. You have lied to Pepper's daughter, wasted her time, and disrespected her before others. Should you feel it necessary to discuss this situation with Mr. Pepper, he will first be put in possession of those salient facts."

The tone was pleasant, the observations almost cordial. The crew, who had been shuffling about, collecting tools and donning jackets, had gone still and silent. The two youngest workmen, mere boys, were as pale as Holland covers, gaping at Valerian open-mouthed, while Emily wanted to applaud.

"Out," she said, pointing toward the door. "Either send a final invoice to my attention within fifteen days or don't send one at all."

The oldest workman left first, pausing to tug his cap at Emily. Ogilvy had snatched up his hat and coat and joined the line of retreating men when a thought punctured Emily's sense of righteous victory.

"You two," she said as the boys made for the door. "Stay here. Somebody will have to tidy up this mess and inventory the material on hand. Can you do that?"

The larger boy, a sandy-haired youth with prominent front teeth, nodded. "Aye, miss. I can read and write, and Jasper can too. We'll do a proper job for you." He still had the high voice of a child, but the worry in his eyes was that of a young man who desperately needed his wages.

"See that you do," Emily said. "You have been subjected to a very bad example. You can either follow it to perdition or learn from it."

The last of the men left, and Emily's sense of triumph left with him. She'd just *sacked an entire crew of men*, in the middle of the day, without permission from Papa or anybody.

"What wages was Ogilvy paying you?" Valerian asked the boys.

They named a paltry sum, and Valerian sent Emily a questioning look.

She nodded. "You will take your meals in the kitchen. The household generally sits down for midafternoon tea at half four. Behave as if you're in church, and the rest of the staff will treat you well. Violate my trust, as Mr. Ogilvy did, and your parents will hear of it before sundown the same day."

"Jasper don't got no parents," the taller boy said. "He's my cousin. I'm Tom."

Jasper stared at the floor, and Emily was angry all over again. "I will leave the tidying up and inventorying to you two. You'll find paper and pencil on the mantel. Ask in the kitchen if you need anything else."

She left with more haste than dignity and kept right on going across the corridor, Valerian at her side. She barreled blindly into a linen closet before the first tear had the effrontery to trickle down her cheek.

"I am upset," she said, feeling equal parts foolish and angry.

Valerian accompanied her into the closet, and closed the door before passing her a handkerchief.

"I suspect you have been upset for a long time," he said, leaning against the door with his arms crossed. "I also suspect, in your situation, anybody would be upset."

Had he taken Emily in his arms, the tears would have overcome her, but he stood across the little chamber, looking as if women cried in linen closets regularly, which—come to think of it—they probably did.

"I've never sacked anybody before."

"He needed sacking, Emily. Badly. The lot of them did. Why did you spare the boys?"

Emily dabbed at her cheeks. The handkerchief was worn to exquisite softness and lightly scented with roses. The fragrance blended with the thick aroma of lavender in the linen closet, the combination clean, domestic, and soothing.

She might have used that moment to tell Valerian about Adam, laboring for his very existence thousands of miles away.

"Suffice it to say," she began, "that I did not think those boys should suffer for the sins of the elders in charge of the situation. Neither boy has had enough to eat. Neither one is wearing clothes that fit him." They were both pale, not as Saxon youth who tended to have fair complexions were pale, but as children who toiled indoors hour after hour were pale.

Valerian pushed away from the door, grasped Emily about the hips, and hoisted her onto the counter running beneath the closet's sole window. He hiked himself up to sit beside her, and a small, dimly lit room took on the quality of a secret hideaway. A safe place where friends could enjoy some much-needed privacy.

"The lads are local," Valerian said, "probably hired at the last minute when Ogilvy brought his pirate crew up from Bournemouth or Portsmouth. Keeping the boys on is both kind and just. Also very shrewd."

"Women aren't supposed to be shrewd. Ladies aren't." They weren't supposed to argue with tradesmen or with much of anybody. Weren't supposed to raise their voices, intrude on men's business, and cite contractual terms. "Lately, I haven't made a very convincing lady."

"My sisters are ladies, as are my sisters-in-law. They are all very shrewd. So shrewd most men will never catch them at it, except for the fellows who adore the ladies for how effectively they use their wits."

"My brother didn't adore me, but neither did he treat me like some porcelain angel." She hadn't meant to say that, but then, Adam hadn't written to her in weeks, and her concern for him was at least part of why she'd grown so impatient with Papa, Caleb, and Tobias.

And Mr. Ogilvy.

And Briggs.

But only part.

"I adore you," Valerian Dorning said, hopping off the counter. "I hope the sentiment is sufficiently reciprocal that you'll go for a hack with me in the direction of Dorning Hall."

He helped her down, and Emily stood for a moment, wondering why a man who adored her wasn't stealing a kiss in a linen closet. Adoration of the adult sort entailed more than kissing, though, didn't it? Much more.

"You'll want to convey this to your father." Valerian gave her the bank draft, which, upon examination, was for an appallingly paltry sum.

Ogilvy had, indeed, needed sacking. "I am no sort of horsewoman, but I suspect riding is another skill needed for life in the country."

"We won't go far, and we're in no hurry." Valerian opened the door, looked both directions, and preceded Emily into the corridor. "Miss Pepper, I will await you in the informal guest parlor, if you'd like to change into your riding habit?"

Valerian *adored* her—perhaps that was teasing—but he also held doors for her, ensured no nosy servants were patrolling the corridor at inopportune moments, and asked questions that were genuine questions, not polite masculine commands.

Those considerations alone would have provoked Emily to sincere respect, but add to them both honesty and an ability to admire feminine shrewdness, and she was moved to adoration too.

And that was without any mention of Valerian Dorning's dancing, conversation, or kisses.

"I'll need a quarter hour, no more," Emily said. "And thank you."

"For?"

For so much. For holding his tongue when Emily had exerted her authority, for standing *with* her rather than *for* her. For having a ready handkerchief and a penchant for honesty, for noticing how hard women worked to be both agreeable and effective, and for admiring that quality.

"Thank you for being yourself." She was tempted to follow up that compliment with a kiss, but instead turned on her heel and left him smiling in the middle of the empty corridor.

YEARS AGO, the oldest of the two Dorning daughters, an estimable female by the name of Jacaranda, had declared to her seven brothers that if she was to drudge all day for the sake of heedless males, she'd at least do so for pay. She had quit her role as the de facto manager of Dorning Hall and gone into service as a housekeeper.

An earl's daughter did not go into service, ever, and had Grey known where to find Jacaranda, her plan would have been thwarted on the instant. Jacaranda, however, had declined to take a post in Town and had instead immured herself at the neglected country estate of one Worth Kettering.

Valerian, along with all of his siblings, the entire Dorning Hall staff, and very likely the hounds, pantry mousers, and livestock, had been frantic.

Frantic not with worry in his case, but with shame.

Like his brothers, he'd blustered for a time about female foolishness and unnecessary drama, and also like them, he'd finally seen what Jacaranda had tried to convey for years: A gentleman did not take advantage of a lady's devotion to family, such that she was expected to handle every chore, from planning menus to dipping candles and beating rugs, while the gent went for a pleasant morning hack, chatted away the afternoon over a pint in the posting inn's snug, sat down to a hearty meal at the end of his day, and caught up on the London papers in the evening.

The day Jacaranda had turned up missing, Valerian had found a renewed determination to make something of himself, something *gentlemanly*. Something honorable and worth respecting.

For, as the days had turned into weeks, months, and then years without Jacaranda to civilize the household, the brothers had suffered. Humor had turned more grim, the Hall had become subtly less gracious. The tenants were polite but not quite as friendly as when Jacaranda had been on hand to fuss over a new baby or commiserate with an elder over sore knees.

She had taken a light of integrity and decency with her and left behind—for Valerian at least—a lesson in valuing others, especially the ladies.

Sitting in the Pepper Ridge guest parlor, he pondered that lesson as it applied to Emily Pepper. She and Jacaranda would get along famously, which was no small compliment. But then, Emily had the knack of getting along well with people generally, and that skill obscured how truly observant and insightful she was.

The door opened, and Emily strode in, wearing a habit of dark blue velvet. "This will have to do. It's the only habit I brought with me, though I have two others in Town."

Valerian rose. "The color is quite becoming."

"But?"

"No buts. The gold embroidery about the buttonholes and collar is in good taste. The cut is flattering without impeding your movements. The hat is appropriately whimsical."

"Silly, you mean."

The thing affixed to her hair was a few peacock and pheasant feathers set at a jaunty angle. "You are still upset," he said. "Let's talk about that on the way to the stable." Valerian wanted to get her out of this house, which was at once too quiet and too full of other people.

He also wanted to kiss her. That impulse was a low hum in his blood that followed him even into slumber.

"I am annoyed," Emily said, stalking from the room. "With Ogilvy and with myself for allowing his thievery to go on for so long. Did nobody offer you refreshment? Of course not, because the only useful footman we have sits outside my father's study, waiting on him and his acolytes."

She took a left turn. "If we go out through the conservatory, we won't be visible from the study. Briggs is doubtless watching from the east turret, and I do believe I finally understand why occasionally a good, hard gallop has some appeal."

"Sacking Ogilvy might inspire your staff to be more attentive to their duties." Or more attentive to the lady of the house.

They entered the conservatory, a comfortably warm space illuminated by skylights, glass walls to the east and south, and glass doors opening onto a side garden.

"Margaret Dorning came to call last week," Emily said, bootheels rapping on the flagstone walkway. "She brought more medication for Papa and offered to send me some plants for my herbal, but I hadn't any notion what I was supposed to *do* with them. Everywhere, I am faced with the reality that country life involves more than fresh air and clean laundry."

"Some things are the same in both Town and country, Emily."

She came to a stop before exiting into the side garden. "Such as?"

"I wanted to kiss you in Town, I want to kiss you in the country." *Here and now.*

Emily gazed off across ferns, orchids, and potted lemon and orange trees. A fountain trickled somewhere among the greenery, and a swallow flitted overhead. Perhaps Eden had been like this, sheltered, private, quiet, and green.

"I resist the impulse to stare at your mouth," she said. "I deliver a tirade to Caleb Booth about insurance and Papa's good name, and all the while, I'm thinking: I would not have to explain this to Valerian Dorning. I swill tea with your sister-by-marriage and discuss some weed that's supposed to be a tonic for the female humors. I want instead to ask her if married life is as wonderful as I suspect it could be."

To hell with kissing, Valerian wanted to *belong* to this woman, heart and hearth.

"My mind takes me down similar paths. What is Emily doing right now? Could I send her a book without appearing too forward? Could a woman who has had the pick of London's dandies and heirs hold me in high regard when I am of such limited means?"

"Means matter little if they are in the hands of someone without the sense to use them wisely." Emily leaned near enough that Valerian could catch a whiff of camphor from her velvet riding habit and see the exact spot on the largest pheasant feather that matched the brown of her eyes.

She should not have to be the one to take the next step with him, not only because convention required the male to do the pursuing, but because any man worthy of her notice ought to put forth *effort*, ought to risk at least his pride for the sake of winning her hand.

Valerian pressed a slow kiss to her temple. "Come with me. What I have to show you bears on the present topic."

She lingered near, driving him halfway to Bedlam with the temptation to lock the doors and turn the conservatory into a private paradise in truth.

"Very well," she said, smiling slightly. "Share with me the bucolic splendors of rural Dorsetshire."

"Rural Dorset is not exactly foremost on my mind just now."

She patted his cheek. "Nor on mine."

Valerian stood for a moment, gathering his wits and admiring her retreating form—and her tactics—before following her out to the stables.

CHAPTER EIGHT

The pale southern shoulder of Britain had come into view an hour ago, a thin, hazy line at first, then more and more distinct as the ship neared its destination. The cliffs were bright and proud, ramparts that had stood unchanging against time and tide. Adam Pepper's heart, by contrast, remained a morass of shifting and uncomfortable feelings.

He was bitter, of course, toward the homeland that had shown him only the pity of transportation over the brutality of the rope, though a convict's life was brutal enough and pity stretched the bounds of credulity. Britain sought to hold the Antipodes away from France's imperial ambitions. If that meant using the powerless to subjugate and populate an inhospitable wilderness, Britain regarded that as a fair bargain. English jails were perpetually full, and convict labor could be put to use in the heat and misery of far-off lands.

That many of those transported died of privation, disease, and despair was just another sort of pity.

Threading through the bitterness was determination, for Adam hadn't endured four months of ocean gales, appalling rations, monstrous waves, and his equally monstrous self-doubt to be thwarted now.

He was enough at peace with himself to admit to sadness. His homecoming shouldn't be like this, a furtive, dangerous violation of the law, when in another two years, he might well have earned his ticket of leave honestly.

"You do not have the look of a man gazing fondly on his homeland." Mrs. Helen Thelwell took the place beside him at the rail, the breeze fluttering the ribbons of her straw hat. "You can find a ship sailing for Le Havre on the next tide."

They had spent endless hours playing piquet, reading to each other, and debating politics, but Adam did not entirely trust Mrs. Thelwell. Like many who'd spent time in *Terra Australis*, she kept most of her past to herself. Perhaps her late husband's business had failed, perhaps he'd been a convict. Perhaps there'd never been a husband, late or otherwise.

That was none of Adam's business. "Are you a woman gazing fondly on her homeland?"

She untangled a skein of coppery hair from the brim of her bonnet. The breeze snatched it right back.

"I have been homesick since the day I lost sight of England, Mr. Carmichael. The southern climate is unkind to pale complexions, and I was not a good sailor on my outbound voyage."

Some unspoken sorrow lay in that admission. "You apparently conquered your mal de mer for the homeward journey."

Her smile was slight and feline. "I've conquered much. What are you setting out to conquer?"

Guilt perhaps? "My father is gravely ill. I hope to see him before he goes to his reward." The truth, ironically.

"That explains why you look upon England with such ire. She threatens to take your family from you. We English value family."

Some of the English did. "What of you? Is your family awaiting your arrival in Portsmouth?"

"No, they are not. My house is in Bournemouth. I will find lodging in Portsmouth for tonight, then make my way down the coast tomorrow."

Bournemouth was more than halfway to Adam's destination. "Have you an escort for that journey?"

"I am a widow. I need no escort for a day's penance on a stagecoach."

Adam had done well for himself in New South Wales, which wasn't unusual for a man with education, skills, and ambition. He had the means to get himself wherever he pleased to go. If anybody was looking for Adam Pepper, a convict who'd broken his parole to return to England, they would not expect him to be traveling with a woman.

"I have business in Devonshire," he said, though spouting false-hoods still sat ill with him. "I will hire a coach to take me west, and I am more than happy to share that vehicle with you."

The details onshore were becoming discernible, ship's masts, buildings, the controlled confusion of busy wharves. Seagulls patrolled from the sky, their cries becoming a constant chorus. The men aloft were reefing sails, and the captain stood on the forecastle, his spyglass for once not in evidence.

An odd ache started up in Adam's throat.

"I will accept that generous offer," Mrs. Thelwell said. "And assuming my house hasn't burned to the ground, you will accept my hospitality in Bournemouth."

He ought not. Anybody abetting a man who returned to England before his sentence was finished could be in a heap of trouble. Emily had pointed that out in several letters.

But refusing Mrs. Thelwell's generosity would be ungentle-manly, and then too, Adam liked her. She was good company, she knew something of where he'd been and what he'd faced there. For a man whose homeland would cheerfully hang him for setting foot on his native soil, Mrs. Thelwell's gracious gesture was hard to resist.

"You refer to it as your house," Adam said, "not your home. I gather you weren't raised there."

"You gather incorrectly. I was born at Toftrees and spent the first fifteen years of my life on that estate. A cousin inherited the place, but as fate would have it, the property belongs to me now. Sometimes, justice does prevail."

On that enigmatic observation, she pushed away from the rail and left Adam alone as the shore—and the commission of a hanging felony—came ever closer.

VALERIAN DORNING WAS PAYING A CALL, on his own initiative and at an earlier hour than most social visits occurred. Emily savored the sense of being *of interest* to a man who interested her in return. She liked Valerian Dorning, she was attracted to him, but he'd mentioned the word *esteem*, and in doing so he'd put his finger on the ingredient that made this outing important.

She *esteemed* him.

She respected that Caleb and Tobias worked hard. She had a proper regard for her father's mercantile genius, and she'd had a sister's devotion to Adam—still did—despite sibling squabbles and the difference in their ages.

She *esteemed* Valerian Dorning. He brooked no disrespect toward her, but somehow emboldened her to fight her own battles. When he was on hand, she won those battles, or at least fought them to a draw.

He was kind, not in the clucking, condescending way that a charitable committee member was kind, but rather, with the quiet pragmatism that tended to unspoken needs. Young people lacked a place to socialize, he provided that. Apprentices hired to do an inventory needed to know their wages, Valerian handled the discussion for them.

Emily had needed to preserve her dignity when confronting her father earlier, and Valerian had given her a credible excuse to quit the field. Perhaps Valerian was simply a gentleman, exhibiting the kindness and honor that so many only feigned when convenient.

In any case, she *esteemed* him, and she hadn't been able to esteem *any* of the fortune-hunting heirs and preening viscounts in London.

"Where are we going?" she asked as they turned their horses from a farm lane down a bridle path that ran between two hedgerows. Summer had reached her full glory, and the branches overhead nearly met, making the path shady and private.

"I'd like to show you some of the countryside between Pepper Ridge and Dorning Hall. By the lanes, the two estates are more than ten miles distant. You can halve that if you know the shortcuts."

"Is there a reason I should know the shortcuts?"

"One should always know the shortcuts, Miss Pepper, though when to take them can be a more complicated question. May I discuss a matter of some personal interest with you?"

Better and better. "Of course."

"I am a younger son, a notably impecunious exponent of the breed."

"You've said as much before." And this time, Emily did not argue the point. Valerian Dorning had called upon her for reasons, and he would explain them in his own good time. Emily could think of only one conversation a bachelor and a young lady were permitted to have in private, and she wanted to have that discussion with Valerian.

"Through the generosity of an aunt," he said, "I have claim to a modest acreage, which thus makes me, technically, a landowner."

Very encouraging. "Do go on."

"Men who own property are eligible for certain posts."

The post of husband? "They can vote." Provided the land was worth forty shillings. "They can hunt game." Provided the land was worth at least a hundred pounds, which said something about the relative value of an Englishman's vote versus the worth of a roasted partridge.

"Just so, and land ownership is also a requisite for the post of magistrate."

Emily brought her mare to a halt. "Magistrate?"

"Justice of the peace," Valerian said, drawing Clovis up beside the mare. "The king's man. The fellow who settles the petty squabbles of the neighborhood and chastises the habitual drunkards."

What had *magistrates* to do with anything? "You have habitual drunkards hereabouts?" The surrounds were pastoral, fields and meadows, sheep and broodmares with the occasional milch cow. A pretty fieldstone manor sat at the bottom of a low rise, an alley of lime trees stretching before it.

"Habitual drunkards," Valerian said, "likely grace every corner of the realm."

Emily nudged her mare forward. "I don't suppose I ever gave the post of rural magistrate any thought. Does it pay?"

As soon as she asked the question, she knew she'd erred. Valerian rose in his stirrups and settled back into the saddle, then adjusted his reins.

"Not a salary. Some expenses can be reimbursed. The thing is, my brother is the current magistrate."

Which...? Oh, the brother who owned all the land, of course. "Casriel, you mean?"

"Casriel, and he is not suited for the post. He's too polite, too much the earl, and if he votes his seat, he'll be in Town for months at a time. He would rather be the devoted husband and doting papa, the good neighbor, the meddling brother. I suspect that last position is calling to him particularly."

"Brothers meddle?"

"So do sisters, at least in my experience. Casriel has asked me to take on the post of magistrate, and I am inclined to accept it. I wanted to discuss the matter with you first."

Confusion and more than a little disappointment lifted into insight. Valerian Dorning apparently needed an ally, too, somebody to stand *with* him, rather than *for* him.

"What are the reasons to refuse the post?" she asked.

"I am in need of coin, and it doesn't pay. I'll have less time for my writing, for turning my hand to profitable ventures, to tending my acres, if I choose not to rent them all out."

As the horses ambled along, the sun shone more strongly. "You intend to take up the plow, Valerian?"

"I have walked miles behind a plow, also ridden miles on a hay wagon, which penance I do not seek to repeat. I've wielded a scythe to clear our drainage ditches—my brother Hawthorne can wax poetic on the topic of drainage—and I've taken my turn in the foaling barn under a chilly seed moon. My father regarded the natural world highly and believed children benefited from physical work. By the time Casriel took over the estate, he simply needed the free labor, and we owed him at least that."

"A seed moon?"

"The April full moon. Mares favor it for dropping foals."

They emerged from the bridle path closer to the fieldstone manor, though Valerian kept the horses beneath the shade of the hedgerow. Without dismounting, he was able to open and close a gate, which was fortunate, because Emily wasn't about to attempt to jump a stile.

"Thank you," she said as his gelding fell in step beside her mare. "I was raised to value the appearance of idleness in women—we're to sit about tatting lace and swilling chocolate—and the industry of a man who labors with his mind rather than his hands."

"Show me a successful farmer," Valerian said, "and I will show you somebody who labors with everything he or she has. It's a challenging life, and running an empire without competent farmers is impossible. You haven't answered my question about the magistrate's post. Should I accept it?"

They rode closer to the stone manor, such that Emily could see roses trellised all the way to the overhanging roof of the front porch. A wide swing hung beneath another rose arbor in a side garden, and half a dozen fat geese strutted on the drive.

Pepper Ridge had no porch roses, though the specimens in the garden were impressive. Emily had hung a hammock, but why hadn't she thought to put up a swing? And the geese were a lovely touch...

"I think you want to be useful to your brother," Emily said. "You've admitted that. His lordship probably doesn't ask for much from you, and refusing him would be difficult."

Adam had asked her to look after Papa, when Emily had been so furious with her father she'd not wanted to speak to him, much less take care of him. That Adam had asked, though, meant she'd had to agree. A man facing transportation should not sail away knowing his father and his sister were no longer speaking.

Valerian steered his horse up a path along the rise behind the manor house. "You are correct that I want to be of use to my brother. He's carried many a burden alone, and the rest of our siblings are now scattered to the four winds."

"The English winds," Emily murmured. "You could reach any member of your family within a few days."

Valerian glanced over at her, probably because she'd spoken a bit sharply. "True, but they don't seem inclined to look in at the Hall."

"Which leaves you wanting a reason to remain by Casriel's side. Hawthorne is nearby, but he's preoccupied with a new wife, a family, and *drainage*, I presume."

"Also with growing the herbs and flowers for the family botanical business. You know something about that enterprise."

Even before Papa had benefited so markedly from Margaret Dorning's herbal remedies, Emily had prevailed upon Papa to help the Dornings find shop space in London. Papa was not their landlord, but he'd put in a good word with a competitor, and the Dornings had an emporium that was both affordable and fashionably located.

"Are you involved in the botanical business?" she asked.

"I am, tangentially. I set up the books, I audit them from time to time, I watch the inventories and match them against what's selling, creating the production schedules necessary to meet demand. I developed a budget and monitor actual expenses and income as they compare to my projections. Nothing very taxing, but my brothers' talents lie elsewhere, so I watch the ledgers and reports."

Adam had those sorts of skills, more's the pity. "But do you *enjoy* all that accounting?"

Valerian remained silent as the horses topped the rise. A carpet of gently rolling countryside spread out beneath them, hedges creating a patchwork of pastures, fields, meadows, and farmsteads. The view was lovely in a way Pepper Ridge's prospect was not. Pepper Ridge was a grand manor, but it lacked such a delightful situation.

"I do not particularly enjoy accounting," Valerian said. "One does it, just as one hangs up clothes upon retiring, or curries a horse before putting on his saddle. Adulthood is full of boring duties that must nonetheless be undertaken conscientiously."

Was that Valerian's opinion or a departed tutor's lecture? "Is being a magistrate a boring duty that must be undertaken conscientiously?"

He drew his gelding to a halt and patted the beast on the shoulder. "To the contrary, the magistrate's job is often fascinating. Rendering a legal judgment is only part of the challenge. One must do so in a way that solves the real problem."

"Like Jenny Switzer's situation?" The girl had been forthcoming about what had sent her seeking employment ten miles from her home.

"She told you about the charges?"

"She told me a neighbor of some standing had forced his attentions on her, and she slapped him just as his son came upon them. The neighbor alleged that Jenny assaulted him because he'd refused her advances, and the son was prepared to lie for his father."

"That is more than Casriel was told. Jenny's case wanted not simply a judgment—the wrong crime had been alleged, so the charges could be dismissed—but a solution. The real problem was that Jenny had made an enemy, and thus her removal from the environs became imperative for her own wellbeing."

"Not exactly," Emily said, thinking back to Ogilvy and his gang of thieves. "The real problem was that Squire Rutledge took liberties uninvited and was then such a coward that he couldn't stand for his own son to know what a philandering weasel he is, much less apologize or take responsibility for the wrong he'd committed."

"My sisters would agree with you. Rutledge tried to press his attentions on Daisy when she was about Jenny's age."

"Do *you* agree with my assessment of Jenny's situation?"

Valerian studied the pretty little farmstead below. No people moved about the grounds, though down the hill from the house some horses grazed in a grassy paddock, a few goats interspersed with the equines.

"I agree with you that Rutledge is the wrongdoer, but I know not how to deal with him. I could knock out his front teeth, and he'd still accost unwilling girls. If I charge him with battery or assault, the females suffer by association and the juries are unlikely to do justice in any event. That is what makes being magistrate such an interesting undertaking. Legalities often stand in for more complex human conundrums, and a good magistrate can do much to address both."

"You would enjoy taking on those conundrums?"

"I would, yes, but as I said—"

"Valerian, you would enjoy the work. Somebody has to do it. Your neighbors would benefit greatly if the post were held by a man who likes the job versus somebody who resents it. If the only meaningful remuneration in this life were in the form of coin, no woman would have children, much less raise them to the age of reason, much less keep house for her family.

"No soldier would take the king's shilling, for that matter. Is a life worth only the soldier's meager pay? I would rather see you paid handsomely in both coin and satisfaction, but if survival is not at issue, satisfaction without coin is a better bargain than coin without satisfaction."

His gaze had shifted somewhere in the middle of that tirade from the pastoral landscape below to Emily's face.

"You're saying I should take the job?"

"Yes. You want to, but you're plaguing yourself with doubts because having what you want seems to be foreign to your nature. Not all of adulthood should be conscientious fulfillment of obligations, you know." She nudged her horse back down the path, feeling as if she'd said more than she meant to.

"Emily, a moment, please." Valerian's gelding came up on her right.

She tugged back on the reins. The mare stopped and swung her head to sniff at Emily's boot.

"I have offended you," Valerian said. "That's the last thing I wanted to do. I did want to discuss the magistrate's job with you, but I also wanted to show you Abbotsford."

"Abbotsford?"

"The farm at the bottom of the hill."

"More of a manor, I'd say. It's quite pretty."

"I'm glad you think so. I was hoping you might be interested in sharing it with me."

VALERIAN HAD PUT his heart at Emily Pepper's figurative feet quietly, maybe too quietly.

"Sharing a farm with you?" she asked.

"Sharing a property and a life. I own these acres, that house, those outbuildings." To say that aloud was odd, in a good way. "Have since I was eighteen. My tenant is leaving after harvest, and I'm considering setting up a household here."

Emily guided her mare down the track. "Are you proposing marriage to me, Valerian?"

"I am proposing to ask your father if I might court you. Before that delicate negotiation, I thought to assure myself of your interest. Permission to court is not consent to marry. I know that, but there's no point in my building that particular castle in Spain if you're not willing to dwell in it with me."

"Papa will be difficult."

Valerian took heart from the future tense. The conditional—Papa *would be* difficult—would have been less encouraging.

"To secure your hand, even to secure permission to seek your hand, I must be willing to contend with difficulty."

The horses picked their way back down the slope, and Valerian let the quiet of the summer day sink into his bones. He'd broached the topic. The lady replied if and when she was so inclined. As much as he wanted to beg Emily to *look at him*, to put him out of his torment, he wanted even more for Emily's answer to be her own considered decision.

"You have said you lack the means to take a wife. Did you forget that you own an entire estate, Valerian?"

"Fair question, and yes, to be honest. I had put from my mind that I had either a right to rent or to occupancy where Abbotsford was concerned. The current tenant is a widow with three sons, and she needed every groat to keep the farm going when her husband died. I fell out of the habit of collecting the rent, but she recently caught up the arrears. My tenant is soon to remarry, and her intended is a man of means."

"You *fell out of the habit* of collecting rent. Rent is not the handkerchief we neglect to stash in a pocket, but you... Three boys, you say?"

"They were all under the age of thirteen when their father died. The oldest will soon be eighteen. I expect you'll meet him and the rest of his family at the assembly."

Failing to collect rent probably struck Osgood Pepper's daughter as proof of witlessness. Why hadn't Valerian seen that?

"My brother Hawthorne wants to rent a portion of the arable land, and he will insist on paying his rent timely."

"I should hope so."

Whatever did that terse tone mean? "I'd like to show you the house. The family is away visiting relatives, and I told them I might stop by in their absence."

Emily rode the rest of the way up the drive in silence, and Valerian concluded he'd misread an important situation entirely. The lady hadn't refused him, but Emily Pepper was a considerate, kind-hearted woman. She would let a fellow down gently and choose her words carefully.

Just because a lady enjoyed kissing a man didn't mean she contemplated a lifetime at his side.

The temptation to argue, to scrap and fight for what he wanted, lost the battle to an ingrained habit of gentlemanly consideration. Valerian assisted Emily to dismount and tied the horses to the hitching post.

"You need not indulge me in this inspection of the premises," he said, withdrawing a key from his pocket. "I would like a woman's opinion on the place, though. I've bided at Dorning Hall because Casriel was off in Town, and somebody needed to keep an eye on the ancestral pile."

That was even the truth. Then too, the cottage at the Hall was Valerian's to use at no cost, and that had mattered too much.

"I like the roses," Emily said. "I like that one approaches the front door assailed by a pleasant fragrance. All the roses at Pepper Ridge are planted too far from the house. The scent neither wafts in through the windows most days, nor graces the entrances. One must hike to enjoy it, and for Papa that was nearly impossible until recently."

An odd little speech. Rather than reply, Valerian unlocked the front door. He hadn't been inside this house in more than two years, but Marie was an impeccable housekeeper. The floors gleamed with polish, the windows sparkled, and not a speck of dust was to be seen.

"Stuffing a house full of furniture sucks up the light," Emily said, peering around the foyer. "I like this openness."

What she referred to as *openness* was simply the typical function-ality of a country dwelling. Pegs along the wall of the entranceway provided a place to hang cloaks and hats. A small deal table held a woven reed basket for mail. Several pairs of house slippers were arranged beneath the table. No heavy, elaborately carved sideboard crowded the space, no fancy ferns blocked the windows. A pot of violets sat on one windowsill, a tabby cat with a white bib sat on the other.

"Hello," Emily said, stroking the cat's head. "Are you guarding the castle?"

"He looked to be taking a nap in his owner's absence." What a lovely picture Emily made, petting the cat in the slanting sunbeams. Valerian wanted to tell her that she belonged here, not in the rambling ostentation of Pepper Ridge, but he instead hung up her cloak and bonnet and held his peace.

"Let's start belowstairs," she said. "I always have the sense of exploring pirate caves when I venture into the kitchens and pantries. The staff doesn't forbid me to pry, but neither are they glad to see me where I don't belong."

"You belong wherever you need to be to run a proper household. The cook and housekeeper might not appreciate an unannounced inspection, but one must wonder why. If your expectations are reasonable, then an occasional peek at the larders or scullery should be of no moment."

"Not to hear Briggs tell it. A lady never descends below the main floor. She summons the staff, and they endure the awkwardness of an interview abovestairs."

"How many homes has Briggs actually managed? And how many of those homes were in the country, as opposed to the rarefied confines of Town?"

"Briggs was raised genteelly enough, but her father and then her brother fell on hard times, and their situation did not end well. She tries to help me avoid missteps, but you have a point. A general doesn't send his junior officer to review the troops. That would be bad for morale and give the junior officer airs."

Emily peered at some children's sketches framed above the

mantel of the formal parlor, her expression unreadable. "I believe this is supposed to be a knight charging at a dragon, while a fair maid watches from her tower."

"Boys draw those scenes and then give them to their mamas." Some boys. Valerian's sketching had been so overshadowed by Oak's talent, he hadn't bothered inflicting his art on his mother.

They wandered through the spotless kitchen and tidy pantries, into a pair of comfortable parlors, and then to an estate office. The office struck Valerian as a cross between a lady's personal sitting room and his father's study. He saw stacks of correspondence, a scarred blotter, and glass-fronted cabinets full of pamphlets, treatises, and ledgers, but also lace curtains that let in plenty of light, a crocheted shawl draped over the back of the sofa, and another pot of violets on the windowsill.

"Your tenant has a way with violets."

"She's done a good job with the farm too."

Emily sniffed at the violets and pressed a finger to the soil in the crock. "Did you ever consider marrying her?"

"Yes."

She watered the flowers from a decanter on a credenza behind the desk. "But?"

"But Marie dearly loved her husband, and to yoke herself to another man whom she didn't love, simply to keep a roof over her children's heads, would have been a poor bargain for the lady. She'd be left with the husband of necessity long after the children are grown."

That speech likely did not help his cause any more than forgetting to collect the rent had.

Emily set down the decanter. "Let's look at the bedrooms."

Valerian was not particularly in the mood to look at the bedrooms. He was in the mood to take himself out behind the hog house and beat his head against a tree. If ever a courtship had been given an inauspicious start, it was this one.

He nonetheless trooped with Emily to the highest floor, which held the nursery and children's rooms as well as accommodations for servants. The middle floor included a master suite, a family sitting room, and three guest rooms, all of which were appointed in a tidy, comfortable style.

"What I like most about this place is how unpretentious it is," Emily said, perusing a spare bedroom done up in green and white. "No traipsing halfway to Bournemouth to get from the bedroom down to breakfast and then the same distance to retrieve a shawl. We could turn one of these spare bedrooms or parlors into a library."

She ran a hand over a patchwork quilt done in squares of white and green with fanciful blue embroidery. Valerian was at first too absorbed watching her palm stroke over the bedcovers to catch the import of her words.

"We could? *We* could turn this room into a library?"

"One could. How long did you allow your tenants to live here without paying rent, Valerian?"

One could prevaricate, one could even lie, but not to Emily, not today. "Five years. From the time Mrs. Cummings became a widow. Threatening her with eviction over rent she would struggle to pay was beyond me. Boys need to eat, they outgrow boots as fast as the cobbler can make them, and seed costs money."

"You gave her *five years* to make a go of this place?"

"She paid every penny, Emily."

"Do you enjoy teaching a bunch of clodhopping young people how to dance?"

What that had to do with anything, Valerian did not know. "I do, actually. Somebody needs to teach them, and they enjoy learning."

"You are hopeless," she said, opening an empty wardrobe and sending a gust of cedar scent into the air. "Did you enjoy setting up the books for your family's business?"

Hadn't they already discussed that? "No, but it had to be done, and Kettering, who might have stepped in, has his hands quite full with his own ventures." Or perhaps Casriel had forbidden Worth to stick his nose in Dorning business.

"And you are becoming the magistrate," Emily said, "so that your brother, the almighty earl, can be spared the terrible burden of spending a morning every other week or so sorting out his neighbors' troubles."

"The earl is a busy man, and—"

Emily crossed the bedroom, coming to a halt directly before Valerian. "Do you know what my father does?"

Valerian *knew* the conversation wasn't going at all in the direction he'd hoped. "Mr. Pepper is basically a mercer, trading in wholesale cloth and soft goods, and he's built a very successful enterprise that extends far beyond English shores."

"Papa is a man who looks at every situation in terms of what he can *take* from it. He's patient, and he stays within the bounds of the law, but he is driven by self-interest. His scheme to marry me to a wealthy squire is predicated on the gain his grandsons would reap from that union.

"He promoted Caleb and Tobias," she went on, pacing away, "because they, too, are defined by self-interest. They drive a hard bargain, they are shrewd, they mind their pence and quid. We have any number of phrases lauding the ambition of such men, and what is the result? Some of them eventually do break the law."

She turned and marched back to face Valerian directly. "Others end up like Papa, buying a home that could house regiments, when he hadn't even the energy to inspect his own premises."

From that tirade, Valerian grasped that Emily was upset, though not with him. "Ambition is generally a good thing." He had ambitions, for example, and they included a life with Emily.

"Ambition can be wonderful, if, like your tenant, that ambition is attached to a desire to provide for loved ones, to care conscientiously for property, to make a happy place for one's old age. Ambition attached to greed is honestly boring, if not downright silly. What is the point of fitting out Pepper Ridge?"

"To make a lovely home?"

"For one old man who will likely decamp for Town as soon as he's married me off? *This* is a lovely home. That sketch over the mantel, the slippers lined up in the foyer, this quilt, likely made by some auntie who remembers each nephew's birthday." Emily grabbed him by the lapels. "*You* made this possible for them. You made that whole botanical business possible for your family."

"My father did that, with all of his collections and cultivations. Casriel had the inspiration, and we've all pitched in." They'd had little choice but to pitch in, now that Valerian thought about it.

Emily leaned closer, so he could see the bronze, chocolate, and gold hues blending in her irises. "The lilies of Dorning Hall's fields require somebody to harvest them and market them, which I gather your brothers can do, but to turn that effort into a *business* took somebody willing to mind the *books*."

She shook him gently by the lapels. "*You* make it possible for Casriel to be the earl and doting paterfamilias he longs to be. *You* make it possible for the young couples in this shire to have a bit of diversion away from gossiping tongues and judging eyes. *You* gave a widow *five years* to get back on her feet, and in those five years, her sons grew up enough to learn to help their mama make a go of this place."

Emily kissed him, hard. "You have this... this ability to see what's needed, without prejudice or judgment. You look at a situation for where you can be *of use*, where you can make a contribution. You aren't dodging about, angling for what you can stash in your pocket, even when your pockets are already full. That is so rare, Valerian, so blasted scrumptious I nearly want to gobble you up."

"Gobble me up?"

She nodded, gaze wary as she smoothed her fingers over his wrinkled lapels.

"Gobble me up, as in marry me?"

"The sooner the better."

A breeze fluttered the curtain, and Valerian felt the current of warmth straight to the bottom of his heart. He wasn't sure what all her rhetoric had been about—God willing, they'd have a lifetime to sort out philosophies and family quirks—but for right now, he gathered Emily into his arms and took the space of three heartbeats to thank heaven for his great good fortune.

"Valerian?"

"Let the gobbling begin."

CHAPTER NINE

"This is..." Worth Kettering frowned at the document in his hands. "This is charming, dammit. My love, why did you never tell me you have a brother capable of charm?"

Jacaranda took up a brush from the low table between her chair and Worth's. "Andromeda, come." A large, toothy canine rose from beside Worth's chair and ambled across the terrace's flagstones to prop her chin on Jacaranda's knee. "All of my brothers are charming, when they want to be. My husband is too. Are you reading some of Ash's poetry?"

"Good God, there's a poet in the Dorning forest? Am I to find him a publisher too?"

Jacaranda drew the brush down the dog's back. "If you're not reading Ash's poetry, what are you reading?"

"Valerian's book on social conventions. Sycamore informed me that publishers don't tend to frequent his gambling establishment, having daily opportunities to lose money already handily located in their literary ventures. I am to *have a look at the damned manuscript*, to quote your baby brother, and mention it to the right people."

"Who would those people be?"

The dog's gaze acquired the sort of glazed expression Worth would soon be wearing if he continued to watch Jacaranda grooming the dratted beast. He loved her hands, loved the competence of them, and the grace, and how when she touched him, he knew it was her without looking even if she merely brushed his sleeve in a crowd.

"I have avoided the scribblers generally," Worth said. "Sycamore is right that the publishing business is unpredictable. One year, Byron is all the rage, then he's in complete disgrace, and his maunderings sell even better than they did when he was all the rage. The next year, it's some die-away recluse writing about monks and knights, the year after that a tattling viscountess wielding thinly veiled satire. I can predict prices for wheat and barley or see a trend in demand for lumber or Italian silk. The business of selling books has too much of alchemy about it."

Jacaranda knelt beside the dog to groom its haunches, and what the hell was wrong with Worth, that after several years of marriage and all the delights attendant thereto, he was still *stirred* by the sight of his wife grooming a damned dog on a summer day?

"You've spent most of the morning reading that manuscript, Worth, and I'll wager there isn't a single column of figures among its pages."

"There is, actually, in the appendices. Valerian lays out what a formal dinner for thirty ought to cost and how to economize without being obvious about it. He also has budgets for household wages, at homes, Venetian breakfasts, and even a typical Mayfair ball."

Jacaranda paused in her brushing to gently tug on Andromeda's ears. "Are the budgets accurate?"

"I don't know. I'm too busy reading the parts about how to converse with a chance-met member of the opposite sex in the park. He has lists of questions, about magic wishes, favorite memories, worst fears, and so on that have nothing to do with the weather and everything to do with making a positive impression as a conversationalist. I can hardly believe these clever ideas spring from the mind of a male Dorning."

Jacaranda resumed her seat. "Sycamore is making a killing with his club. Willow turned training dogs into a profitable venture. Casriel has set Hawthorne, Ash, Oak, and Valerian to establishing the botanical venture, which is off to a roaring start. My brothers are shrewd men. Witness, they had me running their household without a farthing of remuneration."

"I would call them out for that, but their dunderheadedness resulted in my wedded bliss. Do we know any publishers?"

"We might." She pulled the dog hair from the brush and let it scatter away on the midday breeze, a country habit meant to give birds material for building nests. "Do you know who gave me the idea to go into service?"

"Whoever she was, she was brilliant. From the day you arrived at Trysting, you've run the place like you were born to manage country manors, which, I suppose, you were."

"Valerian came in from a long day of some thankless task—laying hedges, sawing logs, I know not what—and I scolded him for tracking dirt onto my carpets. He apologized and looked around at the Dorning Hall accoutrements I spent much of my life dusting. Then he opined that his sister ought not to toil like the head maid all day without compensation. Casriel could impress his brothers into hard labor, because he was expected to send them to university and seen them settled, Valerian said, but if I didn't demand better treatment, I'd grow old as an unpaid housekeeper in rural Dorset."

"Valerian said that?"

"He apologized for rendering his opinion, but his words stuck with me. I'm an earl's oldest daughter. I'd barely spent any time in London, I had nothing approximating a trousseau, no local swain had even ventured to walk me home from divine services. Valerian had spoken the plain truth, and I had simply been too tired for too long to see it for myself. Three months later, I was earning a fat salary keeping house for some gouty old cit who never visited his country seat."

"And I had hired a conscientious, venerable besom who wrote the most marvelously detailed monthly household reports."

He'd loved her monthly reports, loved especially when she'd deliberately mis-tallied by a penny or so leaving him a needle to find in an accounting haystack.

"I do not know for a fact," Jacaranda said, "but I suspect the reason my brothers didn't immediately fetch me away from your employ like a clan of border reivers is that Valerian wouldn't allow it. He has a way with a scold, though he rarely resorts to it."

"Much like his sister."

They shared a smile, until Meda stuck her cold nose against Worth's hand. He petted the dog, though the manuscript tugged at his attention too. The scribblers undertook a dodgy business, but society wasn't about to stop reading, were they?

"This book is both informative and entertaining, though it would be expensive to print."

"Valerian is thorough by nature. Perhaps there are chapters he could cut?"

"I'm no editor."

Jacaranda shifted to sit in Worth's lap. She was a generously apportioned woman, and her weight was a marvelous pleasure.

"Your nose has not left those pages for the past two hours, Worth, and more to the point, you've read the prose when the back of the book offered you numbers to study instead. Are you acquainted with Dougal MacHugh?"

"Big, growly Scot? We've been introduced. We have at least one club membership in common."

"His press handles a lot of domestic advice. You might ask him who'd be interested in such a book." Jacaranda drew the pages from Worth's grasp and set them aside. "I'm feeling rather domestic myself at the moment."

Thank the heavenly powers. "Grooming the dog puts you in a domestic frame of mind?"

She drew off his wire-rimmed glasses. "Watching you read does that."

"Then I will make it a point to read more often." He rose with his wife in his arms and marched for the door, Meda trotting at his heels, tail wagging happily.

EMILY FINALLY UNDERSTOOD the fever that could grip her father when he was seized by a notion to buy up a lot of rare fabric or open a shop in a certain location. Papa had learned from long experience that commercial opportunities were fleeting. One ship docking a week before another could mean the difference between a fortune made and a fortune lost.

When Papa became obsessed with a venture, he ate little, slept less, and tended to his other business with an air of impatient distraction. His focus remained on the pet project, even when he was entertaining business associates at supper or reading the endless reports penned by his subordinates.

Valerian Dorning had become such a fever in Emily's heart. She had been mentally comparing all other men to him, from the scurrilous Ogilvy, to high-handed Caleb, to proper Tobias, to the grinning local lads trying to sort out a quadrille with a lady they fancied.

The lot of them came up short compared to Valerian. Tobias was mannerly, but he lacked warmth. The young men on the dance floor were abundantly charming, but a bit rag-mannered. Caleb dressed well, though not quite fashionably. Those outward trappings were not why Emily wanted to seize Valerian Dorning for her own.

He was honorable and trustworthy, he *listened* to her—witness their conversation about the magistrate's post—he *saw* her, he cared for her. Her money mattered to him only in that he was determined not to touch it.

And oh, how that made her hungry to touch *him*, to consume him, to make certain that his offer of a courtship became a proposal of marriage.

Emily went into his embrace on a tide of joy buoyed by determination. He would be hers. She would be his, and the present was a perfect time to impress that truth upon him. Nothing and no one would come between them.

"I want a special license," Emily said, between kisses. "Please, Valerian."

He took both of her hands and gently held them. "I haven't spoken to your father, Emily. You are his only daughter, and I am not what he has in mind for you."

Emily twisted her fingers free of Valerian's grasp, relieved him of his jacket, and began untying his cravat. "He wants me to marry gentry. You own this lovely estate, you're the brother of an earl, your family has excellent connections, and I'll be close enough to Pepper Ridge to keep an eye on Papa if we dwell here. Papa will see reason."

Emily drew off Valerian's cravat and laid it on the clothes press. His shirt buttoned down to the middle of his chest, a dizzying realization. She undid the first three buttons and had to stop to catch her breath. All dressed up, Valerian Dorning was delicious, but half undone, he was... She slid her hand over warm male muscle and closed her eyes the better to savor the feel of him.

"Emily, what are you about?"

"I'm undressing you. You aren't objecting."

"I am barely comprehending. Until your father has given his blessing to the match, we cannot consider ourselves engaged. Even if he allows me to court you, there are settlements to be negotiated, arrangements to be made."

She wanted to rip the buttons free, but suspected Valerian wouldn't understand wanton destruction of a beautiful piece of men's attire. She settled for stroking her palm over the bare flesh of his sternum.

"I am not a pair of oxen, Valerian, to be bargained away in the marketplace over the barrelhead. If Papa refuses to give his blessing, then we marry without it, though I would rather we had it. I am of age, as are you. You have the means to support a family, and what do settlements matter beyond that?"

He took her hand in his and kissed her fingers. "Finances matter, Emily. I wish that weren't so, but they do."

How she loved the warmth of his grip, the seriousness in his eyes. "When Papa was so ill, all his wealth meant nothing. He weakened by the day, and his warehouses and shops and ships only burdened him further. I know what I want, Valerian, and I know that if I had to dwell with you here at Abbotsford, a farmer's wife, economizing as best I could, I'd be happier than if you had buckets and pots of filthy lucre and ten country estates to go with them."

She wanted to beg him to join her in the bed that sat so invitingly three feet away, to make love with her beneath the soft quilt amid the peace and quiet of a home he owned.

"You mean that," he said, sounding puzzled. "You would marry me without your father's blessing?"

To the world, and to Valerian, Emily doubtless appeared to be a doting and devoted daughter, and she did love her father. Ever since Papa had chosen to doubt his own son, her devotion had been tempered by bitter truth. Papa would set her aside if she threatened his standing in the mercantile community, just as he'd tossed Adam aside.

"My father has no regard for *my* blessing," she said. "He makes a good show of holding me in affection, and he would say he loves me. His love comes at a price. I choose instead the regard you show me, in all its honesty and sincerity."

"You shouldn't have to choose," Valerian said, sliding his arms around her waist. "I promise you, Emily, that if we become man and wife, my every waking thought will be for your happiness, and my last breath will be spent safeguarding your well-being. We will work hard and know some want, but you will never have cause to doubt my devotion."

She snuggled into his embrace, a great weight lifting from her heart. "I want a special license, Valerian. I want to evict your tenant tomorrow and put my own dishes in the sideboard."

He held her, and the fit of his embrace was perfect. Secure, warm, comfortable, nothing careful or tentative about the intimacy.

"Rearranging our affairs will take some doing," he said. "Many couples speak their vows some time before they go to housekeeping."

Emily had no intention of rattling around Pepper Ridge as a married woman who saw her husband at services for the duration of the summer, but she'd make that clear later.

"There's something else I want even more than a special license, Valerian."

He stroked her back slowly, easing away all tension and worry. She was where she was born to be, with the man she was born to love.

"If it's within my power to grant it, Emily, you have only to tell me what you desire."

"I desire you," Emily said. "I desire you, as a wife desires her husband, and if you make me wait for a lot of vows and negotiations and whatnot, I will lose my reason."

She pressed closer lest he mistake her meaning. Valerian was no creature of impulse, and she felt him thinking through the ramifications of her demand. Just this once, she needed him to set aside propriety, family duties, gentlemanly hesitation, and whatever else kept his hands above her waist.

"You are certain, Emily? If we take this step, we are all but married in truth. I will consider myself bound to you and expect you to regard me in a similar light."

That chivalrous admonition was belied by the bulge Emily felt behind his falls. "That is precisely the light in which I already regard you."

"Then the matter is settled," he murmured, kissing her with exquisite gentleness. "I am yours to command."

～

A THOUSAND DOUBTS plagued Valerian as he kissed his intended.

Why hadn't he anticipated that Emily might want a very short courtship? Osgood Pepper would be displeased with this union, and Casriel would be less than enthusiastic. Hurrying the nuptials meant less time to bring either of those two worthies around.

The Cummings family would remain at Abbotsford for several more months—months Valerian had planned to spend courting Emily —and a trip up to London to call on various publishers figured on his schedule too.

"Come to bed with me," Emily whispered, twining her arms around his neck. "Who knows when we'll have this opportunity again?"

She kissed him on the mouth, as if to silence any further words of caution, and with the few wits remaining to him, Valerian realized he faced a choice. The lovely bed, with its soft quilt and abundant pillows, sat three feet to his right, a reminder that *this* bed in *this* house on *this* estate was one of very few he owned personally. If he wanted to consummate his engagement to Emily Pepper, this was the place to do that.

And he did want to—very much.

The other option, to demure, to leave the lady frustrated, to claim that some gentlemanly scruple prevented him from indulging their passions was so much cowardice.

"Emily, your father won't stop this wedding."

She smoothed Valerian's hair back, her gaze puzzled. "I beg your pardon?"

"Osgood. He won't scare me off with miserly settlements, bluster, or insults. You have agreed to become my wife, and I would be the greatest fool in all of England not to marry you at the first opportunity. I would rather face every difficulty in life with you at my side in humble circumstances than spend my remaining years in luxury without you."

She rested her forehead on Valerian's shoulder, and the relief conveyed in that gesture spoke volumes. Osgood Pepper was apparently in the habit of buying off any hopeful swain he deemed unsuitable. Valerian didn't fault a papa for keeping his daughter safe, but neither did he think Emily's judgment so lacking that such meddling was warranted.

She knew her own mind, and her own heart.

"That's what I love about you," Emily said, resuming her efforts to unbutton his shirt. "You see clearly. You aren't confused by dross and noise and lies. These buttonholes ought to be larger."

"So my clothing falls off in public?"

"So I needn't damage your shirt in my haste to see you without it."

She'd do it, too—tear the shirt from his body—bless her unrelenting determination. "Do you know what I love about you?"

Emily shook her head. Valerian's shirt buttons were all undone, and rather than look him in the eye, she stared at his throat.

"Everything," he said, kissing her cheek. "I love everything about you. Your honesty, your fierceness, your humor, your nose." He kissed that too. "Your hands and your laugh. I especially love your laugh and your curiosity. I expect once I am better acquainted with them, I will love your breasts too. Might you favor me with an introduction?"

Emily seized him in a tight hug, then stepped back, smiling. "Introduce yourself, Mr. Dorning."

Riding habits were slightly more complicated than other types of women's attire, but between kisses, smiles, and a monumental display of patience, Valerian soon had Emily standing in her shift beside the bed. He was down to his breeches and ready to be free of them.

"Last chance to change your mind," he said, shaping her hips through the fine linen shift. "I can have a special license within a fortnight, assuming my brothers cooperate."

"You are tormenting me," Emily said, starting on the buttons of his falls. "I will have my revenge."

"Is that a promise?"

"A sworn oath." A moment later, she'd finished with the buttons and taken him in her hand. "Perhaps you'd like to wait two weeks," she said, gently stroking her thumb over a *very* sensitive part of his anatomy, "depending on the uncertain cooperation of a couple of London swells. If we wait three weeks, we can have the banns cried."

The pleasant hum of anticipation low in Valerian's belly became the sharp burn of desire before the third stroke of her thumb.

"Under the covers, Emily. Now." Another stroke, this time accompanied by the most exquisite *tug*. "Please."

She played with him a moment longer, during which eternity Valerian kept himself from begging only by virtue of sheer masculine pride. When Emily had thoroughly scrambled his wits, she climbed under the covers and lay back against the pillows.

Valerian etched the picture of her—rosy, smiling, and wearing only her shift—into his memory, for it was a lovely image. He peeled out of his breeches, draped them across the bottom of the bed, and affected a yawn, the better to let the lady have a good gawk at her lover.

"Valerian?"

All manner of questions lay in that slightly raspy utterance of his name. He answered Emily's questions by joining her on the bed and settling himself over her.

"We'll go slowly," he said, kissing her eyebrows. "We'll take our time and meander along the path. Our first time should be without haste, without—"

Emily lashed her legs around his flanks. "Valerian, I treasure your every syllable and sigh, but fewer proclamations, please, and more passion."

She arched up against him, brushing her sex over his arousal. The physical result was a gut-punch to his grand plans for a leisurely joining and a roweled spur to his desire. Clearly, Emily had no anxiety about what was to come.

And neither did Valerian. She was the woman he loved, his prospective wife. He indulged in a nuzzling acquaintance with her breasts, promised himself he'd get back to that conversation, and eased into her heat with a sense of homecoming and joy.

"Better?" he asked, setting up a slow, shallow rhythm.

She hitched closer. "Better."

The lovemaking was glorious for its sense of rightness. They moved together instinctively, and by Emily's breathing, by the hold she took of his shoulders, Valerian knew when she was nearing satisfaction. Her pleasure was silent, a shuddering, thrashing paroxysm that tried Valerian's self-restraint even as it filled him with joy.

This marriage would be successful, for them both. As he brushed Emily's hair from her brow and crouched over her beneath the quilt, he knew he'd chosen the right bride as surely as he knew the panting rhythm of her breathing and the contour of her rosy lips.

"Again?" he whispered, lips against her cheek.

"I knew you'd be a wonderful lover."

"We are wonderful together." He proved the point by pleasuring her once more, though twice was the limit of his ability. When Emily was again a happy, panting heap of drowsy female beneath him, he withdrew and finished on her belly.

Coitus interruptus was a three-quarter measure of fulfillment, and all Valerian intended to allow himself under the circumstances. As a means of contraception, withdrawing was imperfect, but as a means of leaving some final measure of satisfaction for the wedding night, it sufficed.

He tidied up and lay on his back, pulling Emily into his arms.

"We should get up," she murmured, drawing her knee across his thighs.

"We're in no hurry. You've earned a nap." He kissed her temple and marveled at the turn the day had taken. Even though he'd denied himself the last indulgence sexually, he was replete in a sense that went beyond mere sexual gratification.

Emily curled closer, her head on his shoulder, her arm draped across his middle. "I will work on my dancing, I promise. You won't be sorry you married me, Valerian."

What had that...?

"Your dancing is perfect," he said, and yet, he grasped the point she made. She was marrying up socially, he was marrying up financially. They brought different strengths to the union as far as any observer would assess the match.

"My dancing is barely serviceable," she said, arranging herself over him. "I have never hosted thirty guests from titled families at the same table. My spoken French needs work. Your brothers probably won't like me."

Valerian wrapped her in his arms and bowed up, the better to hold her securely. "Did you take me to bed because you think I'll desert the marital regiment over something as silly as my grouchy brothers?"

"No."

He waited.

"Maybe. Our families will be difficult, Valerian."

"Our love is equal to that challenge, and if it's any consolation, I have never hosted a dinner for thirty guests from titled families, nor do I aspire to."

Emily fell asleep on Valerian's chest, while he lay awake, musing at his good fortune. He was to be married to Emily Pepper. They would live at Abbotsford as landed gentry, exactly what Emily's papa had aspired to for her. Valerian would become the magistrate, a calling that added to his standing, and with hard work and luck, he and Emily would have a lovely life.

He drifted off almost convinced by his own imaginings, but for a small niggle of discord that prevented him from surrendering entirely to slumber.

Emily had known he'd be *a wonderful lover*. How had she known that? On what basis was she making a comparison? She was knowledgeable regarding conjugal intimacies, and Valerian strongly suspected her education hadn't been limited to books and barnyards.

Well, neither was his. They were to be man and wife soon, and the past didn't matter half so much as the future, and that promised to be wonderful too.

EMILY DOZED in Valerian's arms, trying to convince herself that she'd just made the smartest decision of her life. Valerian Dorning was everything she could have hoped for in a husband and more—honorable, shrewd, loyal, determined, brave, and unimpressed by wealth.

She had known he was her heart's desire from the first time he'd bowed over her hand.

Her hesitation came not from the challenges Valerian would face —he was certainly equal to a blustering papa and wresting a crop from some Dorset acres—but from the challenges *she* faced.

"You're awake," Valerian murmured, his fingers gliding along her cheek and jaw. "You barely catnapped. Shall I love you again?"

That question, in that soft, teasing tone of voice, had her insides turning to eiderdown. "I am tempted, but Briggs will learn that I rode out without a groom and send the hounds after me."

Still, Valerian continued his lazy caresses. "Is that why you're in a hurry to marry, Emily? You are fed up to the teeth with Briggs's presumption?"

She *was* in a hurry to marry, and yet, she needed time as well, if certain topics were to be calmly discussed with her intended.

"Given a choice," she said, "between spending the summer listening to Briggs subtly complain about everything from fresh air to sunshine, or spending my afternoons sharing marital bliss with you, I must admit the marital bliss has the greater appeal."

He kissed her forehead. "You will please allow me to broach the topic of our engagement with your father before you take him on."

Emily extricated herself from Valerian's embrace and sat back against the pillows. "You think my father is a sweet old fellow who has had some good luck in the cloth trade. That's exactly what he wants people to think, but he has another side." An ugly, close-minded, proud side.

Valerian arranged himself beside her and took her hand. "Osgood is protective of you."

"He's not only protective, he views me as a business asset. I am to marry according to *his* plan, produce children for the sake of *his* dynasty, and in recent years, he's decided I am to keep my nose out of *his* business." To be fair, Papa was entitled to be a little despotic where his only daughter was concerned. Whatever else was true, the situation with Adam had been a sore humiliation to him.

"Then I shall convince your father that I am the best possible connection you could form, and his plans are advanced handsomely by the match."

"You make sense, but Papa isn't always sensible. He can be stubborn."

Valerian kissed her fingers. "Emily Pepper, soon to be Dorning, when the prize is the rest of my life with you, I will make Napoleon's armies look like so many gnats, swatted away with a wave of the hand. Wellington's determination will pale compared to my resolve, and if that doesn't work, I'll rally my brothers and sisters to my cause. Osgood Pepper will blow full retreat. *Stop worrying.*"

"I want to stay under these covers with you for the rest of my life, Valerian. I want to hide here until you bring a parson to marry us right in this very room."

Valerian rose, and Emily knew she ought to look away, but she could not. He was the quintessential healthy male in his prime. Trim, muscular, beautifully proportioned, and splendidly mussed.

And he is mine—almost.

"I never did get you out of that shift," he said, scratching his chest. "Remiss of me." He slanted a glance at Emily. "We can make love in the dark, you know. Go by feel. All the fun without taxing anybody's modesty."

Emily swung her legs over the side of the bed. "Do you *have* any modesty?"

"Not with you, apparently." That conclusion had him smiling. "I am a competent lady's maid. When we are married, you will have to valet me, at least at first."

When we are married... "When we are married, I will be only too happy to get you out of your clothes whenever the need arises."

That earned her a kiss. "The need will arise frequently. What is the best time to call on your father?"

"Late morning. He sometimes takes a nap in the afternoon, and he's not coming down to the office as early as he used to. He already forgets how sick he was." Or Tobias and Caleb kept him from recalling. "Whatever you do, Valerian, speak to him alone."

"One does typically have such conversations confidentially. Hold still." Valerian dropped her blouse over her head, buttoned her up, and used his comb to tidy her hair.

In a very short time, Emily was standing beside her intended before a pier glass in the corridor. Valerian had made up the bed, neat as a preacher's parlor, while Emily had laced her boots and tried to gather her courage.

Valerian was the right man, no doubt about that, but she wanted to pledge her future to him with a clear conscience.

"When will you talk to Papa?" she asked as he locked the front door behind them.

"Not today. The hour grows later than I'd intended, and one wants to marshal one's arguments with a clear head. Monday, I suppose."

"Will you call on me first?"

The horses were dozing at the hitching post, both of them standing with a hip cocked, heads down.

"The usual protocol is for the suitor to call upon the head of the household directly and then convey the outcome of the interview to the young lady if all goes well. Otherwise, he makes a dignified exit without facing the object of his affections."

Valerian tightened girths and led Emily's mare a few paces away from the gelding.

"Such a private discussion is subject to protocol?" she asked.

"Absolutely. I spent a whole chapter of my book on it."

"When can I read that book?"

He boosted her into the saddle and arranged her skirts. "I'll bring the manuscript with me on Monday."

Emily took up the reins. "Because you are confident the interview will go well and that you will be free to meet with me immediately afterward."

"I am hopeful. One doesn't want to invite the smiting hand of the Almighty by evidencing hubris, but I will not lose you, Emily, not to an old man's schemes, not to anything. As of today, I have committed myself to you in every sense. I have only to tend to some formalities before I can publicize my good fortune to the world."

"I do love you," Emily said, gazing down at him. "Very much."

"And I love you." He swung up into the saddle, the grace of that mundane exertion provoking a buzzing pleasure in Emily's vitals.

And I love you. Those were words to treasure, and Emily hadn't heard them since Adam had boarded a ship for Botany Bay.

"Two weeks for a special license?" she asked as the horses ambled down the drive.

"Maybe less. We should be married before the next assembly, and you will save your waltz for me, Emily."

"All of my waltzes, you poor man."

They laughed and talked the whole way back to Pepper Ridge, but at no point did the conversation lend itself to bringing up Adam and the circumstances that had resulted in his transportation. The day after tomorrow, once Valerian had surmounted the ordeal of winning Papa's approval, Emily would explain that her only sibling was a convicted felon.

Adam's sentence would run for another two years. It wasn't as if he'd turn up at the wedding. Every family had a few secrets, and Valerian wasn't the judgmental sort.

Emily reassured herself with such platitudes all the way back to Pepper Ridge and was still vainly repeating them as Valerian bowed correctly over her hand, climbed back onto his horse, and trotted off down the drive.

CHAPTER TEN

"I have considered the magistrate's position," Valerian said. "Might we discuss the particulars?" He stood before Grey's desk, looking every inch the country squire in spotless riding attire. Actually, Valerian looked more impressive than a country squire, and Grey had yet to figure quite how his brother did that.

A touch of lace at his wrists, a particular shine to his boots, the exact cut of his riding jacket... and only Valerian could ride around the countryside on a dark horse and never sport a single horsehair on his linen.

"We can discuss the magistrate's job only if your answer is yes," Grey replied, putting down his pen. "Beatitude says if I must bribe you to take over from me, any inducement other than our firstborn is fair game."

"You're that miserable?"

"Yes, which doesn't matter. Beatitude is that anxious for me to be free of the bother. The demolition on the family wing should have started a month ago, I have no idea what Oak has got up to over in Hampshire, and my new land steward seems to exist only to ask me questions I can't answer. Then I must impose on Hawthorne for answers, and that good fellow is entirely absorbed in his own situation. Beatitude says we're to invite you for supper."

"Let's enjoy some fresh air, shall we?" Valerian passed Grey a morning coat, which Grey had slung over the back of a reading chair.

Valerian's polite suggestion that they take the air could be his way of ensuring that a difficult conversation wasn't overheard or interrupted by a well-meaning countess. With Valerian, manners served as so many fig leaves shielding all manner of awkward moments.

Grey shrugged into his coat and accompanied Valerian onto the back terrace.

"What do you hear from Ash and Sycamore in London?" Valerian asked.

"Not a blessed thing. Jacaranda has reported to Beatitude, however, that our brothers appear to be in good health, and their enterprise is thriving. Thank God for a sunny day. That damned library manages to be dreary even in high summer."

"Then don't work there," Valerian said, ambling down the steps into the formal parterres. "Use the earl's study, which has the southern and eastern exposures."

"Papa's old study is Beatitude's private parlor now. She needed the light for sewing baby clothes." And Grey loved to drop in on her, catching her at her needlework in the window seat, or perched at her desk going over household accounts.

"Why can't you both work in Papa's old study?"

A fine idea. Perhaps Beatitude had been waiting for her husband to think of it? "Because I own everything you see, the lot of it, and my countess deserves to have a few spaces entirely under her dominion."

"How do you suppose a humbler couple would divide up that dominion, Grey? Couples who have only a few rooms to call home?"

"What has this to do with you becoming the magistrate?"

"Maybe nothing." Valerian took out his pocket watch as they approached the sundial. "I've proposed to Emily Pepper, and she has accepted."

A significant burden, composed mostly of guilt, lifted from Grey's heart. Grey had told his brothers to make their way in the world. Valerian could have joined Ash and Sycamore in Town, could have prevailed on Worth Kettering to find him a post as somebody's man of business, could have become a tutor of British deportment in Paris, or done quite well in government.

Like a loyal old hound unwilling to wander beyond the foot of the drive, Valerian had refused to abandon his post as brother-in-residence. The others had all found someplace to be, *someone* to be, but Valerian's job had been the family manager, the one who anticipated troubles, mediated squabbles, and handed down the uncomfortable truths.

The magistrate's post was a good fit for him, but it was hardly a path to domestic happiness. Emily Pepper could provide that —Grey hoped.

"Congratulations," Grey said, clapping Valerian on the shoulder. "Miss Pepper is a fine young woman, and I know you will make her an excellent husband." And yet, a weight of worry had replaced the guilt in Grey's heart.

"You approve of the match?" Valerian asked, flipping open his watch.

"You aren't asking for my blessing."

"You are my brother, not my great-grandfather." He snapped the watch closed. "I will marry Emily regardless of anybody's opinion on the matter. Mr. Pepper is likely to be difficult."

"Then he's an idiot."

Valerian's smile was pained. "He is my prospective father-in-law, and I gather it is the province of fathers-in-law to be idiotic on occasion. He moved down to Dorset to see his daughter introduced to influential gentry families. I am an earl's son. I'm of a suitable age. I can keep Emily in fairly decent comfort at Abbotsford, and I'm not entirely without prospects. But Pepper will withhold his approval, and that will be hard on Emily."

A pair of reed warblers were making a ruckus in the birdbath over by the snapdragons, flinging water in all directions and nattering at each other. As Grey watched their antics, it dawned on him that Valerian was *asking for his help.*

Of course he was, and Grey had little enough help to offer. "Pepper struck me as a reasonable man, but he has only the one child. Perhaps a long engagement would allow him to accustom himself to the notion of a Dorning for a son-in-law." Or allow Grey to get the family wing demolished and the salvage sold off.

"Before Margaret started dosing Osgood with the foxglove," Valerian said, "he was desperate for Emily to marry. Now his health is improved and he can afford to be choosy. I am not wealthy, Grey. I have discussed Abbotsford with Hawthorne and reviewed the subtenants farming there now. I know what the estate can earn. We won't starve."

Not what a wealthy papa wanted to hear from his prospective son-in-law. "Perhaps if Pepper has time to get to know you, he might be won over by your charm. I learned half my manners from you and the other half trying to set an example for our brothers. What I learned by rote discipline, you seemed to know through instinct."

The warblers flitted away, leaving an abrupt stillness in the garden.

"I have enough manners to fill a book," Valerian said, gaze on the fleeing birds. "What I lack is coin, and that is what Osgood Pepper values and understands."

And what few Dornings were able to amass in abundance. "What does Emily value?"

"Her father's regard." Valerian settled onto a wooden bench across from the roses, which were finished blooming but for a few stragglers. He managed to look elegant and relaxed even in that setting.

"Something has gone amiss between them, Grey. I'm not sure what. I suspect Osgood paid off a previous suitor or two, or he urged unsuitable matches on Emily. I'm not sure which. He and Emily are not at peace with each other, which is all the more reason to avoid additional conflict. Emily wants her own household, and she wants me."

Grey took the place beside his brother. "Your smile suggests she's already sampled the goods. Was that well advised, Valerian?"

"You and Beatitude were as chaste as a pair of monks prior to your nuptials?"

"That was different. Beatitude was a widow."

"She was a lady who knew what she wanted and a woman in love. Emily wants to be my wife. I do worry that she's not entirely realistic when it comes to matters of finance."

Worse and worse. "She'll expect a coach and four, frequent jaunts up to Town, accounts at all the fashionable shops, and the annual sojourn to Paris?" Grey kept the list short, though a spend-thrift wife could beggar a man in mere weeks.

"Maybe the rural equivalent to that? She's in charge of the house at Pepper Ridge, but that's an established estate, and Osgood's pockets are bottomless. Married life will be an adjustment for her."

"For you too."

Grey had never seen quite that smile on Valerian—pleased, bashful, determined, and something else. Tender?

"I've sent a request to Ash to get us a special license."

"Was such haste *necessary?*" Hawthorne and Margaret had resorted to a special license, and while they'd had reasons for their precipitous courtship, Grey would rather the banns had been read.

"Yes, it was necessary. I'd like to be married here at the Hall, Grey. The chapel will do, awash in flowers, because in that regard at least, we Dornings are wealthy. When an aristocrat says that standards must be maintained, what they usually mean is that appearances must be maintained, and we do have the appearances. I want Osgood Pepper to see the family Emily is marrying into, the substance we have even if we're only beginning to turn our legacy into a commercial venture of the kind Pepper will respect."

When had Valerian asked Grey for anything? When had he

asked *anybody* for anything? "Ninety percent of what transpires during a Mayfair Season is about appearances, you are quite correct about that. We can festoon the chapel with flowers and put on a magnificent wedding breakfast. It is high summer, after all, and the gardens are producing in abundance. You and Emily really ought to nip up to Town after that, let the staff at Dorning House spoil you a bit."

Valerian shook his head. "I can't afford a trip to Town for frivolities, Grey. I must acquaint myself with the workings of Abbotsford, and if I do go up to Town, it will be to find a publisher for my book."

That damned book. "Does anybody make money publishing books?"

"I suppose the author of *Waverley* made a fair bit."

"An etiquette manual is not a stirring tale of historical heroism. Could you write one of those stories of knights and Highlanders and such?" Not, of course, that Grey had read any of those novels, though he had picked up Beatitude's copy of *Waverley* on occasion, merely to research what held her fancy so thoroughly night after night.

"One doesn't simply take up the pen and order it to produce whatever the reading public madly desires that week, Grey." Valerian rested an arm along the back of the bench, a gentleman entirely at his leisure—to appearances. "We need to talk about the settlements."

Hence the need to have this discussion privately. "I am happy to negotiate with Pepper on your behalf, but there's not much to discuss. You have Abbotsford. Our brother Willow can send you a fine puppy, Oak will paint you a wedding portrait, I will stock your larder and toss in that rattletrap gig you've been using, but as a family we truly haven't much to contribute in the way of settlements."

If Valerian had expected anything more encouraging, he was too well bred to show his disappointment.

"We have consequence. Osgood Pepper will understand that. We have a business enterprise that's off to a fine start. I will happily add my share of the proceeds to Emily's portion."

"Then how will you build up your own investments, if all your cash goes to securing the future of a wife who will be wealthy in her own right?"

Valerian rose. "First, I must secure the wife, mustn't I? Pepper's approval matters to Emily, and Emily matters to me. Good day."

A proper host would have seen his guest to the front door, but Grey stayed where he was. A brother with a grain of sense knew when a disappointed sibling needed to make a dignified exit. The Dornings were land-poor, at least at present, and no amount of fine manners or social polish could change that sad fact.

not land poor/ —cash poor— they hae tons of acreage (britanically?)

∼

THE LONGEST DAY of Emily's life commenced at breakfast, which she took in her room rather than deal with Tobias over ham and eggs. She was not in the mood to be interrogated for sacking Ogilvy, or for anything else, come to that.

"You are awake," Briggs said, unnecessarily, for Emily was seated by the window in her private parlor, enjoying a pot of chocolate and some cheese tarts while she read the London papers.

"Good morning, Briggs. Won't you join me?" Emily gestured with the pot, though she'd been saving the second cup to enjoy along with the Society pages. She set aside the paper, planning to ring for another cup and saucer.

Except, her tray already held a second cup and saucer. Who had given that order and why?

"Perhaps half a cup," Briggs said, taking the opposite seat. "I trust you slept well?"

Emily had slept miserably. She'd alternated between girlish glee to be the woman engaged to Valerian Dorning and dread of the row Papa would doubtless stir up, to say nothing of the awkward discussion she must have with Valerian regarding Adam.

And now Briggs was apparently intent on an awkward discussion of her own.

"You sacked that Ogilvy creature," Briggs said, helping herself to the last two tarts. "Might I inquire as to your reasons, Emily?"

Emily passed over a full cup of chocolate. "Ogilvy was stealing from Papa, and as long as that was tolerated, nobody else could take on the job. I intend to spend my morning calling on the vicar, who will be well acquainted with the local tradesmen."

"You'll call before noon? I suppose I should change into my carriage dress then."

Emily did not want Briggs's company, and she did want privacy with the vicar. She needed to discuss with him the situation with her apprentices, among *other* topics.

"I'll walk to the village, Briggs. You needn't accompany me."

Briggs gently set her cup on her saucer. "Emily, I understand that you are no longer seventeen. You have learned, to your sorrow, the result of yielding to a young girl's impulses, but your standing and wealth mean you must comport yourself at all times with a view toward your reputation. I will accompany you to the vicarage, and we will take the carriage."

How would Valerian handle this confrontation? For that's what this was.

He would be polite, logical, and firm—utterly firm. "I appreciate your concern, Briggs, but ladies in the country are held to a different version of proper standards than ladies in Town. If I affect Town ways here in Dorset—hitching up a coach and four for a jaunt of less than two miles, for example—I will be seen as arrogant and pretentious. We will ride to the village, and you can visit the apothecary and the lending library while I call upon the vicar."

Emily bit into a tart, though her appetite had fled. Briggs was facing unemployment, did she but know it. Emily would ensure that Briggs had a generous competence on which to retire, but for Briggs, dismissal on any terms would be a blow.

"You are still corresponding with your brother," Briggs said, as if sending a few letters was tantamount to spending the rent money on gin. "You sacked a crew your father himself chose to handle renovations here, then yesterday you rode out with that Dorning fellow, an impecunious younger son who can only be fortune-hunting, and you didn't even take a groom. I'm tempted to ask Osgood to confine you to your room until you rediscover your common sense, Emily Pepper. Instead, I must plead with you to be more moderate in your behavior, or not even a bumpkin will marry you, regardless of your fortune."

"That answers one question," Emily said, dusting her hands over her plate and rising. "You've been spying on my correspondence, which I ought to have expected, but more to the point, you've shared what you learned with Tobias, regardless of what taradiddles he spins about happening upon my letters at the coaching inn. *Might I inquire as to your reasons, Briggs?*"

A silence followed, during which Briggs bowed her head. That display of martyrdom made Emily's blood boil. She took another leaf from Valerian's book and kept her tone civil.

"Briggs, Tobias will tuck away for his own benefit the fact that you knew I was writing to Adam, and that you chose not to tell Papa. When it suits Tobias, *he* will tell Papa. In fact, he has already threatened to do that, and Tobias will ensure that your secrecy reflects poorly on you. You can assume that if Tobias knows, Caleb is likely privy to the confidence you violated, and what Tobias will keep under his hat, Caleb could well blurt out in a fit of pique. Well done, Briggs. You've stepped neatly into Tobias's trap, and the only way I can rescue you is to tell Papa myself that I maintain a correspondence with the brother who was transported *for a crime he did not commit.*"

Emily expected resentment, defiance, another attempted scold, or at the very least, a silent retreat from Briggs. She got the silence, but also an expression of pure, bewildered misery.

"We don't belong here," Briggs said. "We don't belong among these squires and yokels, trying to maintain the business through the post, trying to fit in where nobody wants us."

The comment was decidedly odd, a lament, and perhaps—maybe?—a sidewise apology for having bungled. Badly.

"We will ride into the village," Emily said. "I need the practice in the saddle, and you will enjoy a visit to the lending library. I will meet you in the stables in an hour."

Briggs finished her chocolate, rose, and curtseyed. The gesture struck Emily as an unsuccessful attempt at irony. Briggs wasn't elderly—far from it—but this discussion had toppled her from a pedestal of authority years in the making.

"You owe me an apology, Briggs," Emily said, just as Briggs put a hand on the door latch. "You intruded on my privacy and failed to keep my confidences. If you cannot admit to remorse for that betrayal, you will nonetheless pay restitution."

Briggs turned, hands behind her back. "Miss?"

This show of meekness was temporary, but Emily would take advantage of it while she had the chance. Briggs had miscalculated, probably complaining to a sympathetic Tobias about Emily's letters, never realizing Tobias would use the complaint against the informer herself.

"I want to know every detail of my mother's marriage settlements. You and she were friends of a sort. I expect she shared the arrangements with you."

Briggs drew her white shawl more closely around her shoulders, a shawl Emily had knit for her as a Yuletide gift. "I'd have to consult my diaries, but I'm sure I have most of the terms written down somewhere."

"I want every detail. Every last groat and footnote. Mama herself told me to never sign a document without reading it, and Papa has said the same thing many times. She knew what her portion would be, and I want to know those terms."

A spark of condemnation flared in Briggs's eyes. "Does this have to do with that Dorning fellow?"

"Maybe I'm preparing to decamp for the Antipodes, Briggs. Did you ever consider that? Perhaps that's why I sent Adam those letters. Papa is regaining his health, and I'm fed up to the teeth with polite society, family intrigues, and a companion who cannot be trusted.

Meet me in the stables in an hour, or I will go to the village without you."

Emily crossed her arms and waited until Briggs withdrew, then resumed her seat by the window. She'd spoken the absolute, plain truth for once. She was utterly fed up with Papa, Caleb, Tobias, Briggs, scheming contractors, lazy housekeepers, and a household where she had to sneak about even to send a letter to her only brother.

All of which suggested that she'd best explain to Valerian exactly what Adam's situation was, the sooner the better.

THE SHIPWRIGHT EMILY had insisted Osgood consult pointed out a half-dozen problems with Tobias and Caleb's clever plan, each one worse than the last.

"You may be excused," Osgood said when the litany of mistakes was complete, "and I'm sure the kitchen will be happy to offer you sustenance before you return to Bournemouth."

Mr. Popplegruber directed one last, troubled glance at the plans unrolled on the reading table. "And my fee, Mr. Pepper?"

Tobias fetched a blank bank draft from the open safe built into the sideboard. Caleb uncapped the ink. Osgood had forgotten the exact sum owed, or perhaps nobody had told it to him. Under the guise of moving the standish closer to Osgood's elbow, Tobias murmured the figure.

Osgood added a very generous two pounds and passed over the completed draft. "Your honesty is much appreciated, Popplegruber, and your discretion would be as well."

"Of course, sir." He clicked his heels like some damned Hessian officer and withdrew.

"He's exaggerating," Caleb said, propping a hip on the windowsill. "The weather between here and Lyon is seldom all that bad, and a ship plying the Mediterranean trade can simply put into port if the wind kicks up."

Tobias, predictably, had a rejoinder ready. "Even I know the Bay of Biscay is a sailor's nightmare, and who says we'll be trading exclusively with Lyon? In five years' time, the Americans might be making good, cheap silk."

"Or," Osgood said, "silk might go out of fashion." The infernal Austrian army, or perhaps the French, or possibly the Italians themselves, had cut down Tuscan mulberry groves for blasted firewood. Silk was dear to begin with, and the havoc of the war years had made it only dearer.

"So we make some adjustments," Tobias said, moving the standish and capping the ink. "Our plans were only a first draft, after all, and Popplegruber wasn't about to tell a trio of businessmen we'd done a fine job of designing a ship. Let us consider his suggestions and—"

"He's back," Caleb said, gaze on the drive beyond the window. "That damned dancing Dorning is back. Are social calls really conducted at such a beastly early hour in the countryside?"

Tobias and Caleb exchanged a look. They'd begun these silent conversations when Osgood had first fallen ill. He'd been too weak and angry to care that he was being nannied by a pair of jumped-up clerks. Their campaign hadn't stopped there, though, witness Tobias's casual self-promotion to *businessman* and his equally casual assumption of first-person plural pronouns.

We, our, us...

Our money sure as hell wasn't paying their handsome salaries, for all the pair of them worked hard and knew the business well.

"If Dorning is here to call upon Emily," Osgood said, "that is her affair. He knows the local gentry, which we do not, and she'll make a good impression on them if Dorning handles the introductions. His brother is an earl, and that counts for something."

Emily's brother, by contrast, was a convicted felon. Osgood had left London before the rumors regarding Adam's disgrace had reached flood stage, but old scandal still carried weight among high sticklers, no matter that the case had been heard two hundred miles from London and five years ago.

A rap on the door interrupted those unhappy recollections.

"Mr. Valerian Dorning to see you, Mr. Pepper." The butler passed over a fussy little silver tray with a rather plain card on it.

"Tell him Mr. Pepper is out," Caleb said, shoving away from the window. "We've better things to do than entertain rustics who don't even know when a proper call is to be paid."

"Turning away an earl's son," Tobias said, "regardless of the hour, is not the done thing, Caleb. Dorning is doubtless here to talk business. His family sells—what is it?—tisanes, patent remedies, sachets? They are genteelly dipping their toes in trade, suggesting they have a grain of sense between them. Show him in."

The butler, an old fellow who'd conveyed more or less with the property, stood with his silly silver platter by the door. "Mr. Pepper?"

Respect for one's employer was a fine quality in a retainer. "Tobias, Caleb, you will excuse me. I will meet with Mr. Dorning in the first guest parlor."

A very different sort of look passed between Caleb and Tobias, resentful and impatient rather than knowing and smug. If Adam were on hand...

But he wasn't, and never would be again.

Osgood joined the butler in the corridor. "What is the local opinion of young Mr. Dorning?"

"The Dornings are held in highest regard, sir. The family has been at Dorning Hall for centuries, and they are enlightened stewards of the land."

"So they don't raise the rents when times are hard?"

"They do not. They pitch in when there's work to be done, and they entertain their neighbors generously. Their botanical venture has yielded income for a good dozen of the ladies, but then, they always hire locally whenever possible."

Meaning they didn't hire a gang of rogues from Bournemouth. Osgood wasn't sure whether to praise Emily for sacking Ogilvy or berate Tobias and Caleb for hiring the man in the first place.

Probably both. "And what of this particular Dorning?" Osgood asked. "Is he the family wastrel?"

"The Dornings haven't a family wastrel, sir. Lord Casriel wouldn't allow it, and neither would his countess."

Not long ago, this hike down the Pepper Ridge corridors would have been too much for Osgood, and a hike while conducting a conversation would have been utterly beyond him. The foxglove medication mixed up by Mrs. Margaret Dorning had changed all of that. Saved his life, or at least added good years to it.

"Shall I bring a tea tray, sir?"

"Is that how these things are done in the country? Tea trays at dawn?"

"As far as I know, a tea tray is always considered good manners." The butler paused to dab his handkerchief at an imaginary smudge on the face of a longcase clock.

Eleven o'clock already. Where had the day gone? Where had the *decades* gone? "Very well, then. Young men are bottomless pits when free food is on offer. Send along some comestibles with the tea. I like Mr. Valerian Dorning, you know."

"Sir?"

"He as good as told me to go to hell, and he was polite about it. One values honesty in one's old age. Honesty and health."

"If you say so, sir." The butler shuffled away, still carrying his fussy little tray.

Osgood took a moment to assess his reflection in the pier glass outside the formal parlor. "I'm an old man." Which didn't particularly matter if he was a healthy old man. More to the point, he was an old man looking forward to putting a young man in his place. He liked Dorning, and he didn't want to offend the Dorning family, but if Dorning had come with courting on his mind, he was due for a serious set-down.

How long had it been since Osgood had had the pleasure of putting a dashing swain in his place?

Too long. Too damned long.

CHAPTER ELEVEN

Valerian chose a chair with a view of the gardens in hopes that Emily might be strolling out of doors. His seat likely dated from the time of Queen Anne and was a handsome piece of furniture, though the cabriole legs weren't quite even, and the pink velvet of the cushion showed signs of wear.

Why had Pepper set Emily to refurbishing the master suite when a public room such as this so clearly needed attention?

"Mr. Dorning." Osgood Pepper stalked in, his eyes alight with something other than welcome.

Valerian rose and bowed. "Sir, you're looking well."

Pepper closed the door. "I am, aren't I? I intend to stay that way, too, but my illness left me with much business to catch up on. While I am always happy to greet a neighbor, I'll ask you to state your business and be on your way."

As an opening salvo, that move—declaring oneself to be in a hurry—was rather unsophisticated.

"I won't keep you long, sir, though Emily did tell me just the other day how relieved she is that you've put a higher priority on rest and repose. This season of the year, between planting and harvest, is when time in the country can be the most enjoyable, don't you think?"

Pepper took the seat Valerian had vacated. "Emily has time to rest and repose, but if I'm to keep the girl in the style she's come to expect, the same cannot be said for me."

Valerian was a guest, but he was not a supplicant. He availed himself of the sofa, sitting on the end closest to Pepper's chair.

"Is Emily a girl, sir, or has she earned the right to be referred to as a grown woman?"

Pepper's chin came up. "What business of yours is that?"

The question required a choice, between tact and indirection on the one hand and blunt honesty on the other.

"Your time is precious," Valerian said, "therefore I will be forthright. Emily has agreed to become my wife. She is of age, and I have the means to support her. Your blessing is unnecessary, but it would mean much to both Emily and me."

Valerian was reminded in the next instant that Pepper's health had truly been delicate not long ago. The older man put a hand to his chest and leaned forward as if somebody had delivered a blow to his back.

"Who the hell do you think you are, Dorning? Apologize for your presumption this instant, or I'll have you thrown from the premises."

Threats of violence were also an unimpressive negotiating tactic. "I do not think, *I know* I am the man fortunate enough to have earned your daughter's esteem, as she has surely gained mine. In the normal course, I would have first asked your permission to court Emily, after having secured her assent to such a measure. Emily has indicated that she'd rather dispense with such protocols. She knows her own mind, and she has asked me to procure a special license."

Pepper opened his mouth as if to speak—or perhaps shout—then snapped it shut. A fraught moment passed, the silence broken by a tap on the door.

"Begone!" Pepper barked. "Damned servants and their damned

tea trays, and damn you too, Dorning. If you think I'll permit my only daughter to elope with some pockets-to-let bounder in fancy breeches, you are sadly mistaken. You barely know my daughter. Take yourself off, and don't come back."

Valerian stayed right where he was. "Mr. Pepper, you have had a shock, but I beg you to consider the facts. Emily has made her choice based on several months' acquaintance with me. She is not a schoolgirl who can be banished to some auntie in the north for kissing the footman. I have standing in this community and have been introduced at court. My family is titled, and I can support Emily adequately. On what basis do you object to the match?"

Beneath Pepper's ire, Valerian detected a note of true dismay. Emily grasped that her father regarded her as a strategic asset, but Osgood was also an aging papa with only the one child under his roof. He would miss Emily, though he'd likely never admit that to her.

"You damned puppy. She's all I have left, and you think to spirit her away, then live on her money. You turned her head with your flattery and fine manners, and you took advantage of her kind nature. I'll not have it."

Of all the accusations, the notion that Emily would leave her father's side never to be seen again was doubtless the charge of greatest substance. Pepper's admission also, however, suggested that he and his son were on quite bad terms.

"Emily and I plan to dwell at Abbotsford, my estate. The manor lies not three miles from the front door of Pepper Ridge if you take the bridle paths. In addition to sizable acreage attached to the home farm, Abbotsford has five tenancies of a hundred acres each. I will happily show you the estate books and the property itself if you like. Emily deemed the house an adequate place to begin married life."

"You'd put *my Emily* in a farmhouse? A girl who has danced with dukes, had the best tutors, gone to the best school, and you'd have her hoeing peas and feeding chickens."

Pepper was truly upset, which might be why he had conveniently forgotten that his plan had been for Emily to marry into an influential gentry family.

"I would have Emily be happy, sir. She is not happy here. She has little purpose now that your health is restored, and though she would bring much to your business endeavors, there's apparently no place for her there."

"Damned right there isn't. I'll not have it said she bears the taint of the shop."

Of course Emily bore the taint of the shop, and of course that slight had already been directed at her. Pepper, a merchant to his bones, could have no notion of the viciousness Society gossips turned on an heiress with new money.

"She was supposed to put this house to rights." An element of lament had entered Pepper's voice, an element of defeat.

"But you didn't let her choose the crew, didn't allow her to develop the renovation plans, schedules, or budgets. You are alive today, very likely because Emily was stubborn enough to seek help for you after the doctors told you all hope was lost. She has been loyal to you, and I gather that's despite areas of significant contention. She is of age, sir, and you cannot stop this wedding, but you can make it a happier occasion for her."

Had Valerian not thrashed through a thousand arguments with his siblings, had he not spent hours teaching farmhands how to dance, had he not known how dearly Emily valued her father's regard, he would have excused himself and planned to be estranged from his papa-in-law.

But family mattered, and Emily had so little of it.

Pepper's bony finger traced the claws carved into the arms of the chair. "She did a damned sight more than kiss a footman. That girl led me such a chase as no father wants to endure."

"Ancient history, sir. I was no saint at university, which I gather is half the point of sending young men to such institutions. Emily saved your life."

"Did she see my heart repaired only to break it? Emily thinks you are what she wants, but she's merely bored with country life and at loose ends. I'll take her back to Town and have done with playing the country squire. Wretched lot of nonsense anyway. Name your price, Dorning."

Valerian had dreaded this aspect of the conversation most of all, but he'd thought through his reply and remained at his ease on the somewhat lumpy sofa.

"I haven't a price. I have offered Emily marriage, and she has accepted. She is my heart's desire, and I am apparently hers."

Pepper snorted. "I've heard that before. Cost me a bit, but I ran the young scoundrel off, and he promptly married some wealthy widow. You can use a bit of blunt, no shame in that, but you will agree to leave Emily in peace for the rest of your days. What do you say to five thousand pounds? You can leave here with the signed bank draft in your hand."

No wonder Emily was exasperated with her father. "What you have that I value, sir, is the ability to send Emily into married life with your blessing. Your money will gain you nothing in this discussion, and Emily would be disappointed to learn of your offer."

"Emily's disappointment is bearable. I will not have her endless misery on my conscience, though, and that is all you can promise her. You doubtless do like her—who wouldn't?—but it's easy to like a young woman awash in money. Ten thousand pounds should console you on your failed marital aspirations."

Valerian had never been destitute, but he'd never been rich either. Perhaps that was an ideal perspective from which to approach life, for obviously Pepper's wealth hadn't made him happy or wise.

"Is Emily so content here at Pepper Ridge?" Valerian asked, rising. "She's dwelled in Dorset now for several months. Is she calling on friends? Involved with the social committees at church? Helping to plan the next assembly? Are her friends visiting her here? Has she a few investments she likes to manage for her own amusement? Has she earned the regard of the staff at Pepper Ridge and taken on the redecoration scheme like a woman settling into her lifelong home?

"No," Valerian said, answering his own questions. "No, no, no, and no. She's restless, bored, lonely, and ignored by the man who now claims to have her interests so very much on his mind. My family has called on her. My sister-in-law in particular keeps an eye on you, the better to safeguard your health, and that is at Emily's request."

Pepper gazed off into the garden, though Valerian knew by the way the older man gripped the chair arms that he was listening.

"You are not concerned with her happiness, Mr. Pepper, you are concerned with your own. Emily has for once put her wishes before yours, and I am the fortunate recipient of her decision. You can either be a gracious and loving father about our engagement, or you can destroy what warm feeling Emily yet harbors for you. I'll bid you good day and hope to see you at the wedding."

"Twenty-five thousand pounds, and that's my final offer."

Emily's stubbornness had apparently been learned at her father's knee. "Mr. Pepper, your commercial experience vastly eclipses my own, but I beg leave to inform you that this is not an auction, and neither my honor nor your daughter's happiness is for sale."

Pepper came out of his chair like a man half his age. "Dammit, Dorning, you have no idea of Emily's situation. She can't marry into a titled family. They'll eat her alive."

"My titled family will not, or they will have me to deal with."

A longcase clock bonged the quarter hour. Valerian waited, for the true issue, the true reason for Pepper's intransigence, had yet to be broached. Perhaps Pepper was much poorer than he let on—business reverses had brought down many a new fortune. Perhaps his heart was troubling him again. Perhaps he was simply a tired, lonely old man with too many regrets and only one child left to love.

"Has she told you about the boy?"

"Emily has a child?" Valerian would rather have learned of that situation from Emily, if so.

"And if she does?"

"My brother has a by-blow. Tabitha is a delight to us all, and we miss her when she's off at school. Emily's wishes regarding her offspring must control on this issue, but I would hardly cry off over such a matter."

Pepper ran a hand through thinning hair. "No child, thank the Almighty. She has a brother." The admission seemed to cost Pepper all of his bluster. "You will have my blessing, Dorning, but you won't get a penny to go with it. Insist that Emily tell you of her wayward sibling before you speak your vows, and if you are still willing to marry her, I will attend the wedding."

No man should consent to his daughter's nuptials with such an air of sadness. "Sir, are you well?" But then, Pepper hadn't admitted to having a son. He'd referred to Emily having a brother.

"I am as well as a man can be when he contemplates his daughter's broken heart."

"I will not abandon Emily over another family member's errors, any more than she would hold my siblings' indiscretions against me."

Pepper headed for the door, his step considerably slower than when he'd made his entrance. "Talk to her about her brother. Tell her she's not getting a single groat from me in settlements, and if the pair of you are still determined to marry, I will lend my paternal imprimatur to the resulting farce."

He closed the door quietly behind him, leaving Valerian alone in the faded splendor of the formal parlor. The negotiation had concluded successfully, the primary objective achieved. Emily would have her father's approval, which was all she'd claimed to want.

The lady chose then to emerge from the terrace into the garden, and the sight of her in a plain straw hat, a frilly blue parasol over her shoulder, should have filled Valerian with elation.

The prospect of marrying Emily did fill him with joy, and the knowledge that he had secured Osgood Pepper's blessing was greater cause for happiness. The absence of settlements was either a test or an old man's stinginess, but of no matter to Valerian. He was confident Emily would eventually forgive the slight.

That Emily was concealing some material information from him regarding her brother was troubling, though, and the notion that she'd done *more than kiss a footman*—long ago, doubtless, and in the heat of youthful intemperance—was not exactly cheering news either.

"MR. PEPPER." The butler, minus his tray, paused at the foot of the stairs. "Sir, are you well?"

Dorning had asked the same thing, and Osgood's sense was that the impudent puppy's concern had been real. "I am in fine health, thank you."

Though did a man in fine health sit on the footman's chair, staring blindly into a past that included so many regrets?

"Shall I help you up, sir?"

Osgood rose, feeling decades older than he had an hour ago. "You shall not get above your presuming self. When's luncheon to be served?"

"Miss Emily usually has the kitchen bring up luncheon at one of the clock. We can move that forward, if you'd—"

Osgood waved a hand. He wasn't hungry, for all he'd just gone toe-to-toe with a man half his age. "And where is Miss Emily?"

"Walking in the garden, Mr. Pepper."

Wasting no time, clearly. "Mr. Dorning will doubtless join her. They are to be left undisturbed, do you hear me?"

"Quite well."

Was the old fellow smiling? Osgood felt a reluctant urge to smile too. He'd been trounced, utterly, and by nothing more than romantic foolishness. Perhaps Dorning would cry off when he learned of the family scandal, but for Emily's sake, Osgood hoped not.

"I spared Dorning's manly dignity, let him strut about and make sentimental declarations. Young fellows enjoy that sort of display."

"They assuredly do, sir."

Osgood had also tested Valerian Dorning, to the tune of twenty-five thousand pounds, and Dorning had passed easily. Emily might take some consolation from that news if Dorning deserted her over the scandal involving Adam.

A gentry family could have absorbed that scandal, the countryside having better things to do than circulate gossip and dig up old news. A titled family, though, constantly traveling to and from London, overly concerned with appearances and tattle... Emily would not fare well in such a situation.

Dorning faced a hard choice for an earl's son, and by taking Emily's inheritance out of the equation, Osgood hoped to make the choice less difficult—for Dorning. If Emily was about to yoke herself to a penniless prig who valued gossip more highly than Emily's happiness, she needed to know that now, and her old papa would be on hand to console her if Dorning abandoned her.

Osgood started in the direction of the office, considering how severely to castigate Caleb and Tobias for their folly over the merchantman, when the butler's voice called to him.

"Miss Briggs has requested a moment of your time, Mr. Pepper, if that's convenient."

"Veronica Briggs does not request a moment of any man's time," Osgood retorted. "She issues a parliamentary summons. She can join me for luncheon in the breakfast parlor."

The butler glanced up the steps, then down the corridor. "I gather the nature of the discussion is private, sir."

"No matter. My loyal henchmen will be plotting another means of wasting my money, and Miss Briggs and I will be undisturbed at our meal."

"Very good, sir."

EMILY HADN'T HEARD any shouting coming from the formal parlor, but then, the windows were kept closed in there, for the room was seldom used.

Why was that? Why, after several months of biding at Pepper

Ridge, did so few people call on her? The vicar had promised to drop by and look in on Papa, but yesterday's entire discussion in the cluttered, book-filled study at the parsonage had been awkward.

The silence from Briggs had been more awkward still. Emily had had to endure no reproachful looks, no muttered asides. Briggs had retreated into a vast, unreadable quiet, the very boon Emily had so often wished for. Perhaps Briggs, who had lost at least one sibling to debtor's prison, realized that parting from Emily on good terms was more likely to result in a generous pension than would an acrimonious end to their relationship.

Valerian emerged onto the terrace, his stride brisk and confident. Emily waited by the fountain, both so she could enjoy the sight of him in the late morning sun and because—if the interview with Papa had gone poorly—there was no need to hasten the bad news.

"My dear." Valerian took her hands and kissed her knuckles, the right hand then the left. She'd forgotten her gloves—she'd nearly forgotten her hat and parasol too—and his lips brushing over her bare skin sent sensation rippling through her.

His romantic gesture had doubtless been seen by anybody spying from the house, and being Valerian, he would have known that.

She curtseyed. "Mr. Dorning, good day. You've been in discussion with Papa."

Valerian bowed and offered his arm. "More like a verbal brawl, but you will be pleased to know that Osgood approves of our union. He will attend the wedding and lend what he called his paternal imprimatur to the nuptials."

Emily sagged against her escort. "I am relieved. I ought not to admit that, but Papa can be so very set in his ways, and once his pride is offended, he's more arrogant than a duke."

"That determination has served him well in commercial matters."

Valerian slipped his arm around Emily's waist, which would have been a shocking intimacy except that they were *an engaged couple,* and Emily was honestly feeling a touch unsteady.

"Let's have a seat in the shade, shall we?" Valerian suggested.

He would always be like this—steady, considerate, sensible. How she treasured those qualities. He led her to a wrought-iron bench among a grouping under the laburnum alley. Most of the bloom was over, but a few golden clusters yet cascaded from the greenery overhead.

"The flowers remind me of lanterns," Emily said, closing her parasol and leaning it against the bench, then taking a seat. "Margaret claims they are poisonous to people and animals alike. Does Papa know about the special license?" She untied the bow at her chin and removed her straw hat, perching it atop the handle of her parasol. "I am babbling."

Valerian took the place beside her and wrapped an arm around her shoulders. "Are you about to cry? My handkerchief is available for the purpose, if so."

He brandished his linen, and Emily did feel a tear trickle down her cheek. "I have no idea why I'm being such a goose."

Valerian dabbed at her cheek and passed her the handkerchief. "It's not every day a lady's engagement becomes official. Osgood made a few remarks that led me to believe he's meddled with your romantic choices on a previous occasion."

How delicate, how tactful that inquiry. Not even a question, really. "I fancied myself in love with the second coachman." In this peaceful garden, with Valerian's arm around her shoulders, that confession felt merely foolish, not the great scandal Briggs insisted it had been. "Papa would send the coach to fetch me home from school and so forth, and Edward and I developed a flirtation."

Valerian's silence was patient and untroubled.

"More than a flirtation," Emily went on. "I was seventeen and wanted very much to come home from school for good. Papa insisted on another year, and Edward was so very understanding."

"He understood his way right under your skirts, I take it?"

No censure colored that remark, no ire. "He did. Edward loved me beyond telling, and I was the dearest, the wisest, the most beautiful, the smartest... I was an idiot. Papa paid him off, and he emigrated to Philadelphia with a pretty widow. I went back to school a sadder and wiser heiress."

"You had a narrow escape. I fell in love with a tavern maid at Oxford. I proposed to her at least twice a week. We planned to run away to Ireland, where my talents as a dancing master or tutor would support us in fine style. That my true love asked for money regularly and laughed off my earnest entreaties escaped my lovesick notice. I was sixteen. No use to talk sense to me."

"You aren't ashamed of that sixteen-year-old?"

Valerian hugged her a little with the arm around her shoulders. "Of course not. He was innocent of the world, terribly lonely, and trying to be a man in somebody's eyes, but without a man's abilities or perspective. The tavern maid earned a tidy sum entertaining the lovelorn scholars, and I, too, had my narrow escape."

At Abbotsford, Emily had rejoiced to become intimate with Valerian. He was a demon between the sheets, tender, patient, passionate, and inventive. But this sharing of past follies, this letting go of regrets... such confidences were in their own way more intimate than a physical coupling.

"I was terribly lonely too," she said, the realization coming only as the words formed. "Briggs was no sort of company either. She made the loneliness worse. Papa hired her when I finished school, and then I had no solitude, unless I was in my very bed."

"I take it Briggs will not accompany us to Abbotsford?"

"God, no."

"Good. Newlyweds are entitled to some privacy, though we'll be married for several months by the time Abbotsford is vacant."

Emily left off sniffing his handkerchief. "We will?"

"Abbotsford is an agricultural property. The lease expires after the harvest is in."

This did not appear to trouble Valerian. "So you'll live with me here at Pepper Ridge?" Meals would certainly become livelier, and Tobias and Caleb would have to polish up their manners considerably.

Valerian lifted his arm from about Emily's shoulders. "I'd planned on you joining me on the grounds at Dorning Hall. The cottage is humble, but there's only the two of us, and it will be for a mere few months. Weeks, really."

Emily folded up his handkerchief and passed it back to him. "*What* cottage? I thought you lived at Dorning Hall?" The question sounded more querulous than she'd intended, but where they lived mattered.

"I live *at* the Hall; I do not live *in* the Hall. Casriel and his countess need privacy, and I have my own modest dwelling else-where on the grounds. Is this a problem?"

His tone suggested it had better not be.

"How modest?"

"Very. I have a cook-housekeeper who does not live in, and for any other tasks, I request assistance from the Hall."

"No maids? No footmen?"

He refolded his handkerchief into precise eighths and tucked it away. "I don't need them, and servants cost money."

Emily rose, snatching up her hat and parasol. "If that's the prob-lem, then we'll use my money, just until we get on our feet at Abbots-ford. We haven't chosen a date yet. Wednesdays are said to be good luck for weddings."

Valerian got to his feet more slowly. "As it happens, you have no money. Osgood will bless the union, but he had two conditions. The first was that he make no contribution to your dowry."

Emily abruptly dropped back onto the bench. "*He what?*"

"Your father agreed to approve our marriage, but on condition that he make no contribution to your settlements. You won't be penniless in the event of my death." Valerian paced before the bench, hands behind his back. "I will leave Abbotsford to you, and my share of the family business as well. I have some cash, more than enough to keep the property out of debt through a bad year, and my brother Hawthorne suggested I sell some mature timber from my home wood. Then too, my book—"

"Papa is refusing to release my settlements? Can he do that?"

Valerian remained three paces away. "What does it matter? I did not intend that we live on your settlements, Emily. I thought you approved of me in part because I'm not a fortune hunter."

Some element of masculine pride had entered the discussion, in addition to whatever high-handed game Papa was playing.

"Those settlements are *mine*, Valerian. I earned them, one French conversation, one deportment lecture, one formal ball at a time. I understand that you expect us to live within our means, but should I be widowed, those settlements are for me and our children." For their daughters, especially.

Valerian gazed off down the laburnum alley, a pretty, shady path curving beneath poisonous trees.

"Who was it that said she'd rather be a farmer's wife than the lady of ten manors, provided she could be married to me? Who warned me that our families would be difficult? Who accused Osgood Pepper of being overly proud and stubborn?"

Emily plunked her hat onto her head. "I did, blast you."

"Will you let Osgood's pride and stubbornness win, Emily? If you cry off, I will wish you well and keep you in my prayers. It's one thing to be told your suitor has only modest means, it's quite another to face the reality. Osgood is doubtless counting on you stumbling over that distinction."

The recent altercation with Tobias had been unsettling. The conflict with Briggs was unsettling. Papa's latest ploy was worse than both of those upsets combined, but as Emily's intended stood at his ease, tall, handsome, and self-possessed, her emotions calmed.

Papa was simply up to his usual tricks. She ought to have expected as much.

"You are quite right," she said, going to Valerian and taking his hand. "Papa must have his little games, and that's all they are. At least he didn't try to buy you off."

Valerian drew her close. "He did, actually. Offered me a grand sum to decamp for parts unknown. I do believe Osgood is terrified of losing you, for all he makes noises about marrying you into some family awash in wool money and blood stock."

Emily went into Valerian's embrace with a sense of having crossed the threshold that separated a girl's dependence on her father from a woman's loyalty to her mate. "I will kill Papa. He had no business offending you like that. Was it a very great sum?"

"A pittance compared to the joy I will own when I speak my vows with you."

A very great sum indeed, then. "I love you, Valerian Dorning. I love you more than I can say."

He kissed her, a brief, fierce reminder of their joining at Abbotsford. "I will never give you cause to regret your choice, Emily. That, I vow."

A perfect moment ensued, full of hope and determination and not a little desire. Emily stepped back before the desire became unmanageable. She moved off down the alley, hand in hand with her fiancé, wanting to gain distance from the house.

"You said Papa had two conditions. What was the second?"

Valerian ambled along at her side, ducking the occasional cluster of fading blossoms. "Nothing of any great significance. He insisted you tell me about your brother."

Emily stumbled, catching her toe on a rock. She would have gone down to her knees or worse, but for Valerian taking a stout hold of her arm.

"LET ME RETRIEVE YOUR PARASOL," Valerian said, mostly to give Emily an opportunity to compose herself. Mention of her brother had put an uneasiness in her eyes, and she'd clutched Valerian's arm like a woman tottering on the brink of a sea cliff in a high wind.

Then too, parasols cost money. Frilly, lacy parasols dyed to match the color of a lady's gloves and reticule cost a great deal of money.

The idea that this particular parasol might be left out in a passing shower weighed on Valerian. He could replace it, but he'd rather not spend his limited coin on a frippery.

And most of all, he dreaded explaining that reasoning to his bride. He'd also prefer he and Emily did not spend their honey month at Pepper Ridge, and he most assuredly would never ask Osgood Pepper to relent about the settlements.

Valerian fetched the parasol, rejoined Emily, and offered his arm. "Would you like to see where I'm living now? As a lovers' retreat, I think it has potential."

"I'm sure it will be fine."

Truly, something had the lady upset. "You might prefer to rearrange the bedroom." And if he showed her that bedroom on Sunday, the cook-housekeeper would not be on the premises.

"We won't be living there for long, so what matters... oh. Well, yes, I'd like to see your cottage. And your bedroom."

Emily clearly didn't give a hearty heigh-ho about the cottage, much less the bedroom where they'd embark on married life.

"Emily, what's wrong? At Abbotsford, you couldn't get my clothes off me fast enough. Now, my naughtiest flirtation only annoys you."

"I'm fine."

Like hell she was. Valerian examined the clasp on her parasol. The mechanism was flimsy. The handle looked to be stained pine rather than a sturdy hardwood. Pretty, but not a high-quality product after all.

"I am anxious." Emily tromped a few paces away, then back to his side, then away again. "My brother's name is Adam. He's five years older than me, which is a perfect age difference for a big brother."

Sycamore might argue with that characterization. "Where is this Adam?"

Emily huffed out a sigh. She twiddled the ribbons of her straw hat. She gazed past Valerian's shoulder. "Botany Bay, or somewhere thereabouts. He works for the governor's secretariat."

A position in a colonial government was often a stepping stone to solid wealth and influence—for those who had no other means of gaining them.

"He didn't want to work for your father?"

Now she stared at Valerian's cravat pin. "Adam did work for my father and was quite good at it, but then he was accused of stealing from the business, and charges were brought."

Charges were never a good thing. "Brought by whom?"

Emily stomped off again. "By my idiot, stupid, infernal, bloody-minded father. He brought charges against his own son. Thievery is a capital crime, and Adam would never steal. Never. Why take money when you have more than enough of your own, and the penalty for your crime would be so very severe?"

Rich people took money all the time. Some of them delighted in their swindles and wagers, confident that their wealth was sufficient to spare them legal repercussions.

"Osgood accused his own son of a capital crime?" Some distant day, Valerian might be impressed with Pepper's integrity—assuming Adam was the guilty party. The Hanoverian dynasty was rife with fathers who'd done everything possible to sabotage their sons, and conversely. For the present, Valerian was appalled at the dilemma Emily had faced.

"Adam didn't do it," she said. "He's not like that. He's not stupid enough to commit such a crime and get caught at it, and he had no motive. Nobody has ever explained to me why a man in line to inherit a thriving business—and I do mean thriving, Valerian—would risk his life over a few hundred pounds. Adam loved the business, and he was far better liked by the staff and the customers than Papa will ever be."

A few hundred pounds was a fortune to most. "Did Adam have debts?"

"No. Did I? Yes. Did my father? Of course, as do most people. Not Adam."

Innocent or not, a convicted felon in the family was a problem, but at least in this case he was a problem many thousands of miles away.

"Your father thought I'd abandon you over this situation." Many men would have. The fellow was never supposed to withdraw his offer of marriage, but given the circumstances, nobody would blame Valerian if he done just that.

"Adam is a person," Emily said, "not a situation. I meant to tell you, but Papa stole a march on me. I would never have married you without disclosing the facts, Valerian. Besides, Adam is innocent."

Valerian passed her the parasol. "I applaud your loyalty, Emily, but I've sat through enough parlor sessions to know that virtually every person ever charged with a crime protested his or her innocence."

She grabbed the parasol, and the light in her eyes suggested she'd like to wallop him with it. "You don't know my brother. You don't know the details. Somebody put Papa's signature on that bank draft, but it wasn't Adam. I saw the trial, Valerian, and the only evidence supporting conviction was a signature on a bearer bank draft that Papa claimed he didn't sign."

Worse and worse. "You think your own father arranged for his son to be tried and convicted of a hanging offense?" Casriel would take a very dim view of a scandal of these proportions. For that matter, *Valerian* took a very dim view of it.

"Adam did not steal," Emily said, snapping open her parasol. "Papa did not connive, but each is convinced of the other's wrongdoing. For the past five years, I have been silently railing at them both. Adam will earn his ticket of leave in less than twenty-four months, and then they will have to confront one another. For now, Papa refuses to speak Adam's name, and Adam's letters contain not even a polite inquiry about Papa's health. I told him Papa was failing, and even then, Adam would not relent."

To return to England after a sentence of transportation was rare, but it did happen. To return prior to the end of the stated sentence was another capital offense.

"Who knows about this?" Valerian asked, already composing his half of the discussion he must have with Casriel.

"Here in Dorset? Nobody outside my father's staff and you. The case was heard all the way up in Durham, and most of the gossip was confined to mercantile circles. When I was in London, I listened for any hint that the scandal had become common knowledge. I gave the tabbies so much else to criticize me for, they apparently didn't bother hunting through my past for more ammunition."

They hadn't yet. No wonder Osgood was distraught at the idea of Emily marrying into a titled family. Had she snagged a titled heir, the sniping would have turned into a full-on cannonade.

"I am compelled to disclose these particulars to my siblings."

Emily marched off in the direction of the fountain. "Why? This is old news and will soon be no news at all."

Valerian fell in step beside her and did not offer his arm. "Because I have agreed to become the *magistrate*, Emily. A magistrate with a convicted felon for an in-law will be a novelty at least."

"Then don't become the magistrate. The post doesn't bring in a salary, and those duties would involve you in all manner of sordid squabbles."

Sordid squabbles, like a father, son, and daughter at daggers drawn? "I have given my brother my word that I will relieve him of the burden of the petty sessions and all that goes with them. I do not break my word, Emily."

She had doubtless had her fill of stubborn, inflexible men, and Valerian winced at his own tone.

"I know you keep your word," she said, steps slowing. "I love that about you. You are trustworthy and honorable, but, Valerian, my brother has lost years of his life over what was very likely a lapse in recall on Papa's part. I cannot be bothered with Lord Casriel's distaste for scandal when I know Adam has been the true victim here."

A knot in Valerian's belly eased. Emily was being reasonable. She was allowing that his perspective had validity, as did hers. Sibling loyalty was a fine quality, most of the time.

"We will muddle through this," he said. "Osgood has bet against us twice, and we will prove him wrong on both counts. If and when Adam returns from the Antipodes, he will be welcome in our house." A magnanimous compromise, but if the boot were on the other foot, and Sycamore had been sentenced to transportation, Valerian would hope for the same generosity of spirit from Emily.

She paced along in silence until they emerged from the laburnum alley. "Have we had our first disagreement?"

Had they? "I wish you hadn't been pushed into this disclosure by Osgood's meddling, but I also wish you'd told me sooner. I might have refused the magistrate's post."

She gave him a wan smile. "The talk will be awkward if your neighbors learn of the connection, won't it?"

Our neighbors. "We'll manage. The magistrate's post tends to rotate among the landed men, and I'm merely taking a turn." Besides, what were the chances that a five-year-old court case heard three hundred and fifty miles away would become common knowledge locally?

Emily slipped her arm through his. "The whole situation haunts me, Valerian. I know my brother is innocent. I know it, but I also know Papa truly does not recall signing the bank draft. I have nightmares about the whole business."

He patted her hand. "I'm sorry, and particularly sorry that you've carried this burden alone. Let us agree that we won't have secrets, Emily. If my brother Sycamore suffers a financial reverse, I'll tell you. If you are feuding with the vicar, you will tell me. Nobody will drive a wedge of suspicion between us. Agreed?"

She kissed his cheek. "Agreed. I have hated sneaking my letters into the post, hated keeping all the worry to myself when Adam doesn't write back. The first two years were very hard, when the work he was assigned was mostly manual labor. He's doing much better now, but I still worry."

"I worry for my siblings, and they aren't serving sentences of transportation."

"I worry to the point of distraction, Valerian. I lose sleep over Adam's situation, and sometimes I think I'm losing my wits as well. Just yesterday, I thought I saw him across the street from me in the village, and we know that cannot have been the case."

CHAPTER TWELVE

Dorset was beautiful in the way much of England was beautiful—verdant, peaceful, settled. Adam had missed that quality most of all. England had history for him in a way the Antipodes never could. His mother was buried on English soil, his sister bided here—not two miles away—as did his father.

Osgood Pepper was apparently much recovered from a brush with death. Adam's entire justification for returning to England was thus moot.

Or was it? Caleb Booth and Tobias Granger had used Papa's illness to tighten their orbit around him and Emily, and Adam had had five years to consider exactly who had benefited from his downfall.

"Your horse, guv'nor," a scrawny boy said, leading a leggy chestnut gelding across the inn yard. "Name's Topsail. Hostler says he loves a good gallop and will clear anything up to five feet. Seems a bit sleepy to me, and you know how hostlers talk."

Adam eyed the horse, who eyed him back. "He looks sound enough." Horses were at a premium in Australia, and the sleek conformation of a hunter hack had been a rarity when the empire's agenda for most of its colonies was work, work, and more work.

"Has good manners," the boy said, patting the horse's shoulder. "Makes you wonder how a fellow like this ended up in the village livery."

"Bad luck can happen to anyone." Adam checked the girth and swung into the saddle, then tossed the boy a coin.

"So can good luck, sir! Thankee!" The boy skipped off, coin clutched in a dirty paw. He'd learn soon enough that bad luck was more abundant than the other kind.

Though at least the weather was accommodating today. Adam had gleaned directions by pretending to be interested in buying property locally. An older woman and her niece in the inn's common room had been eager to tell him that Pepper Ridge had recently changed hands— Summerfield House, until the sale. The gent who owned it was a *London type*. Not long for the country, in their opinion, and his daughter was probably eager to return to Mayfair's ballrooms and carriage parades.

Miss Emily Pepper had a lady's airs and graces, despite her origins. That last was offered grudgingly, as Emily had no doubt been given grudging credit in Mayfair for the same hard-won airs and graces.

If Adam had the coin, the ladies opined, he could very likely lease the place. He'd endured a careful perusal after that observation, during which he'd smiled genially and thanked the women for their kind assistance.

He had the coin, as it happened. His wealth was a result of his own hard work, the opportunities a new colony presented, and Emily's cleverness, for he hadn't arrived to Australia entirely penniless. Transportation could make a man rich, if it didn't kill him.

He turned the horse from the market green and left the village at a sedate, unremarkable walk. Topsail was content to saunter along under the blue summer sky, while Adam seethed with conflicting emotions.

To be home was to be reminded of everything that had been taken from him, everything he'd never get back. Years with his family, his standing in the community, the right to hold his head up in any company. The greatest theft had not been the money—a sum too large to overlook—or even the years spent thousands of miles from home, but his own father's trust.

Adam guided Topsail down a shady bridle path, one that would keep him out of sight of the Pepper Ridge manor house. If he was lucky and vigilant, he might find a laundress or scullery maid willing to summon Emily to the garden.

Luck had abandoned him five years ago, but he'd become expert at vigilance. He was thus heartily surprised to spy Emily parting from a tall, dark-haired gentleman right at the edge of a long bed of roses. She and the fellow embraced in the tight, unself-conscious manner of spouses or lovers, which was interesting. Emily kissed her swain on the cheek, and then he strode off around the side of the house before Adam could get a decent look at his face.

Emily, bless her eternally, repaired to a small folly overlooking the garden.

Adam tied Topsail's reins to a sapling and used the folly to keep his approach from the view of anybody in the house. He stood beneath the side of the little structure, offered up the first prayer he'd composed in five years, and spoke softly.

"Emily, don't move. Please."

Being Emily, she did move, though she made the gesture about collapsing her parasol and setting it aside. "Who's there?"

Adam rose enough that she could see him above the edge of the folly. "It's Adam. For the love of God and England, don't scream."

She studied him and, with a composure she'd never have claimed five years ago, turned her gaze back on the garden. "What in all of perdition are you doing here now?" She laid the parasol across her lap. "You look well."

He looked like he'd been baked in a southern sun, which he had, and like he'd accustomed himself to unrelenting physical labor, which he also had.

"I came home because I feared Papa would go to his reward with our differences unresolved."

"Papa is much better. He's found a medication—foxglove—that routed the dropsy. He's healthier now than he's been in years. You took a terrible risk, Adam."

"As did Papa when he set the law on me. You're looking well too, Em." Beautiful, really. Emily was not a diamond of the first whatever the term was, but five years ago, she'd been pretty. Her regular features and thick brown hair were complemented now by self-possession and composure. Witness, she'd not screamed—yet.

"I am well." She fussed with her parasol and stole another glance in his direction. "Adam, you must leave. I have every confidence that if Papa lays eyes on you, he'll set the law on you once more."

"I didn't take the money, Emily." He shouldn't have to tell her, of all people, that he was innocent.

"I never believed you did, but anybody could have put Papa's signature on that bank draft."

"Including you?" That question had to be asked. After five years of wondering and doubting, of considering the innuendos and the unspoken conclusions, Adam was owed an answer.

Emily opened the parasol and twirled it gently over her shoulder. Bad luck to open a parasol indoors, but then, a garden folly wasn't exactly indoors.

"Of course I know Papa's signature," she said. "So do you, so did a half-dozen clerks. His penmanship is not hard to copy, but the law is the law, and you have been convicted. Two more years, Adam, just two more years, and you can come back."

"The governor takes a dim view of those who violate their parole, Emily. England is no longer at war with France, and the United States presents many opportunities for a man with my skills. I was hoping you'd come away with me, even if Papa refuses to put aside my differences with him."

The parasol abruptly halted. "I love you, Adam, and I have longed for your safe return, but not like this. I refuse to go anywhere with you."

She had always been stubborn, but then, with Osgood Pepper for a father, stubbornness was a must.

"I can have us on a ship by tomorrow morning, Emily. Leave a note telling Papa you've eloped with some squire's son. He'll believe it, and we'll be well away before Papa knows any different."

"I break the law if I leave with you. I'm probably breaking the law by failing to raise the hue and cry at the sight of you. I beg you, Adam, please leave as quietly as you can and don't come back."

For all that she spoke calmly, her grip on the parasol was tight, and her cheeks had gone pale. She was preparing to bolt, and Adam hadn't had so much as a hug from her, hadn't held her hand, hadn't seen her smile. The temptation to join her in the folly, to shout, to damn the consequences tore at him.

"I am innocent, Emily. Do you know how hard it was to jeopardize what I've achieved over the past five years to try to reconcile with our father?" Of all people, she should be able to calculate that toll.

She snapped the parasol closed. "Do you know how hard it has been pretending Papa's treatment of you is a mere bygone? How I've longed to tell him that his failing health was exactly what he deserved for betraying his own son? Osgood Pepper can spare tens of thousands of pounds without flinching, but he couldn't set aside his damned scruples for the sake of a paltry bank draft. I have wished his businesses would fail, Adam, and worse than that, but when it was clear that he was dying, I couldn't let that happen. He had to live long enough to welcome you home. And now..."

She rose, and Adam nearly leaped over the railing to grab her by the wrist.

"I must be going," she said. "I wish you the best, but please don't come back. As it is, if you even tell me where you end up, I am bound by law to disclose your whereabouts."

Her response was understandable—also all wrong. "Emily, you'd betray me too? Does this have to do with that fellow taking such a fond leave of you five minutes ago?"

Her posture would have done a grenadier proud. "I am to be married, Adam. Valerian Dorning is all I've ever longed for in a husband. He's honorable, kind, considerate, and willing to work hard for his coin. Papa does not approve of him, but will accommodate appearances for his own purposes."

"Do you love this Dorning fellow?"

"Passionately, and you are right: I am choosing to be Valerian's wife rather than become the sister you'd make into a fugitive."

Well, damn Valerian Dorning, then. "I promised myself I would make things right with Papa, Emily. Now you tell me he's thriving, and you intend to remain here in Dorset, some squire's wife, while I drift about the world without even letters from you. I can't do that."

She bowed her head. "Because you are innocent."

Her admission was something, not quite a vindication, but an olive branch of some sort.

"You must believe me, Adam. I long for your safety and wellbeing, and you shall ever be dear to me, but I cannot see you again."

"Because of the squire's son."

"Because my intended is the new magistrate and an exceedingly honorable man. He will arrest you on sight rather than betray an oath of office. I love you, and I will pray for you until my dying day. Farewell, and may God go with you."

VALERIAN WAS NOT in the mood to gallop back to his cottage, which was by no flight of the imagination a *lovers' retreat*. Ye gods and little fishes, what had possessed him to characterize it thus? Four rooms plus a kitchen and scullery, a terrace, and a muddy garden suited mostly to foraging chickens was no place to bring a new bride.

Clovis steered himself not onto the lane, but rather, onto the bridle path, choosing the shorter route back to Dorning Hall.

"And back to your grassy paddock and your mates," Valerian murmured.

He'd forgotten to give Emily the copy of his manuscript that he'd tucked into his saddlebags. But then, Emily hadn't been in a very manuscript-reading mood, had she? She had been upset with her father, fretting over a long-lost felonious brother, unhappy with Briggs...

Not an auspicious beginning to a marital union. "And how on earth am I to explain this to Casriel?"

Clovis's ears pricked up as another horseman came into view down the bridle path. Valerian did not recognize the fellow, a good-sized specimen who sat his chestnut gelding easily.

"Greetings," Valerian called. "Pretty day for a hack."

"That, it is. I hope I'm not intruding on your land."

A stranger to the neighborhood, then. "Not at all. This bridle path is old enough to qualify as a common right-of-way. Have you family in the area?"

"Business connections." He turned his horse alongside Clovis. "And family, of a sort. Yourself?"

"Dorset born and bred, though most of my family has left the area." Valerian did not want to make small talk with a stranger, but ignoring the man would be rude. Besides, Valerian had the rest of the day, week, and possibly his life to brood over Osgood Pepper's schemes and Emily's moods.

"I've never lived in the shires," the man said. "I thought English country life would be quiet. The birds alone create an endless racket."

"In spring and summer, they do tend to sing. You've traveled some distance from the Dales or coalfields of the north." Traveled a great deal, very likely.

"How can you tell?"

"Your complexion is not that of somebody biding in Northumberland, and your diction gives away your origins."

Valerian's companion laughed, though the sound conveyed little mirth. "Your powers of observation are keen. If I were inclined to set up a household in this vicinity, am I likely to find any properties for sale?"

"What sort of property?"

"A modest, comfortable manor. Someplace a woman could call her own, with enough tenancies that she need not worry for her old age. A solid edifice, well maintained, and nicely situated."

He described Abbotsford, which Valerian was not about to part with. "Are you in contemplation of holy matrimony perhaps?"

Another bark of laughter. "For a man like me? Perish the thought. If my business dealings can be concluded amicably, then that family I mentioned will require some attention."

Family, of a sort, whatever that meant. Perhaps he was somebody's by-blow, or a lady in the neighborhood was raising his illegitimate child.

"The only property in the area to recently change hands is Pepper Ridge," Valerian said, "but that's a sizable estate with many tenancies and much in need of refurbishment. If you're willing to rent, your options might increase."

He shook his head. "I'm not after a farm for hire. The property is not for me, but for a relative, as a dower household, more or less. I am hopeful that I can redress an old misunderstanding while I'm in the area, but the party from whom I parted on bad terms is a stubborn old gent and set in his ways."

Much like Osgood Pepper. "You have my sympathies. I find with men of that ilk a campaign of charm, persistence, and relentless common sense can advance my cause."

"Alas, I left my charm somewhere off the coast of India."

Whoever this fellow was, he was not happy. This unresolved business weighed on him, just as Emily's unsettled mood weighed on Valerian.

"I take the next turning," Valerian said. "I'll wish you best of luck with your business ventures."

The fellow touched a finger to his hat brim. "And good day to you too, sir."

"Might I have a name?" Valerian asked. "If I hear of any properties for sale, I'd like to pass the information along." Then too, Valerian was about to step into the magistrate's shoes. Any stranger in the area was of interest to him, even one passing through on personal business.

"A name." He patted his horse. "Ad—Addison Topsail. I'm at the posting inn in the village and will be for another day or two."

"Pleased to meet you and good day, Mr. Topsail. Best of luck." Valerian cantered away, the little encounter adding to his store of uneasiness. According to Hawthorne's most recent gossip, Squire Rutledge had lost his prime morning hunter in a card game to Devin White, whose father owned the livery. In a display of stupidity such as only young men are capable of, White had sold that very high-quality gelding, a glossy chestnut, to his father for use in the family livery business.

A prime hunter ought never to fall so low, and that horse's name was Topsail.

Who was this Addison person, what was his business in the neighborhood, and why had he been idling along the bridle path not two hundred yards from Emily's back garden?

"YOUR COTTAGE IS... COZY," Emily said, though *cramped*, *humble*, and *dark* had come to her mind first. "For a temporary home, it will do splendidly." The housekeeper, whose half day it was, kept the place clean, but no amount of beeswax and lemon could compensate for a lack of sunshine.

"Nothing about this place is splendid," Valerian said, propping a hip on a windowsill, "except that I'm to share it with you. What bothers you about it the most?"

Honesty came naturally to him, and Emily would have said the same about herself, but for that encounter with Adam in the garden.

"It's dark," she said. "I hadn't realized how thick walls steal the light, no matter how many windows a house has." And this cottage hadn't nearly enough windows. The walls were of fieldstone, built to stand for ages against all weather, and thus nearly two feet thick. That was fine for creating window seats or growing an occasional fern, but such sturdy walls turned the inside of a room gloomy.

"We do have a terrace," Valerian said. "I'll show you."

He rose and extended a hand, though Emily was reluctant to touch him. Her intended was so perceptive, she feared he would feel the secrets she was keeping and the turmoil they created. Why had Adam come home now, and what was to be done about him?

But then, she knew why he'd come home: She'd told him in many letters that Papa was mortally ill. At the time, she'd believed that to be the truth.

"How did your first parlor sessions go?" she asked, settling for a hand on Valerian's arm rather than taking his hand.

"Not that well. Casriel says it gets easier, but I served as secretary for many of his hearings, and I did not observe that the job grew easier from week to week."

Valerian led her down a narrow corridor to a squeaky door that opened out onto a stone porch. Perhaps a Lilliputian would consider the dozen squares of flagstone a terrace. Emily took one of the two seats arranged at a wrought-iron table.

"It is sunny out here. Tell me more about the parlor sessions."

He took the other seat, the chair legs scraping against the stone. "When Casriel handed down his decisions, he did so from a certain distance. He's been the earl for years, he nips off to London, he corresponds with half the peerage. I'm just... me. Valerian Dorning from up at the Hall. I've translated recipes for the menu at the coaching inn. I taught Woodmore Troke's older brother how to smoke a cheroot."

"And has Woodmore's brother been brought up on charges?"

"Public drunkenness."

This troubled Valerian, apparently. "If he was drunk in public, then he was a disgrace to his family and a nuisance to his neighbors."

"I said as much, then I took the case under advisement and told Elmer I'd hear it again next month. If he stays out of trouble for four weeks, I'll dismiss the charges because they are based on only Olive Cheaverton's accusations."

Talk of charges and arrests was hardly cheering. "Why is that name familiar?"

"Because Maysie Cheaverton is sweet on Woodmore, and Olive is May's mother. Mrs. Cheaverton does not approve of the match."

Four yards away, a half-grown rabbit lolloped between overgrown beds of sweet pea. No vegetables grew here, and what flowers there were had gone weedy and unkempt.

Much like Emily's emotions, and perhaps Valerian's too. "Do you disapprove of your own decision?" she asked.

"I am to apply the law to the facts, Emily. I took an oath to do that much and no more. I swore to do right by all manner of people according to the laws and usages of this realm, not according to my own fancies."

The words chilled her, for they brooked no exceptions or lenience. "You think you should have fined Mr. Troke? Sentenced him to hard labor over a few pints too many on the word of a woman who has a motive to slander him?"

Valerian stretched out his legs and crossed them at the ankle. "I reasoned that this time of year, the family needs Troke's muscle to tend the crops and maintain the farm. He has small children, after all. So I gave him a reprieve, but what if I have to lock him up next month, when we'll be that much closer to harvest? Besides, if he can lollygag at the inn for hours swilling summer ale, his labors aren't that pressing. I should have simply applied the law and let him suffer the consequences of his own stupidity."

What would Valerian say about a man who'd been not merely sighted stumbling down a public byway, but convicted of stealing?

"Valerian, you had only the one witness to condemn Mr. Troke. Surely if a man is drunk in public, then more than one witness ought to have come forward."

"Nobody wants to come forward against a neighbor, my dear, and yet, everybody knows Elmer Troke is fond of drink. Mrs. Cheaverton testified against him, and now I'm left with a choice between calling her a liar—a perjurer, more like—or letting a drunk pull the wool over the eyes of the law. I should have locked him up and been done with it. He'd be home by harvest, sober and more respectful of the law."

"Is that what Casriel would have done?"

Valerian peered at her. "Very likely. A man who can boot his own brothers from the nest develops a certain resolve."

As Papa had resolved to see Adam held accountable for a wrong he had not committed? "Well, thank goodness I'm not marrying Casriel, then. As I see it, you brought the weight of the law down on Troke by maintaining the charges against him. That suggests you took Mrs. Cheaverton's testimony seriously. You can still lock Troke up the instant he lapses." She rose, which caused the rabbit to dash into the overgrown sweet peas. "Why has nobody looked after this garden?"

"I was too busy finishing my manuscript and enforcing some accounting discipline on the family botanical venture." He came to stand beside her, lacing his fingers with hers. "You haven't seen the bedroom."

His grip was warm and firm, and the exact timbre of his voice caused a fluttering in Emily's vitals. She had dreamed of their interlude at Abbotsford, and she'd lost sleep over it too.

"Hold me, please." She leaned into him, and he wrapped his arms around her.

"Having second thoughts, Emily?"

"Not about marrying you. Never that."

"About?"

She was so tempted to tell him: *I did see Adam in the village.* Five years older, leaner, more weathered, and mature. Thousands of miles from where he was allowed to be and seeking to make peace with a father he believed to be mortally ill. In other words, committing a capital crime simply by going about his business in England.

"Matters at Pepper Ridge are growing somewhat contentious."

Valerian kissed her brow. "Oh?"

The day was mild, with the sun beaming down on the overgrown garden, and yet, Emily tucked in closer to Valerian's warmth.

"Papa is yelling again. For months, I longed to hear him ranting and shouting, and now that he's regained his vigor, his temper is reemerging."

Another kiss, more lingering. "You think our nuptials have set him off?"

"Yes, in a sense." Oh, how lovely to be held, to be listened to. "Papa is trying to run a complicated business by correspondence. He thought having his two lieutenants, Caleb and Tobias, at Pepper Ridge would make that arrangement workable. Instead, with only a few clerks and secretaries to order about, Caleb and Tobias compete with each other and bicker the livelong day."

Valerian turned her under his arm and strolled with her back into the house. "That's not the whole of the problem, is it? Has Briggs been difficult?"

"She's been silent. A silent Briggs is far more worrisome than a Briggs who's delivering scolds and lectures. I haven't told her we're engaged."

Valerian drew Emily to a halt in the dim corridor. "Shall I tell her? Tell her you've stolen my heart and all my wits too? Shall I tell her I stare down the drive by the hour in hopes the boot boy is bringing the special license along with the post?"

Why did Adam have to be making an appearance now? And why did Emily feel so utterly miserable for behaving toward her own brother as she had? Why did English law have to be so bloody-minded and unforgiving?

"It's too soon for the special license to be arriving in the mail, Valerian."

"Casriel sent a pigeon. It's not too soon. We should be married by this time next week, my love."

My love. My dear. How she craved those endearments and craved the man speaking them.

And how disappointed he'd be should he learn of her dishonesty. "I'd best arrange for my trousseau to be sent here if the ceremony will be in less than a week."

"Have your trunks sent to the Hall," Valerian said, resuming their progress down the corridor. "We'll unpack what's of immediate use and store the rest for when we remove to Abbotsford. Behold, Miss Pepper, our soon-to-be marital bed."

He opened a plain wooden door and bowed.

The bed took up most of the room, leaving space for a hearth, a privacy screen in the corner, and a wardrobe next to the privacy screen. A chest that was very likely cedar-lined sat at the foot of the bed, and one window looked out on the overgrown garden.

The whole room was about the size of Emily's dressing closet. The bed hangings were indigo, the curtains burgundy, the carpet woven of black, blue, and red with an occasional gold flourish. The wainscoting was oak gone dark with age, and nary a gilt frame or burnished sconce reflected what light there was. The window was open, bringing in much-needed fresh air.

"I know what you're thinking." Valerian closed the door. "The room is dark. Recall what I said about making love without illumination. The experience has much to recommend it." He crossed the carpet in two strides and wrapped his arms around Emily's waist. "Shall I demonstrate?"

Emily's heart said yes, her body said yes *please*, but her conscience shrieked no.

"Kiss me," she whispered, touching her mouth to his. "And lock the door."

He smiled against her lips. "We're alone here, and nobody with any sense would disturb us."

"Valerian, people without sense are thick on the ground in some locations. I may soon become one of them."

His smile was wicked and merry. "I live in hope."

Emily turned to present him with the hooks of her driving ensemble—she had handled the reins from Pepper Ridge all the way to Dorning Hall's driveway—and still the battle between her conscience and her heart raged.

She had promised Valerian honesty, but what relationship could withstand the constant weight of bald truth? That would be like applying the law without any grasp of human nature, wouldn't it?

"We need only dwell here for a few months," Valerian said, deftly undoing her dress. "Weeks, really, and if you'd rather dwell at the Hall for those weeks, I will arrange it."

And if Adam should accost her on the very grounds of Dorning Hall? While the earl, his countess, or one of their legion of servants peered out a window?

"I will be happy with you here, Valerian."

He turned her gently by the shoulders. "You wouldn't lie to me, would you, Emily? I would rather have your honest discontent than sham smiles and feigned happiness."

She pressed her forehead to his chest. "I will be happy with you here. I am not lying." *About that.* "Quarters such as these will be an adjustment, but I am absolutely certain I'd rather have a modest cottage to share with you than a whole palace without you."

He enfolded her in a hug so complete and sheltering that Emily nearly started crying. *I do not deserve this. I do not deserve you.* But Adam did not deserve to be treated like a criminal just because the king's justice had served him an evil turn.

Which was why Emily would meet her brother once more, exactly as he'd asked her to in the note she'd found in the morning mail.

CHAPTER THIRTEEN

Valerian unlaced Emily's stays with the same sense of awe and wonder that had buoyed him ever since she'd consented to be his wife. They were to be married, possibly within a week as he'd said, and still, he could not trust that fortune had smiled on him to such a degree.

He was the Dorning brother who always made do with his lot, consoling himself with philosophical platitudes while heartily encouraging his more daring and talented siblings. But this time, he'd won all the games, taken top honors, and claimed the only boon that mattered—Emily Pepper's heart.

"Into bed with you," he said, patting her bottom when she was wearing only her chemise. "I can undress myself." He wanted to see her in the bed where he slept every night, the better to dream of her there.

She passed a slow caress over his falls. "Be quick about your disrobing, please, and do not think of hiding behind that privacy screen."

Her comment reminded Valerian that his bride had experience, and that was a good thing. She knew what to expect and knew how to ask for what she wanted.

"You are not to bring Mr. Troke or Mrs. Cheaverton to bed with you," she went on, folding back the quilt and climbing under the covers. "I shall be quite severe with you if you are a distracted lover."

"Perish the thought." Though Valerian sensed that *Emily* was distracted. The cottage really was dark, now that she'd pointed that out, and she'd mentioned discord between Osgood and his underlings. She'd also made no move to remove his clothes here in the bedroom, and her kisses had been restrained.

Tender, rather than demanding.

Valerian pulled his shirt over his head and draped it across the cedar chest. "Is Briggs to retire upon our nuptials?"

Emily thumped a pillow rather soundly. "At this moment, I would rather share our bed with Mrs. Cheaverton's goats than hear a mention of Briggs, Valerian."

No attempt at false cheer there, none whatsoever. "So we're to share the bed with Briggs, Mrs. Cheaverton, Troke, Caleb, and Tobias?"

Emily flopped onto her back. "A rather crowded undertaking. I am simply not accustomed to trysting. I desire you with all my heart, Valerian, but my mind is chattering on fourteen different topics at once. Kiss me some more, and I'm sure the noise will stop."

He stepped out of his breeches, which made it apparent to any observer that he was not yet overcome with desire, much to his own consternation. He'd pleasured himself twice since rising, and that had been merely to take the edge off his anticipation.

"I have heard a grand total of eight cases as magistrate," he said, considering his nearly flaccid member. "Two of them I dismissed for want of evidence, and one I took under advisement, but all eight are demanding a rehearing right this moment. How is it judges and barristers have any children?"

Emily's smile was crooked. "I truly do love you, Valerian Dorning. That you care about your cases means you are the right person for that job."

And he loved her. Madly. "Let's have a cuddle, and you can tell me about the fourteen topics that plague you."

Emily shifted to the side of the bed nearest the window, and Valerian spooned himself around her. For form's sake, he wished she'd protested—no, you must make passionate love with me!—but for the sake of their future dealings, the alacrity of her assent was a relief.

As his suggestion had clearly been a relief to her.

"Briggs can afford to retire," Emily said, wrapping Valerian's arm about her waist. "Her menfolk were very bad managers of money, so she's careful to a fault with her own funds. But she's pouting because the decision to retire will be taken from her, or that's my best theory."

"Are you sure she's well fixed?"

"Positive. Papa had me read her contract so I would know exactly what her duties are. I read the whole thing—one should always read the entire agreement—and she can't possibly be worried about money. Papa knew her family could be no use to her financially, and thus he was uncharacteristically generous."

"But something troubles her."

"She thrives on frustration. Tell me about your other cases."

Valerian told her, and in the recounting, they lost much of their weight. Mrs. Tolliver was convinced her companion had stolen half a ream of vellum, while the companion insisted she'd used only a few extra sheets because cheap ink blotted so terribly, and one could not send out blotted invitations, could one?

"How did you resolve that situation?" Emily asked, drawing a lazy pattern with her fingers on his forearm. "Briggs hated writing invitations for Papa, but she had such beautiful penmanship, and she was much faster at it than I was."

Who would do Osgood's invitations once Emily and Briggs were both gone? "I pointed out to Mrs. Tolliver that the coin saved because of the cheap ink was very likely comparable to the coin spent buying extra paper. I suggested she buy better-quality ink and monitor the paper consumption more closely. Casriel says Mrs. Tolliver and Miss Grimstead get into a dust-up about twice a year, so they will likely come before me sometime over the winter."

"And already, you dread that."

"I don't dread it." Not as much as he would have before sharing the particulars with Emily. "What do you suppose Caleb and Tobias are feuding about?"

She was silent for a moment, then she pulled the covers up over them both. "Who knows? I am surprised to find I am actually tired enough to take a nap. You will think me a terrible *fiancée*, Valerian, but might I close my eyes for a bit?"

He patted her shoulder. "Have a rest, and I'll do likewise."

The intimacy was real and precious, and yet... this was not what Valerian had planned. Not at all. Married life was, according to Casriel, a series of adjustments, but what sort of besotted couple was too preoccupied to take advantage of the present opportunity?

Emily either fell asleep or feigned slumber, while Valerian held desire at bay, for of course, now that they weren't to make love, the flesh was once more willing.

The parlor sessions had been a disappointment, true, and Emily's situation with Briggs and Osgood sounded vexing as well. Had this cuddle turned into something different, Valerian might also have found a way to tell Emily that instead of a special license, the post was bringing him rejections of his manuscript. Some terse, some polite, each more disappointing than the last.

And at the edge of all that fretting, he was also still wondering about that Addison Topsail fellow. Why ride a distinctively impressive horse if subterfuge was the objective? Why lie so clumsily about a name?

This last annoyance Valerian could at least investigate. If Addison Whoever was still in the area, Valerian, as the magistrate, had the authority to get some answers out of him. On that decision, he drifted off and dreamed of a light-filled house made entirely of glass.

"THIS IS A DISASTER, I TELL YOU." Caleb paced the confines of the library, his boots thumping annoyingly on the carpet. "You should have foreseen this, Tobias. You claim to be the superior tactician of the two of us, and you let that bumpkin yokel Dorning waltz off with my Emily."

Caleb had been ranting all morning, ever since Osgood had explained to them that the bumpkin yokel was to be his son-in-law, a situation about which Osgood had seemed quite pleased.

"Dorning is the son and brother of an earl," Tobias replied, "and he's a local landowner, apparently. Had you bothered to acquaint yourself with those facts, you might not be in such a pet now."

Caleb tossed himself into a reading chair. "I'm not in a damned pet."

No eight-year-old could have sounded sulkier. Tobias poured two brandies, though the hour was barely past noon.

Caleb accepted the drink with a wan smile. "I'm not in a pet, damn you to blazes, but thanks for the brandy. What can Emily be thinking?"

"I don't know as her brain is the organ making the choice, but if you'd consider the situation rationally, you'd see that her upcoming nuptials work to our advantage. The happy couple is to be married by special license, by the way."

The brandy was merely mediocre, probably the last of the stores that had conveyed with the Pepper Ridge property. Emily would never have laid in such unimpressive stock.

Caleb paused before taking a sip. "How could you possibly know about a special license? Briggs has acquired the silence of the tomb lately, and she doesn't care for either of us enough to let such a detail slip."

"So you do occasionally notice what's right in front of your face. I account myself impressed."

"I could dash this drink in your impressed face, Tobias. Emily rejected you too, you know."

This point apparently consoled Caleb as indifferent brandy could not. "Osgood was the party we courted," Tobias said, "more or less. Between Emily's inherent discernment, the limitations imposed on her by polite society, and the threat of old scandal, she wasn't about to find a husband among the fortune hunters and younger sons in London."

"She's *marrying* a perishing younger son, you dimwit. By special license, if your intelligence is accurate."

"But she's not taking any settlements with her into that marriage, Caleb. The whole pot remains in Osgood's clutches, and that does not bode well for Emily's prospects as an heiress, does it?"

Caleb put his drink aside and sat up. "I beg your pardon? One of the foremost heiresses in the realm is going into her marriage with the clothes on her back? Has Osgood gone barmy?" Caleb rose and paced the length of the carpet again. "I'll not have it, Tobias. Emily is dear to me, and while I'd like to shoot Dorning off his horse at close range, I won't see Emily humiliated like that."

He strode for the door as if he had every intention of telling Osgood Pepper to fritter away a quarter of a million pounds for the sake of paternal duty.

"Stop, Caleb, or it won't be Dorning coming off his horse. The whole point of wooing Emily's favor was to secure her fortune."

"Not the whole point, Tobias. Never the whole point. I couldn't do that to her."

Truly, there was no greater impediment to common sense than romantic notions. "While I applaud your tender sensibilities, I applaud even more Osgood's shrewdness. If Dorning is a fortune hunter, he'll abandon Emily at the altar. Then she will be used goods, furious with her father, and even more in need of a husband."

Caleb stalked back across the carpet. "Don't call her used goods. No gentleman refers to a woman in those terms. If Dorning cries off, Emily is the wronged party, and the fault will lie with Osgood for not seeing Dorning's motives before the situation became an engagement." He resumed his seat and finished his brandy in a single gulp. "Vile stuff."

"We are still clerks at heart, aren't we?" Tobias said, eyeing his own untouched glass. "We drink Osgood's brandy because it's free, even when we know the difference between quality spirits and hog swill. Osgood did more than refuse to fund Emily's settlements."

"How do you know these things?" The look in Caleb's eyes said he was calming down, regathering his focus on his perennial lodestar —his own self-interest.

"This old house has seen many renovations," Tobias said, "and will likely see many more. Just off the formal parlor is a closet that served as a warming pantry when the formal parlor was the formal dining room. When Osgood received Dorning—"

"You declared that you were peckish and would take an early tray for luncheon. You bounder, you went to eavesdrop."

"I gathered intelligence. Osgood was plainspoken with Dorning. He said Emily could marry Dorning with her father's blessing, but without a penny of his money. Dorning was satisfied to have Osgood's approval of the match." Which ludicrously romantic gesture was proof everlasting that the aristocracy was daft.

"You can't eat a blessing," Caleb observed. "Can't use it to keep warm of a winter night. I hope Emily knows what she's getting into."

"If the marriage ever comes about."

Caleb leveled a look at Tobias that suggested the lovestruck-suitor, hotheaded-young-fellow, and conscientious-man-of-business roles were all just that—roles that Caleb put on and took off like so many well-tailored jackets.

"Whether or not the wedding happens is no business of mine, Tobias. I will not be a party to any more of your schemes. That business with Adam beggared my peace and put me in fear of eternal damnation. If I did not know that Adam thrives handily in the Antipodes, I'd be unable to sleep at night."

"Life is spectacularly unfair, and we are to attribute that great truth to the will of the Almighty."

Caleb picked up both glasses and took them to the sideboard. He poured Tobias's untouched drink back into the decanter and set his own glass far enough away from the tray that nobody would mistake it for clean.

"Life was unfair to a pair of overworked clerks, but Osgood Pepper has been more than fair to us."

"And we have toiled for him more conscientiously than any pair of clerks ever tended their ledgers," Tobias said. "Adam is once again proving to be a problem. Osgood warned Dorning to speak with Emily about her brother. Briggs has confirmed that no letters have come from Adam for months, and I have reason to believe that Adam has returned to England."

Caleb turned slowly, making a fine picture in this elegant old room, surrounded by books and brandy. Emily might one day wish she'd not been so dismissive of Caleb Booth, not that Tobias could afford to speculate on that possibility now.

"How the hell could you know what Adam Pepper has got up to?"

"I am nearly certain I saw him striding out of the livery yesterday, as bold as the 15th Hussars on parade."

Caleb's expression became uncharacteristically serious, while somewhere in the house a door banged closed.

"Adam can only be here to make trouble, Tobias. He'll hurl accusations at Emily, impart entirely unacceptable theories to Osgood, stir up all manner of scandal. We can't have that."

"No," Tobias said, feeling genuine regret and even more genuine determination. "We certainly cannot have that."

ADAM WAS PACKING what few belongings he'd brought, ready to admit that returning to England had been a mistake. Well intended, but a serious mistake, and he'd overstayed his planned visit for no good reason. Emily would ignore his summons, because what could she possibly gain by admitting the truth now?

To continue lurking in the hedges was risky, and by tomorrow night, Adam could retrieve his luggage from Helen Thelwell and be on a boat for—

A soft tap on the door had him reaching for the knife he kept in his boot at all times.

"It's me," said a female voice. "Open the dratted door before half the village comes to gawk."

Adam sheathed the knife and opened the door to find Emily standing in the corridor, heavily veiled and radiating impatience.

"You came."

"You are my brother. I will always come. I cannot stay long, and you were an idiot for breaking your parole, but I don't want you thinking that I'm—"

He snatched her into his arms and kicked the door closed. "I should not have surprised you at Pepper Ridge," he said, hugging her to him. "I lacked the patience to arrange a meeting, and I hadn't planned to find you in the garden, but there you were."

She hugged him back, though Adam sensed hesitance in her embrace.

"Had you arrived five minutes earlier," she said, "you would have come upon me with my intended. What possessed you, Adam? And why are you still here?"

She let him go, pinned back her veils, and treated him to a pensive perusal, and that was all wrong. She had no smiles for her long-lost brother, no tears of joy—also no apologies.

"I wanted to make peace with Osgood," Adam said, "and also with you." Emily had played the part of the loyal sister, sent letter after letter, probably in defiance of Papa's orders. Every one of her epistles had hit the perfect notes of concern, reassurance, family news, and hopeful wishes. He'd replied in the same light, because a convict's mail was seldom private.

Now they could be honest with each other.

"I have been so angry," Emily said, "angry with Papa, angry with Tobias and Caleb for stepping into your shoes, angry with myself for being unable to reason with Papa. I have missed you, Adam. You could talk sense to Papa and to me, and the past five years have been very long without you."

She didn't know the half of what a long five years could be. "Is Papa truly on the mend?"

"For now. If he takes his medication and uses common sense, he's in quite good health. He's back to yelling and threatening lately, when for months he was appallingly meek."

"And your fiancé deals well with Osgood?" That mattered, because once Adam left England this time, he could not return, not after having broken his parole.

"Papa looks at a situation and asks, 'How can I gain from this?' Valerian's approach is, 'Where can I be of service here? Who needs aid? What needs doing?' Papa has no idea what to make of Valerian, but Valerian is exquisitely competent at managing Papa. I will learn from Valerian's example, and I wish I'd met him much sooner."

Osgood Pepper's outlook was simply that of competent business-men. Adam had learned to despise them as a class, for they exploited convict labor without mercy and saw the colonies as so much booty waiting to be plundered—while never missing divine services, of course.

But Adam could not hate his own father, not even now. Osgood had done what most any parent would have done in the same situation.

"Does your Valerian know the details of my conviction?"

Emily had not taken a seat, though the room boasted both a reading chair near the window and a chair behind the writing desk. She instead began inspecting the contents of Adam's valise.

"Valerian knows the generalities. Papa's approval of the match came with two conditions. This is a very well-made shirt."

"Italian."

Her smile brought to mind the younger Emily. "Tuscan silk, Adam? From one of our mulberry orchards?"

"I have established a commercial venture with some of Papa's contacts in the Italian states."

Her smile disappeared as she refolded the shirt. "You'll compete with Papa?"

"No, I will handle mulberry seeds and mulberry seedlings. Certain parts of the world can't get enough of either."

She sat on the bed beside his open valise. "Certain parts of the world far away. I wish I knew who signed that bank draft, Adam. I would set the law on them before you could say Adam Smith Pepper."

She sounded so forlorn, so sincere. "Emily, you need not dissemble with me. Caleb explained the whole of it before the trial began, though he was delicate about the details."

"What *whole of it*?"

"I know you signed that bank draft. If I had raised that defense, I'd have your transportation or possible demise on my conscience. As it is, I am in a position to assure you that you would not have fared well at all in Botany Bay. Women are scarce there, and their—"

Emily was off the bed in the next instant. "Caleb told you that *I* signed that bank draft?"

"He didn't put it in plain English, but he puzzled it out. I have to say, I'm glad he shared his suspicions with me. I'd otherwise think that Papa brought charges simply to get rid of me."

"Adam, *what are you talking about?* I had no motive to steal from anybody. Papa insisted I handle my own pin money, and I had more than ample funds. I would no more have signed a bank draft for my own use than I'd strut naked down the Strand. Has the southern sun baked your wits?"

Her consternation was real, as far as Adam could tell. "Please keep your voice down."

"You accuse me of a hanging felony and tell me to keep my—"

She paused and let out a breath. "I did not sign that bank draft, and even if I had, why did you cash it?"

"Because I did the Friday banking. The bearer draft was with the stack of notes I was to deposit or cash, the same as I did every Friday. I assumed Papa wanted to add to the cash in the safe."

Emily sank into the chair behind the desk. "I don't like this, Adam. I don't like it at all. For five years, I've told myself that you were caught up in a terrible mistake, that Papa forgot he'd signed a draft, or he'd signed it months previously and mislaid it. Anything, rather than believe the worst of you or Papa. I had no idea I was among the suspects. Caleb never hinted, and he's not that good at keeping secrets."

Adam took the place she'd vacated on the bed. "He's apparently very good at keeping secrets—possibly for selfish reasons—though this development changes nothing. Perhaps it's as you said, and Papa simply laid aside a signed draft, and some clerk added it to the banking. I'm still a convict who broke my parole, and Papa still believes I'd embezzle from my own father."

A considering silence ensued. Beyond the window, the sound of hoofbeats clip-clopping along the high street punctuated the jingle of a harness and the music of an English village going about its business.

"Is Caleb the culprit?" Emily asked, rising and wandering to the window. "Tobias? A clerk who took you into dislike because you scolded him for tardiness? Did one of Papa's competitors connive to see you sent away? Papa claims everybody spies on everybody else in the cloth business, and sometimes I think—"

"Emily, no." Adam gently drew her away from the window. "You cannot wade into this like some avenging angel of justice. Caleb *saw you* in Papa's office."

"Any number of people frequented Papa's office, Adam. That is hardly conclusive evidence of guilt—mine or yours. *Caleb* spends nearly his whole day in Papa's office of late, as do Tobias and a pair of clerks. The footmen are in and out of there. A maid cleans first thing of the day. Caleb should have known better."

And yet, Caleb's theory had made such perfect sense to a man in jail. Caleb had been so convincingly hesitant to share his theories, so reluctant to point any fingers, so careful to deal only in hints and innuendo.

"If you are innocent," Adam said slowly, "then *I* didn't know better than to blame you. The idea that Papa would set the law on me rather than on you explained the whole business. Papa could not cover up the theft entirely—the bank records showed the money withdrawn—and the next day, I was still in possession of the funds. At the trial, I put on what defense I could without implicating you."

Emily crossed her arms. "Meaning you didn't implicate Tobias, Caleb, the clerks, or Papa himself. You didn't hint that Papa and his associates always have spies in one another's warehouses. You became the victim of a nasty scheme and thought you were heroically saving your larcenous sister in the bargain."

"You suspect *Papa?*" In thousands of miles of brooding, in years of revisiting the facts, Adam had never considered that possibility.

"If Tobias hadn't noticed the discrepancy, by Monday morning, you would have put that cash into the safe, where Papa could have removed it without anybody the wiser."

"Why steal from himself?"

Emily went back to wandering the room, the best the inn had to offer and still quite modest. "Stealing from the business to use the money for personal gain isn't the same thing as stealing from himself. He has partners, Adam. They are silent investors, true, but it's their money too. I thought to come here to say good-bye to you. Now I have a headache to go with my heartache."

"Papa didn't need the money either, Em. He'd have no motive to steal from anybody." Caleb, Tobias, and any number of clerks did have motive, however.

Emily rubbed a gloved hand across her brow. "I want answers, Adam. I wish I could discuss this situation with Valerian."

"You must not. He'd be honor-bound to arrest me first and ask questions about the original crime later. The answers to those questions have had five years to hide. Tell me where to write to you."

"Abbotsford," she said. "Valerian's estate is not far at all... No, you can't write to me there yet. Valerian and I will bide in a cottage at Dorning Hall until harvest, then you may write to me at Abbotsford. Valerian said you'll be welcome there, once you have your ticket of leave."

Magnanimous of him, but that ticket of leave would never be granted now. "Promise me you won't poke your nose into the past, Emily. Let me leave here with at least that much consolation."

"We could ask Papa what he knows."

"Stubborn," Adam said, wrapping her in another hug. "Stubborn, stubborn, stubborn. I cannot ask Papa anything. He had me arrested once before. What makes you think he'd give me a fair hearing now? If I was confronting a dying father with a chance to put the past right, he might be more understanding. You tell me he's in good health and still believes me guilty."

Emily had no retort. She leaned against him, a precious, dear sibling of whom he should have thought better.

"I'll walk you to the livery," he said. "I enjoy the fresh air, and they have a horse for hire whom I'd like to buy for a friend who lives near Bournemouth."

A small, heart-weary part of Adam hoped Emily would argue with him as an excuse to stay longer, but she dropped the veils over her face, gathered up her reticule and parasol, and let him escort her to the walkway through a blessedly empty common.

"I notice you did not tell me where to write to you, Adam."

No, he had not. "Write to me in care of a widow, a Mrs. Helen Thelwell, who dwells at Toftrees Manor just west of Bournemouth. I will acquaint her with my next port of call by letter once I leave England. I am Mr. Adam Carmichael to her. She knows me to be a businessman returning from the Antipodes after making my fortune there for the past five years. She herself has spent time in Australia."

Why hadn't Adam had the presence of mind to call himself

Carmichael when questioned by the man on horseback the other day? Because deceit, ironically, was not part of his nature, that's why.

"I want you to go," Emily said as the livery came into view, "and I hate that you must."

"Promise me you won't breathe a word of my whereabouts to your suitor."

Emily walked along at Adam's side, to all appearances a matron, perhaps even a widow, out and about on a summer day.

"I promised Valerian honesty, Adam. I certainly won't volunteer particulars to him, but he's never lied to me, and his esteem is my greatest treasure."

That was probably as much assurance as Emily would give, and it was something. "You drove yourself here from Pepper Ridge?" he asked.

A stable lad darted off at Emily's nod.

"I am becoming a competent whip, thanks to Valerian's efforts. A lady in the country often drives herself. Briggs will doubtless be appalled that I came into the village on my own."

"Are you marrying to escape her companionship, or because this Dorning fellow has truly turned your head?"

"I wasn't sure myself," Emily said as the stable boy brought up a sturdy dog cart, and stood silently holding the reins. "But I love Valerian and look very much forward to being his wife. He's patient, kind, sensible, and more understanding than any prospective husband should be. I am delighted to be marrying him, but when I leave you, I will cry all the way back to Pepper Ridge."

Adam drew her into the privacy of the livery stable's shadowed interior. "Don't cry, dearest. I am for all intents and purposes free to wander the world now. I am a person of means, and I honestly wasn't happy spending most of my days in another man's counting house. I am cheered to know you no longer have an ailing father to fret over, and that you and I can put aside the mistakes of the past."

A fine speech, for a fellow who flirted with a noose simply for the privilege of visiting a sibling.

Emily stepped closer and seized him in a long, tight hug. "I love you so, and I will always keep you in my prayers, but I will never, ever stop missing you." With that, she turned on her heel and walked out. She kept right on walking, climbing into her vehicle without assistance. She took up the reins and clucked to the horse, not glancing even once in Adam's direction.

～

EMILY DEVELOPED an intimate acquaintance with the verb *to seethe* over the next twenty-four hours. She very nearly confronted Papa at dinner, despite Briggs, Caleb, and Tobias looking on, but she had nothing specific to confront him *with*, save suspicions, fears, and worst nightmares.

Then too, Caleb and Tobias had sat through the meal, swilling Papa's wine and eating his beefsteak. Emily had not resolved for herself who the guilty party was, much less what exactly that party had hoped to gain. She'd taken a tray in her room at breakfast and barely touched it, for she'd woken with the headache to end all headaches.

Which was of no moment when she was preparing to leave Pepper Ridge for a humble cottage and to cast Papa upon the mercy of a lazy housekeeper.

"You've done a very thorough job," she told Jasper as he and Tom shifted from foot to foot before her in the master's suite's parlor. Emily had given orders that the boys were to be properly clothed and shod, so at least those nervous feet sported well-fitted boots.

"We checked it all twice," Jasper said, "to be sure, miss. Every board and nail."

And they'd probably counted as slowly as possible, bless them. Some of their pallor was gone, and both boys looked less gaunt.

"The butler will pay you for your efforts, and I am happy to recommend you to any household in need of junior footmen or men-of-all-work. I was hoping, though, that you might assist me to move my trousseau to Dorning Hall." That hope was of very recent vintage.

"Beg pardon, miss?" Tom asked.

"My bride clothes, linen, silver, and such. I'll be leaving Pepper Ridge for the Dorning estate in the next week. Somebody must carefully count and pack up the lot of it."

Jasper became fascinated with the boards stacked in the middle of the room, and Emily realized the first people she'd told of her upcoming nuptials—outside of family—were a pair of local lads she barely knew.

"Shouldn't your maids be seeing to your trousseau, miss?" Tom asked.

Emily did not exactly trust her maids, now that Tom had raised the question. They had doubtless carried tales to Briggs.

"The butler would typically tend to the silver, porcelain, and linens. That is most assuredly not a job for the maids. Let's start there, shall we? You'll have to do another inventory to avoid confusion about what's leaving Pepper Ridge with me."

The boys exchanged a look. "We're good at inventories," Jasper said. "We'll do a fine job for you."

"I know you will." And who else could she trust in this oversize, dusty monument to rural ostentation? Valerian's tiny cottage truly had begun to take on the qualities of a haven, if not exactly a lovers' retreat.

The door swung open, and Papa stood in the corridor. "I thought I'd find you here."

"Off to the kitchen, boys," Emily said. "Tell Cook you're to have a proper tea break to reward a job well done."

They scrambled for the door, barely giving Papa time to step aside.

"Ah, youth," he said. "Defined by bodily appetites, just as old age is defined by bodily discomforts."

"I've asked the boys to inventory my trousseau and pack it for me. Valerian expects the special license to arrive any day."

Papa sauntered into the parlor, peering about as if he'd never seen the place before. "You've told your Mr. Dorning about your brother?"

"My brother has a name, and yes, I have acquainted Valerian with what I know about Adam's situation." The headache pounding at Emily's left temple became a battle drum. "The question becomes, Papa, what do *you* know about Adam's alleged crime? Your signature was on that bank draft."

Papa left off examining the dusty, ornate ceiling plaster. "My signature was forged on that draft, Emily. Forged, I tell you. I know when I've committed hundreds of pounds on a bearer draft, and I never signed that damned thing."

Emily fisted her hands rather than upend the bucket of nails sitting atop the lumber. "Then why not absorb the loss quietly, keep a closer eye on your accounts, and stop allowing half the clerks in Durham to frequent your office? Why risk the life and ruin the reputation of your only son over a few hundred pounds?"

Papa sat on the stack of boards, huffing out an old man's sigh. "Adam's life was never at risk. I bribed the guards at the jail. I bribed the captain of the transport ship. I had Briggs sew money into the blankets your brother took on board with him. I made sure he had a store of medicines and good, well made clothes. Boots too. A man's life can depend on whether he owns a single pair of sturdy boots."

Interesting. Emily had sewn money into the lining of Adam's trunks. "People who accept bribes are not to be trusted, Papa. You taught me that." Consternation replaced a small portion of Emily's ire. "If you thought Adam guilty, why take these measures to ensure his safety? For all you know, he could have been sentenced to death."

Papa shook his head. "Judges have discretion. It's not fair to say I bribed a member of the bench, but I certainly did all I could to minimize the possibility of a death sentence. His Honor and I have known each other for years, ever since his daughter tried to steal a length of silk from our warehouse. The young lady had a little bad habit, so we arranged a system whereby she could steal all she pleased, and her papa would cover the losses. That's not as unusual as you might think."

"I do not understand," Emily said, barely managing to keep her tone civil. "A judge's daughter steals valuable cloth for a lark—repeatedly—and it's *a little bad habit*. My brother is accused of a theft he did not commit, and you send him halfway around the world in disgrace? For all you know, Papa, Caleb signed that bank draft, or Tobias, or I might have done it myself."

Papa hunched in on himself, abruptly looking not only old, but once again the frail, failing man he'd been just a few short weeks ago.

"Daughter, I well know that the culprit could have been you. Anybody familiar with our business could see at once that you were as likely to be guilty as your brother—more likely, in fact."

His gaze was sad, disappointed even.

The unspoken conclusion presented itself to Emily's mind as a horrid fact: Papa had chosen between his children, believing *Emily* to be the guilty party, and *Adam* the one best suited to take the punishment.

"I cannot fathom..." she began through clenched teeth, "Why, Papa, didn't you simply *ask* me what I knew about the matter? Why would you leap to the least likely... I don't know whether to be furious with you—more furious with you—or thank you for not slapping me onto a transport ship without a trial. Suffice it to say I will not be a frequent caller here at Pepper Ridge after next week."

And to think she'd given up her entire bride portion to secure Papa's approval of her marriage.

Emily had much more to say on that score, more to shout very likely, but Valerian rapped on the doorjamb with his gloved knuckles and strode into the room.

"Haven't we a butler to announce intruders?" Papa asked, rising. "Or has the old boy gone to his reward at last?"

Valerian bowed to Emily—formally—and then nodded to Papa. "My business is somewhat urgent and private. A word with you, please, Miss Pepper."

No hint of affection colored that greeting, and Valerian's version of *Miss Pepper* was downright ominous.

Papa shuffled for the door. "He's come to cry off, see if he doesn't. I knew he would. Thank heavens few will learn of this farce, though the rumors will eventually reach the wrong ears. They always do where you're concerned, daughter."

As this vituperation rained down, Valerian's expression remained remote. Papa stopped at the door and sent Emily a pitying glance.

For Valerian, Papa's gaze held sheer contempt. "Coward."

"Papa has had a shock, Valerian, please forgive him. The day has been exceedingly trying, and I know you did not come here to cry off."

Valerian closed the door and locked it. "I regret to inform you, Miss Pepper, that your conclusion might well be in error."

CHAPTER FOURTEEN

Valerian had tossed and turned for half the night, tried getting drunk, and then set the decanter aside before the third brandy. He'd wandered his dark little cottage and sat out under the summer moon, his thoughts refusing to form up into logical squares.

Emily had lied to him, by omission if nothing else, and after giving him her word that they'd have honesty between them.

"Did I steal from you too?" Emily asked, picking up a hammer laid across the top of a bucket of nails. "Embezzle from your botanical venture? Perhaps I forged your signature on a magistrate's order, though I would have had to disguise myself as Mrs. Cheaverton to do that. Maybe I impersonated Miss Tolliver, or did I venture into your cottage in the dark of night and purloin your silver?"

Indignation, hurt, and fatigue bore down on Valerian in a crushing weight, and yet, he had wits enough left to know Emily wasn't reacting as a guilty bride about to be jilted for her subterfuges.

"I have little silver worth purloining. What on earth are you going on about?"

She tossed the hammer from hand to hand as if it weighed no more than a riding crop. "Somebody wants to know what I'm going on about, as if my thoughts, my feelings, my opinions carry any weight. Send an express to the *Times*."

"Emily, are you unwell?"

"Yes, Valerian, I am unwell." She swung the hammer and sent the bucket of nails toppling to the floor in a spectacular crash. "My own father thinks I'd steal hundreds of pounds from him when I already had hundreds of pounds at regular intervals to do with what I pleased. My darling brother thought I'd steal, Caleb was convinced of it, Tobias doubtless also agreed with the opinion of the male mob, and here you are, looking ready to add to the merriment. Pardon me if my *female humors* are in something of an uproar."

She kicked the bucket hard enough to send it rolling across the floor, leaving a trail of nails in a wide arc.

Whatever reaction Valerian had steeled himself for—tears, apologies, begging—it wasn't this.

"What did Osgood say that upset you so?" *And could you please put down that hammer?*

"I told you my brother was transported for theft," she said, turning a gimlet eye on him. "Papa just now confirmed that he allowed Adam to be charged and sent away because Papa thought he was protecting me, the actual culprit. Apparently, they *both* believed they were protecting me. Had they *asked* me, I would have told them I would rather have protected myself. I want to throw this hammer right through a window, Valerian. I want to hear glass shatter."

He went to the window, then stood back. "There's nobody below."

Emily positioned herself two yards from the window, wheeled her arm like a champion cricket pitcher, and let fly with the hammer. The bottom frame of the window smashed, the glass tinkling onto the flagstones below, followed by the soft thud of a heavy weight hitting turf.

"Now that we are both unarmed," Valerian said, "perhaps you could tell me what has sent you into such a rage."

"I *am* in a rage," she said, her expression satisfied as she surveyed the broken window and the spilled nails. "That is exactly the word. Are we still to be married?"

"That depends," Valerian said, "on why you were in a passionate embrace with some fellow at the livery yesterday, a fellow who uses a made-up name and addresses you as *dearest*."

"You saw us?"

"That is not a denial, Emily, or an explanation. Such is my besottedness that I would likely settle for either."

"I would never play you false, Valerian, and yet, I have lied to you. Your doubts are understandable. I am sorry for that." She picked up the empty bucket and gave it a stout heave through the top portion of the window, shattering that pane as well.

Her apology was a start, toward what, Valerian did not know. "Sometimes a falsehood is necessary for the sake of kindness. I wrote that in some book or other." A book nobody had read save perhaps Casriel. "Are you thinking of heaving me out the window next?" In her present mood, she could do it.

"If I tell you the truth, I am all but condemning to death somebody I have loved my whole life. If I refuse to confess the falsehood to you now, I lose a future with the only man to give me his honest regard. This room needs more windows."

The situation needed more light. "I came to you, Emily, because I want to hear the truth. I care for you deeply, and I want to hear what you have to say about your behavior in the livery stable."

He'd settled on that course as the birds had chorused their greeting to the dawn. Another pretty summer day in the country, following the most miserable night of his life.

"You are being the magistrate," she said, dropping onto a sofa draped in a Holland cover. "I am not a prisoner in the dock, Valerian."

He took the place beside her. "You have the power and the right to keep your own counsel, Emily. I know that. I came here to understand rather than accuse. I cannot imagine my future without you, cannot see how to get on in any meaningful... I love you."

Loved her with a fierce yearning, a bottomless affection, and a boundless respect, which made the present situation *unbearable*. Still, she sat silently beside him, very likely planning more property destruction, for which Valerian could never have arrested her, no matter how many charges Osgood Pepper brought.

"Emily, I will do all in my power to avoid sending anybody you care for to the gallows, short of breaking my oath as magistrate. Even if we cannot be man and wife, I would have the truth between us. What did I see in the livery stable?"

Emily gazed out the broken windows, where borders of jagged glass framed a pretty summer sky. "Why didn't you simply show yourself in the stable?"

Did her question bear a hint of relenting? "I nearly greeted that fellow with my fists, but I wanted time to consider what I saw. Through happenstance, I briefly met the man enjoying your embrace, and he seemed a gentleman. More to the point, I owe you discretion. Your dignity matters to me, and the encounter obviously left you upset." Valerian would have said *heartbroken*, but even honesty had to cede some ground to diplomacy.

Perhaps he should put that in a perishing unpublished book too.

"You could have broken off the engagement by letter," Emily said. "Could have sent your titled brother to inform me you'd departed for the capital. Another man would have taken the easier course. You are the most mannerly person I know, Valerian. Why confront me like this?"

She was angling for some confession, for some bit of his soul that eluded his notice. "We are having a discussion, Emily, rather than a confrontation. I can only ask you to trust me. If you tell me to take myself off and cease troubling you, that is exactly what I'll do."

"I lack your courage," she said, toeing at the scattered nails with her slipper. "You face the truth, while I busy myself selecting a parasol to match my reticule, and my idiot father hides in his office."

Valerian had heard Osgood Pepper's muttered insult—*Coward*—and had known it for a bitter old man's Parthian shot. Still, the epithet had stung. How much courage did it take to translate recipes in a dark little cottage? To teach dancing to rural swains? To set up ledgers for a commercial venture carried out by others? To settle the village squabbles?

"You think I'm brave?"

"I know you to be," Emily said. "You view life honestly, not through a lens of your own convenience. You deal in truth and don't put on airs or suffer fools. You simply march forward into any situation, confident of *yourself*. I don't know how you do it, but you inspire those around you to be a little better than they'd otherwise be. Or a lot better."

Emily's somewhat grumpy benediction settled on Valerian's heart like a warm blanket on a cold night. She cuddled against his side, drawing her feet up, and Valerian wrapped an arm around her shoulders. He could think now, could manage logic and reason once again. Emily would not play him false, but she was protecting somebody she cared for greatly.

He mentally sorted through the shards of facts, emotions, and impressions, matching edges and puzzling over missing pieces.

Well, of course. The obvious conclusion was upsetting, inconvenient, and better off ignored, but Emily had seen Valerian's nature more clearly than he'd seen it himself. Some men had the courage to ride into battle, sabers swinging. Others treated illness without regard for their own health. Others stood up in the Lords, knowing they'd be ostracized by the peerage for speaking the truth.

Valerian had been given the gift of wading through the messy, painful, complicated realities necessitated by ordinary relationships. His family was better for it, and Casriel had handed him the magistrate's job as a result.

The bloody, bedamned magistrate's job. "You met your brother Adam in the livery, didn't you? Met him and wished him farewell."

Emily nodded. He passed her his handkerchief—the soft old handkerchief that wasn't for show—and then she began to cry.

"DORNING IS PAYING another call at an ungodly early hour." Tobias had taken the precaution of shooing the clerks from the office, something Osgood was unlikely to even notice lately. "I suspect the almighty special license has arrived."

"The Earl of Casriel has pigeons," Caleb replied, sprinkling sand across an offer to purchase cloth from an Italian silk trader. "We ought to have some pigeons if we're to be stuck out here in Beelzebub's hog wallow for much longer." He rose and closed the door. "Have you confirmed that you saw Adam Pepper in the village, and if so, has he had the good sense to decamp for parts unknown?"

Caleb clearly hoped that was the case, while Tobias prided himself on a more ruthless sense of order.

"If Emily is ever to have any peace of mind, Caleb, if she's to raise a family with her doting Dorning, she needs to know her brother won't bother her again."

"Next, you'll say we did Adam a favor by putting him on that transport ship, and I doubt Emily considers it a bother to lay eyes on her only sibling for the first time in five years."

A conscience was a fine thing, in moderation. "They had a touching reunion yesterday, and one can only hope they didn't spend too much of their time together parsing out the details of Adam's conviction. I've made arrangements for Adam to be escorted to Portsmouth, where he will be given the opportunity to sign on to a ship of the line as a landsman facing prosecution."

Caleb twiddled his pen between his palms, making the feather twirl. "And if he declines that option?"

Offering a stint in the Navy in lieu of a criminal sentence was a common practice among rural magistrates. Everyone benefited, in theory—the miscreant avoided incarceration, the Navy avoided the distasteful practice of impressment, and the local jail was spared the burden of another mouth to feed. Peacetime meant the press gangs had less to do, but because of Britannia's determination to rule the waves, willing recruits with some experience at sea could still find a berth.

"If Adam rejects a post on a naval vessel," Tobias said, "then he has chosen to take his chances with the law. A few years in the Navy never hurt a fellow in good health. The seamen are reasonably well fed, the Navy isn't fighting any wars at present, and Adam is well acquainted with life at sea."

Caleb set aside the pen and rose. "Sailors die of scurvy, Tobias. The poor sods are always dying of scurvy, or plague, or typhus, or whatever scourges afflict foreign ports. They are lost at sea, they are taken captive by pirates."

"Your belated display of conscience ceases to be entertaining, Caleb. Adam is healthy, and he's spent plenty of time in foreign ports already. If he was going to succumb to disease, he would be dead by now. My men will accost him on the road to Portsmouth this afternoon, and we needn't fear any awkward father-and-son reunions."

Caleb took the place behind Osgood's massive desk. "Why not allow that reunion? They can agree it was all a misunderstanding, Adam can be about his business, and nobody need die of a dread disease. I don't think Adam will implicate Emily, not at this late stage."

"Of course he won't." Tobias spoke as gently as he could when addressing a dunderhead. "He will implicate *you*."

"*I* didn't sign anything," Caleb retorted. "I doubt you did either, but you were the one who suggested Emily was at fault. I've had five years to consider the matter and five years to consider Emily. She's not a thief. It's more likely *you* spun that tale to cover up your own criminal wrongdoing."

"By the throne of heaven, I ought to call you out for that."

Caleb picked up a silver letter opener engraved in Celtic knot patterns. "You are planning on having a man all but impressed, a man whom we strongly suspect to be innocent, whose downfall gained us much good fortune, and now you want to meet *me* on the field of honor?"

He turned the letter opener end over end, the silver gleaming. "The country air is making you daft, Tobias. I did not forge Osgood's signature, you claim you didn't either, and Adam is also likely innocent. That leaves Emily—whom I personally have come to doubt as a suspect—or Osgood himself as the author of this drama. The question is why, and what shall we do about it now?"

Caleb was a glib liar and a competent forger, at least where Osgood's signature was concerned. Nonetheless, if he *had* falsified that bank draft all those years ago, he should have been well away from Dorset on any pretext he could summon, given Adam's reappearance.

And yet, Caleb had much to gain by sticking to his guise of innocence, if he was the guilty party.

"Who signed the bank draft matters little at this late date," Tobias said. "Somebody wanted Adam out of the country five years ago, and they achieved their aim. For his own sake, the sooner Adam is sent packing the better, before he can point any fingers at you, me, Jacob, or Emily."

"Good of you to think of the lady now, Tobias. I own I am touched by your consideration."

Before Caleb could embroider on his insults, Osgood pushed through the door. "Where are my clerks, and why are you two idling about when there's work to be done?"

Caleb rose from the seat behind the desk. "We were discussing a remove to London, though of course, we defer to your judgment on the matter. Emily's nuptials are likely to be uppermost in your mind, but I'm sure you'll be returning to Town once she's settled. I am happy to trot up to London and ensure the warehouse office is in readiness for a resumption of business from that location. The weather looks to hold fair for a few days, and I'm happy to make the journey now."

"As am I," Tobias said. "In fact, Caleb and I could travel together. Just say the word, and we'll be packed to leave in the next hour."

HAWTHORNE AND MARGARET had taken the children into Dorset for a day of shopping, meaning Valerian had only one brother left in whom he could confide—the worst of the lot for present purposes.

"I must speak in hypotheticals, Casriel, but your full attention would be appreciated."

"I'm listening." Casriel continued to sort through a stack of correspondence.

He was half listening, which was perhaps meant as a sop to Valerian's dignity. "I am faced with a choice. I took an oath as magistrate to uphold the law without respect to a person's station or standing. I have also offered marriage to a woman whom I esteem greatly. I cannot uphold my magistrate's oath without serving that lady a devastating blow, which I am loath to do. She has entrusted the matter to me, and I hardly know... Have you heard a word I've said?"

Casriel propped his boots on the edge of his desk and tossed a folded and sealed epistle across the blotter.

"Before I forget, that came for you yesterday from Worth Kettering. I didn't realize he was investing on your behalf."

"He would be, except I haven't sent him any funds to invest." Valerian stuffed the letter into his pocket, because the missive was very likely from Jacaranda rather than Worth. She was doubtless exhorting her brother to jaunt up to Town and admire her offspring. "Grey, the contretemps I'm in is serious. If I betray my oath of office, I bring shame upon myself and my family."

Mention of family ought to inspire Casriel to put aside his damned bills and letters. Instead, he hefted a package wrapped in heavy brown paper. The paper was torn, and no ribbon or string held it closed.

"This came for you too. It's your manuscript."

Valerian paced before the desk, even knowing that a gentleman did not pace or fidget lest he disturb those around him.

Casriel could use some damned disturbing. "I do not care to discuss my book just at the moment." Nor to speculate on why his brothers had returned it to him.

"You don't?" Casriel spared him a glance over the rims of his glasses. "I started reading your tome—not simply skimming a page here and there. I ought not, when I have work to do, but you did put in a few hours with the writing of the damned thing. I've never regarded manners in the light you present them, as consideration, as kindness to one's fellows, a duty of decency and respect to all of the Creator's handiwork. I like that notion much better than a set of arbitrary rules by which we judge each other."

"Grey, for God's sake, forget the rubbishing book!" Valerian snatched the manuscript away from his brother, who was grinning at him like a sibling much in need of pummeling.

"You shouted," Casriel said. "*At me.*"

Valerian set the sheaf of papers on the mantel rather than smack his brother with it. "Consider hypothetical facts: A man is transported for felony theft. He forges a ticket of leave two years before his sentence is up, travels under false colors, and returns to England, ostensibly to bid farewell to his dying father."

Casriel was no longer smiling. He sat up, his boots thumping to the floor. "Go on."

"The father is not, as it happens, dying, but that hardly matters. His death did at one point appear imminent. The punishment for the transported fellow's return to England is a noose. If I do as the law requires, I will break the heart of a woman who nearly lost her father not long ago and who has very little family to call her own. She maintains that the convict is innocent, but she cannot tell me who the real culprit is, and that hardly matters once a sentence has been passed."

Casriel held his glasses up toward the window, then polished the lenses with an embroidered handkerchief. "So as long as I use the correct fork, I can say anything I damned well please at table?"

"*What* are you going on about?"

"Yonder book." He gestured with his glasses. "The author makes a good case that gentlemanly deportment is not a set of behaviors, but rather, a set of values that inspire behaviors. Seems to me if a man's been wrongfully convicted, then sending him to the gallows for being a dutiful son is rather harsh."

"The law is harsh, the better to deter malefactors."

"How many times did Sycamore steal from Oak's collection of nude drawings?"

"Countless times."

"And yet," Casriel said, donning his spectacles again, "Papa punished our baby brother severely. Made him memorize Bible verses by the score, confined him to the countess's sitting room by the hour, put him on bread-and-cheese rations, denied him time in the saddle. Did Sycamore stop peeking and snitching?"

Casriel was making a point with this parable. "Cam grew diabolically clever at his sneaking and peeking."

"Precisely, so let us dispense with the fiction that harsh punishments serve some higher purpose, particularly when applied to those who are innocent. You can simply turn a blind eye to this man's violation of parole, and the world will be no worse off."

"No, I cannot. I took an oath and a man's word is his bond. I am not wealthy, Grey. I am not particularly learned. I have not studied for the bar like Ash. I cannot paint wondrous canvases like Oak. I have no aptitude for husbanding the botanicals, as Hawthorne does, and God knows I cannot turn one penny into three, as Worth Kettering manages to do in his sleep. I am merely that unremarkable species we refer to as a gentleman, but my honor has value to me. An oath is an oath."

"You are a capital fellow—" Casriel began, rising.

"I did not take an oath to be a capital fellow!"

The earl sat back down. "That's twice now you've hollered at me. Very well, I shall holler back, albeit figuratively. Papa told me that you are the only one of his offspring—the only one of the *nine* of us, Valerian—whom he never worried over. He was convinced you would succeed at anything you turned your hand to, and forever be a credit to his house. I will deny the admission in the company of our siblings, but Papa was in this regard absolutely correct."

Valerian stared at him, even as he wondered what this recitation had to do with bringing charges against Emily's brother.

"When did Papa—?"

Grey waved him to silence. "On any occasion when he'd had more than a bit to drink, and our brothers had been particularly troublesome. *Valerian is a son any father would be proud of. Why can't you lot be more like Valerian?* I heard that question frequently, and resolved to become more like my mannerly, decent, self-possessed, younger brother."

Valerian sank into the chair across from the desk, an unexpected warmth filling his heart. "He saw me. He knew I was there." Perhaps Papa hadn't known Valerian had been spying in that tree all those years ago, but Papa had *seen* him, nonetheless.

"We all see you," Grey continued. "You are a capital fellow who always seems to know how to go on in the midst of controversy. You sort out the haying crews before they come to blows. You sort out your brothers *while* they are coming to blows. You are universally liked and respected, but you don't appear to share in the general opinion of your own worthiness.

"Be that as it may," he went on, "whatever choice you make in the present instance, I will support you and proudly claim you as my brother, as you have claimed us in return, no matter how vexatious we are. I suspect your Emily has chosen the same course, which explains why she confided in you."

Grey hadn't raised his voice, but he'd raised an interesting point.

"Emily once said that I always look for how to be of service." Valerian had not regarded that as much of a compliment, likening him to an overeager footman, but he'd been wrong to be so dismissive. "I believe the greatest service I could render to my prospective wife and in-laws, and also to the cause of justice generally, is to determine who *ought* to have been on that transport ship, if Adam Pepper was not the appropriate party."

Casriel once again propped his boots on the desk and resumed sorting mail. "If I were this *hypothetically* transported fellow, I'd be on the fastest ship out of Portsmouth I could find. He likely knows more about the situation than he thinks he does, not that you ever mentioned him to me by name."

Valerian rose, grabbed his brother by the ears, kissed him on the crown, and marched for the door.

"Adam who? I know of no Adam. Please inform me when the special license has arrived."

His hand was on the door latch when Casriel picked up a thick epistle. "I do believe this is it."

"Guard that document with your life, Casriel, and prepare to stand up with me before sunset tomorrow, or get me mortally drunk in the alternative."

Casriel saluted with the license. "Your servant, Valerian, as ever."

Valerian didn't bother bowing. He made for the stables at a dead run.

TO DETERMINE what was needed in a situation meant studying that situation, not merely spouting platitudes and bowing to a proper depth. As Valerian galloped back to Pepper Ridge, he sorted through what facts he had and what answers he needed. Rather than take the turn that would lead Clovis down the bridle path connecting to the Pepper Ridge property, Valerian instead sent his horse onto the road that led to the village—and to Adam Pepper's last known whereabouts.

Thirty yards later, Valerian encountered Mr. Prentiss Ogilvy and a trio of his disreputable minions. One of the fellows held the reins of a dog cart, his compatriot beside him on the bench, while Ogilvy and the fourth man were mounted on skinny hacks. The four of them were lounging in the shade around a bend in the road half a mile outside the village.

"What a coincidence," Valerian mused, drawing Clovis to a halt.

"Mr. Dorning." Ogilvy tugged at his hat brim. "Fine day to take the air, isn't it?"

"Fine day to loiter on the road," Valerian countered, "when last I heard, you were to be looking for honest work in Portsmouth."

The fellow in the cart who wasn't holding the reins casually propped his fist on his hip, which had the effect of pushing back the flap of his jacket. Valerian would have bet his favorite cravat pin that a knife was tucked into the man's waistband, just out of sight.

"Nevertheless, Mr. Dorning," Ogilvy replied, "we're here now and free to remain here for as long as we please. A prudent man would leave us in peace." Ogilvy smiled, though his eyes held a whipped dog's resentment and a rat's cunning.

Would Osgood Pepper arrange for his own son to fall into Ogilvy's hands?

Yes, he would. More likely Pepper sought to forcibly banish his son from England rather than have him turned over to the magistrate. But was Osgood Pepper foolish enough to trust this lot yet again?

Valerian didn't think so. "In point of fact, Mr. Ogilvy, you are in error regarding your rights. You, sir,"—Valerian gestured to the fellow on the cart—"turn out your pockets, please."

The man shot a questioning gaze at Ogilvy, who sat up straighter in the saddle. "He'll do no such thing. Smithy there is minding his own business, while you are intruding into matters you'd best leave alone."

"There you are mistaken," Valerian said. "As *magistrate*, I am duty-bound to inquire of all strangers regarding their means and intentions. Vagrants are still subject to arrest, you know, and some backward-thinking souls yet believe itinerant unfortunates should be whipped at the cart's tail and forcibly returned to their home shires."

"I don't fancy no whippin'," the man muttered. "You never said nothin' about the king's man stickin' his beak into this job, Ogilvy."

"Hush," Ogilvy snapped.

"Well, you dint," the fellow on horseback said. "Had me enough of the lash when I was at sea."

"As a courtesy," Valerian said to Ogilvy, "I will provide you some advice. Clovis here looks like a sleepy beast, but he's quite fit, more than a match for the nags you've hired. I can outride you should you attempt to elude me as I go about a lawful inquiry. I'd enjoy the exercise, to be honest, and enjoy even more the legal puzzle of what to charge you with. Assaulting or otherwise bothering a magistrate on his appointed rounds is a serious error in judgment, fleeing and eluding are equally ill-informed. Some might regard those bad choices lethal errors."

The fellow on horseback edged his mount away from Ogilvy's.

"We are as free to take the air as any other Englishmen," Ogilvy retorted. "That's the law."

"But you aren't taking the air, are you?" Valerian replied as the fellow on the cart whispered something to his friend holding the reins. "You're up to no good, and I've caught you at it. Again. Whatever you've been paid"—he sent a meaningful look at the minions—"or *promised*, you are already known in this area as untrustworthy and unemployed. Three of you have come back here with empty pockets and no employment. That makes for three easy arrests, and I will have pointed conversations with all three of my suspects before deciding how to charge the fourth."

"No more arrests," the man holding the reins said. "I'm done with that, Ogilvy. My missus will beat me to flinders if I'm sent up again." He backed the cart awkwardly onto the verge, while the man on horseback directed his mount into the road.

"I'm for Portsmouth," he said. "Shoulda known better than to take up with you again, Ogilvy. You don't pay, and yonder swell is right. You're crooked. Worse than that, you're lazy, takin' all the blunt and leaving the lot of us to fend for ourselves."

The cart creaked off in an easterly direction, the horseman plodding at its side.

"The smart thing to do is to go with them," Valerian said, "or I could arrest you for fraud upon Osgood Pepper. You never did transport his used books to Portsmouth, and yet, you charged him for haulage."

That was pure speculation on Valerian's part, but a simple enough conclusion.

"Damn your meddling," Ogilvy retorted. "Damn all you high-and-mighty prigs and your—"

Valerian crossed his hands over the pommel of his saddle and surveyed the pretty summer sky.

"—self-important, nosy, arrogant poking about. You think the world exists for you, but you've never had to work for your living. You've never known what it is to have no place in life, nowhere you're fussed over and made welcome. You and your fancy—"

A pair of horsemen trotted around the bend, substantial bundles rolled behind each man's saddle.

Caleb Booth and Tobias Granger drew rein, and Ogilvy's features underwent a progression of emotions. An obsequious smile died aborning, a flash of consternation followed, a sneer came after that, then a shrug.

"To hell with the lot of you," Ogilvy said, driving his heels into his horse's sides. He jostled off in the same direction the cart had taken.

"Gentlemen," Valerian said, "good day. Are you also intent on enjoying the fine Dorset air, or are felony arrests in order? Perhaps we ought to share an ale at the coaching inn while we discuss that question?"

Valerian had no idea which of them was responsible for hiring Ogilvy—very likely the pair had conspired, or maybe they'd done Osgood Pepper's bidding—but it was Caleb Booth who first turned his horse back toward the village.

"A good summer ale is not to be missed," he said. "Come along, Tobias."

"You go without me," Tobias said. "I haven't spent nearly enough time appreciating the beauty of rural Dorset."

Caleb appeared to consider that, while yet another horseman rounded the bend, a bundle of worldly goods also affixed to the back of his saddle.

"Mr. Addison Topsail," Valerian said. "A pleasant day to you. Granger, Booth, and I were off to the coaching inn for a friendly chat. I suggest you join us, there being ruffians loose on the road hereabouts, and I further suggest we make our destination Pepper Ridge rather than the inn."

Mr. Topsail studied the road. "Ruffians?"

"At least four of them," Valerian said, "and I suspect they are armed. They drove a somewhat disreputable though sizable dog cart, and the compartment under the seat would easily, though not comfortably, hold an unconscious grown man. One would not wish such a fate on an otherwise blameless wayfarer."

Valerian could make Adam Pepper no promises, but he owed it to Emily and to his conscience to determine who was blameless and who was not.

Tobias Granger shifted his horse to the edge of the road, and Adam Pepper swung his mount around to block the path.

"To Pepper Ridge," he said, "and if you are tempted to bolt, Tobias, please know that for me to be the pursuer rather than the pursued would be a sweet relief, and my hunter can outrun anything in the shire without breaking a sweat."

"Anything," Valerian said, kneeing Clovis forward, "except the king's justice. To Pepper Ridge, gentlemen."

The three of them trotted along behind him as he led them to the bridle path winding past the Pepper Ridge garden. They reached the stable yard in silence and handed the horses over to grooms who scurried into the stables without offering so much as a greeting.

CHAPTER FIFTEEN

Valerian had spent a precious quarter hour with Emily in the master suite's sitting room, patting her hand and assuring her all would be well. Then he'd trotted away to Dorning Hall, claiming he needed to consult with the earl.

Emily had not liked the sound of that, but then, how many magistrates were faced with the challenge of arresting prospective family members? Nonetheless, Valerian had asked for her trust, and what was marriage, but an exercise in mutual trust?

She made another circuit of the music room, which had a good view of both the front drive and the side garden, though no matter how hard she stared at the white shell lane circling the fountain, no handsome horseman on a big bay gelding appeared.

"If you are determined to marry your current preoccupation," Briggs said, "you would be well advised to learn to cope with his absences. Men have better things to do than while away their days dancing attendance on spoiled young ladies."

Adam's life was in peril. Papa's life had recently been in peril. A special license was on the way from London, and Papa was withholding the marriage settlements for reasons Emily could not fathom

—and Briggs thought the issue was schoolgirl impatience over a doting swain's absence?

"For the past five years," Emily said, swishing past the great harp, "I have *coped*. Even before that, even while I was at school, I coped. I coped with my mother's death. I coped with betrayal from my first love. I coped with my brother being sent to the ends of the earth for a crime he did not commit. I coped with a Society where I did not fit in. I coped with waltzing partners who loathed me. I coped with my father excluding me from his business even as he expected me to serve as his hostess."

Briggs remained on the piano bench, calmly sorting music. "A second coachman is nobody's first love, and a lady never pace—"

"Briggs, I am to marry the son of an earl, which suggests I'm lady like enough for those whose opinions matter."

Briggs set a Mozart sonata on the music stand, happy, confectionary music that Emily wanted to tear into a thousand pieces. Smashing glass, kicking over a bucket of nails, and weeping all over Valerian had unleashed some dragon inside her, and though the dragon was angry, it was also a confident, determined beast.

"Had you attended more closely to my lectures," Briggs retorted, "you might not have to settle for an impecunious younger son. Your father is disappointed in this match, Emily. It's taking a toll on his health, if you ask me."

Which I did not. "Papa's guilty conscience is likely taking a toll on his health, and heaven knows it's taking a toll on my spirits too. What plans have you made for your future, Briggs?"

Emily wanted Briggs gone, which was unsettling. Briggs was a link to the past, to the time before Adam's supposed crime had rent the family asunder, to the years before Papa had grown so ill. To send her packing now was ungracious, *unladylike*.

And yet, some instinct warned Emily that Briggs needed a nudge out the door if not a heave out the window.

"Until you have taken up housekeeping with Mr. Dorning, I will make no plans for my future. To do so would display an optimism regarding your nuptial choice that I do not feel. He is pockets to let, has little presence in Town, and few prospects other than some farm or other. When you come home to your Papa, hat in hand, I will still be here to ensure you have proper companionship, though I vow your present prowling about will prostrate me with a megrim before this day is through."

I'll show you a megrim. Emily trailed her fingers over the harp strings, the result a discordant arpeggio. "Have you done the one thing I asked you to do, Briggs?"

Briggs pretended a frown of puzzlement. Emily knew that expression, knew precisely how long Briggs would hold it before the frown became a vaguely bewildered, questioning gaze.

"I beg your pardon?"

"I asked you to locate the terms of my mother's marriage settlements, and you said you'd do it."

Briggs put her hands in her lap and bowed her head. "I will, I most assuredly will, but lately, the household has been at such sixes and sevens that your request slipped my mind."

Emily closed the lid over the piano keys lest Briggs think to afflict her with some dirge or lament. "Nothing slips your mind. You have Debrett's nearly memorized. You know every person who has been granted vouchers at Almack's for the past decade. If I must write to the family solicitors and forge Papa's signature, I will do it to learn the terms of those settlements."

All pretensions to martyrdom disappeared. "You mustn't. No forging of signatures, Emily. Your father would learn of it and be appalled. Your word to me on this."

Emily stalked away, taking the place in the center of the music room lest she be tempted to smash the violins, violas, and guitars hanging on the walls.

"Does everybody think me a felon? Either you tell me the terms of Mama's marriage settlements, or I won't need to forge Papa's signature. I will have my prospective husband-*the-magistrate* confront my father-*the-liar* and force Papa to disclose the sums I am entitled to under the terms of Mama's settlements."

Briggs rose, hands fisted against her skirts. "How could you contemplate turning the law on your own father? To compel Osgood to adhere to those old agreements would be unseemly."

Where was a bucket of nails and a stout hammer when a woman needed to make a point? "For Papa to sign marriage agreements decades ago, then break his word to his only daughter now, when he neither needs the money nor has reason to object to my choice of spouse, is *beyond unseemly*. My mother's family would have made provision for her unborn children at the time of her marriage, particularly her daughters. Mama was an heiress, and half the purpose of marriage settlements is to ensure family money is used for the well being of family members."

No girl from a family of any means was ignorant of the workings of marriage settlements. Mama had doubtless inherited money or property from her own antecedents. If her arrangements were typical, that wealth had been put in trust for her children upon her death, and Emily would do the same for her own offspring.

"This is not the right time," Briggs said, re-tidying the music that was already neatly stacked. "When your father is less upset, when your own situation is resolved, then perhaps the topic of settlements can be revisited. Timing matters, Emily. How often have I had to remind you of that?"

"Timing matters exceedingly, which is why you will go straight up to your room, locate the terms of Mama's settlements, and deliver them to me today, or I will see you and your effects put on the next stage for wherever in Britain you choose to go. Don't think Papa will stop me from doing it either. I am beyond vexed with him, and he knows it."

Briggs left off fussing with the music. "*You* are beyond vexed? *You are beyond vexed?* For years, I've put up with your moods and missteps, your ingratitude and unwillingness to heed my guidance. I've tried to protect you from the repercussions of your upbringing, guided you to the best of my ability, and now you are *vexed*? Emily Pepper, I am ashamed of you."

A few weeks ago, even a few days ago, that most cutting of judgments would have destroyed Emily's resolve. Now, she had Valerian's example to fortify her. Noise, bluster, and uncomfortable emotions were inevitable if a confrontation was to be productive.

Emily ran a finger down the mantel and rubbed the dust away with her thumb. "Very dramatic, Briggs, and not at all to the point. You are evading direct questions, breaking your word to me, and trying to sabotage my marriage before I've spoken my vows. Consult your diaries, or start packing. In fact, I can send Jasper and Tom to assist you, if you like. They are hard workers and entirely to be trusted with whatever task they're given."

The consternation in Briggs's gaze was real this time and more than a little satisfying.

"I am tempted to wash my hands of you," Briggs said, starting for the door. "I truly am."

"Then jot down the settlement terms before you go and tell me where I'm to send your final wages."

That occasioned a sniff and a slammed door.

"A lady never slams doors," Emily mused aloud to the empty room. "Perhaps Valerian should put that in one of his lovely books."

Emily would not miss Briggs, a realization that occasioned neither sadness nor guilt. Briggs had been more finishing governess than companion, and she had grossly overstayed the need for her particular talents.

"Will I miss Papa?" Emily murmured. Her next confrontation would be with Osgood, and for that, Valerian's steadying presence would be appreciated. Somebody had to unravel the crime that had been committed five years ago—the crime committed against Adam, not by him.

∾

VALERIAN KNEW two things as he herded Tobias, Caleb, and Adam up the steps to the Pepper Ridge front door. First, the mystery regarding Adam's guilt had to be solved. Second, Emily was owed the opportunity to hear those answers in person.

The lady herself stood at the foot of the main staircase, her expression wary. "I thought Tobias and Caleb left for London."

"On horseback," Valerian observed, "when a comfortable coach-and-four was available to them. I asked myself why that should be. Good day, Miss Pepper. I believe you know this fellow." He gestured to Adam, who was peering around at the foyer's appointments over Caleb's and Tobias's shoulders.

Emily nodded serenely, though to Valerian's eyes, her composure was underscored by a touch of pallor. "It appears we're to have a discussion," she said. "Shall I ring for tea?"

Emily might enjoy smashing a teapot and some saucers before the *discussion* was concluded. "Tea would be appreciated. The formal guest parlor is large enough to accommodate this gathering. Mr. Osgood Pepper and Miss Briggs should be summoned as well."

Emily spared the steps a fulminating glance. "I'll send a footman."

"If you'll excuse me," Tobias murmured, "I can fetch Miss Briggs."

Interesting bit of courtesy from a man who'd shown toweringly few manners on previous occasions.

"I think not," Valerian said. "The guest parlor, if you please." Had he been among his brothers, he would have cuffed the nearest sibling on the back of the head. But these were Emily's menfolk, and she deserved to do any cuffing the situation called for.

The parlor had sufficient seating, but rather than avail themselves of it, Caleb and Tobias remained standing. The room had only the one exit, and Valerian gestured Adam into the chair nearest the door. Emily's brother would stop anybody intent on bolting.

When Emily joined them, she took one of two wing chairs near the fire. "Briggs will be along shortly. I told the footman to haul her here bodily if need be."

Briggs arrived a moment later, looking as annoyed as a hen dethroned from her nesting box. "What is the meaning—*Adam?*" She sank onto a tufted chair near the door.

Adam rose and bowed. "Miss Briggs."

A footman brought in the tea service, and Valerian took the chair opposite Emily's and poured out while he considered theories. Who benefited from having Adam sent to the Antipodes? Osgood, Tobias, and Caleb all benefited, while Emily did not. As for Briggs...

Osgood Pepper's arrival interrupted that speculation. "What the hell is going on here?"

"We're having a discussion," Emily said. "Valerian is pouring out. Have a seat, Papa."

Pepper had marched right past his son when he'd stormed into the parlor. Adam remained standing by the door, and Pepper caught sight of him apparently for the first time in five years.

"You're here," Osgood said, studying his son intently. His countenance gave away no emotion, no joy, no relief, no sorrow.

"Hello, Papa. I'm pleased to see you looking well."

Pepper blinked several times. "You are looking quite well, too, you fool."

"Papa." Emily's tone was mild, even sweet. "Have a seat. Now."

Pepper sank into a corner of the sofa. "Whatever course you embark upon, Dorning," he said, "I ask that you undertake it with discretion. Old rumors were flying around London when we decamped several months ago. After all these years, I have no idea why ancient family scandal should rear its ugly head so recently, but my business dealings rely on a reputation for scrupulous probity."

"Your son's life hangs in the balance," Valerian replied. "Your daughter's happiness might well be at stake, and you are concerned with your *business dealings?*"

"My business is all I have to leave them."

"Don't be foolish," Briggs muttered. "Your health is quite improved, and your children have no need of your funds."

Emily picked up her cup and saucer, holding them before her. "You'd know that *how*, Briggs?"

Briggs scooted around on the cushion, again bringing to mind the image of a broody hen. "Your mother left you both well-off. The money has been collecting interest for years. I did review her settlement terms. I simply wasn't ready to reveal them to you without first consulting your father."

Emily took a slow sip of tea, her very calm portending doom for the porcelain—or perhaps for Briggs.

"Veronica," Osgood said softly, "that will do."

"That," Valerian said, "won't nearly do. Miss Briggs has removed yet another motive for Adam to have forged any bank drafts. His mother left him funds, which he very likely learned of when he came of age. When do the funds disburse?"

Briggs sent Osgood a look that appeared to convey the sentiment *you tell them, or I will.*

"For Adam," Osgood said, gaze returning to his son, "the funds were to be made available on his twenty-eighth birthday, which has passed. For Emily, upon her marriage or her twenty-eighth birthday, whichever first occurs. I dared not risk sending the money to Botany Bay, travel over that distance being perilous for anything of value."

Caleb Booth was studying the carpet, Tobias Granger the crown molding. They either knew of these terms or had no reason to care about them.

"And these funds were in addition to any pin money Emily could claim?" Valerian asked.

Osgood nodded, and he, too, appeared to become fascinated with a slightly worn carpet.

Adam sank into the chair near the door. "So Emily had no need to forge a bank draft. Papa similarly had no motivation, unless he took me so much into dislike he'd risk my life on a transport ship, which I am loath to believe."

"I took every precaution," Osgood retorted, his veined hand grip-ping the arm of the sofa, "every measure, every possible safeguard for your welfare. The damned governor of the colony intervened on your behalf, and I hate to tell you what that cost me."

"The damned governor of the colony shouldn't have *had* to inter-vene on my behalf," Adam said, "but I grasped that you and I were protecting Emily."

"You most assuredly were not," Emily said, tapping her spoon against her teacup. "Not for a moment, Adam. I had as little to gain by forging Papa's signature as you did. For Caleb and Tobias, the same cannot be said."

She smiled at them, teeth gleaming over her cup and saucer.

Valerian moved the tea tray a few inches closer to her knee. "Booth, Granger, you both had motive and opportunity. This very day, I found you headed away from the village on horseback, rather than taking the Pepper family coach and four to London. The coachman would have reported your destination back to your employer. That suggests you weren't aiming directly for the capital. What say you?"

"We wanted to have a look at a merchantman for sale in Portsmouth," Tobias replied. "We were bound for London, but I suggested a detour to Caleb that we could make discreetly without arousing Osgood's ire. Redesigning a ship is not a cheap or simple undertaking, and an inspection of the vessel itself was in order."

"No," Emily said, "it wasn't. I had a look at the plans you drew up, as did a master shipwright. He scotched your foolish notions thoroughly."

"Give me the name of the ship," Valerian said. "I'll verify that it's in port and that it's a merchantman for sale. Mr. Pepper's trust in you will be vindicated, and we can focus our attention on the events of five years ago."

A tense silence ensued. Nobody was drinking the tea except Emily, and Briggs was perched on the very edge of her seat.

"It won't wash," Caleb said, tossing himself onto the sofa. "We were going straight to London, where I suspect Tobias was about to withdraw every penny he's hoarded away for the past five years, leaving me to make awkward explanations, except I haven't anything to explain."

"Try," Emily said. "Try very hard, Caleb."

He sat forward, his forearms propped on his thighs, his gaze on the empty hearth. "Here is what I know. Somebody signed Osgood's name to a bank draft for three hundred and fifty pounds. The bank draft was blank on Friday morning, the funds were in Adam's keeping by the end of the day, and Adam took it to the bank to be cashed. Osgood swears he didn't sign that draft. Tobias says he didn't either—not that he's much of a forger. That left Emily or Adam as the culprit, both of whom know their father's signature well. I wasn't about to point a finger at Emily. Tobias and I agreed that Emily must not be implicated."

"I had no motive," Emily snapped. "Tobias had more motive than I did. He was a former clerk earning a manager's wage, with few funds to invest and a long, hard climb to amassing any sort of fortune. You had more motive than I did, Caleb. The clerks in the counting room had such a motive, but Adam did not."

"How was I to know that?" Caleb retorted. "How was I to know that your pin money was adequate, that you had no private debts you could not mention to your father? How was I to know Adam wasn't frittering away his funds on vice or gaming? Tobias is too careful to commit such a blunder, and I'm not brave enough."

"You're brave," Tobias said. "Sometimes stupidly so."

"Thank you," Caleb replied, smiling slightly. "While you are merely stupid, but not stupid enough to steal from the hand that literally feeds us. You were convinced Emily was to blame, though—an erroneous conclusion, it seems."

"Perhaps even a stupid conclusion," Valerian mused. "Mr. Pepper, what have you to say about this matter?"

"I didn't sign that bank draft, but I made a holy commotion when I learned somebody had. That was foolish of me. The clerks heard me, and they were questioned accordingly, but if one thing is certain in my business, it's that the competition has spies everywhere. I had to hold somebody accountable, or I would have lost the custom of the Italians, and at the time they were crucial to my endeavors."

They had also very likely been under a French blockade, meaning Osgood had been doing business with smugglers. Not exactly a genteel lot.

"Then why," Adam said quietly, "hold *your only son* accountable for another's wrongdoing? If you were convinced of Emily's guilt, why not confront her and give her an opportunity to explain?"

Emily's gaze grew thoughtful, then she set down her cup and saucer. "Papa is protecting somebody," she said, "but that somebody isn't me."

Valerian had reached the same conclusion nearly at the same moment Emily had. He passed Emily his cup and saucer, and noticed that Adam was standing directly in front of the only exit.

"Briggs," Valerian said, "you need not admit to anything, but after all these years, airing the truth would be a profound courtesy to those inconvenienced by your lies."

VALERIAN SPOKE GENTLY, not as a man passing judgment, but as a man pronouncing *sentence* on one already condemned. Emily suspected his courtesy was not for the criminal—for Briggs was clearly the culprit—but for Emily herself, for Adam, for Papa, and even a little bit for Tobias and Caleb.

And maybe a little bit as a nod to the inherent gentlemanliness owed even to a felon.

Briggs spread her soft, pale hands in her lap, the hands of a lady, and yet, Briggs was not a lady, was she?

"Veronica, hold your tongue," Papa said. "We can attribute this whole contretemps to a grave misunderstanding."

Briggs met his gaze, volumes being exchanged between them in silence. Emily could parse out the despair and the regret, but other emotions too subtle for labels hung in the air as well.

"I needed the money," Briggs said. "My brother was in the Marshalsea prison, already showing signs of consumption. If I didn't get him out of there, he would have been lost to me. You lot can't know what it's like to lose your only sibling. No man wanted me for a wife, my parents were long gone, and Jemmy was the only kin I had."

Osgood shook his head. "I would have—"

"No, you would not have, Osgood Pepper." Briggs's tone was more sad than angry. "You are eloquent on the topic of impecunious debtors. You give no quarter, unless it's in your commercial interest to do so. A judge's daughter goes free, but my brother was to rot away his life in a foul prison he had no hope of leaving."

"I do not make the laws," Osgood said. "I had to buy a property to even qualify to vote for the scoundrel of my choosing. I didn't put your brother in debt, but, Veronica, if you'd come to me, I would have made you a loan, something. You need not have tried to steal from me."

"You forged Papa's signature," Emily said, needing to hear an admission of guilt. "You had plenty of practice addressing invitations, as I did, and you saw a chance to solve your problems with the stroke of the pen. When would you have retrieved the money?"

"The safes are often left open," Briggs replied, "both here and in London. Failing that, Osgood always jots the combinations on the underside of his blotter. Retrieving the money on Sunday morning while the rest of the household was at services would have been easy enough."

Tobias and Caleb were quiet for once, while Valerian spoke up. "But the bank ledger would have shown the money withdrawn. How were you planning on hiding that fact?"

"I had asked Tobias to bring the weekly reckoning directly to me," she said. "I told him I wanted to use it to acquaint Emily with commercial ledgers. I could document the transaction half-illegibly, and nobody would have looked too closely."

Tobias looked uncomfortable. "Emily was already well acquainted with ledgers of every sort, and had she wished to peruse more ledgers, they were stacked six deep in the office cabinets. I was thus suspicious, but in any event, Osgood was at his desk early Saturday morning when the bank reckoning for the week arrived. I had no means of retrieving that document before he was poring over it. When the theft became apparent, I concluded Briggs was trying to protect Emily."

"And Briggs," Emily said, turning her gaze on her companion, "doubtless realized the advantage in fostering your error. Papa might well send an embezzling lady's companion to the gallows, but not his own daughter. Briggs, did you decide that if you were to lose your brother, I should also lose mine?"

"She pleaded with me," Osgood said. "Begged me not to pursue the matter, but Tobias had made a few remarks that implicated my own daughter. Emily has often copied my signature on social correspondence, on regrets, on any manner of documents. Emily was frequently my amanuensis for business correspondence and well knew my office routines. Then too, the clerks were alerted to the theft, as were Tobias and Caleb. What sort of merchant would I be if I allowed my own offspring to steal from me with impunity? An example had to be made."

And that was Papa, trying to talk himself out of blame for a stupid decision. "You could have made an example of a clerk, tossed him out without a character and had Tobias quietly slip him a few pounds. You are complicit in this, Papa. You never gave me a chance to speak for myself. You simply chose for me how the matter was to be resolved."

"And you chose for me too," Adam said. "Why, Papa? I denied my guilt, I'd never broken my word to you, and yet, you let me be put on a transport ship and sent to the ends of the earth."

"Did you good," Osgood said, chin coming up. "Look at you now. Hale and fit, possessed of more than a bit of blunt. You were bored witless with the business, and I wasn't about to slip off to some garret to slurp porridge so you could take over what I'd built with my own two hands. Caleb and Tobias were always trying to pit us against each other, and you were starting to run about with titled fellows and idle heirs I couldn't approve of."

"They were *my friends*," Adam shot back. "Young men from good families whom I'd met at school. That's precisely why you subjected me to university. Now they dare not acknowledge me on the street, even assuming I complete my sentence."

But Adam hadn't completed his sentence, and therein lay a terrible problem. "You sent my brother away for a crime he didn't commit," Emily said, "and you kept in your employ a woman who betrayed your trust. What will you do about that now, Papa?"

It wasn't really for Papa to say, there being a magistrate present. Emily darted a peek at Valerian, but his expression gave away nothing. He might have been enduring another tea tray with the new neighbors, so calm was his countenance. He even smiled at her ever so slightly.

I won't lose him over this. The relief of that realization was physical, a lightening of a heavy burden, and it gave Emily the courage to press for further answers.

"The rumors that started earlier in the year in Town," she said. "They originated with you, Briggs, didn't they?"

"Veronica?" Papa prodded.

She nodded. "Once Emily found a husband, I'd have no post. No reason to remain under your roof. I'd be just another aging companion in want of a position."

"So you encouraged me to wear the wrong dresses," Emily said, thinking back. "Engaged incompetent French tutors for me, suggested I walk out with the fortune hunters rather than the young men of means and character. You sabotaged my success socially to keep your salary."

Briggs looked away. "Not only to keep my salary. You would write me an excellent character, I know, and I might have found another post. I betrayed this family's trust in one regard, and sooner or later you'd find a spouse—witness, Mr. Dorning sits among us now. I simply wanted to be..."

Near Papa. Who'd almost died, while Briggs had watched and worried in silence.

Valerian held out a plate of cakes to Emily. She took one to be polite, but the gesture conveyed more than simple guest-parlor civility. The Peppers and their retainers were having a discussion, much to her surprise, a quiet, albeit sad, but honest discussion.

"When did you begin to suspect that Emily was not the guilty party?" Valerian asked, directing the question to Osgood.

"That took a while," Osgood said. "The wheels of justice turn swiftly when the matter is criminal. I was much taken up with ensuring Adam's passage would be safe and his situation as comfortable as I could make it. My suspicions eventually fell on Tobias and Caleb, but they weren't behaving any differently, and they are in their way loyal, if not to me, then to each other. They would not jeopardize long-term gain for the short-term return of three hundred and fifty pounds.

"Then Emily went through yet another London Season without securing a match. She's pretty, well dowered, smart... Any man should be proud to call her his wife. I am a mere merchant, heavily tainted with the smell of the shop, but I am a wealthy merchant. I control several seats in Parliament, and Emily's inheritance will be considerable. Somebody was interfering with her search for a spouse, and the most logical somebody put her feet under my table every night. By the time that realization dawned on me, I was quite ill, Adam had only another two years to serve, and the rumors regarding his crime had reached London.

"Worse yet," he went on, "in my desperation to convince everybody that the right culprit had been found, I adopted an attitude toward Adam appropriate to a betrayed father. I am sorry for that, son. Very sorry, but at the time, I thought I was safeguarding your sister."

"So you came to Dorsetshire," Valerian said. "To the back corner of nowhere, thinking to die in peace?"

Osgood's gaze returned to Adam. "Veronica told me Emily had been corresponding with Adam, and my eyes and ears in Botany Bay told me Adam had slipped the leash. I suspected he was coming home to set matters right with me, thinking me at death's door."

"You were at death's door," Emily interjected. "You could be again if the medication stops working."

"I was, but you and your stubborn determination to see me well prevailed. By then, all I could do was wait here to see if Adam had in fact violated his parole. The London rumors made decamping to the country a reasonable choice, and this place came up for sale."

"You owe Adam an apology, Papa," Emily said. "You owe me an apology, but the worse harm was done to my brother." Briggs owed Adam much more than an apology, though Emily refrained from pointing out the obvious.

Valerian chose a lemon tea cake. "Perhaps Adam ought to share his thoughts with us."

"I can forgive my father," Adam said, still standing like a sentry before the door. "He believed himself to be protecting Emily, as I believed myself to be. I am less charitably disposed toward Miss Briggs, who not only condemned me to the ignominy of transportation as a felon, but interfered with Emily's future as well."

Emily regarded her former companion, whom she'd once thought a formidable ally. "I leave the matter in your hands, Adam. My future could not be more promising, while yours will always carry the shadow of a wrongful conviction."

Papa had taken to examining his pocket watch, a plain gold article Emily's mother had given him. "Of course, I am sorry for having mistrusted my son. I am sorry for having believed the worst of you, too, Emily, but I'm not sure, given what I knew at the time, that I'd handle the matter any differently if allowed the chance."

"You might have told me of your misgivings," Adam said. "Might have written to me."

"I considered a good case of rage against your papa might help you endure the tribulations of a colonial life. Emily kept you informed of our situation, and I did not want you tempted to return prematurely, though here you are."

Adam ambled to the window and stood half in profile to Emily. "All these years, I thought I might one day hear my sister apologize for her crime and thank me for my sacrifice. That was all the reparation I sought—an acknowledgment of the harm she'd done me, an expression of remorse. Now I find Emily has also been sinned against. Perhaps the king's man has some idea how we're to go on, for I am at a loss when I cannot legally remain here in England."

Adam turned to regard Valerian, who lounged at his ease across the low table from Emily. "Mr. Dorning, you're the magistrate, and a criminal sits among us unpunished. What say you?"

Emily was glad Adam hadn't asked for her opinion, for Briggs had been both confidante and betrayer, both friend of a sort and felon.

"I'd like to hear your perspective too," Emily said. "Like Adam, I am torn by conflicting emotions, most of them unpleasant."

Though, amid all the chaos in her heart, one truth stood clear: Valerian would sort the situation out if anybody could, and then Emily would marry him, and by God, nobody would disturb their peace ever again.

CHAPTER SIXTEEN

Nothing Valerian had read in his brother's law books, nothing he'd encountered settling family or neighborhood squabbles, prepared him for the situation Veronica Briggs had wrought on the Pepper family.

The wronged parties were Adam, Emily, and Osgood, though none of them was willing to suggest a sentence for the wrongdoer.

"Miss Briggs," Valerian said, "have you any apologies to offer?"

Briggs glowered at him, which was to be expected. She was cornered, possibly facing a noose, and without allies.

"I am not sorry I tried to steal that money," she said. "My brother *died* in that stinking sewer of a prison, died miserable and alone because he trusted wealthy customers to pay their bills on time. His trust was repaid with suffering, death, and injustice. Any sister would have done the same."

"No," Valerian said, "she would not. Another sister might have asked Osgood Pepper for a loan, might have enlisted Pepper's aid to see those wealthy customers held accountable, might have admitted her wrongdoing before an innocent man was transported for it. Adam Pepper has spent five years as a convict, thousands of miles from what little family he has. Emily's social standing has been undermined by your meddling, and who knows, but Osgood's health was nearly ruined by worry over his children's well-being. You chose to commit a crime. You chose to lie about it."

That needed to be said. Aristocrats who failed to pay their bills were a sad fact of mercantile life, and if the debtor was titled, he could not be jailed for his cheating. That problem—and Valerian very much saw it as a problem—wouldn't be solved by letting Briggs get off with a scolding.

"I was desperate," Briggs said, her voice low. "I was new to my position. I had no hope Osgood would make me a loan that would have taken me years to pay back. For all I know, he would have turned me off on the spot, and then I'd be in worse circumstances than my brother."

"I would never—" Osgood began.

Emily held up a hand. "Hush, Papa. You turned off two companions in the space of a month before Briggs joined the household. I'm sure the hiring agency let her know that."

Valerian was not particularly interested in arguments that mitigated Briggs's guilt. "Are you sorry for any part of this situation?" he asked.

She gazed around the room like Boudica surveying the smoldering ruins of Roman Londinium. If she felt any remorse, that sentiment was nowhere evident in her expression.

"I am sorry I am poor," she said. "Sorry Emily was willing to settle for a younger son with little more than a farm to his name. I'm sorry Adam was too witless to stay where he belonged in Australia. I am sorry for much."

But she was not sorry for her victims, at least not that she'd admit, and that made Valerian's decision easier.

"*You* belong in Australia," he said. "I can charge you with forgery. I suspect Osgood would testify against you, and Caleb and Tobias would support his version of events by further recounting how you threw suspicion on both Adam and Emily. The charges alone would mean you will never find decent work again in Britain, and they would be valid charges. The quarter sessions aren't scheduled to start for weeks, and in the intervening time, you'd enjoy the hospitality of the local posting inn —unless Osgood is willing to maintain you under house arrest here."

Briggs's mouth closed with a snap. "You would not dare arrest me after all this time."

"I would dare. Your behavior offends the law, decency, and conscience. To allow you to lark about, wrapped in injured dignity and righteous ire, would be to offend common sense as well. You have committed multiple crimes and paid no price."

"Dorning," Osgood said, "is this really necessary?"

"No," Valerian said, sitting back. "If Briggs gives me her word that she'll put herself on a ship bound for Botany Bay and remain there for at least seven years, I'll consider the matter adequately addressed. I suspect Mr. Granger and Mr. Booth would willingly accompany her to the Antipodes."

Caleb glanced up sharply at Osgood. Tobias, interestingly, looked immediately to Caleb.

"New South Wales?" Caleb said. "You want us to escort Briggs to Australia?"

Emily's expression was arrested, while Caleb looked curious.

"I don't trust Briggs to keep her word and leave the country," Valerian said. "If she'll take Osgood's money while consigning his son to transportation and his daughter to disgraced spinsterhood, she bears supervision."

Tobias scrubbed a hand through his hair. "Australia? You expect me to travel halfway around the world, for what?"

Caleb took the seat Adam had vacated. "For adventure? For opportunity? Adam appears to have prospered, and he's a convict."

"He prospered," Tobias retorted, "because Osgood smoothed his way."

Adam crossed his arms. "I did well because I was lucky and

worked hard. Papa could bribe half the governors in Australia, and that would not have made me wealthy."

Tobias peered at him. "You're *wealthy?*"

Osgood was looking at Adam as well. "Well?"

"Australia wants for everything," Adam said, "from vineyard grapes to sturdy livestock, to looms, mills, agricultural implements. Anything human society needs can probably find a buyer in the older settlements."

"Have they mulberry trees?" Osgood asked.

Adam nodded. "Macarthur planted some at his property at Parramatta. Nearly twenty years on, they appear to be thriving."

Valerian rose. "This is all very interesting, but I've yet to hear from Miss Briggs. Madam, will you accept an informal banishment, or must I bring charges?"

"Don't be a fool, Briggs," Emily said, rising as well. "You have left a trail of misery and could do with a fresh start. I hear there aren't many women in Australia. Papa might offer you some severance if you can swallow your pride long enough to ask. Adam doubtless has a few words to say to you."

Oh, precisely. Valerian was willing to bet his saddle that Adam and Briggs would come to terms no magistrate wanted to be privy to. Important terms that allowed each of them to look forward and put the past behind them.

Osgood snapped his timepiece shut, and Emily speared him with a look. "Papa, have you something to say?"

"Adam, Briggs, and I will discuss terms."

"Briggs?" Valerian prompted. "What's it to be? The assizes or a new start?"

Briggs looked bilious, while Caleb and Tobias were exchanging whispers at a furious rate.

"I'll go," she said. "I'll go, and good riddance to England."

And good riddance to you. "Emily," Valerian said, extending his hand, "might you favor me with a turn in the garden?"

He wanted to leave Osgood, Adam, and Briggs to work out details of their arrangements in private. More to the point, he wanted to be alone with Emily, wanted to hear all the words she'd bit back in the midst of this difficult and taxing exchange.

"Try smashing the teapot, Briggs," Emily said as she took Valerian's hand. "Works a treat for improving a lady's mood. Mr. Dorning, some fresh air sounds lovely."

~

"YOU TWO," Adam said, causing Tobias and Caleb to cease their whispered quarrel and regard him owlishly. "Take yourselves off, and do not think of decamping for London until Papa and I have settled matters with you."

Papa's brows rose, but he for once held his tongue as Caleb and Tobias scuttled out the door. Miss Briggs sat in her wing chair, silently fuming like a deposed queen.

"I have to wonder," Adam said, "if the hard labor I did in Australia, and the tribulations I bore before the governor took notice of me, were anywhere near as difficult as the years Emily spent with you as her companion."

"I did my duty by her," Briggs said. "She will manage splendidly. Mr. Dorning dotes on her, and she on him. Those prancing ninnies in Town weren't worth her notice."

Adam had met many of Briggs's ilk in the penal colonies. They had, most of them, committed flat-out crimes, but in their exalted opinions, no wrongdoing merited banishment from Merry Olde. The criminal thus viewed himself not as the recipient of royal mercy, but rather, as the victim of a heinous injustice.

Anger sustained a beleaguered soul. It also trapped that soul. The smart convicts—the majority of them—learned that and made the best of their fate, as Adam had. Briggs did not have the look of a smart convict about her—yet.

"You made Emily's life harder," Adam said, "and mine and Papa's as well. Here's what I want from you, and I suspect Dorning well knew what I'd demand: You will write out a full confession, witnessed by two of the upper house servants here who have no vested interest in this whole mess. You will make a copy for me, one for Papa, and one for use as we see fit. We will agree to do nothing with those confessions until you've arrived in Australia. Take up a new identity there—it's easy enough to do—and the law won't find you when I petition for a full pardon."

"And if I am not inclined to stick my neck in a noose?" Briggs retorted. "As it happens, the money never went missing. The money was recovered from you, not me."

"But the forgery," Papa said quietly, "was yours, Veronica, and forgery is a capital offense. You stole *five years*, from Adam, from me, and from Emily. Five years we could have been a family. You lost your brother to his own intemperance and foolishness. You nearly cost me my son and cost Emily her only sibling, when all I've done is offer you employment at generous wages."

Briggs surged out of her chair. "*You pitied me.* I never wanted your pity, you idiot man. You needed somebody to look after you so you didn't work yourself to death, but your regard for me was that of a superior for a subordinate. 'Look after Emily,' you told me, as if that woman needs anybody to tell her what to do. I watched you sicken and nearly die, and all you had to say to me was, 'Look after Emily.' Well, now Emily has found a husband, and you are left with nobody to fret and fuss over you. I wish you the joy of your lonely old age."

Adam would have offered a sharp rebuke, but two tears trickled down Briggs's cheeks. A woman not *even* scorned—merely pitied—was entitled to a tirade.

"I never misled you," Papa said, passing her a plain white handkerchief. "When I began to suspect the enormity of what you'd done, I kept my own counsel rather than involve the authorities. You were a woman alone, grieving for your brother, and there was no undoing your mischief. My choices were rage or pity. Be glad you got the pity from me, for very few do. You will write those confessions, and then we'll discuss other terms that might make your view of me less severe."

Before Briggs could descend into outright weeping, Adam opened the door. "I'm sure you'll find the library a commodious place to put your thoughts on paper." A house this size had a library, and that library would have paper, pen, ink, and sand.

Adam waited until after Briggs had marched away before raising the next question. "Papa, when you mention *other terms*, you're not considering—?" Briggs as a step-mother was unthinkable.

"Of course not. Your mother was the only woman for me, as I told Briggs when she first attempted to alter the nature of our relationship."

Ye gods, Papa felt guilty for having rebuffed the woman who'd stolen from him. "I don't know whether to be more impressed with Briggs's audacity—attempting to court the favor of one of her victims —or your unwillingness to see her charged."

"She loved her brother, as Emily loves you. I ought to have given Veronica that damned money unasked, though Jemmy Briggs would simply have drunk himself to death before the consumption finished him off. He was a lazy, charming, drunken schemer, and she couldn't see that."

"A tangled web?"

Osgood fingered the gold chain affixed to his pocket watch. "Old business, which I hope to put behind us. Might you track down Caleb and Tobias before they come to blows? They lack your business instincts, lack your ingenuity at the bargaining table, but they certainly have a full complement of ambition. A few years adventuring in the colonies will do them good and go some way toward restoring my peace."

The compliments were inordinately heartwarming. Papa might never apologize for having shielded Briggs from guilt, never apologize for having suspected his own children, but in a small way, he'd admitted to regrets.

"I need to leave England," Adam said. "Nothing can change

that."

"You won't need to stay away for long. Your dear sister is marrying into a titled family. That family is connected to a fellow named Kettering, and *he* is rumored to have the sovereign's ear. My own wealth will be brought to bear on the situation, and do not underestimate the skills of Emily's intended. He comes across all harmless country squire, but Valerian Dorning could tell King George to leap into the sea and make it sound like friendly advice from a trusted confidant."

Or tell a man with a noose all but around his neck to come along for a spot of tea with the local magistrate and make that sound like a cordial invitation.

"Do you approve of Dorning, Papa?"

"He did not so much as bat a handsome eyelash when I told him Emily had no settlements. I more than approve of him. I admire him."

"So what are those additional terms you'll discuss with Briggs?"

"The less you know of those the better, but suffice it to say, I don't intend to reduce your inheritance by any substantial amount for her benefit."

Meaning Papa would reduce that inheritance by a modest amount, because he still felt sorry for a woman driven to desperate schemes and bitter measures.

"I'll find Caleb and Tobias," Adam said. "I would like to attend Emily's wedding and invite a friend too, if that's permissible?"

"A friend?"

"She lives near Bournemouth. I think she and Emily will get along. I'm in discussions with her regarding some mercantile investments."

Papa smiled, looking for a moment like a younger and more devilish fellow. "You never were one to let grass grow under your feet. I'm sure the bride and groom will welcome your friend—as will I."

And that was better than hearing Papa express a mere regret and better even than a royal pardon. That was a welcome back into the family.

"I FEEL ODDLY PROTECTIVE OF BRIGGS," Emily said, her hand still clasped in Valerian's, "and I want to strangle her."

"You needn't do either," he replied, though he knew exactly how she felt. "Let's take advantage of the shade in the folly."

"I don't hear any shouting. Papa can shout with the best of them now, and Adam is no slouch in a yelling match."

To blazes with Papa, Adam, and Briggs. "Will we have yelling matches, do you think?"

Emily paused at the foot of the steps that led up to the folly. "I want to yell when you pleasure me. Want to yodel to the heavens."

Valerian slipped her hand onto his arm. "As a change of subject, Mrs. Dorning-to-be, that will do nicely."

She kissed his cheek, which had the agreeable effect of pressing her breast against his arm. "What do you suppose they are discussing, Valerian? I can't imagine Papa is sweet on Briggs, but he seemed to feel some guilt where she's concerned."

"He likely does. If he'd intervened in her brother's situation, the whole matter might have been avoided."

Emily led the way up the steps. "Might have been?"

"Some debtors are habitually unable to manage their money. Perhaps Osgood knew that about Briggs's brother. She did not ask for a loan, and Osgood did not rescue the unfortunate Jemmy, so we will never know what might have been, but are you prepared to rescue your Papa, Emily?"

Emily took a seat in the shadows, her back to the house, and Valerian came down beside her.

"In what way does Papa need rescuing? He's healthier than he has been in years, the business is thriving, and with Caleb and Tobias sailing away to the South Seas, I'm sure he'll have all manner of projects to hatch up with them. Then too, Adam has returned, and while he might have to bide in Lisbon or Tuscany, Papa is fit enough to travel those distances." Her gaze became somewhat forlorn. "Adam and Papa can discuss business for hours."

Valerian tucked an arm around his beloved's shoulders, for he was feeling somewhat forlorn too. Good manners were nothing more than consideration for one's fellow creatures, and Valerian owed Emily much more than good manners.

That his obligation would likely leave him missing his wife much of the time, and feeling *de trop* among the business-minded Peppers was of no moment.

"You read contracts, Emily mine, every word of them. You brought in a shipwright to stop a conflagration of male arrogance that could have resulted in lives or fortunes lost. You have handled Osgood's correspondence, you know his business, you *wear* his products. Modistes purchase more silk and fine wool than tailors do, and modistes are female."

"Valerian..."

He kissed her. "My family is titled, and we're embarking on a venture that involves peddling soaps and sachets, mixing up herbal tisanes, and opening shops, which we dearly hope become fashionable. My baby brother runs a glorified gaming hell. My brother-in-law is up to his wealthy ears in finance. The days when younger sons, or even titled families, could disdain trade are fast fading. That my wife has a hand in a successful cloth business would be a source of pride to me, Emily."

That was the truth. Emily would always be a source of pride to him, but on what grounds could she be proud of him? He'd make a go of Abbotsford, of course, he'd be a devoted husband and father, God willing, but would that be enough?

"Ladies don't run businesses, Valerian. Briggs was implacably clear on that."

Perhaps Australia wasn't far enough away for Miss Briggs. "Briggs was as self-interested in the telling of that lie as she was in the rest of her dishonest endeavors. Lady Jersey is not merely involved in a bank, she's the senior partner. A woman up north by the name of

Mrs. Mountain owns more than two thousand coach horses and enough inns to stable them, as well as a shop that makes coaches. She's merely turned her hand to the family trade and done quite well at it. Women own mills, schools, farms, shops, and more. They run charitable endeavors of significant complexity. They run most every household in the realm."

He took her hand. "I would be loath to think that my wife shied away from a family business at a time when that business needed her expertise. Your father won't ask for your help, but I think you are in a position to bargain with him."

Emily leaned into him. "Bargain how?"

Valerian closed his eyes, the better to enjoy the scent and feel of his intended, the better to accept a fate that he'd never anticipated.

"Tell Osgood to keep his settlements in lieu of a share of the business."

"Mama bequeathed me money, Valerian. Papa can be as parsimonious as he wants, but he had no business being difficult about what my mother left to me."

Well, no, but Valerian was fairly confident Osgood would have turned the money loose after the ceremony. "What would your mama tell you to do?"

"Box Papa's ears. Mama and Papa talked business all the time. She more than once raised her voice to him over a commercial matter. He learned to listen to her too. It's as you say: Women do most of the purchasing of fine fabrics, and we wear them by the yard."

Without moving, something about Emily's posture shifted. Instead of a woman drained by a difficult family confrontation, she seemed energized by the thought of taking on her father's stubbornness. Perhaps her mother's memory had done that, though Valerian hoped his encouragement had contributed as well.

"I will inherit an interest in the business," Emily said. "I suspect Papa intended for Adam to manage it and send me reports."

"Adam won't be on hand for some time, if ever, Emily. Your brother has seen the world. He cut ties with England and came back only to reconcile with you and Osgood. You cannot expect him to reverse course on the day of Osgood's choosing and leave his own affairs adrift. He should quietly collect the funds your mother left him and make haste away from England. Caleb and Tobias are off to conquer the Antipodes, and that leaves only you."

"Papa could hire—"

"*Papa* hired Ogilvy."

That had her on her feet and pacing. "He did, and he never once bothered to look in on Ogilvy's progress. I suspect he didn't even read the blighted contract, and now he's talking about buying ships that aren't fit for his purposes."

"Ships—plural?"

She came to a halt, gaze on the house. "Where would we live, Valerian?"

"I would need to spend some time here in Dorset, but I can let out Abbotsford, if that's what you're asking, and Hawthorne will serve as my steward." Valerian didn't want to give up on the peace and quiet of his own acres, a place to call home near his family seat. An English gentleman owned property in the usual course.

But the usual course would not suit Emily, and thus the usual course might have to be abandoned.

She faced him, her expression quite fierce. "I am asking what you need to be happy, Valerian. I can bury myself in Papa's business affairs, but I expect we will be blessed with children. They don't raise themselves, and I have no respect for the aristocratic practice of treating offspring as a burden to be shouldered by servants, rather than as treasures to be lovingly reared."

Oh, how he adored her. "My father was an aristocrat. He and his countesses raised their progeny, though they had help." Valerian rose, because he sensed Emily had made as much progress with the notion of managing Osgood's business as she was going to make for the moment.

"I will be a good mother to our children," Emily said, closing the distance between them. "My mother managed to keep Papa in line and look after me and Adam. Will you take an interest in the cloth business?"

He considered a well-meant lie, considered shading the truth. Neither would serve for the woman he esteemed above all others.

"I will of course never refuse a family member's request for assistance, Emily, but I know nothing of the cloth industry. I like to be of use doing the work others neglect, and yet, I can't very well be effective in an area where I'm toweringly ignorant. My expertise lies with diffusing arguments, managing complicated social situations. Petty diplomacy, I guess you'd call it."

For which no real profession existed, other than that of gentleman at large.

"What of your book?" she asked. "Did you enjoy writing your book?"

His book. On what fanciful day had he ever thought himself capable of authoring a book? "I loved every minute of it. When I took up my pen, all other worries and cares disappeared, and I absorbed myself in the challenge of effective and meaningful communication."

Which was the problem. A gentleman brought means to his marriage, but he should also bring *meaning.* While Emily was keeping Osgood's mercantile empire from floundering, what meaningful effort could Valerian turn to, other than calling upon the Abbotsford tenants?

"You must write more books." Emily looked absolutely certain of her conclusion. "You persisted with your manuscript when nobody encouraged you. You sent it out to publishers for consideration when another man would have set it aside as a mere pastime. You have ideas for more books, Valerian, I know you do."

"How do you know that?"

She slipped her arms around his waist and rested her head against his chest. "Because I love you. Because I know you don't need to bleat your every idea for all the world to hear. You keep your own counsel, but your mind is never idle."

He wrapped her in his arms, glad that embracing meant she

couldn't see his face. "I would like to draft something like *Aesop's Fables* to teach children the point of good manners. Why do we wait our turn? Why do we offer courtesy to everybody we meet, irrespective of station? Why do we never take more from the tray than is polite? Children love stories, and when we're young, we're especially impressionable and good-hearted. Teach a boy his manners, and he'll become a gentleman, regardless of his calling or station."

And such a book would be *meaningful*. Perhaps not enormously lucrative, perhaps forgotten in a few years, but it would be meaningful.

"Then that is what you will do," Emily said. "And you will help your family with their botanical venture, and manage your brothers, and see to Abbotsford's holdings, and serve as magistrate, and be a papa to our children. I will be their mama, and Papa's business conscience, and the lady of our household." She took a firmer hold of him. "This will be complicated, Valerian. We will be endlessly busy."

Valerian hoped they would be endlessly happy. Not according to the conventional expectations for an earl's son or a wealthy heiress, but according to their own hearts.

"You forgot the most important part, Emily."

She peered up at him. "The assemblies? I am happy to be your dancing partner at the lessons, Valerian, though that's entirely selfish of me. My dancing wants work, I know."

"You will be my partner at the lessons and for all the good-night waltzes, but the most important part is that I will love you, and I hope you will offer me a reciprocal regard, and thus all the busyness and complication will be manageable."

He knew it would be, because he knew Emily, and he knew his own strengths and abilities.

"You are right, of course. Do you hear yelling?"

Caleb, Tobias, and Adam were apparently going at each other, their strident tones wafting across the garden. "They are merely being emphatic. When they are truly hollering, we will intervene."

Emily sighed, Valerian kissed her brow, and the moment became all the sweeter for the knowledge that whatever had sparked the difference of opinion in the house, Valerian would enjoy sorting it out, and Emily would likely take a hand in that too.

They were to be married, and they were to be partners in any number of adventures, business and otherwise.

"What's in your pocket?" she asked, easing her grip. "You usually look all dapper and perfect, but I can hear paper crackling in your coat pocket."

Valerian shoved his hand in his pocket and found the epistle Grey had passed along to him earlier in the day.

"A letter from my—" He opened the missive, expecting to see Jacaranda's tidy script. Instead, Worth Kettering's scrawl greeted him. "From my brother-in-law."

"Well, what does it say? Papa claims Mr. Kettering is scandalously wealthy, which from Papa is high praise indeed."

Valerian opened the letter, expecting a terse warning that Sycamore was getting in over his head, or perhaps a command to appear in Town to make a fraternal obeisance at Jacaranda's feet.

"He likes my book," Valerian said slowly. "He showed it to King George himself."

In the next moment, Valerian found it imperative to resume his seat.

"Go on," Emily said, sinking down beside him. "The king fancies himself quite the arbiter of manners, doesn't he? Europe's first gentleman or some such. Patron of the arts, courtier without compare."

"The king was 'impressed with both my wit and the breadth of my subject knowledge.' His Majesty suggested I divide the book into two volumes, one aimed at a masculine audience, one at a feminine audience... That's not a bad idea."

"You can do that? Just chop a book in two?"

Valerian tried to make his mind focus on Emily's question, but *the king liked his book.* The sovereign of the realm *liked his book.*

"I can revise the material," Valerian said, thinking through his arrangement of chapters. "I can add a bit for the ladies, a bit for the fellows. The notion is actually clever."

The noise from the house grew louder, not quite to the threats-of-violence level, merely the music of a lively difference of opinion.

"Is there more?" Emily asked, peering at the letter. "His penmanship is terrible."

"Much about Worth lacks polish, but he adores Jacaranda, and she him. He says..." Valerian looked more closely at the slashing script. "He says..."

He put the letter down and purely hugged Emily.

"What?" she demanded, hugging him back. "What does he say?"

Valerian fumbled the letter into her hand and went right back to hugging her.

Emily managed to get the epistle up to eye level. "Who is Dougal MacHugh?"

"He's the most successful publisher of domestic advice in London. His books are in every shop that wants to attract trade from the households with means and aspirations to social betterment. He's... perfect for my book. For my books."

"The king's endorsement persuaded him to..." Emily tossed the letter onto the bench. "I'll read it later. Perhaps we should frame it. If Adam uses his fists on Tobias and Caleb, will you arrest him?"

Valerian kissed her, because what else could a man do when his dreams came true, except kiss the woman who'd share those dreams with him?

"Do you want me to arrest him?"

"I like it when you subtly threaten legal retribution as you offer up the tea cakes. That's very dashing and ever so—"

He kissed her some more, and as it happened, nobody came to blows that day, but only because Valerian and Emily interceded, brandishing both tea cakes and threats, and having ever so much fun doing both.

EPILOGUE

Valerian peered at Emily over the rims of his spectacles. "Sycamore is threatening to visit. He sends his love."

Valerian in spectacles inspired Emily's imagination in all manner of marital flights. He was in the habit of reading in bed late at night, wearing nothing *but* his spectacles, and ye gods...

He was fully clothed now, and the fire cracked merrily in the hearth of Abbotsford's study, but no wonder Emily's first born was due to arrive in less than four months. A woman could withstand only so much scholarly nudity from a husband, after all.

"Tell Cam to pay his call when we can take him with us to the next assembly," Emily said, peering at the hem of the infant dress she was embroidering. "The local ladies will enjoy standing up with him."

Valerian put aside his brother's letter. "I also had news from Kettering today."

"Good news?" Worth Kettering had taken over managing Emily's funds, though she and Valerian had refused any sort of settlements from Osgood other than the money Emily had inherited from her mother. From the Dorning family, they received a modest percentage of the quarterly profits from the botanical business, the ledgers for which remained under Valerian's supervision. The "flower money" and the proceeds of Valerian's writing were set aside for savings.

"Worth sends very good news," Valerian said, taking off his glasses. "The king has agreed to pardon Adam, though I gather Osgood had to first gift acres of silk to Carlton House and the Pavilion."

"Papa could cover both buildings in silk and barely feel the expense. For Adam's sake, I am relieved, though justice should not require a bribe in silk. Perhaps Adam can attend the baby's christening."

Adam had attended their wedding. The ceremony had been a quiet gathering in the Dorning family chapel, with only family as witnesses. Margaret Dorning had stood up with Emily; the Earl of Casriel had served as best man, and the wedding breakfast had been a hearty family meal on the back terrace of Dorning Hall. Adam had taken his leave before sunset the same day, though he wrote regularly from Milan, and appeared to be conducting an epistolary courtship of Mrs. Thelwell too.

"Do you still want to travel up to London next week?" Valerian asked, rising and going to the window. The latest snowfall had been a mere six inches. Enough to be pretty, not enough to stop travel.

"Once the baby arrives, I'll be disinclined to travel for some time. If we don't look in on Papa now, he'll get up to mischief."

Valerian turned and braced his hips against the windowsill. "Do you regret hiring Mrs. MacLellan, Emily? We can still move to London, you know. We could stay at Dorning House, or even buy our own property."

Valerian's books had done exceedingly well, and his children's book subscriptions were piling up apace though the manuscript wasn't complete yet. He told her frequently that he could write anywhere, and Emily believed him.

"Come sit beside me," Emily said, folding her embroidery atop her work basket. "I have a confession."

"This sounds interesting." Valerian joined her on the sofa and rested an arm along her shoulders. "Have you been naughty?"

"Not since I was naughty with you before breakfast. This has to do with Papa's cloth business."

Valerian leaned his head back against the cushions and closed his eyes. "You want to move to London. Very well, we'll move. I can let out Abbotsford, though finding the right tenant might take some time, and—"

Emily put two fingers over her husband's lips. "I thought I wanted to run Papa's business, Valerian, to be the manager Papa never allowed me to be."

He wrapped her fingers in a warm grip. "And?"

"Not *and. But.* But, I find I am not all that interested in cloth. Papa was trying to keep me away from the business at first because he worried that I'd stolen from him, then because he realized that even a very large and wealthy business was still the dreaded mercantile *shop* in the eyes of polite society."

"Polite society is changing, Emily, and you excel at business. Moreover, your father needs somebody to curb his enthusiasms, because Caleb and Tobias are apparently having a grand time becoming cloth nabobs in Australia."

"My condolences to Australia." Briggs had found a husband within a month of setting foot on Australian soil, and Emily had not heard word of her since—nor had Emily inquired, nor did she intend to. "As for Papa, Mrs. MacLellan curbs his enthusiasms, and she doesn't even have to raise her voice to do it."

Valerian peered at her. "Are you saying you'd rather *not* go up to London?"

"Yes, I'm saying I'd rather stay here at Abbotsford. You have books to write, I'm learning the herbal recipes from Margaret, the renovations at Pepper Ridge require our supervision, Hawthorne hardly makes a decision regarding the botanicals without consulting you, Casriel is forever asking your opinion on his demolition and rebuilding at Dorning Hall. We are busy, we are happy, we have family nearby, and we are soon to become parents. I will at some point become responsible for Papa's business by virtue of his passing, if nothing else. For now, let's *stay home*, Valerian, and let London roar along without us."

"You're certain?"

How she loved him. How she loved that he listened to her, that she could tell him anything, that she was to have a child with him.

"I am competent to run a household the size of Abbotsford," she said, "and I enjoy doing it. I enjoy the company of our tenants, I enjoy haggling with the factors in Dorset over the price of seed and horseshoes. That's business too, you know."

She maneuvered up off the sofa—an increasingly ungainly effort —and straddled Valerian's lap. "You ambushed me," she went on, kissing him. "I thought I knew exactly what I wanted, and exactly what I did not want. I thought Dorset at the ends of the earth, but now... you are here, and home is here, and"—the baby kicked, which Valerian had to have felt—"the baby agrees with me. This is home."

"You are home," Valerian said, returning the kiss. "You are my home, and if we never spend another week in London, I will be content. That child is quite lively."

Emily snuggled close, so she and Valerian could enjoy their lively child together. "What shall we name this baby?"

"Do we favor a botanical name," Valerian asked, pressing a kiss to Emily's temple, "in the Dorning tradition, or have you a Pepper family name you'd like to bestow?"

"I like classical names. Do that again, please."

He did it again, and added a gentle caress to Emily's breasts, which had become marvelously sensitive. From there, matters tended in a horizontal direction, and it wasn't until a good hour later that Emily was able to resume the discussion of the baby's name.

Over the ensuing months, many similar discussions took place, until the child was born and—with her Uncle Adam standing as godfather, and her Aunt Jacaranda as godmother—christened Calantha Terpsichore Dorning. She loved flowers, she loved to dance. She had exquisite manners, and quite a head for business too!

TO MY DEAR READERS

To my dear readers,

Valerian has been charming me and straightening out his brothers for several books now, and I did wonder who could successfully charm *him*. Emily Pepper stepped forth, and the wild rumpus was immediately under way. But what of our dear Oak, all on his lonesome in the wilds of Hampshire?

What do you know, Oak's not so lonesome. Mrs. Verity Channing, a widow formerly married to a very successful artist, has hired Oak to restore some paintings for her. Oak has his eye fixed on London as the only address for a successful portraitist, but he cannot refuse the coin or the cachet that working for Verity might afford him.

Then he finds some scandalous art hidden among the widow's treasures, and matters grow exceedingly delicate. Smooching happens, which only complicates the whole situation even more. Excerpt below, and ***A Lady's Dream Come True*** will be available from my **webstore** in May, and on the **major retail platforms** in June.

Which is just too far away, isn't it? Fortunately, my next **Rogues to Riches** story, ***A Duke by Any Other Name***, comes out in

April. Lady Althea Wentworth, having failed miserably in Mayfair's ballrooms, is determined to wedge her way into Yorkshire's rural society. Her plan hinges on the cooperation of a grouchy, reclusive neighbor who just happens to be a duke. Nathaniel, Duke of Rothmere, wants no part of polite society, but neither can he countenance anybody treating Althea badly.

What's a duke to do? Well, yes. More smooching, which again, only complicated matters. Excerpt below.

I'm also busy, busy, busy bundling up previously published novellas from anthologies no longer in circulation (*A Duke Walked into House Party* is my first venture in this regard), pondering stories for Ash and Cam Dorning, and noshing on my Regency whodunits, the *Lady Violet Mysteries*. To keep track of all my upcoming releases and pre-orders, simply follow me on *Bookbub*. You might also check out my **Deals** page, where I always have some title or other discounted. (I went a little overboard for *True Honor's* release—it's a triple discount for all of February.)

Wherever you find the books, happy reading!

Grace Burrowes

Read on for an excerpt from *A Lady's Dream Come True*!

EXCERPT—A LADY'S DREAM
COME TRUE

Oak Dorning has accepted a temporary post restoring old paintings for Verity Channing, widow of a very successful artist. Oak's ambitions lie squarely in London, the only venue for successful English portraitists, while Verity wants nothing to do with art, London, or portraits. Then Oak finds fascinating treasure lurking amid Verity's art collection, and possibly in a few other unexpected places too...

The tub was a trifle cramped for a man of Oak's proportions, but he made do, and the heat of the water was exquisite after the day's chilly, interminable journey up from Dorset. He scrubbed off and lay back, happy to soak until the water had cooled a bit more.

Night had fallen, hastened by the miserable weather, and thus Oak's chamber was illuminated only by candles and the fire roaring in the hearth. Mrs. Channing apparently did not skimp on fuel, nor did she believe artists ought to be housed in drafty garrets.

Oak's bedroom came with a cozy sitting room, and both chambers sported lit fires. A dressing closet off the bedroom added further to the sense that Oak was a guest rather than an itinerant tradesman.

He took another nibble of a pale, blue-veined cheese and washed it down with a sip of excellent port. He'd begun the argument in his head—to doze off in the tub or climb out before the water grew cold—when a quiet snick sounded from the other side of the fire screens.

"I'll unpack the valise myself," he said, giving up on the nap. "You needn't bother. I can see to it later." God willing, his clothes weren't entirely soaked. His trunks would probably not arrive at Merlin Hall for another few days and damp shirts were a misery not to be borne.

He expected a footman's cheery greeting, or maybe a disapproving comment from the butler, Bracken. Instead he heard a quiet rustling.

"Halloo," Oak said, sitting up, though the fire screens blocked his view of most of the room. "Who's there?" Had a maid stumbled into his room by mistake? Did somebody think to rifle what few belongings he'd brought with him?

He stood reluctantly, water sluicing off him into the tub, and cold air chasing the drowsiness from his mind.

"Show yourself," he said, grabbing a towel and wrapping it around his middle. "I already have an extra bucket of coal in both rooms."

Over the top of the fire screens, Oak saw the door to the corridor open. Soft footsteps pattered from the room, though in the gloom, all he could make out was a shadow slipping into the greater darkness beyond the doorway.

"Bloody hell." A thief stealing his razor would not do. Oak extricated himself from the tub and bolted for the open door. "Get back here, whoever you are. Stealing from a guest is not the done thing." Though Oak wasn't quite a guest. He was an employee at Merlin Hall, an artisan rather than an artist.

The air in the corridor was even colder than the air in the sitting room had been, and Oak hadn't gone two yards from his doorway before it occurred to him that he was racing about a strange house wearing nothing but a towel.

He came to an abrupt halt just as footsteps faded around a carpeted corner. "Christ in swaddling clothes. What was I—?"

A throat cleared.

Oak turned slowly, clutching his towel about his waist with one hand.

"I see the swaddling clothes," the lady said. "I rather doubt the son of the Almighty stands before me."

She wore an aubergine dress so dark as to approach black in the corridor's shadows, and she held a carrying candle that flickered in the chilly breeze.

"Oak Dorning, no relation to the Almighty. I would bow but as I am a man wearing only a towel, I've no wish to look yet more ridiculous."

She cast an appraising eye over him. "I assure you, Mr. Dorning, you do not appear ridiculous, though I can understand why you'd be a bit self-conscious. I am Verity Channing."

Oak considered himself too slender, at least when compared to his brother Hawthorne. Compared to Valerian, his toilette and manners were unpolished. He lacked Casriel's Town bronze. He hadn't Ash's head for business, Sycamore's cunning, or Willow's imperturbable calm.

But Verity Channing apparently saw something in Oak's nearly naked form that held her interest. Her gaze conveyed no prurient curiosity, but rather, the sort of assessment Oak made when he considered sketching a subject. How did the light treat this particular complexion? Was a slightly different angle more revealing? More honest?

Candlelight was said to be flattering, but in the few instants Oak took to study Verity Channing, he concluded that she needed no shadows to obscure her flaws, if any she had. Her eyes tilted ever so slightly, the perfect complement to a strong nose, full lips, and swooping brows. Her features had a rare symmetry and came together in ideal proportions. Brows, chin, jaw, cheeks... all the structures of a human face were presented in her physiognomy on the balancing edge between grace and strength, beauty and perfection.

She was, quite simply, stunning. So lovely to look at that for a moment, Oak forgot he was wearing only a towel, forgot this was his employer, and forgot that he stood gawking at her in the middle of a chilly corridor.

"I owe you a favor, Mr. Dorning," she said, lowering the candle. "You extracted a gig from the muck earlier today, and spared Dante a long, chilly walk back to the Hall. For that reason, I will promise never to mention to another soul the circumstances of this meeting."

Oak could not tell if she was teasing him, but he believed she'd keep her word, and thank God for that, because his brothers would never stop laughing if they learned of this encounter.

"I don't suppose you might *forget* the circumstances of this meeting, ma'am? Wipe them from memory, perhaps?"

He'd have to pass her to return to his room. Her smile, so slight, so devilish, suggested she knew that.

She approached and handed him the candle. "When I am an old woman who hums under her breath to the distraction of all who must endure my company, I will still recall the sight of you clad in only a towel." She made a slow inspection of his chest, his arms, his shoulders, then his face. "The memory will make me smile. Good evening, Mr. Dorning. I'll see you at breakfast, though—lamentably, for me—somewhat less of *you*, I trust. One wouldn't want such a fine specimen coming down with a lung fever."

She sauntered off into the darkness, and Oak remained in the corridor, sorting through his thoughts. He could not recall anybody—male or female—regarding him with such frank appreciation. The attention was unnerving, but also... gratifying in an odd way.

And besides that lingering sense of gratification, he had the artist's aching need to render on paper something he'd experienced mostly through his visual senses—but not entirely. A hint of cinnamon hung in the air, a throb of awareness such as a man feels toward a woman who has impressed him viscerally.

"That smile," he murmured, gathering up his toweling and returning to his sitting room. "That knowing, impish, female..."

When three footmen arrived to deal with the tub, Oak barely noticed. He sat swathed in towels on the sofa, trying to sketch Verity Channing's smile.

Order your copy of **A Lady's Dream Come True**, and read on for an excerpt from **A Duke by Any Other Name**!

EXCERPT—A DUKE BY ANY OTHER NAME

The usual polite means of gaining an introduction to Nathaniel, Duke of Rothmere, have failed Lady Althea Wentworth utterly. Being a resourceful woman, she's turned to unusual measures to achieve her goal...

Althea heard her guest before she saw him. Rothhaven's arrival was presaged by a rapid beat of hooves coming not up her drive, but rather, directly across the park that surrounded Lynley Vale manor.

A large horse created that kind of thunder, one disdaining the genteel canter for a hellbent gallop. From her parlor window Althea could see the beast approaching, and her first thought was that only a terrified animal traveled at such speed.

But no. Horse and rider cleared the wall beside the drive in perfect rhythm, swerved onto the verge, and continued right up— good God, they aimed straight for the fountain. Althea could not look away as the black horse drew closer and closer to unforgiving marble and splashing water.

"Mary, Mother of God."

Another smooth leap—the fountain was five feet high if it was an inch—and a foot-perfect landing, followed by an immediate check of the horse's speed. The gelding came down to a frisking, capering trot, clearly proud of himself and ready for even greater challenges.

The rider stroked the horse's neck, and the beast calmed and hung his head, sides heaving. A treat was offered and another pat, before one of Althea's grooms bestirred himself to take the horse. Rothhaven—for that could only be the dread duke himself—paused on the front steps long enough to remove his spurs, whip off his hat, and run a black-gloved hand through hair as dark as hell's tarpit.

"The rumors are true," Althea murmured. Rothhaven was built on the proportions of the Vikings of old, but their fair coloring and blue eyes had been denied him. He glanced up, as if he knew Althea would be spying, and she drew back.

His gaze was colder than a Yorkshire night in January, which fit exactly with what Althea had heard of him.

She moved from the window and took the wing chair by the hearth, opening a book chosen for this singular occasion. She had dressed carefully—elegantly but without too much fuss—and styled her hair with similar consideration. Rothhaven gave very few people the chance to make even a first impression on him, a feat Althea admired.

Voices drifted up from the foyer, followed by the tread of boots on the stair. Rothhaven moved lightly for such a grand specimen, and his voice rumbled like distant cannon. A soft tap on the door, then Strensall was announcing Nathaniel, His Grace of Rothhaven. The duke did not have to duck to come through the doorway, but it was a near thing.

Althea set aside her book, rose, and curtsied to a precisely deferential depth and not one inch lower.

"Welcome to Lynley Vale, Your Grace. A pleasure to meet you. Strensall, the tea, and don't spare the trimmings."

Strensall bolted for the door.

"I do not break bread with mine enemy." Rothhaven stalked over to Althea and swept her with a glower. "No damned tea."

His eyes were a startling green, set against swooping dark brows and features as angular as the crags and tors of Yorkshire's moors. He brought with him the scents of heather and horse, a lovely combination. His cravat remained neatly pinned with a single bar of gleaming gold despite his mad dash across the countryside.

"I will attribute Your Grace's lack of manners to the peckishness that can follow exertion. A tray, Strensall."

The duke leaned nearer. "Shall I threaten to curse poor Strensall with nightmares, should he bring a tray?"

"That would be unsporting." Althea sent her goggling butler a glance, and he scampered off. "You are reputed to have a temper, but then, if folk claimed that my mere passing caused milk to curdle and babies to colic, I'd be a tad testy myself. No one has ever accused you of dishonorable behavior."

"Nor will they, while you, my lady, have stooped so low as to unleash the hogs of war upon my hapless estate." He backed away not one inch, and this close Althea caught a more subtle fragrance. Lily of the valley or jasmine. Very faint, elegant, and unexpected, like the moss-green of his eyes.

"You cannot read, perhaps," he went on, "else you'd grasp that 'we will not be entertaining for the foreseeable future' means neither you nor your livestock are welcome at Rothhaven Hall."

"Hosting a short call from your nearest neighbor would hardly be entertaining," Althea countered. "Shall we be seated?"

"I will not be seated," he retorted. "Retrieve your damned pigs from my orchard, madam, or I will send them to slaughter before the week is out."

"Is that where my naughty ladies got off to?" Althea took her wing chair. "They haven't been on an outing in ages. I suppose the spring air inspired them to seeing the sights. Last autumn they took a notion to inspect the market, and in summer they decided to attend Sunday services. Most of our neighbors find my herd's social inclinations amusing."

"I might be amused, were your herd not at the moment rooting through my orchard uninvited. To allow stock of those dimensions to wander is irresponsible, and why a duke's sister is raising hogs entirely defeats my powers of imagination."

Because Rothhaven had never been poor and never would be. "Do have a seat, Your Grace. I'm told only the ill-mannered pace the parlor like a house tabby who needs to visit the garden."

He turned his back to Althea—very rude of him—though he appeared to require a moment to marshal his composure. She counted that a small victory, for she had needed many such moments since acquiring a title, and her composure yet remained as unruly as her sows on a pretty spring day.

Though truth be told, the lady swine had had some *encouragement* regarding the direction of their latest outing.

Rothhaven turned to face Althea, the fire in his gaze banked to burning disdain. "Will you or will you not retrieve your wayward pigs from my land?"

"I refuse to discuss this with a man who cannot observe the simplest conversational courtesy." She waved a hand at the opposite wing chair, and when that provoked a drawing up of the magnificent ducal height, she feared His Grace would stalk from the room.

Instead he took the chair, whipping out the tails of his riding jacket like Lucifer arranging his coronation robes.

"Thank you," Althea said. "When you march about like that, you give a lady a crick in her neck. Your orchard is at least a mile from my home farm."

"And downwind, more's the pity. Perhaps you raise pigs to perfume the neighborhood with their scent?"

"No more than you keep horses, sheep, or cows for the same purpose, Your Grace. Or maybe your livestock hides the pervasive odor of brimstone hanging about Rothhaven Hall?"

A muscle twitched in the duke's jaw.

The tea tray arrived before Althea could further provoke her guest, and in keeping with standing instructions, the kitchen had exerted its skills to the utmost. Strensall placed an enormous silver tray before Althea—the good silver, not the fancy silver—bowed, and withdrew.

"How do you take your tea, Your Grace?"

"Plain, except I won't be staying for tea. Assure me that you'll send your swineherd over to collect your sows in the next twenty-four hours and I will take my leave of you."

Not so fast. Having coaxed Rothhaven into making a call, Althea wasn't about to let him win free so easily.

"I cannot give you those assurances, Your Grace, much as I'd like to. I'm very fond of those ladies and they are quite valuable. They are also particular."

Rothhaven straightened a crease in his breeches. They fit him exquisitely, though Althea had never before seen black riding attire.

"The whims of your livestock are no affair of mine, Lady Althea." His tone said that Althea's whims were a matter of equal indifference to him. "You either retrieve them or the entire shire will be redolent of smoking bacon."

He was bluffing, albeit convincingly. Nobody butchered hogs in early spring, for any number of reasons. "Do you know what my sows are worth?"

He quoted a price per pound for pork on the hoof that was accurate to the penny.

"Wrong," Althea said, pouring him a cup of tea and holding it out to him. "Those are my best breeders. I chose their grandmamas and mamas for hardiness and the ability to produce sizable, healthy litters. A pig in the garden can be the difference between a family surviving through a hard winter or starving, if that pig can also produce large, thriving litters. She can live on scraps, she needs very little care, and she will see a dozen piglets raised to weaning twice a year without putting any additional strain on the family budget."

The duke looked at the steaming cup of tea, then at Althea, then back at the cup. This was the best China black she could offer, served on the good porcelain in her personal parlor. If he disdained her hospitality now, she might...cry?

He would not be swayed by tears, but he apparently could be tempted by a perfect cup of tea.

"You raise hogs as a charitable undertaking?" he asked.

"I raise them for all sorts of reasons, and I donate many to the poor of the parish."

"Why not donate money?" He took a cautious sip of his tea. "One can spend coin on what's most necessary, and many of the poor have no gardens."

"If they lack a garden, they can send the children into the countryside to gather rocks and build drystone walls, can't they? After a season or two, the pig will have rendered the soil of its enclosure very fertile indeed, and the enclosure can be moved. Coin, by contrast, can be stolen."

Another sip. "From the poor box?"

"Of course from the poor box. Or that money can be wasted on Bibles while children go hungry."

This was the wrong conversational direction, too close to Althea's heart, too far from her dreams.

"My neighbor is a radical," Rothhaven mused. "And she conquers poverty and ducal privacy alike with an army of sows. Nonetheless, those hogs are where they don't belong, and possession is nine-tenths of the law. Move them or I will do as I see fit with them."

"If you harm my pigs or disperse that herd for sale, I will sue you for conversion. You gained control of my property legally—pigs will wander—but if you waste those pigs or convert my herd for your own gain, I will take you to court."

Althea put three sandwiches on a plate and offered it to him. She'd lose her suit for conversion, not because she was wrong on the law—she was correct—but because he was a duke, and not just any duke. He was the much-treasured dread duke of Rothhaven Hall, a local fixture of pride. The squires in the area were more protective of Rothhaven's consequence than they were of their own.

Lawsuits were scandalous, however, especially between neighbors or family members. They were also messy, involving appearances in court and meetings with solicitors and barristers. A man who seldom left his property and refused to receive callers would avoid those tribulations at all costs.

Rothhaven set down the plate. "What must I do to inspire you to retrieve your *valuable* sows? I have my own swineherd, you know. A capable old fellow who has been wrangling hogs for more than half a century. He can move your livestock to the king's highway."

Althea hadn't considered this possibility, but she dared not blow retreat. "My sows are partial to their own swineherd. They'll follow him anywhere, though after rioting about the neighborhood on their own, they will require time to recover. They've been out dancing all night, so to speak, and must have a lie-in."

Althea could not fathom why any sensible female would comport herself thus, but every spring she dragged herself south, and subjected herself to the same inanity for the duration of the London Season.

This year would be different.

"So send your swineherd to fetch them tomorrow," Rothhaven said, taking a bite of a beef sandwich. "My swineherd will assist, and I need never darken your door again—nor you, mine." He sent her a pointed look, one that scolded without saying a word.

Althea's brother Quinn had learned to deliver such looks, and his duchess had honed the raised eyebrow to a delicate art.

While I am a laughingstock. A memory came to Althea, of turning down the room with a peer's heir, a handsome, well-liked man tall enough to look past her shoulder. The entire time they'd been waltzing, he'd been rolling his eyes at his friends, affecting looks of long-suffering martyrdom, and holding Althea up as an object of ridicule, even as he'd hunted her fortune and made remarks intended to flatter.

She had not realized his game until her own sister, Constance, had reported it to her in the carriage on the way home. The hostess had not intervened, nor had any chaperone or gentleman called the young dandy to account. He had thanked Althea for the dance and escorted her to her next partner with all the courtesy in the world, and she'd been the butt of another joke.

"I cannot oblige you, Your Grace," Althea said. "My swineherd is visiting his sister in York and won't be back until week's end. I do apologize for the delay, though if turning my pigs loose in your orchard has occasioned this introduction, then I'm glad for it. I value my privacy too, but I am at my wit's end and must consult you on a matter of some delicacy."

He gestured with half a sandwich. "All the way at your wit's end? What has caused you to travel that long and arduous trail?"

Polite Society. Wealth. Standing. All the great boons Althea had once envied and had so little ability to manage.

"I want a baby," she said, not at all how she'd planned to state her situation.

Rothhaven put down his plate slowly, as if a wild creature had come snorting and snapping into the parlor. "Are you utterly demented? One doesn't announce such a thing, and I am in no position to..." He stood, his height once again creating an impression of towering disdain. "I will see myself out."

Althea rose as well, and though Rothhaven could toss her behind the sofa one-handed, she made her words count.

"Do not flatter yourself, Your Grace. Only a fool would seek to procreate with a petulant, moody, withdrawn, arrogant specimen such as you. I want a family, exactly the goal every girl is raised to treasure. There's nothing shameful or inappropriate about that. Until I learn to comport myself as the sister of a duke ought, I have no hope of making an acceptable match. You are a duke. If anybody understands the challenge I face, you do. You have five hundred years of breeding and family history to call upon, while I..."

Oh, this was not the eloquent explanation she'd rehearsed, and Rothhaven's expression had become unreadable.

He gestured with a large hand. "While you...?"

Althea had tried inviting him to tea, then to dinner. She'd tried calling upon him. She'd ridden the bridle paths for hours in hopes of meeting him by chance, only to see him galloping over the moors, heedless of anything so tame as a bridle path.

She'd called on him twice, only to be turned away at the door and chided by letter twice for presuming even that much. Althea had only a single weapon left in her arsenal, a lone arrow in her quiver of strategies, the one least likely to yield the desired result.

She had the truth. "I need your help," she said, subsiding into her chair. "I haven't anywhere else to turn. If I'm not to spend the rest of my life as a laughingstock, if I'm to have a prayer of finding a suitable match, I very much need your help."

Order your copy of **A Duke by Any Other Name**!